The Nine Lives ʻ

CW00507590

Jay Margrave has been writing both fiction and non-ficton for many years but the author's recent fiction has concentrated on what could be described as mystoricals – novels that combine a love of history and literature to solve mysteries.

Also by Jay Margrave

The Gawain Quest
Luther's Ambassadors

The Nine Lives of Kit Marlowe

Jay Margrave

to Chas

Margrave

Goldenford Publishers Ltd
Guildford
www.goldenford.co.uk

First published in Great Britain in 2010 by
Goldenford Publishers Limited
The Old Post Office
130 Epsom Road Guildford
Surrey GU1 2PX
Tel: 01483 563307
Fax: 01483 829074
www.goldenford.co.uk

Cover design by Penelope Cline from an original ceramic by Iris Davies

Printed and bound by CPI Antony Rowe, Eastbourne

ISBN-978-0-9559415-1-1

This is the final book in the Priedeux Trilogy

Prologue

'All the world's a stage..
and one man in his time plays many parts.'

I gave them clues. I said one man *plays many parts,* which should have told those willing to discover the truth, that I, and my alter-ego - or my living nom-de-plume or alias or what you *will,* I - and he - played our parts well.

All through the Sonnets - those playthings we devised to keep in touch through code - all through the plays, I double-entendred. I punned at the reality but, so far, no-one from my old life has discovered me hidden in my lady's robes. In a way, I wanted to be found out, although it was dangerous, for how else could I attain the lasting fame I craved?

Yet despite that, it was too dangerous to be centre stage and let someone else take the limelight. Now I am glad I wasn't discovered in my multi-disguises. Dear Will lived on tenterhooks with it, for he was really a lowly peasant who wished for nothing more than an Alderman's robes and a large house in his local swans-town. Which he has now acquired in his dotage thanks to my whisperings in his ear and scribblings in secret.

But I must away soon, too, for as I age and reach that time women become men with straggling beards and thinning white hair revealing white pates, sans teeth, etc., the big fear is that, sans mind as well, I'll give myself away - when a government spy will see through the mist of my created illusions and I'll be assassinated *again.*

After nearly twenty years of living like this, so much in my role, it would be a great shame to give my enemies what they thought they had achieved many years ago. And poor old Shakespeare would be discovered for the old country bumpkin he is - and the biggest fraudster of all time. But maybe that will be no bad thing for his old retainer Kit, catty kit, the old maid, who shambles through the attics of Will's London lodgings. The only measure of luxury I have is Will's best bed; he can leave his second-best to that witch his wife, with whom he never lived. Indeed he *lived* with me and fed off the food of my brain far more than he ever was fed by her. So if I was to be discovered? Kit would then be known for what she is truly: a magician of sorts trapped like the old namesake, Merlin, (some said another old spelling of the family name) not in a cave but in constricting robes of womanhood - and truly - Christopher Marlowe. He who should have died at Deptford.

Forget the upstart crow and see the graceful merlin, then, bird of prey, silently swooping on the most apt word, the exact pentameter; so that all who hear rejoice in the excitement of the structures built in the air of anonymity.

Chapter One

London, 1593.

'Murder, murder! Fetch the constables - Mister Marlowe has been stabbed!'

All was noise and screaming from the house of Widow Eleanor Bull, in Deptford Strand. Mistress Bull's voice was the loudest. In the street, men looked at one another and started running. There was confusion before her house, no-one knowing what to do. At the bottom of her garden two men hurried away to the quay, unnoticed.

'Well killed, Kit?' the taller of them asked his companion.

'Indeed, I have been, no thanks to you, my dear friend Priedeux. There was a clean eye-view of the knife and my first life gone - but eight more of my nine lives left.' Kit Marlowe laughed as he stepped into the boat as Priedeux loosened it from moorings and jumped in opposite Kit. It was a small Thames craft, with a waxed covering at one end where provisions or wares could be safely stored from the weather. Priedeux took the oars and used one to push the boat from the jetty as Marlowe bent low and was lost beneath the dark awning. The dusk aided his disappearance.

As the boat moved slowly out into the mid-tide, he stripped off his men's clothes and shivered in the chill spring sun of the English late afternoon. Cries of panic still reached them in eerie echoes across the river. Tom Priedeux set to, rowing quickly away from the mayhem. If truth were told he was also rowing away from the horror of the dead body, putrid with plague, that they had pulled out of the bushes of Mistress Bull's neat garden and heaved over the shoulders of Skeres and Poley. The horror of the dead weight which had been dragged back into the house would stay with him

3

as nightmares for many a year. Marlowe's substitute had not been a pretty sight.

They could see nobody scanning the river even though the hue and cry continued; a woman screaming, men arguing and the crowd goading, the voices fading as the little boat headed towards the north bank of the Thames.

'Now let's go and live a true life without watching for traitors. I'll find my foes, kill them, too. There's too many men telling tales.' Kit's voice was muffled as he struggled with the women's clothes. He added, as he looked out, adjusting a wig, 'Prison is not good cheer, dear Tom, and I'll never want to be there again.'

He grinned. 'Thank God for those fellows, Skeres, Poley and Frizer. They surely played their parts well in our life-giving plot.'

Priedeux did not answer, using all his energy to row the boat across the tide. Marlowe continued to speak in a staccato manner as he stretched his neck and scraped the man's shadow from his chin and chest with a cut-throat made deadlier by the unsteady lilting of the rowboat.

'And we'll find those who betrayed me. *Me,* who truly served the Queen well. And, Tom, I cannot understand why Cecil did not believe I was loyal to her Majesty, but, God preserve me, I will *not* spend time in jail again even if it was meant to make the Catholics believe I was one of them.'

'Shush, Kit, we're coming now to the north side. There may be listeners.'

Despite the high tide, they soon crossed the river to the safe spot at Limehouse, called, appropriately, the Devil's Tavern.

As they approached the great loop in the river, Kit sat down, acting the woman now, and stared forward, thinking of the lime that quickened the bodies of the dead. He likened it to his situation; *he* would be no more and a young lady of uncertain heritage would be born as he carried the beginnings of her before him in the guise of a farthingale and numerous skirts, bodices and wigs. The land they headed towards, the Isle of Dogs, was a flat outcrop, mainly marsh land, with a few buildings along the river bank, a dead piece of land, fit for losing people. Before he landed on the steps of the Devil's Tavern, he would have to forget that he was the man Christopher Marlowe, scholar, playwright, and a roustingman about town. Instead, a young lady would be helped up the slippery slopes of a new life by Tom Priedeux, once a Cambridge scholar, but now the shadowy servant and tutor to this young charge. They both knew the game would be risky and perhaps questions asked about the strangeness of a male tutor with a young girl to care for but hoped it would not be so bad in other countries. Kit knew that the woman he hoped to become, would have to trust Tom Priedeux.

'You have to be careful here, Kit, this inn is used by all sorts of reprobates, sailors, pickpockets, and others, usually waiting a sailing to escape from something,' Priedeux whispered as he eased the boat to the mooring. After securing it safely against the swell, he helped his companion, a delicate, green-eyed lady, bewigged and richly clothed with flowing robes, to step on land. On the boarding platform, *she* - now called Christabel - waited. Priedeux held out his arm which the young lady leaned against gratefully. She seemed to have difficulty walking in the heeled pattens she wore. Apart from this, the only clue that this *woman* was not a lady born was the deep chuckle which came from the throat.

'Aah Priedeux, a great freedom floods me. No longer prey to my debtors; no longer a person with hidden enemies, perhaps one of them the great Raleigh. It was said I spied on him, but it was not so. There's no more need to rely on the Queen's goodwill, fickle as she is. Now I will find those who betrayed me, who forced me to flee like this, if I have to chase them half-way across Europe and back again to the new Amerikey-lands in the west.'

Priedeux was about to hush his companion, as they neared the inn, but Kit continued, in a savage whisper, 'I'll be avenged for betrayal of me. And I *will* write more great plays. A new life - a different life - awaits us.'

Chapter Two

'Look, try that man over there; the one with the buckskin boots. I'll wait here in the shadows. I know my place now that I'm a woman.' Kit pushed Tom forward, towards a group of men, one of them obviously in charge.

It would not be difficult to get a passage on board, leaving the next morning. Amongst the bustle of a merchant ship taking on parcels of good English wool, of pewter pots and plates, a couple of passengers would not be thought unusual. The Devil's Tavern was a place where captains took on extra loads without their merchant owners knowing, so long as sufficient gold passed palms.

Kit watched as Priedeux negotiated. Playing his part, he shrank into a corner, seemingly cowed by the rough language and boisterous laughter of the inn's customers. Eventually the negotiations were completed and Tom returned.

'The captain is in charge of a small craft which slips up and down the coast of England and, luckily for us, will brave the Northern Sea to the Netherlands tomorrow. He has agreed to take us. We sleep here for the night. We will, of course, have separate rooms, and you, poor Kit, must go to bed now, for women don't stay up drinking, unless they expect to earn a penny or two from the rough sailors hereabouts and,' Tom continued with a wicked twinkle in his eye, 'they may have quite a surprise if that occurred. Go on, bed with you, woman.' The last was said loudly and Kit, fuming, obeyed. He was surprised at Tom's sudden authority but realised he must have learned this in his job as tutor. He had certainly changed from the adoring youth who had always fawned around Kit at Cambridge.

The next morning they headed for the harbour to find their

ship. Kit eyed it from the quay; he had travelled before and was well acquainted with the different types of vessels that sailed across the Channel. He saw before him a well-kitted merchant ship, not one of the great sailing ships that took part in the new trade, loaded with hoards of English merchandise, pewter platters or glass beads, to bribe the Afrique Moors for slaves to transport across the dangerous wastes of the new ocean in the wake of Drake and Hawkyns. No this was a small barque that sailed the Channel, transporting bales of cloth from one member of a family to another for a special occasion; that took samples from the wool merchants of East Anglia to the weavers of Fleming to tempt them to buy more; that brought small loads of coal down the long coastal eastern routes before risking the Northern seas to reach the flatlands of the nether-lands, hiding from Spanish warships.

Jetsam of humans, a young man and his companion, a young, shy woman, would not be noticed amongst the many labourers running hither and thither.

It was cold and drizzly and there was no officer checking passengers, only an old sailor supervising the labourers. All hands were busy rigging the ship and stowing the wares. A quick exchange of silver, instead of the gold that was paid to the captain, and they were aboard, the weathered seaman hardly glancing at them as he tried the coin between broken teeth. He pointed them to the tiny cabins reserved for passengers.

Before they went below, they both lent on the prow and watched the men working. Priedeux turned to Kit, 'I've been thinking in the night. It is dangerous to head for the Netherlands, what with the Spanish constantly on watch. We may be safe; you as a woman would deflect any curiosity, but we must be extra careful. You'll be guided by me?'

Kit laughed, 'Of course, I'll be as docile as you like.'

Priedeux looked sharply at his friend, as they moved on, Kit stepping carefully over the sodden ropes that snaked across the deck. Was his friend being sincere? How could he tell? They passed a family group, the mother holding a wailing babe, being herded by the father towards the stern. Tom had no time to think before Kit pulled on his arm, 'I don't want to share with others, Priedeux, I hope you have asked for a private cabin.' He sounded like a petulant woman.

Tom laughed. 'Of course, already arranged. We must, get you out of the country in secret.' He lowered his tone, 'we can't have others seeing your early morning stubble, can we?'

Kit stomped forward, annoyed at his friend's teasing. It was hard enough for him to learn to walk and uncomfortably hot wearing a wig; he didn't need to be ribbed about it. Tom followed and stopped him.

'Come Kit, dear, you are displaying unladylike temper.'

He then became serious and pulled Kit to the seaward side where there was less activity. 'How do you know our ploy will work? Will a stab in the eye, a distortion of half a face, be enough to fox your enemies? Will all the world believe you are dead? They are not fools. I hope you can trust your friends to put up good evidence.'

Kit said quietly 'My so-called friends will persuade the coroner with gold and silver, what will he care about a body that is too disgusting to touch or investigate?' He shrugged and, looking towards the family which was not far from them, said, 'Let's get below, it's drizzly here; I don't know yet how this powder on my face lasts. I'll explain when we're alone.'

When they were settled in their room, Tom stared out of the thick glass of the ship's tiny window; it was mottled green and dirtied with globules of dried seawater, so he could see little of the activity on the quay except vague shadows moving quickly. He turned back to his friend.

'You need to trust me now, Kit, and explain. All I know is that you are in trouble with the authorities. And what you said yesterday, about not going to jail again? What did that mean?'

Kit sighed, hesitating. 'I realise I owe you an explanation. I know you eagerly agreed to help when you thought it was just a matter of escape. I think you suspect there is far more to it than that.'

'Now what have you got into? I have always believed in you Kit, you know that. Remember, it was I who warned you about that scheme to discredit you.'

'Oh, yes, the question of my not paying my buttery bills, how clever of you to spot that it was quite another person – even the name was different – Marley. Yes, Tom, I will ever be grateful for that. And I will ever forgive you for invading my privacy.'

Tom was surprised when the woman in front of him came and kissed him on the cheek, and then stepped away quickly. His surprise turned to annoyance. Kit was always teasing him as if he was an oaf.

All right, he might be a year or two younger than Kit, but he had always been one of his prime admirers among the students. So much so, that Kit had once told him to stop following him around like a pet dog. This Tom had forgiven because he was grateful that, when there were secret meetings, Kit had invited him. Now it was Tom to whom Kit had turned when he needed a confidante and fellow conspirator. But the thrill was rapidly wearing away. He grabbed Kit by the shoulder and forced him to face him again.

'Come, tell, tell me all.' Tom knew he sounded sulky.

Kit put his arm round his shoulder, 'Oh, dear Tom, don't become an unpleasant companion. We are in this together.'

Tom turned away this time. 'I only promised to get you out of England. I have made arrangements with my relative in Flushing, and after that, it depends on your future plans – I might just go back to my tutor's post, and be safe.'

Kit laughed. It was an unpleasant laugh and made Tom remember that Kit had a hold over him, as Kit was quick to remind him. 'But Tom, there are favours on both sides. You owe me – not just for saving you from your dull little post but what about all those gambling debts? What about those roughnecks who visited your rooms at Cambridge and threatened to get you? They could as well find you in that dull country mansion in Yorkshire, as I did.'

'Are *you* blackmailing me now Kit? Will I never be free?'

'Blackmail. In faith, Tom, you underestimate me. I'm your friend remember? You were eager enough to take up the challenge of our little escapade at Deptford, and run from your dull life. What else was there? Back to the manor house in Walthamstou, to care for your father's farms?'

Tom sighed. He was aware that he could never become the country squire his father wanted him to be, nurturing the lands his father proudly explained the mother of the Queen, Anne Boleyn, had given him, 'for services rendered.' Kit was far cleverer than Tom, and he knew he was outwitted every time by his older, more sophisticated friend. 'Very well – remember you promised to explain – let me hear it.'

Kit approached him and rested his hands on the taller man's shoulders making him sit. Kit remained standing, folding his arms as if he were to commence a soliloquy in one of his plays.

'You ask if I trust my conspirators in Eleanor Bull's house. I trust them only because they have an interest in the result. All three, Poley, Skeres and Frizer have something to hide, and will do what they think is right for themselves. Of course I'm not safe, and can ask for nothing. But they have been heavily bribed and their association with me was getting a little too hot for them as well. They will have enough to retire now. I'll wager they'll not be seen in London town once the inquest has finished.'

'Yes but who paid them? Surely not you?'

'Tom, you're a good pup and I'll not put your life in danger; best not to ask. You never did ask questions when I kept coming and going when we were at Cambridge.'

'But that was different. I was not involved in what you did then, now I am. I think I deserve more than that. I know there's nothing for me in England except a tutor's life but at least I had a roof over my head, and food on the table. We have no idea where our next meal is coming from…' He added peevishly, 'And don't call me a young pup.'

Kit moved towards him. 'Tom, it was meant as a sign of

affection. I asked you because I knew we could work together.'

Kit stepped away at Tom's look of distrust, and walked around the cabin, leaning against the sloping walls, where he pushed himself off to eventually sit on the bunk next to his companion. He pulled off the high heels he'd been wearing, and loosened the ribbons as he continued. 'Even so, I would not trust them to take the Queen's purse if it was offered.'

'So it was not the Queen?'

Kit shook his head, and carried on. 'They would betray me if the price was right; perhaps only the Queen can afford to so pay. I cannot tell you who provided the silver for this enterprise, dear Tom, and even if I did you would not believe me.' He paused, and then said brightly, 'We will find a way to live.' He said it with such confidence that Tom was not reassured. He was suddenly suspicious of what Kit had arranged.

Kit was now adjusting the wig. 'So, I had to protect myself with one more ploy. Those three "murderers" do not know about the women's clothes. Only you know that, Tom, and I thank you for it. It is a good disguise even from them, if they think to come and find me and use blackmail against me, they would never dream that I am now a woman. That's why I don these frowsy clothes and must practise my walk.' He minced up and down the tiny cabin, barefoot. Tom smiled, it was such an affected action that he wanted to laugh aloud. Kit turned to him and raised a hand in a flourish and curtseyed. 'Do what they will, dear friend, and I will pray to the Devil to help us.'

Priedeux winced at the reference. He remembered Marlowe's play *Dr Faustus*, and knew that his companion had already been condemned by the Queen's spymaster as a necromancer and atheist. He turned away, to hide his fear and made himself busy, setting their things in some order in the tiny space they had.

Then he stood, set his face in a light smile and said, 'Very well, I've burned my boats. I have agreed to follow you in this enterprise, and now I'll stick to it.'

Marlowe tapped Tom's sleeve in a peculiar feminine manner.

His previously elegant moustache had given way to a pinkish tinge beneath his well-shaped nostrils, and he was smiling so that his pouting lips looked every inch that of a flirtatious woman's. Tom realised it was *that* smile that made friends give in to him every time.

'Come, friend, we will have a great time on the Continent, wherever we go. Do you know when we sail?'

'Aye, when the tide turns at ten; it hoves over to Flushing first, where we will disembark if you agree to my plan to stay with my coz, Bridget, but if not, we can remain on the boat as it follows the coast down to Calais. We can choose whichever port you wish, *dear lady,* and I will bow to your desires.'

Kit stopped practising, his hand held arched in the air in the comical way that an actor would use to depict a flirty woman.

'To Flushing. But we must watch the Sidney faction. Even there I have enemies.' He lowered his voice so that Tom leaned forward to hear what he was saying. 'But it could be good. Perhaps I can call on a few friends, to even the score with false coin.'

He faced Tom. 'Take no note of my ramblings. I forget, I am to be dead to the world and Christabel must cover for me. Even so, I would not want to meet my cronies in that little scheme again. Though they might be skeletons, they might blame me for their lack of skin.'

Tom had turned away, and was helping himself to wine but looked over his shoulder and gave his friend a quizzical look. He had no idea what he was talking about. Kit was known to ramble so, as if he were constantly hatching plots. That was another reason why Tom had agreed to accompany his friend, whatever it might entail. He loved to hear Marlowe speaking – and then find, some time later, the very words transported into drama on the stage. But this made no sense and he hoped Kit would elaborate. Kit saw the look, smiled and said,

'As I said, dear Tom, just ignore my ramblings, let us look to the future. Tomorrow our adventure starts.'

* * * * *

12

In the night Priedeux woke suddenly to find the cabin door banging and Kit gone. He swung his legs over the bunk and headed outside. He knew Kit was unpredictable, but Tom was worried that he had forgotten he was a woman and was now roaming at will amongst the sailors. What was he up to now, even before they had arrived in a new country?

Outside, the night was chill and the ship was scudding through white-tipped waves. Priedeux held on as he lurched along the deck. It was his first time at sea and he found the movement deeply unsettling. He concentrated on avoiding the ropes and other paraphernalia. At first he could see nothing except the night lamps swinging on the prow but then, as his eyes adjusted he could see land on either side and realised they were still on the Thames. He felt unsettled by the slight sway. If this was what it was like in the wider reaches of the river what would it be like in open seas? Then a dim light in the furthest cabin caught his attention. The captain's cabin, he guessed. Would Kit be there? And why? He decided to approach. The door was ajar as if someone had hastily entered and had not bothered to latch it. Priedeux stepped to one side and pressed his ear in the gap between the hinges and the door-jamb. He strained to hear. The roar of the sea in the sails and the creaking of the ship meant that there was no way an eavesdropper could hear. Nobody else would be about at this time of night, except for the watchmen, one high up in the rigging, another at the prow. Their jobs would keep them away from the captain's cabin and besides they would think nothing of the captain having a visitor.

As the door swung further open, Tom peeped through the gap. Sure enough there was Kit, talking to the captain. The same man Kit had pointed out in the inn. So Kit had known who to use to plan his escape and had guided Tom to his accomplice. Tom was not surprised; he knew Kit was always good at such plans. The two men were drinking together. Priedeux realised now why their boarding had not been questioned. He watched, and guessed from the way they moved that a deal was being negotiated. The captain

13

bent down behind him and handed Kit a wide leather belt on which hung several pouches. It was obviously heavy and Kit took it gingerly, pulling it around his waist, hitching his skirts awkwardly. Priedeux watched as Kit hitched up his heavy skirts and positioned the pouches on his hips and stood up, pulling the heavy skirts down over them. He glided away to a part of the cabin where he could not be seen, the walk a parody of a mincing harlot, the belt enhancing the feminine shape.

Priedeux waited and, after a while, Kit came into view again, standing in front of the captain, who had been grinning at the little parade before him. Kit nodded and shook hands. Priedeux turned and hurried away, reaching their cabin and hiding behind the door. He waited, holding his breath. He noticed that dawn was breaking, giving the cabin a shadowed hue. When Kit returned he gripped him in a lock around the neck and whispered, 'Oh now my pretty, you are going to tell all.'

Kit went limp and did not struggle as Priedeux threw him onto the bunk, and fell with him, loosening his neck hold and spinning Kit round in one rapid movement so they faced one another. Tom held fast, his knees either side of Kit's hips, pinning down the skirts and holding him by pushing his shoulders into the hard base of the bed. Kit breathed heavily and for a moment stared at Priedeux. Then he lunged upwards. Priedeux had anticipated the move and shoved him down again and held him fast.

'No! Don't make me give you bruises on that comely face. You speak. Now.'

Kit taking another deep breath, protested. 'What you don't know can't hurt you. Let it go, its private business. You said you trusted me.'

'Kit, I need to know what's happening. How can I protect you as a woman if I don't know what you're going to do next?'

There was a pause while both men stared at each other. Tom tightened his grip. 'I may be only a poor scholar, but father took great pains to teach me how to fight, how to protect myself, and- if I need to - use a knife. So, Kit, now tell all.'

14

His captor looked away and then sighed. 'Very well, I suppose I do owe you an explanation.' He tried to take a deep breath, and then said, 'I know the captain of old, and he granted us passage in exchange for a favour.' He then said rapidly, 'We act as couriers…'

'No, you act as courier – go on.'

'*I* act as courier, then. But dressed like this, as I must, not only to keep myself safe, but also the items I carry, you have to help me.'

'Exactly, so when were you going to tell me?'

Kit did not answer the question but continued. 'If I deliver my package to Antwerp safely there will be a reward. You must trust me on this one Tom, it will mean we can travel anywhere on the Continent, have money to buy fine velvets, brocades, good wines, and bribe our way into good company…'

'What is it you carry?'

'That I will not tell – it could put your life in danger.'

Tom lifted one arm to slap Kit around the face but Kit, suddenly free on one side, jerked his shoulder and Tom nearly fell off him, unbalanced. It was not just Kit's movement though, he realised the ship was now sailing in the swell of open seas. Tom suddenly took fright realising they were crossing the Channel. He could not turn back. He fell heavily beside his friend, and lay there, subdued. What could *the package* be? Letters probably. The belt seemed too heavy for letters though. Gunpowder? Letters could be dangerous for the carriers if discovered. Gunpowder, even worse. But who would lift a woman's petticoats to search for such?

Kit watched him, a small smile on his face, as if he were the very devil waiting to see if the temptation he offered was good enough.

'You promise me it is nothing that would have us hanged?' Tom asked.

Kit laughed. 'I cannot promise that, I know not what could happen.' Then he voiced what Tom had already realised. 'But think, who would dare to look under a young lady's petticoats? We are as safe as we could be.'

15

Tom gave in. After all, he was as trapped as Kit was now, he couldn't jump ship. Now the adventure had begun, he would have to go on, at least as far as Flushing. He pulled himself off the bunk and walked to the window, not facing Kit. Resigned, he said, 'Very well, Kit, I have come this far, I cannot leave now. You win. You are the very devil. But, I insist you tell me all, before you get into any more scrapes.'

Tom could hear Kit approaching him and when he spoke, Tom heard glee in his companion's voice. 'I will tell you all you need to know, dear Tom.'

'That is not enough. I know you. You must promise to tell me everything.'

'But that's the only answer you will get from me tonight. I'm dead tired; having to be a woman is exhausting.' As he spoke he removed his outer garments, but left the petticoats which hid the bulky packages on the belt. Tom threw himself onto his bunk, exasperated, and faced the wooden bulwarks, away from Kit.

They settled down. Whatever Kit carried around his waist was heavy, but it didn't seem to affect him for he soon fell into a deep slumber, his staccato snoring disturbing his companion.

It was a long time before Priedeux managed to sleep. As he drifted off, great waves of fear, accentuated by the noise from Kit, made him alert again. With whom and what had Marlowe got involved?

Chapter Three

Kit recognised immediately that they had landed by the jolt and the reverse motion as the anchor was dropped and the pilot, shouting incoherently, manoeuvred the heaving vessel into dock. Like a cat, Marlowe was totally alert, even though his body might not show it. It was still dark and he moved gently at first so as not to disturb his companion. He always woke in the same sudden way, but then lay there, feline, half-open eyes absorbing the new day slowly. As soon as he was awake he knew who he – she – was and languished in the new identity. Christabel would, he thought, stretch languidly, enjoying the curves of a feminine body accentuated at the hips by the tightened waist of the clothes and the thick padding belt. The bunk was small and as he stretched he felt the hard sides of the ship; landlubbers were not given hammocks.

Then he unfolded himself and stretched to see through the window. He recognised the port of Flushing; he had been here once before, on the Queen's business. Even though it was not yet day he knew where they were berthed and was pleased to note that it was not near the port's castle defences but in the spur on the southern side; the southern gate was easier to enter by than the one nearer the castle which was always heavily guarded. Kit knew he had to be careful; it would not be the English soldiers and administrators in charge here that would be a danger but those he had tried to infiltrate. The Catholics. The Spaniards.

On top of that was the cargo he had collected from the ship's captain last night. If they were discovered with *that*; certain death. He shivered. He could not have told Tom, he would have refused to help probably jumping ship here. Kit had to get to Antwerp, and he knew he could only do it with Tom in attendance. An uncharoned woman travelling would not be left alone and he would be vulnerable. He could not revert back to Kit in this town; he was too well known.

Neither could he tell Tom how dangerous it was for him to be discovered by his enemies. When he was last here, Sir Robert Sidney had been in charge and had written a note, which he knew would be intercepted by Catholic spies, to say that Kit had been taken in the act of counterfeiting coinage. A small spell in the Tower and Kit's loyalty with the Catholics had been satisfied. They had trusted him and he had discovered secrets which went back to his Queen, and several Catholic priests had quickly been arrested on landing in England. He suspected they he had realised the reason for the arrests was Kit, so he could only expect certain death from them. If he had his way he would strike first.

The double-dealing! He was a-tingle with anticipation of the danger and of finding out what might have happened to those he had known a few years past. The harbour excited him too; all was bustle, the men lit up by torches as the day had still not broken, as they waited for the ship's cargo to be unloaded.

He could wait no longer, he was impatient to be gone, and turned to the still sleeping Priedeux. 'Come, *wake up,* sleepy head, we're here.'

Priedeux groaned, and sat up rubbing the sleep from his eyes.

'Where do we go now, Priedeux? Do we put up at an inn or do we go straight to your cousin's house?'

'Oh, wait. First, where are we? Have I slept through?'

'Flushing, we're at Flushing'. Kit was moving around the room, noisily, collecting an overskirt that he had discarded in the night, and tidying his petticoats as if they were trews. He almost tripped on the skirts as he hurried and was annoyed for he knew Tom watched him from the bunk. Kit could not disguise the belt which was still in place beneath although he tried to cover it before Tom noticed.

Tom grinned. 'Oh, all your ladylike ways are forgotten in your sleep.'

He stood up and gave Kit a peck on the cheek. 'Come dear lady, let me help you to dress.'

They both laughed as Tom adjusted the overskirt and blouse, pulling the drawstrings tight and patting him where the belt was. 'Wha-at?' he exclaimed in mock surprise, and was pleased to see Kit looking embarrassed.

'Tell me.' Tom said firmly. Kit could see he was determined to know and would brook no nonsense. He sighed. 'I have to fund the trip somehow.'

'Fund the trip?'

'Yes, I get ten per cent if I deliver it to a merchant at Antwerp who is waiting for it.'

'It?'

'Gold.' Kit paused. 'And silver.' Tom sat back on the bunk in shock. Yes, he could see now that the belt would be full of bullion; that was why it was so heavy.

'Where from? How? Come, Kit, we're in this together.'

Kit paused. He remembered last night; Tom could not 'jump ship' now. It would do no harm to tell and it would not be good to have Tom sulky and refusing to help. Whatever happened he needed Tom as an ally.

'There is a plot throughout Europe, there are many involved, you need not know...'

'*Kit,* you promised. Do not gainsay me now.'

'Very well, I will tell you of what I carry so long as I can keep my secret as to why.'

'Kit, tell me.' Tom was almost panting and Kit smiled to himself; his young companion was almost jumping up and down in anticipation.

'It is Spanish bullion, reals, pieces of eight, stolen by Dutch pirates in the Indies.' He paused, but before Tom could say anything he went on. There is a convoluted route which ends up in Antwerp where the money merchants use it to fund the Spanish *and the Dutch* armies; who fight each other! I think it has a poetic beauty about it that meant I could not refuse to help.'

'And the ten per cent.'

'Well yes, that as well, it is all part of what I carry around my waist.'

'How much is ten per cent?'

'One hundred ducats and more.'

Priedeux stood up, saying nothing, but reached for the next layer of Kit's clothing and placed the farthingale over his skirts. He tied it tight, still saying nothing. One hundred ducats! It was a King's ransom. Kit could see by Tom's face what he was thinking. Tom could buy a small estate for that and stock enough to become a squire in his own right, without waiting to succeed his father.

Kit interrupted his reverie, 'Yes, you could travel the world.'

Tom laughed, 'It's tempting.' He had followed Kit because he admired him and now he was painfully aware that he had thrown in his lot with Kit. Besides, there was the knowledge that all knew he was part of the rebellious faction at Cambridge; he had already been warned. Now that he had left his tutor's post suddenly without explanation he would be even more suspect, and could not return to that job. Life had become uncomfortable for him as well as Kit.

One hundred ducats. He tried to envisage it. With that amount of gold and silver, they could travel wherever they wished. With no officious cellarer to complain of non-payment of their bills. As he dreamed, he attended to Kit's attire. He tied a bow at each shoulder to attach the bloated sleeves to the robe, still saying nothing. Kit stood still, willing to be dressed, waiting for his friend's reaction. After some time Christabel emerged; trying out a few steps in the high-heeled shoes.

It was Kit who eventually broke the silence. 'Where to then?'

It was his original question and Tom now started thinking of how they could find his cousin. 'My cousin's husband acts as secretary at the English garrison; they live in the Street of the Scribes, so should not be hard to find. We'll go there and I'll explain that I am escorting you to your husband in Italy, that'll do for her. But I would not have you endanger them, you must behave yourself, Kit.'

Kit nodded. 'But of course, I can do nothing else in these skirts.'

Tom glared at him. Could Kit really metamorphose simply by changing his outer layers?

They soon left the harbour and entered the city gates with the first of the farmers and their carts of wares; chickens and eggs, ducks and cheeses, fresh greens and haunches of hams for the early morning market.

Tom accosted one of the farmers, and asked, 'Tell me, Sir, where will I find the Street of the Scribes?'

The man scratched his head and looked at the woman with him.

'Wife, where be...?'

'I know, I heard. The Street of the Scribes. We would not know that, not having any need of such things. Ask Madge there. She had to have papers prepared when the Spaniards wanted her farm.'

The person they referred to came up to them and looked quizzically at the two strangers. She was a bent over old woman, her face as wrinkled as an old winter-stored apple.

'You not be Spanish?'

Tom laughed, and answered. 'No, we are...'

But Kit interrupted, 'We be from Walloon, down the road, we need to meet our family...'

'Oh, that be all right then. The Street of the Scribes is at the back of the town, near the city walls. Take that road there, and keep going, near the church turn left, then right and then left and you should find it, look out for the city walls.'

They thanked the group and moved off the way indicated. Tom led his companion away from the main thoroughfare, avoiding the main square where everyone else was heading. He took the route suggested by the old crone, without really knowing where he was going except it was quiet, being the opposite way to everyone else. They continued without speaking, past the church, through narrow streets that hid behind the larger houses and warehouses

21

along the quays. They soon left the market bustle behind.

As they turned into a narrow street, they heard the thud-thud of heavy feet. The regular rhythm was like a death knell. Kit and Tom stopped; the sound was a fore-runner of what they feared; a troupe of soldiers, six of them. It was too late, they had rounded the corner and were heading straight for them, their red and yellow tunics dull in the early morning grey. They marched in formation, their pikes, small pendants flying from the tips, held upright to form an artificial wall that threatened to hem Tom and Kit in. The metal of the pikes glowed in the flares they carried.

Tom whispered, 'don't run, Kit, they'll not expect a woman to run. Lean back against the doorway as if you're shy. I'll try to shield you.'

'Ho, what goes here?' It was the captain, a heavily bearded man, with lowering eyebrows. He held up his hand and his men stopped as one. As he spoke two of them came forward and stood at either side of Kit and Tom, criss-crossing their pikes, so they could not escape. 'What are you doing out so early?' Then his eye moved from Tom to Kit, who shaded his face. 'Or should I say so late? What have we been doing with the young lady, Sir, and are you about to smuggle her back to her cold bed after warming her all night?'

Tom stepped forward to explain to the leader, leaving Kit. He tried to raise himself higher and look dignified. As he was about to answer some of the other soldiers broke rank and moved round to peer at Kit's hidden features. Whisperings of 'Come on, don't be shy, you doxy' and 'Give us a peek of your beauties' reached him. Tom turned to see Kit squirming away as one of the men grabbed his buttocks but Tom could not reach Kit, his way blocked by two of the other men. The remaining two stood either side of their captain, impassive.

Without answering their leader, Tom stepped back and took Kit's hand, and said, 'Leave h...' but he stopped short, stuttering; he had nearly said 'him'. He continued, 'her alone, you bullies, come...'and he pulled Kit away. The sudden movement surprised the two soldiers who had been harassing Kit, and they involuntarily stepped back. As Kit moved between them one of them put out a warning hand and it rested on the breasts which had been so carefully made of old rags; his hand tightened. He exclaimed, 'What! What have I grabbed here; nothing at all but crumpled softness; Let me tell you man, this is either a flatpuss or not a woman at all.'

'Run, just run.' Tom was moving as he gave the cry, stamping on two of the men's feet as he went. They dropped their weapons as they involuntarily gripped their injured feet.

Kit lifted his skirts and kicked the man nearest him between the legs. He gasped and fell back with shock onto three of his companions, not expecting such force from a woman. One leering companion, grizzly bearded, made a grab at Kit as he pushed past, but Kit leant against him with his full weight and pushed. The heavy belt around his hips must have done for the older soldier who fell, winded, and the men behind him staggered as he landed between them. Kit saw his opportunity and barged through the melee as they tried to close in on him, their pikes intertwining and slowing them down. The two men who Tom had injured were still hopping from their injuries and all of the soldiers were hampered by their pikes which became encumbered in between them. Kit, surprising them with his agility, jumped over the sprawl and now ran faster to catch up with his friend, who hesitated only a moment and then dashed away.

As Kit caught up with Tom, and overtook him, he felt the old excitement rising in him and this gave him added speed, despite the awkwardness of his pattens and the bullion around his waist. Again he was testing himself, just as when he had been involved in spying and plotting. The danger cleared his brain and he could see exactly what was to be done. His thoughts moved as rapidly as his body. Suddenly he remembered the terrain from his days with the Catholics, as if the whole town was laid out as a map before him. He knew Tom was not far behind; he could hear him gasping as he tried to keep up with him.

'Come on,' he gasped, 'I know where to go, and it's not to the Street of the Scribes.'

When he was about his previous business in the town, he had discovered all the taverns with secret back doors; all the safe houses and the alleys which seemed to lead nowhere but had narrow paths where a man could disappear when pursued.

'Quick, they're coming, I can hear them,' cried Tom.

Kit suddenly jumped sideways into an alley as Tom caught up with him. Tom, looking ahead was horrified, calling out, 'Kit, it's a dead end, no! Not that way.' But Kit grabbed his arm and pulled him onward. He pushed against a door which could not be seen at first, which opened and they almost fell in to the darkened interior. They found themselves in a small room with a few barrels for tables, half barrels for chairs and a trestle against which a man stood, wiping a tankard.

'What the...?'

Kit yelled 'Soldiers! They're after us!'

The man did not hesitate, but gestured behind him, eyebrows raised. Kit dashed past him, and Tom followed. They hurled themselves through another thick door into a courtyard cluttered with rows of barrels. Tom could smell the strong odour of ale, malmsey and spilt wine as he followed his companion to the gate out into the road beyond. Then they were in a narrow street of tall merchants' buildings, still quiet at this time of the morning, the only life being a dog curled up asleep on a step. It was as if they had entered another world where there was no occupying army, no soldiers and no fear. It was a pleasant domestic street, just stirring in the early morning. As they passed, the dog lifted his head and wagged his tail forlornly but when he realised they were not approaching his house, returned to his curled up position, head on tail.

Kit and Tom stopped at the same time and lent against a wall to catch their breath. Kit, recovering first, took charge again. 'This way. Your cousin lives in the Street of the Scribes? It's only a few blocks away from here.'

'Kit, how can you be so calm? Wait a second.' Indeed Tom was still gasping and Kit adjusted his skirts which were caught up around his knees and waited. He realised that, for Tom, this was a totally new experience. Up to now he had been but a scholar and his only excitement had been to visit Kit in London who had taken him on nights of carousing in the fleshpots of the city after an afternoon at one or other of the playhouses.

Soon, for the town was not large, they reached a row of tall terraces that ended with the City walls so that it formed a blind alley. Tom headed for one of the houses and rapped on the door. Another small dog sniffed at their heels as they waited. Kit bent down and patted the animal which stood expectantly with them.

'This is a town of dogs, it would seem,' said Tom as they waited.

'Indeed, yes, I noticed that the people here like their spaniels.' Kit concurred.

The noise of the rapping reverberated in the narrow street but soon the door opened wide. There stood a matron, wiping her fleshy hands on a large apron which stretched across the widening hips of a woman who had borne her children and was now waiting for grandchildren. At first she gaped but then there was dawning recognition.

'Tom. Cousin Tom. At last you arrive. Come in.' She stopped, spying Kit, who was holding back. 'Ooh and who is this? You didn't say you were going to bring a bride to show us.'

'No, let me explain.' Tom stepped forward as his cousin ushered them in. The dog followed and Bridget stretched down to stroke it as it wagged its tail and lolloped down the passage, obviously heading for the kitchen. The two men started to follow but Bridget waved them back.

'Nay, not you two. Who is this, I ask again? Please say it is your bride to introduce to me, Tom. And I had no missive of such a thing. Go into the parlour, I'll call Martin, he's still abed.' The glance she gave to Kit was quick and assessing, as she ushered them through the hall. She did not however head for the stairs.

After looking Kit up and down she changed her tune. 'Nay, he was late last night on his business, so we'll let him sleep. You must have come in with the tide. Have you eaten?' She spoke as she moved; quickly, her full bosom heaving. She undid the apron as she walked and dropped it onto a side chair in the dark wood-lined hall. With a continuing movement she reached a panelled door and opened it, showing them into a room at the front of the house, chilly with disuse. She shooshed them in, wiping the mantel with her hand as she settled a pewter plate into a new, more symmetrical position. Tom knew better than to say they would prefer the warm kitchen. He said nothing as Bridget fussed about, plumping coverings, hastily wiping dusty shelves with a lace she extracted from a pocket, but trying to hide the activity as if she were ashamed that she was cleaning. The two men stood, waiting for her to finish, feeling awkward.

Eventually she turned, arms akimbo and surveyed them. Her gaze was penetrating and Tom saw Christabel hang her head as if she felt like a naughty child who would be found out. Suddenly Bridget started moving again, bustling past them saying, 'Sit, sit and I'll be back with victuals. Then you can tell me.'

Tom and Kit were left alone. Tom felt awkward; why was his cousin saying nothing more about his companion? He found this disturbing. Did she suspect?

'Wait there, *Christabel*' Tom accentuated the name and Kit nodded, grinning, understanding the hint. I'll see what my cousin is up to.'

Priedeux had never seen his cousin's married quarters in Flushing before but followed the smell of baking bread to the back of the house through a door where the dog had disappeared. He found a well-stocked kitchen with haunches of pig hanging, cheeses standing on the large wooden bench, and a large bunch of carrots and other vegetables overflowing a basket. There were jugs of milk and ale, of wine and water. Unusually, the kitchen had its own oven. Tom smiled to himself; it would be typical of his cousin to have her own baking facilities, refusing to be like most housewives who used the bakers on the edge of the street, thinking it too dangerous to have such heat in their wooden houses. She probably thought the baker dirty, he thought. The oven which also had a hob on top of it, cast a circle of heat and on top a pan was simmering. The dog had curled into a ball in the large fireplace surrounding the oven. Tom could see Bridget in a store cupboard at the far end of the kitchen, moving large clay pots around. She stood on a ground of flattened earth, strewn with herbs, but here, where he stood in the kitchen, the floor was of large stone flags, polished to cleansed perfection.

'Bridget,' he called and she turned. 'Let me explain…'

'Time enough for that, boy. I always knew you would come to no good.' But she said it kindly.

'What do you mean?' He was grinning. Bridget had been his much older childhood companion and would satisfy her maternal instincts by making him her baby before she was married and left their home. Now she was using the same tone that she had used to him as a child. She came out of the larder and stood before him, holding a large pot. She placed it on the table and stopped moving for a moment, a dramatic stance for one who rarely stood still. She pointed beyond Priedeux.

'That *boy* in there! Do you think he can fool anyone dressed like that? And with his mannerisms.'

'Boy?' He could say no more. Was Kit's disguise so transparent? They had planned it and watched the young actors, boys themselves, playing women on stage; Kit had asked them for their secrets, the rouge and other make-up they had used to give their faces the softer shape of females. Admittedly Kit had not taken easily to the pattens, with their high heels, but to Tom it seemed he had managed well enough today until they had clashed with the soldiers. But here was Bridget seeing right through him.

All he could add was, 'How can you tell?'

After her outburst Bridget had moved back to the larder and he had to wait until she returned, her arms now laden with loaves of bread, and a jug of steaming ale which Tom automatically took from her. She gestured for him to put it down near the fire.

'Ale; it needs to be warmed before it can be drunk,' she explained as if in answer to his question. He waited, knowing that, if he badgered her, she would delay even longer in her explanation. She gathered some herbs and started to chop.

'How can I tell? How can I tell? Well, for one thing,' and here she stopped and put one hand on her hip. 'For one thing the farthingale is not on the right place on the hips, it is too far down; it looks too bulky! For another, he wears his cap as if he would hide his hair; we have a trick to show some of it, not to pull it all back; and for another, did you colour his face? It looks as if he is to break out with plague at any time.'

She turned back to the herbs and between the chop-chop sounds, she carried on talking. 'If he must be a woman you need a woman to show you, Tom. You don't *have* to tell me what's going on, but it would be better if you did; then I will decide whether to help you or not.' She moved round him, shoving him out of the way, and gathered a bowl of eggs to her. 'But as sure as these eggs have shells you'll not get far with the shell of that man pretending to be a woman.'

Priedeux assessed this cousin of his. He had come to her house because he trusted her. He knew her to be a sensible person, one with humour and, underneath the wifely mannerisms, he also knew her to have unconventional views which she kept closely hidden. Her husband was different. He was a seemingly affable man who smiled and offered all courtesies but Tom knew that he was also fussy to the point of fanaticism when it came to carrying out his duties for the Queen. He'd been sent to Flushing to be a secretary, being totally trustworthy in the service of Elizabeth. He was sure that, if Martin thought that there was something wrong with what they were doing, then he would not condone it; he might even tell the English protector and then Kit's secret would be out.

'You'll not tell Martin? We would not want a report sent back to England.'

'I'll not have to tell him. He has eyes, you know.' Then she grinned. 'It's a challenge, if it's worth it. Tell me why and I'll think about it.'

Priedeux, though he did not understand the reference to a challenge, could see that, if he were honest with Bridget she might help. It was the only chance they had if Kit's disguise really was so useless.

His explanation concentrated on Marlowe's helping the Government, how the Government's enemies were now pursuing him, heavily weighting his story on Kit's pro-Government activities. He knew his cousin would never have seen a play, and perhaps never heard of Kit's writings, and suspected she would not approve if she had. But she was a good wife, and he believed that, if she did, after all, tell her husband, Kit's service to the Queen would stand him in good stead. When he finished, she stood back from chopping the herbs, the rhythmic movement of which had followed Tom's story, and once again assessed him.

Suddenly her attention was caught by the bubbling pot on the oven, as it threatened to boil over. She moved quickly and carried it to one side, blowing on it and stirring. When she had finished she stood upright again, came round the table to Priedeux, put her reddened hand on his arm, and said, 'Come, if the man is to become a woman, he must learn woman's ways...' She smiled. 'Like how to catch a boiling pot. I'll teach him. Once he knows how to run a household, for that is what women have to do, he will truly be female. He is but a parody at present.'

Priedeux was speechless. His cousin's generosity astounded him. He admired her perspicacity. At the same time, he was at a loss as to what the proud-hearted Marlowe would say. Would the arrogant graduate, the great playwright, so fêted in London, used to adulation and the patronage of great lords, bow down to being virtually a servant of Bridget?

Chapter Four

'No. No No No!' The last negative was so emphatic that Tom fell backwards as if he had been hit. Before he could explain further, Kit emphasised, 'I cannot do it. Cooking and cleaning? That is impossible, and to stay here, in this provincial place, for more than a few days would kill me.'

He was raving as he stormed up and down, all pretence to womanhood forgotten. Tom said nothing, even though he knew Kit's raised voice must have carried to where Bridget busied herself in the hall outside, to wait on their decision. He just hoped that Marlowe's rantings didn't reach the rest of the household, even though they were still upstairs, asleep.

'Kit, Kit listen, please listen...' But Kit was in full swing now.

'You've led me into a trap, Tom, I'm doomed, I can never escape this hell hole, now your cousin knows about me.'

'My cousin means well, ' Tom was torn between the family love he bore for Bridget, and the loyalty to his friend. 'Perhaps it is best to abandon our plans?'

Tom knew Kit well.

'Abandon our plans? I cannot, I am dead, remember?'

Tom shrugged. He would have to let Kit scream and shout, like Tamburlaine raged at his sons. Eventually Kit would calm down and then Tom would be able to reason with him. He knew, after his talk with Bridget, that it was necessary to train Kit if he was truly to be taken for a woman. It was not only what Bridget had said. Now, as Kit strutted back and forth, his skirts whirling around him, ankles showing, arms on hips, he did not even look like a clumsy washer-woman. How would he pass for a well to do lady travelling with a chaperon? It would be no good; he would soon be discovered if they left this place without some tuition in the art of being a woman.

Kit stopped pacing up and down, and stood breathing heavily, silent at last. There was a long pause.

Tom broke the atmosphere by saying calmly, 'We were nearly caught this morning. Bridget saw through you right away. That's enough for me. If you won't see reason, I'll stop here. I'll go no further with you. '

Marlowe turned his back on Tom and started his pacing again, as if he would walk away himself. Before he reached the window, he turned about and faced Tom, clutching one elbow with his hand and staring straight ahead, as if he were dreaming of another time, another place.

Priedeux tried another tack. 'She is a kind woman, Kit, but she is loyal to her husband; if we don't go along with her, she might tell him and he's a Queen's man. We may be betrayed.'

Kit still glared but Tom did not stop. 'You said your accomplices could not necessarily be trusted, they could be bought at any time. Are you sure they haven't already turned traitor and told of your escape? But they'd never guess that you had the idea of being a woman. Only I knew that part of the plan. *If you can carry it off.'*

He continued, as he saw Kit take breath, not wanting his friend to start shouting again. He would not be stopped now.

'If you are unsuccessful and they hear rumours of a man pretending to be a woman; supposing they guess? They come looking, they know where you're planning to go but all they hear about is the arrival of a man and a clumsy woman. It won't be long before we'll be sought out.'

Tom paused. Kit looked interested but said nothing.

'For you to be a *true* woman, you'll have to learn from Bridget. This is the only way, such a clever way, to lose yourself, Christopher Marlowe.'

Priedeux was cut short, before he could try any more arguments, by a commotion outside.

A banging on the front door was followed by a hysterical high-pitched exclamation. 'Madam. Madam, have you heard? The military are seeking a man dressed as a woman. They have issued a proclamation at market; anyone harbouring him will be imprisoned. Fancy!'

Bridget shushed the maid. 'Where is the produce you were asked to get at market? Come girl, hush, come into the kitchen before you wake the master – he will be none too pleased.'

Her voice faded. Marlowe turned to his companion. His face showed defeat.

'I accept what you say.' Then he smiled, mercurial as ever. 'I am a fast learner, Tom, and we'll not be here too long. I pine to see the Italy of my dreams; the new statue, David, by Michelangelo that everyone raves of; the ruins of Caesar's Rome. I have not been there and I am not known, so will be able to live easily.' He took a deep breath. 'Yes, as a true woman.'

Priedeux nodded, satisfied, and left the room to tell Bridget she had a new servant.

* * * *

'Come, it must be higher; and those breasts just won't do. Tighten it; the whole idea is to make you shapely; and from now on you will be known as Christabel, if that is your chosen name; and Kitty for short by those in your family; never let a strange gentleman call you that until you marry and then only your husband and your immediate family.' Bridget was enjoying herself; she was pulling the laces tight and watching the man grimace, having hitched the farthingale higher. She continued to speak, not letting Kit answer. He wriggled as she patted his waist, embarrassed at the belt he wore beneath it, hoping she wouldn't be too inquisitive.

'My, you've given yourself plenty of padding; that's no bad thing. Good childbearing hips, I'd say.' Bridget had previously accepted that a man was a man and women were women. Now that had been called into question by Kit's disguise and her inventive mind, usually restricted to running a smooth household, was creating many activities she would impose on Kit to ensure he developed womanly ways.

'I've sent my girl to her family for a few days, using the excuse that the plague may be coming. She's a great worrier, as you heard this morning with all her hue and cry, so is happy to go, with all the kerfuffle about men dressed as women That will also give me a reason why you're helping out. Not that Martin concerns himself with household matters, but it's best to allay any suspicions. I doubt he'll have any. If he thinks you're helping me, even though a guest, he'll ignore you. As you serve him, for you will act as serving-maid, he won't notice you, so intent on rushing his food and getting on with his job. Such an industrious man.'

She chattered on as she showed him how to curl a little hair out of his cap, to soften the lines of his face.

Kit was sullen. He seethed at the words 'serving-maid'. How could anyone ignore *him*, Christopher Marlowe?

'First you must learn how to wear the gowns; then you will have to learn how to launder them. Come.' With a last pull at the laces that held the bodice tight, she led him through the back of the house, and into the garden, where there was a pump. She handed him a jug of pungent liquid, which made Kit spasm into a coughing fit.

'Yes, a most onerous task, and the smell of the ammonia is terrible but it is the only liquid that really bleaches the linen; I'll trust no outside washerwomen with my household's finest chemises, collars and shirts. And, mind, when you come to the muslin, use not the ammonia, for it is too strong for such a fine material. You must learn the best way to wash all types of material if you are to be a perfect housewife.'

Kit thought to protest but she prattled on. 'When you've done with the washing, hang it out, and later, when all is dry, I'll teach you how to starch the ruffs that fashion dictates we all wear now. Silly things. In my day, it was all straight collars, so much easier.'

Kit was becoming tired of her constant talk but watched her demonstrations and followed her example. The sooner he learned her ways, the sooner he would be gone.

Later that day, when his hands were red raw from the washing, and his back ached, she began again. 'I will need to teach you to cook, to bake, to preserve; onions are just about ready to be pickled. You'll need to learn about herbs and preservatives. Come, I'll show you the herb garden. And don't believe that because you have a large house and plenty of money you will have to ignore these matters; a good woman teaches her maids by example – any woman will need to know all this if she is to run a good house. Even that famous lady Bess of Hardwick can cook and garden.

'Oh, yes, you'll be taught how I've been taught; only the hard work of a woman will show you how to be truly feminine.'

As she watched Kit chop the vegetables for supper, she worked out how she would organise different varieties of laundering, the collection and grinding of herbs, the cooking of great potages; the plucking and gutting of ducks, hens and geese, the shaking of feather mattresses and the beating of carpets. She would teach him to wait at table.

'Later, you will eat in the kitchen. I will tell Martin you are cold and tired and shy. You are just not fit yet to appear before the men, you'd never remember not to speak until you are spoken to!'

Kit fumed and thought of storming out, but Bridget's firm words, her authority, held sway.

* * * * *

A few days later, Tom hovered in the corridor outside the women's bedroom. He wanted to talk to Kit but Bridget came up behind him and made him jump as she scolded him. 'Now, Tom, you go out and leave me with Christabel; get Martin to take you to his office and see if there is anything you can do. I don't want you men hanging around us women.'

She smiled at her husband who had just emerged from his chamber as she spoke. Martin, slow and bleary-eyed and carrying an open book, as if he couldn't wait to start reading again, had accepted the explanation that his wife's nephew was escorting the young lady to her husband in Italy. And he did not query his wife when the young lady did not appear at morning prayers, or at least he had not made any comment. Now he looked up from his book and surveyed Tom from over reading glasses.

'Indeed, Tom, I could make use of you at the office. You can write some letters for me. And, it will give the girl confidence to be with Bridget. We men are not wanted in the pantry.' Martin joked and his wife was pleased that he had accepted her explanation that the girl was both shy and chilly after her journey, and had decided to stay in the kitchen. Martin, as usual preoccupied with his work, found nothing unusual in this and had never really noticed the newcomer.

* * * * *

'Now the men have gone, let me look at you: walk up and down. You are becoming a proper female. No better still, go into the pantry and fetch the cheeses and more bread; I see that Martin has eaten all the loaf I fetched earlier; go on.'

Kit stroked his chin, and realised it was smooth almost as smooth as a woman's cheek. He had had enough; he would not obey this woman whom he considered his social inferior. He stood, head to one side, not moving. Suddenly Bridget came quickly towards him, grabbed a swatch which was leaning against the hearth and rammed it into his stomach. 'Go, don't stand there dreaming, girl, otherwise the menfolk'll be complaining when they come home for dinner. You'll have to learn to be quick about it, there's a multitude to do. The beds have to be turned down and shaken; your strength will come in well there. And then there's…'

But *Christabel* heard no more. He quickly moved into the pantry away from the tirade, but if he had turned round he would have seen Bridget smiling.

The rest of the time was taken up with household chores and, when Kit thought all was finished, Bridget arranged for some pickling to be done. *That will teach the snooty man, the bitter smell of the onions will soon make him weep like a woman*, she thought. She said aloud, 'The vinegar will soften your hands at the same time.' When she saw he truly did cry, she suspected with tears of frustration, she relented. 'Come, let me shape your nails and we'll also get rid of these dark hairs from your knuckles.

'If you are to be a woman, you must remember the hairs; and those in your nose and ears. Now let me see you walk again.'

Shortly before the men came home, she made *Christabel* mince up and down the kitchen and into the panelled hall. She watched him and laughed.

'No, you'll never do. You still do not move properly. Look, this is how you walk, easily, from the hips, but don't swing them, that's too provocative.'

She took him into the front room and demonstrated how to sit, lifting up her farthingale so it was high on the waist before she sat down.

'Now you must raise your voice, too, but not so that it squeaks; and a young woman would never speak unless spoken to, remember that.'

Christabel grinned and repeated, rote-like, 'And never take part in debate, or for that matter smoke. I remember my friend...' But he stopped. Bridget would certainly know of Sir Walter Ralegh and quite likely have heard the infamous tales that Marlowe had been told when asked to spy on him; that he denied God, that he encouraged young men into dissolute ways and that he made his female servants try the smoking pipe with the richest strongest stuff in it so that it made them go green and puke up; then he would rebuke them and explain that all he was doing was demonstrating to them that smoking was for men.

But Bridget wasn't listening. She was bustling back to her own territory, passing from the hall into the kitchen, leaving Kit to follow from the front parlour. As he entered her domain, she passed him a knife and an already plucked chicken.

'Come, we must prepare dinner. The men folk will be home soon. Chop that up.' She watched as he hacked at the head of the chicken and then at the backbone, and laughed. 'Nay, that's not the way to cut up my poor Matilda. Show her some respect, she has given me many eggs. Look, like this,' and she took the leg and bent it and chopped between the bones and gestured for him to do the same. Kit puckered his lips but took the chicken and carefully followed her example, and carried on dissecting the rest of the chicken.

She set him stirring some broth over the fire while she took the prepared chicken from him and set it on the spit to roast, pushing the sleeping dog away from the hearth. There was a companionable silence which she broke to hammer home her lessons.

'Tonight, you will help serve at table; you will follow me and hand the food to the men folk and stand respectfully by the side of the door in case they ask for anything else. Remember, you do not sit until all the food is served. Take small portions, after the men have had their fill. You do not speak until spoken to.' She was chopping green salads, and placing them in a bowl.

'And you are too shy to talk, and a young woman never interrupts the men anyway. When leaving, when you can see the men are ready for their next dish, you should slide out from your chair and curtsey slightly as I have shown you before leaving the room. Oh, and don't feed the dog from the table.'

Christabel grinned, took the wooden bowl and minced out of the room, one hand on hip. Bridget ignored the exaggerated movement, knowing he was trying to rile her. She was well satisfied with what she had achieved in such a short time. Indeed, the man was a quick learner.

As they washed up after dinner and the men folk smoked, with Kit greedily trying to get a whiff of the tobacco smell, Bridget said, 'Seeing as I had to send my girl away for you, it is about time you learnt how to start a fire. You'll have to get up at five to get it going. I'll knock on your door and show you how 'tis done.'

Kit said nothing but gritted his teeth as he bent over the large sink of filthy suds, determined that his indoctrination would not last long. He was exhausted.

* * * * *

'*Christabel*, wake up, wake up!' Tom awoke to hear rapping on the door next to his, at dawn, and the frantic whispering of Bridget. He listened; Bridget sounded annoyed. He and Kit had been with his cousin for a week and Tom had been impressed by the improvement in Kit's femininity. Indeed, as they were finishing last night's meal Kit had shyly announced, 'Forgive me, but I am tired and would retire early. Is that acceptable?'

Bridget had taken pity, 'You go, lass, I'll finish the dishes.'

As Tom listened, he grew suspicious. Why would Kit not respond to that loud rapping on his door? He knew that Kit was never an early riser, and had suffered from Bridget's insistence that he serve at breakfast table. At first, he thought that the early mornings had caught up with Kit. Now, listening to Bridget's calling, he wasn't so sure.

He heard a door latch being lifted and then silence. He waited, but the silence was worse than any activity. He had to investigate; he recalled some slight noises in the night that had invaded his dreams. The memory made him anxious. Why had Kit excused himself so humbly the night before? Tom suddenly realised it was so transparent; he'd been planning something. He pulled a robe around himself and hurried into the gallery, nearly tripping over the dog who was sitting watching his mistress. Several bedrooms came off the long gallery, with Bridget and Martin's chamber at the front of the house; his was in the centre, with small windows looking out on the side of the house at the back extension; Kit's room was right at the back, with the flat roof of the kitchen beneath and the sloping eaves of the roof cutting it low at one end. Bridget came out of Kit's room and turned when she heard him approaching. 'Where is he?' she whispered. 'There's no sign of him. Your friend has flown.'

Tom pushed past her into Kit's room. He surveyed the small chamber; it looked as if all Kit's feminine attire was still there; the two dresses, the farthingales and petticoats. He caught sight of Kit's trunk and rushed over to it and looked inside, ignoring Bridget who watched him closely. There was the huge belt of silver; but what *were* gone were the sword and dagger, and Kit's doublet and hose. Tom stood up, closing the lid of the trunk rapidly hoping that Bridget could not appreciate what was inside, and started to think.

His cousin was pacing up and down, smoothing the coverlet which was already smooth. Tom followed her actions and caught her gaze as she looked up. They both knew that the bed had not been slept in. She pulled at the curtains which were ruffled and shut the window. Tom eventually broke the silence. 'I don't think Kit has gone far. I believe he has no money, and no-one else he would want to turn to. I suggest you start your day's work, Bridget, and I'll try to find him.'

She nodded. 'Indeed, I now have to light the fire and a mountain of other things to do and if I don't have your friend to help, I have twice the work.'

Tom was inspecting the window and said over his shoulder, 'I'll look round to see if I can find any clues to where he may be.'

But Bridget had gone. He strode to the door and saw her hurrying below, no stairs creaking as she went; a practised housewife starting her day without waking the men folk.

Tom looked round and returned to the trunk. He felt almost guilty as he rifled through the contents. He found, beneath a mixed layer of doublets, hose, farthingales and skirts, some papers and writing materials. He found scraps of poems, some about a dark lady which mystified Tom, for Kit was no more enamoured of women than a dead dog for a bitch. He ignored the belt; it worried him so. What would he do if Kit did not return?

He'd been told it held Spanish bullion; he could, he supposed, just take the silver and return to England, but if it really was so, how would he explain having so much money if he were ever stopped? He could not leave it here; there was always a risk that the Spanish overlords would decide that Flushing was theirs, and he would be putting his cousin and Martin's life in danger. Kit had told him they were to deliver it to Antwerp but where? Could he make enquiries and complete his friend's mission?

As he fingered the belt he heard a scraping at the window. He turned. It was still early morning and it was dusky outside. All he could see was Kit's head and hand, the hand a crablike claw, the face grinning.

He jumped up and rushed over, gingerly pushing the casement open.

'Come, Tom, help me up; it has been a hard job crouching on this low roof these ten minutes whilst your coz made such a fuss.'

Tom, unable to say anything, shocked as he was, did as he was bid. Kit soon stood before him, his clothes filthy, far more than should have been from the dirt on the pipes and roof over which he had obviously clambered. He was still grinning. Tom felt like punching him. Thinking better of this – he did not want to add a bloody nose to his friend's filth - he exclaimed, 'What have you been up to? How am I going to explain this to Cousin Bridget?'

'Just say I was in the privy all the time and too shy to tell her. I came back up while she was in the larder so she missed me. Go, while I clean up.'

Tom thought about what Kit said. It was just possible, just. The privy was at the bottom of the garden and there was a small passage between the kitchen and the garden door; just enough for someone to creep by while the occupants of the kitchen were in the separate room of the larder.

'But what about the bed? She's noticed it's not been slept in.'

Kit laughed, which infuriated Tom but before he could react, he answered quickly, 'If she asks, just tell her I had learned my lesson well, and made my bed before leaving my chamber.'

Tom shrugged, he knew he couldn't catch Kit out when he was at his sharpest. 'Very well. But you'd better tell me what you have been up to…'

'Tom, listen, we don't have time now. Bridget will fuss even more if we don't appear soon.' As he spoke, he was stripping off his doublet, and swung the sword belt off his waist. As he rapidly hid the weapon in his trunk, Tom was sure he saw the stain of blood on the hilt. Kit was deftly pulling on his skirts and Tom, stunned into silence, helped him by tying the laces of his bodice. As they left the chamber, and before Tom could gather his wits to ask about the blood stained sword, Kit forestalled him and turning to the water jug he wiped his quickly and said, in a voice muffled through the cloth, 'This has nothing to do with you, and if you don't know, then you'll not be worried. Come, I must go to my day's chores.'

* * * * *

'They say some Catholics, suspected to be Spanish spies, were murdered in their beds last night...'

Martin was telling them the news on his return for his dinner. He had stopped chewing his meat to tell them about the horror and leaned forward as if to emphasise what he was saying. Bridget and Kit were fussing around him, making sure the cheese was nearby, Bridget, pushing the dog out of the way, offered him a choice apple which she polished on her apron before handing it to Martin.

Tom looked up. He'd gone back to bed after the disturbance and had not gone out with Martin.

'Wha-at...'

'Yes, someone broke into their house, and stabbed to death the two brothers and another who lodged with them.'

'Do you think it might have been one of those robberies that are carried out by mercenaries dissatisfied at not being paid? Queried Tom, trying to deflect any idea of spies and double-dealing, for he remembered Kit's stories of spying in this very town.

Martin shook his head. 'They say not, because nothing was stolen.'

Tom was eager to hear more. He was watching Kit, who seemed totally impassive except that Kit looked down, refusing to meet Tom's eye. To Martin it might seem the young *lady* was trying not to listen to the terrible story of men being murdered in their beds, but to Tom, it was an indication that Kit thought his face might give him away. Had Kit killed the Catholics?

'They were Flemish, the men, stabbed by several sword thrusts, it is said. An assassin's death.'

Martin spiked a morsel of meat and chewed it after imparting this information. Tom was sure that, as far as he was concerned it

41

was another example of the terrible times they lived in, but had nothing to connect it with his household. Tom needed to know more.

'Why do they say they were Spanish spies? How can that be known?'

Martin finished chewing but it was too slow for Tom.

'How can it be known?' he repeated.

Martin eventually swallowed and gave a sigh before explaining. 'Ah – some time ago, was it last year? Or the year before? Time goes so fast…they were hauled before our English overlord here in Flushing, accused of counterfeiting English money. An Englishman was with them; can't remember his name now, Marlin or some such thing. Once I write these names down they drift off from me; it's figures that I remember. The Englishman was shipped back to England, said *he* was spying for Elizabeth. Never knew what happened to him. The Catholics also were released…but such stories persist and now they have been murdered, the old tales are resurrected.'

Tom was furious. So that was what Kit had been doing in the night, wreaking his revenge. He wished now that Kit would learn his lesson of womanhood quickly so they could be on their way. Every day they stayed here he would be on tenterhooks.

* * * * *

It was not until a few days later that Tom managed to collar Kit on his own. Bridget had set him the task of weeding in the herb garden; seeing as it was now high summer and boiling hot, it was no easy task. The courtyard garden, with its squares of herbs, soft fruit and flowers to be cut for the house, was well sheltered from wind and rain but in high summer was a heat trap. Bridget and Martin had gone to a friend's house to celebrate a christening. Tom and Kit were alone. Kit sweated more than usual in the thick garments and wide hat, held on with a scarf, that he was required to wear. He had stood up and was bending backwards, his hands on the wide hips of his skirts, to rest his back, when Tom approached. Kit turned, for the paths were made of broken seashells and nobody could approach silently. The air was heavy with the humming of bees and the soft perfume of late pinks.

'I thought you would come to see me today, Tom. I have watched you brooding and staring at me at mealtimes. Well, let us have it out.'

'Kit you have to tell me all – first the goods you collected on the ship coming over, and now this. I know you said you wanted to get revenge on your enemies. Perhaps you'd better tell me how many enemies you think you have.'

'Keep your voice down, Tom, others might be able to hear; let's go over to that arbour where there's some shade, and I'll explain.'

Where they were sat, the scent of roses mixed with that of the pinks, made them heady. Kit lent back languidly. 'Your coz does believe in making me work, does she not? How think you I'm doing?'

'Don't try to change the subject.'

Kit hesitated; how much could he get away with? He didn't want to tell Tom all; pride, perhaps, or fear that he would not help him further when he knew the risks he was taking?

'Tom, trust me. You trusted me enough to find a body and help me substitute it, and escape from England. Is that not enough?'

'I thought it would be; instead I find myself…' Tom hesitated, looked around, listening, but all was quiet, except for the soft humming of bees.

'…I find myself involved in smuggling bullion *into* the country it is destined for…and now further murders. I don't mind covering for you while you are disguised in this ridiculous dress, but murders. We could be hanged, drawn and quartered.'

'Indeed, and the sooner I satisfy your cousin the better. And I love you, Tom, my dearest friend, and would not want you to be too involved and thereby endangered. You have trusted me, trust me a little more. All you need know is that I have my pledge to carry out in Antwerp and time is passing. Will it suffice, Tom, if I promise not to carry out any further night-time sojourns here in Flushing? I have, I assure you, revenged myself…at least here, in

43

the low countries.'

Tom slammed his fists into his knees in sheer frustration. The reason he admired Kit was his power with words and now he heard those honeyed words and felt he was being confused again.

Kit could see Tom didn't know what to say. 'We could take the bullion, and go to Italy. You know that's where I dream to be.'

'What? Steal it, you mean?'

Kit laughed. 'It's stolen already, remember.'

'But you said there was a way that we would be found out.'

'I would risk it, if you will help.'

Tom thought about it. Murder. Now theft. What lengths would his godless friend go to?

'No, Kit, we honour what you have to do – and then fulfil your wish.' He decided to change tack. 'What are all those writings in your trunk?

Yes, I admit I looked in there; I was, after all trying to find out what had happened to you.'

Kit grinned. 'Don't worry, I knew you had. They are mere scribblings, sonnets. I cannot help myself, I must have some release after my day's labour. I was asked to write some before I left and I continue the series, that is all. Shall I read some to you?'

'Nay not here, it might be thought strange that a young woman like you should be writing such things – they might think you have ideas above your station. I know it is said that Queen Elizabeth writes poetry and the Lady de Vere and even Lady Sidney – but a girl such as you are pretending to be, no.'

Tom put his hand on his friend's shoulder and Kit patted the hand; they were friends again.

They leaned back and savoured the soft humming from the bees and the scents of the garden. After a companionable silence Kit suddenly said, 'You know, I am beginning to admire your cousin Bridget; she is introducing me to so many new things. I had never thought about gardens and plants and flowers before and she has opened up a whole new world for me. Did you know that different flowers can be associated with the different humours?

No, nor did I.'

Tom looked at his friend, and thought of his plays; all about hard men who ranted against the world and their fate. His characters might use classical allusions or refer to alchemical mysteries, but never to the world of botanics.

He teased Kit. 'Oh, a Canterbury Scholar, and a university man, and one who has lived in the flesh-pot of the City of London now becomes the countryman? I can't believe it, Kit. You could never become such a one, surely?'

Kit laughed with him. 'It is a whole new *field*, I admit – a field of poesy and humming bees, Tom, which gives me ideas for sweet poems.'

Tom grinned back. 'Well, Kit I truly believe you are having a change of heart – a more feminine and country-wise one.'

*   *   *   *   *

After that, the days passed with Tom seeing little of *Christabel*. Indeed it was obvious that *Christabel* was avoiding him. Martin commented to his wife one morning as they lay abed that the young lady was exceptionally shy and well mannered and Bridget pecked him on the cheek and turned to her own side of the bed to hide her smile of satisfaction. The late summer burned into autumn.

*   *   *   *   *

'It is said that the Dutch will win at Geertruidenberg.' Martin said suddenly at dinner one day, and added, 'It is not so far away, either. They hold the town to siege and have constructed some clever mats to stop them sinking into the marshlands around the town. You know what that means, Tom?'

Tom carried on chewing, nodding, and waving his fork into the air to indicate he would answer when he had swallowed. He glanced over at *Christabel* and waved his fork even more violently to serve as a warning to Kit, who was opening a pouting mouth as if to respond to what Martin had said.

Bridget looked up from her food, and was quick-witted enough to notice the exchange. She had been only too aware of unrest in the streets and had heard tell of rebellion when she was in the markets. *Christabel* had been with her and had heard all the stories, and they had made their own conclusions. She placed her hand on *Christabel's* arm as if to comfort a young woman frightened by the men folk's talk, and interrupted before her husband could continue. 'Come, Martin, not before the young lady, you'll frighten her. You and Tom can discuss it afterwards when we are washing the crocks.'

Martin looked contrite and smiled at *Christabel* who shyly smiled back. The moment passed, but later, when Martin and Tom were alone, sitting in the small yard, and Martin puffed at the clay pipe he had taken up like his Dutch neighbours, He explained. 'It could turn bad, Tom. The Spanish Road is slow and the Spanish may decide to come by sea. If they do they'll head for their garrison town and could well pass Flushing on their way to break the siege. That means the English troops will be obliged to march out to protect our position here. You and the girl should be gone soon; you should not be involved. But I fear that your journey could be a dangerous and long one. What plans had you for reaching Italy?'

Tom had no plans except for the vague ideas that he and Kit had discussed in the garden on that hot summer's day. He did not answer immediately, thinking about what Kit had explained during those few precious moments alone. They had to reach Antwerp for Kit to deliver to Merchant Robstein, that was all he could think of but realised it would not be wise to tell Cousin Martin. So, part-truthing, he said, 'We must go via Antwerp, where Christabel has relatives she is expected to visit, and from there through France.'

'Yes, that would be your best plan. There are many bands of dissatisfied troops from the Spanish army. King Philip finds it difficult to pay them and they live on promises. When silver is sent it is stolen by brigands and when consignments eventually arrive the paymaster-generals take their cut and there is little left for the infantry. At least our soldiers fare better – until they are too old or injured to fight. There have been stories of more unrest in Zeeland and Friesland so avoid those places if you can.'

Tom nodded and excused himself. If he could he would have a private word with Kit, who would be pleased at what he had to tell him. He could see that his companion was a perfect female now, thanks to his cousin Bridget's training. They could leave soon, confident that Kit could play his part in the world.

Chapter Five

'You'll need this pass to get out of town. It will provide you with safe passage to Antwerp, to take messages for me. From there you should be able to go on your way safely.'

Tom couldn't believe his luck, Martin was helping them on their way. Did he know? He glanced at Bridget, but she was busying herself brushing her husband's coat, ready for him to go out. 'You can go by the next trading boat. It is none too soon. Winter will soon be here and travelling become nigh impossible.'

He handed Tom some papers. 'Go soon, I insist.'

Tom was convinced now that Bridget had told Martin something, but what?

Then Martin surprised him again by adding, 'Look after your young lady – I'll not ask anymore.' He looked serious. Tom said nothing. Bridget *must* have told him a story, realising that matters were getting serious and if Kit was found in their household they would all be in danger. Better to get rid of us quickly, he thought. But how much did Martin know? If he were interrogated, would he be able to tell all?

'Very well, we leave today.'

Bridget nodded. 'Come, I'll provide you with food for the journey and tell Christabel to ready herself. '

'Goodbye, then, Tom.' Martin shook hands. 'I have a great deal of work to do now that our troops are mustering.'

When they were on the steps of the house, the dog standing next to Bridget, its tail between its legs, Bridget hugged the young woman she had moulded. 'You have done well, young man,' she whispered. 'I'm sure you're doing what you're doing for a good reason. Do not let me down. And no more disappearing at night, it is not seemly.' She leant back and smiled at him. Kit pecked her on the cheek.

'Thank you, dear Bridget, I will remember you…'

Tom hugged his cousin and whispered, 'Thank you and God care for you.'

He turned away, embarrassed at the tears in her eyes. He knew she was wondering if she would ever see him again.

*   *   *   *   *

The barge sailed slowly up the River Scheldt, leaving the sea behind as they sailed eastwards.

'It's as wide as an ocean,' exclaimed Kit as he leant on the side and looked past Tom. There was nothing but grey foaming water and a thin line of land on one side. They could not see the further bank. 'It must be a furlong wide.'

Slowly though, the river narrowed as they moved closer to Antwerp. Here, they could see church steeples breaking the flat sky-line, and a few trees looking thin and windblown, as the leaves were falling. Herds of well-fed cows bunched together in the corners of fields, as if they waited to be herded in and penned for the winter. Kit and Tom stayed on deck to watch the flatlands on either side. It seemed peaceful, with no threat of the unrest which they knew was threatening, with rushes on the foreshore and grain growing high in the late warmth of summer, stretching as far as the eye could see. Soon the harvest would be gathered in. Then there would be dark days and no growth or movement in the land.

'It truly is a land that has no gradations.' exclaimed Kit. 'Not what I want at all. I dream of towering mountains and magical waterfalls, of great forests and lowering landscapes, places fit for princes to roam and princesses to be lost and then found; of tyrants conquered and good kings wronged. Great lands, so different from our gentle hills and the winding rivers of England. Instead I find myself stuck in this uninteresting wetland. After spending weeks, or so it seems, in slave labour. It has truly been a discipline for me, Tom.'

'What say you now, *dear lady?*' asked Tom, 'You truly speak nonsense.' He mocked, reverting to their bantering ways which had to be hidden in Martin's household, where they had hardly met.

'I mean, being a woman. It is truly hard not to join in a political discussion and your coz Martin would bring up such interesting matters. He is so partisan to his own country I wanted to yell at him sometimes. But to be a woman is interesting; outside the conversation of men, listening, instead of joining in. At first it was very hard to contain my great anger and you probably noticed I nearly burst out with the need to make a point on many occasions. Then something happened. As if the clothes I wore wrapped me in a veil of invisibility. I realised I could listen. It meant I could think more, give consideration to what was being said *and* appreciate the undercurrents.'

'Undercurrents? What do you mean?'

Priedeux turned away from the landscape, leaning on the prow behind him, so he could face the man who was Christabel.

'Well, who do you think ruled that household?'

'Do you mean who is in charge of the finances? Who decides what?'

'I mean, who decides how they live, where they live, what each of them do.'

Tom thought. Martin was the head of the household, of course. But Kit's question, like the riddles he would pose when they were at college, made him reflect before he answered. He knew Bridget ran the household, but surely Martin would tell his wife when things were wrong; surely he had been ordered to Flushing by his superiors and all the family had gone. Bridget would not have been able to stop him. She might have stayed at home, but that was a different matter. Martin would have had to agree to that, surely? Martin was the man of affairs, the one who knew what was going on because of his job; he knew what happened in the world, not Bridget. He decided there was no trick to Kit's question.

'Martin, of course – he is the man, he is in charge.'

Kit laughed and watched a woman as she led her cow by its tether to the water's edge and allowed it to drink.

'Look at that; who is in charge there?'

'The woman. The cow is tethered to her.'

'Yes, exactly. If the cow is not led to the water, will it not die of thirst?'

'Oh, Kit, you're being provocative – just like a woman.'

'No Tom, it is true. You may think Martin was in charge but I watched, *I was involved* – as Bridget organised him. We worked together, remember. She knew all about the siege of Geertruidenberg long before Martin officially heard. The women have their own ways of finding out information and I know that if she had thought it necessary, she would have brought up the subject earlier. Women have a great way of gossiping in the market place, of listening at tables when the men think they are not there. Bridget is intelligent; she would have made a good general if she had been a man.'

Tom tried to protest, it sounded ridiculous, but, just like a woman, he thought, Kit breezed on. 'She had already warned me that we should be on our way soon, and why. She then told me not to say anything. *Men don't like news told them by women, they call it gossip and scare-mongering; you have to let them find out in their own good time and then not say anything. Let them tell you as if they are all knowledgeable. But in the meantime, get yourself ready. The men won't think of food and water, of stocking up for the future. You'll soon work out how to do it when you watch the other women in the market.* And I saw it for myself; they were panic buying when they heard about the Spaniards coming, Tom. Bridget has plenty of stocks put away if Flushing is besieged, I assure you.'

'But you were going to say something at the table when Martin spoke about it, I saw you.'

'Yes, only to say that we knew anyway. But Bridget caught my eye and so I stopped.'

Tom thought about what Kit was saying and answered lamely, 'But you have only that one example.'

Kit looked away over the banks of the river and said nothing. Tom followed his gaze and saw the woman and the cow on the horizon as silhouettes as the sun went down in the west, the woman leading the cow away. Tom smiled and shrugged. Kit said nothing but continued to stare. Tom watched his profile and was surprised at what he saw. For the first time he saw a young woman, looking pensive, as if in love, knowing something that others didn't know, keeping it to herself, hugging her secret.

*   *   *   *

Before they reached Antwerp Kit showed Tom a small map, drawn on a scrap of paper closely folded, which he produced from an inner lining of his bodice. 'We must perform my delivery first, Tom, we're long overdue, and then we will carry out Martin's instructions, what say you?'

Tom nodded. He would much rather get rid of Kit's contraband. They were now in foreign territory and would certainly be killed if discovered.

He studied the map and said, 'Yes, the street of the merchants. I agree, we'll go there first.'

Kit allowed Tom to lead them.

'A matter of necessity, Tom; I'll have to be truly female now.'

After asking a few people, Tom returned to Kit, who sat on a low wall, patiently waiting, eyes down, the very picture of a bashful woman waiting for her men folk to collect her.

'The street of the merchants will be easy to find, I am told. They hold a fair there twice a year where dealings are done. Any stall holder will know where it is,' Tom explained helping Kit to rise, as if she were exhausted.

They pushed through crowds of coster-mongers, young servants, apprentices in the bright colours of their guilds, like bright strutting cockerels, stern-looking lawyers in their raven-robes, merchants in their fur-lined gowns fussing like pecking starlings. If they had thought Flushing was busy in the early morning, Antwerp was bulging. The harbour was a heaving mass of bobbing ships, tiny ferrying craft looking as if they would be crushed by the great seagoing vessels. Men threw great bales onto the quay from the ships, while others took note and scribbled away in great tomes. Labourers stacked the huge heaps, while great horse-drawn carts, piled high with goods, rumbled past them. Poorly dressed women and urchins mingled amongst the workers, the children diving for the stray piece of grain or merchandise that fell as the goods were being hauled ashore and scurrying away before they could be beaten about the ears. There was a great muttering, and a soft rhythmic singing among the workers, the rhythm of their tune forcing a beat by which they worked. One group disturbed the friends by roughly pushing between them and Tom ushered Kit into a side alley, away from the river.

Soon they had left the lowering warehouses and the wooden cranes jutting out, like giant noses of the quay, and found themselves between tall buildings, with stepped frontages. Here the way was narrow, barely wide enough for one cart load, with twisting lanes. After a short while, they found themselves in a wide space. At one end, facing them was the tall façade of the cathedral, spire rising heavenwards, way above the shops, which hugged its sides. There were stalls being erected, fruit piled neatly in boxes, fish being laid out. The crowds were thickening and Tom edged around these to avoid a group of vicious looking men who gathered before a large imposing building at the side of the square. They looked like fighting men, some had scars ruining their faces, others had cabbage ears or misshapen noses. They were murmuring, a low angry sound, leaning against their pikestaffs as if they would pummel the very ground into submission. Kit, with a soft feminine movement of his arm, stopped Tom from hurrying past.

'Hush, listen to what they're saying.'

One of the men had forced his way to the front and was berating a man who sat at a makeshift desk before the imposing door of the building.

'Dear God! We'll not serve any longer. We want to be paid.' The accent was guttural and Tom guessed these men were mercenaries.

A placating hand was placed on the shoulder of the

complainant. Another man shouldered past and demanded, 'Let me go talk to the paymaster-general once again. Make him understand'.

Banners waved in the wind, showing which company was now disaffected by lack of pay. The man at the desk was stony faced, not even answering, merely shaking his head.

Kit murmured to Tom, 'Oh dear, once again the Spanish King has no idea. It is as your cousin says; his army marches on promises, despite his great wealth, and it is not until a group breaks out and refuses to fight that money is grudgingly unloaded from the great treasury and sent north. Since Palma died last year, the new governor has been kept short of funds.'

Tom hurried on, saying nothing. How could Kit speak like that when he had Spanish coin hidden beneath his skirts? Tom was furious and did not even turn round to see if his 'woman' was following. He knew Kit had to keep with him, but felt sure he would do so reluctantly, knowing that Kit wanted to stay and listen. Tom led him into side streets to leave the angry murmurings behind, knowing they could not afford to get involved in a riot. Hungry and disaffected soldiers had a way of forcing funds from the local populace and sometimes the women were left with bellies full of revenge to nurture for nine months. If they caught Kit, what would they do when they found their victim was not a woman?

They came out onto another open square where there were large trees shading the centre, even though the sun was riding high in the sky. At this time of day only a few men bustled by, ringlets and sashes showing them to be Jews.

'We must be near the mercantile centre.'

'Ask one of them for Robstein's house. He is well known and they must be used to such a question in this place.' Tom nodded and accosted one of the lingerers in the square, a pocked man with one leg. He held out his hands for alms, and Tom gave him some coin while asking for directions.

'Over there; that's Robstein's place. But make sure you keep your hands in your pockets, for he's a sly one.' The beggar limped away cackling.

Tom warned, 'Leave things to me, remember you're female'.

Kit nodded, resigned. He knew he would have to be led by Tom at least in such a public place. He let Tom rap on the heavy door, made more imposing with large iron bolts and hinges.

A panel in the door was opened with a rattle of keys and a half face appeared, the forehead and eyes only, and stared at them. It was framed with a dark tonsure and closely fitted skullcap.

'Yes?'

'We come to see Robstein. On business.'

Kit was whispering something. Tom tried to ignore the whisperings but his companion eventually pulled on his sleeve. 'There's a word I must use. Let me speak, I have to say it quietly.'

Tom shrugged, resigned, and stood aside. He listened hard as Kit, using a soft feminine voice, whispered. It sounded to Tom like 'Puss, puss.' Tom grinned at the ridiculous password, which suited his companion.

The panel was snapped shut. They waited. They could hear shufflings but the door was not opened immediately. Kit had time to turn to his friend and smile, as if the delay was his fault and he should apologise. Tom tried to edge him away from the door.

'You must remember you are a shy and retiring female,' he had time to whisper before the rasping of bolts being slid back told them they were being allowed entry. Kit's only response was to raise his finely shaped eyebrows and smile. Then came the noise of a key being turned. This was a well-secured house. The door was opened slowly, showing how heavy it was, and the face they had seen half-revealed now looked down on them from the high steps inside. The house was obviously built so that its entrance was high above the road, leaving visitors at a disadvantage. Kit raised his skirts as he entered, pushing past the man who stood in the entrance, who was dressed all in black except for white ruff and cuffs. The man hurriedly closed the door and skipped past them into the gloomy interior but said nothing, keeping his head down.

Here was a small covered courtyard, a grimy glass roof

allowing a dim greenish light into the interior so they could not make out the decor. They were led through another door, up some wide richly carved stairs and down a long narrow gallery. Their guide scurried before them, his hands folded in front of him, holding himself close, revealing nothing. They followed mesmerised, not taking in their surroundings at all. When they reached the end of the gloomy gallery, their guide knocked on another heavy, wood-panelled door and then stepped aside. Tom wondered about the building; when they had entered from the street, it appeared to be only one room deep but they had certainly gone further and further back. He guessed that the house went back a long way, even having another entrance at the rear, onto a parallel street.

They entered the room and the door was shut behind them. They now found themselves in a brightly lit chamber, the light coming from the late autumn sun, angled so it shone through the large bay window, with leaves of the trees outside obscuring any view. Were they facing the square from where they had entered? It was as if they had entered a maze and had no idea of their orientation.

Papers were strewn on a huge desk which dominated the room. It smelt heavily of wax and Tom noticed spent candles in sconces placed around the desk. The walls were lined with shelves on which were huge ledgers. A room of business, he guessed, where those who worked needed a great deal of light, either from the large window or from candles, to study or write entries in ledgers. Both Tom and Kit were initially dazzled by the strong sunlight after the gloom of the gallery but as their eyes adjusted to the light, they saw that, behind the desk sat a heavily jowled man, a mop of greying curly hair and a beard hiding his features, except for the eyes. They were large and deeply brown and caught the light from the window so that Kit and Tom could almost see their reflections in them. He stared at the newcomers and it was as if his heavy eyebrows had risen before they had come in the room and frozen there. He wore a long dark robe, furred at the edges. Hanging around his neck was a tiny pair of spectacles.

Kit stepped forward but Tom restrained him and bowed.

'We have come to deliver something…'

But he was cut short. 'At last you've arrived. I expected you some months ago.' The voice was low as if the man was reluctant to spare his breath.

Tom answered, trying to keep his voice as steady as possible. 'Yes, we were told to deliver as soon as possible, but we were delayed.'

'I know that, but it is still far too long, we have great troubles brewing because you are late.'

'How do you know about me?'

'You think you were given such a package by my agent and then just let loose? Do you not know that we have our own systems for monitoring such as you? You're not of the chosen people. Until you can be trusted we will watch over you and always know where you are. Except that we did not expect such you to spend such a long time in Flushing.'

Kit shivered. He thought he had left all that behind at Deptford, along with his male-ness. Walsingham's eyes, Ralegh's intrigues, the streetmen watching and scuttling behind him in the dark alleys of London. The duplicity of the priests at Reims. Those who plotted not only to promote their papist ways, but threatened the very life of England's queen. The Dutchmen who would be friends but were really enemies. The dealings, and the double-dealings and even the triple-betrayals.

He had hoped his 'murder' would have left him free of all that. Now he felt a new web insidiously weaving about him. Perhaps he should have let himself be assassinated by those enemies who were encircling him in England. What was life worth if he was constantly being spied upon? He began to wish he'd never accepted this assignment. It was necessary, though; otherwise how were they to live this new life? And Kit – even in his new guise – could not bear to be in beggar's rags. He loved good lace, fine velvets, good food and wine. He *needed* the money in order to have the life he envisaged, to do the work he wanted to do. Even so, a gleam of an idea was forming, but he would not want Tom to know.

The man had addressed Tom, and Kit realised he did not know that Kit was really the carrier. He nudged Tom and nodded. Tom realised what was going on and explained, 'Very well, we can deliver now. I would ask that my lady here has a private room in order to divest herself of the items.'

'Ja?' It was a guttural uncompromising answer that sounded more like a question. The man pulled himself upright, slowly, and it could be seen that his hands were curled in crablike shapes, as if frozen in the act of permanently fingering and trying the coin that passed through them. He moved slowly from the table and gestured to a panel between the shelves. His voice, when he eventually spoke was a low.

'She can go in there, a small cubicle but that is all she will need, ja?'

The words seemed to hang in the air. Tom was not sure whether the man normally spoke so quietly or whether he suffered from a phlegmatic disease which meant his breathing did not come naturally. Kit moved to the door and opened it quickly, peered inside and turned to Tom, saying shyly, 'It's a privy. I won't be long.'

The man's eyebrows moved again and his mouth twitched as if he would stifle a smile. Tom noticed it and was perturbed. Did he know what had gone on in Flushing? Did he know the true identity of *the lady*? His host gestured to a chair and Tom sat and watched as the man returned to his position behind the desk, and picked up a scroll, and held it high, ostensibly reading it while they waited.

It wasn't long before Kit emerged. Tom immediately noticed that his bustle was not quite so thick. He thought that he looked less of a woman now. Over his arm he held the leather belt, which hung heavily. As he moved into the room, it knocked against the arm of a chair and made a jangling noise. He swung it on the table before the man.

'I come to deliver this. I wait for you to count it. I was promised ten per cent if I delivered it safely.'

The old man looked up, clearly surprised at the determined way the 'woman' spoke. Tom decided that it was best to explain. 'My *lady* will do the negotiating; she has more of the man in her than you can know. I am surprised your spies did not discover that.'

'I take things as I find them,' said Robstein. He scrabbled for the belt and started to unbuckle the panniers. He continued, 'A pound of flesh, is that what you want?' The crabbed hands reached out slowly and took the bags from the pouches. 'I will count in front of you.'

He examined the seals carefully, and then ripped them open and emptied the contents onto the table. Priedeux gaped as gold doubloons cascaded between the dusty papers and scrolls, the old man quick now as his hands moved to contain those which rolled away from his reach. Tom believed they had been carrying silver; now all he saw was glinting gold. Stolen Spanish gold. He stood and watched as the man counted, the crabbed fingers moving rapidly as he moved the coins into piles, and then lined up the piles into lines. It glinted in the mid morning sun and Tom wondered whether the reflection could be seen in the windows, for all to see below, it seemed so brilliant. Certainly the man's eyes also glinted with tiny gold flecks.

A thought flitted through Tom, like a cold shiver, but then disappeared: *supposing he and Kit were to kill this man and steal it all.* He knew they would never escape from this house; bankers such as this man would be well protected and he remembered the long corridors and creaking doors through which they had passed to reach this inner chamber; the skull-capped man who had led them here. So he waited, not daring to catch his companion's gaze. *How much would be theirs?* So far the man had twenty piles in front of him, made up of ten doubloons each and he was still counting. Even now Tom could see that Kit would be taking a sizeable portion, enough to keep them in luxury for several years. And still the man gathered coins and piled them. There was no movement in the room except for the hands gathering, counting and piling, which seemed to create a breeze all its own. Tom was sure he could smell the sweat of men who had gathered the gold; the sea salt of the journey it had taken to reach this spot, the acrid odour of spilt blood in sacrifice, and, over it all, the smell of sour tallow of candles which were needed to write in dusty ledgers the final sum which did not calculate the human misery such wealth generated.

Finally the last coin was handled and piled up. One thousand or a little over and Kit's share would be a hundred. A king's ransom! Robstein pushed a pile representing ten percent towards Kit. He said nothing. He started to put the remainder into bags which he took from a drawer. Kit did not move. Tom said nothing. Eventually Robstein looked up, surprised at the lack of movement.

'Have you anything to carry it with?'

Kit shook his head. 'I found the belt useful, could I keep it?'

The banker smiled then, showing browned teeth. *Stained with tasting coin,* thought Tom. Slowly the old man placed his hands together, in a strange painful looking movement. Then he said slowly, whispering again, 'You can have it – for two of your coins.'

Tom gasped; such a leather pouch would cost but a shilling in the market – a doubloon, hardly ever seen by a peasant, was worth many times that. The man was nothing but a thief. Kit though, smiled, that rare smile he had given his companions at college when he enjoyed a good philosophical debate or when someone had agreed with his theory that God was but an empty vessel; he was enjoying this.

'No, only one coin, just one and that is too much, old man.'

Kit had taken one of the coins from the pile in front of him, and held it out, flat in the palm of his hand. Slowly the crabbed hand reached out and took it, pushing the leather belt across at the same time. Quickly Kit gathered the coins and stashed them neatly and evenly into the bags.

'One moment my friend, while I replace the belt in its hiding place.' He disappeared into the privy and soon emerged again with his womanly curves. Tom nodded and smiled.

As Kit returned, the door they had entered opened as if by some hidden signal and their guide stood there and gestured for them to follow. Before they did so, Kit said, 'Wait, I would have a private word with our banker here, Tom, would you leave us?'

It was said with such authority that Tom shrugged, annoyed but finding himself in an impossible position. He did not want to show that there was any disagreement between them. The banker looked up from his writing. His eyes narrowed. He nodded to his servant who gestured Tom out into the corridor.

When the door was closed behind Tom, Kit said,

'I would ask a boon of you, sir.'

'Ja?' The way he said it, Kit knew he would have to do some hard bargaining.

'I have great respect for your people, the way you deal with matters. Discreet, but intelligent.'

Robstein gestured for him to sit, but said nothing.

'I know your people live on the outskirts of society. Yet you are successful as I can see from your house. For that, I admire you.'

Robstein's brows raised. 'You should not use false flattery, *young woman.*'

Kit understood, by the way he had said it, that Robstein knew who he was and again a shiver ran through him. Still, he continued, 'You said you have your networks; your systems. Watching people. Presumably your networks stretch to England?'

'And why do you want to know? Such knowledge is dangerous.'

'Do you?'

'We bargain here, my friend. We bargain with an exchange of information. You tell me why you want to know and I might tell you.'

'I need to return letters, manuscripts…to England.'

'You must tell me more. I cannot allow my systems to be interrupted if waylaid, to be found to be carrying treasonous papers.'

'Indeed not. Not treasonous. Just letters, treatises between intellectuals; poems, mere whimsies.'

'Such things can be written in code.'

Kit smiled. 'Indeed not. You must know from your systems who I am?'

The man lent back, his hands moving into a webbed pattern, fingers interlacing in front of him. He nodded slowly and Kit was sure he saw a twinkle in those secretive eyes.

'Indeed, Ja, I know.' Kit noted that he had pretended ignorance earlier. This man was as slippery as a snake but Kit revelled in their bargaining.

'Then I will admit – I need to write plays. I have an idea, and believe it can work if I can use an efficient system.'

It was true that Marlowe had succeeded in his old life of play-writing and spying because he knew how to manipulate words and actions to persuade others and here he was conscious of never having used the skill so carefully before. His opponent was not to be underestimated. Kit watched him, noting the eyes closing and waited as he considered.

It was a slow process. He wondered if he needed to say more, but decided not to. There was a long silence and Kit was about to give up when Robstein nodded:

'So long as you promise me there will be nothing in them that will identify *you* – for obvious reasons – or that will be seen to be sedition and against your Queen.'

Kit nodded eagerly. 'But of course – the Queen I revere.'

Robstein stood and offered his hand. Kit took it and was surprised at the firmness of the old man's handshake.

The door opened silently, at the conclusion of their business, as if an invisible hand had pulled a chord to summon the black-clad clerk again. Without any further farewells Kit stepped out into the corridor and joined Tom, who looked at him questioningly. Kit ushered Tom before him, keeping his head down, in a gesture reminiscent of a humble woman. Nothing was said, as they followed the clerk, retracing their steps, their guide unlocking and locking doors after them. Soon they stood on the steps in the open air again.

It was an anti-climax. A cat stalked past, a peasant girl carrying the morning's vegetables from the market wandered away from. Cooking smells came from some of the houses; lunch was being prepared. All was calm.

'Where to, now my friend?' asked Tom, knowing he would have to bide his time if he were to find out what the private interview was about.

'We travel to France next, for I must find someone. And it would not be safe to remain in the empire of King Philip. But I tell you this, dear Tom, do not underestimate the Jews; they can be very good friends if you understand them. But they suffer not fools gladly. Now we go to where there are many fools.'

Chapter Six

'I must go to confession – now!'

'What?' Tom was so taken by surprise that he dropped the book he was reading. They had been sitting peaceably in their lodgings, *Christabel* at the window to catch the light on the papers before her. Anyone in the street below, if they had looked up, would think she was a pretty maid, scribbling letters home. But Tom had noticed the young lady had not been writing. Every time he'd surreptitiously glanced towards Kit, he was astonished to see him chewing the end of his quill, forehead furrowed, the very picture of a nervous woman penning love poetry to a secret admirer and puzzling to ensure each word would be well received. With the rich clothes made to order, of fine lace ruffs at collar and cuffs, and layered skirts, Kit carried off being a maid well. But Tom could see that the feathers at the end of the quill were shiny and stuck together, for being sucked so long. The parchment before him seemed blotted and unevenly filled. Instead of frantically jabbing with staccato movements to catch more ink from the inkwell, as was normal for Kit, Tom caught him each time daydreaming.

'What, now? Why?'

For days they had stayed in this room which Kit had insisted they take, opposite the great west portico of Reims Cathedral. Respecting his friend's need for solitude after the turbulent time in Flushing and Antwerp, Tom had readily agreed. He, too, was glad of a few days to read and think. During those days, he'd realised Kit was not studying the great sculptures on the entrance of Reims cathedral when he stared out, but had left him to it, and immersed himself in his own reading. Still Kit was silent, and, in an effort to get him to respond, Tom said, 'You deny the church. How is it you suddenly feel the need for confession?'

Kit did not turn as he answered, but, still staring out of the window, said decisively, 'Confession may cleanse the soul, young friend, if not for me, for others. Let's go now.'

'I cannot believe you mean this, but if that is what you want.' He watched and wondered as Kit put his papers away in a leather case and started to smooth the feminine clothes. 'How can you, the rebellious playwright, who has denied that God existed, arguing against all accepted beliefs at drunken student debates, want to go to confession?' Tom shook his head as if to clear it of such a thought. 'You always maintained to those who secretly practised the faith that confession was useless, so how come now?'

In all the time he had known Kit, he had never voluntarily mentioned going to church. If Kit believed in anything, it had to be in a rational type of doctrine, miles from the ritual of the Catholic Church.

'You can't be influenced by the beauty of this very Cathedral city of Reims, this den of Catholicism?' Tom knew that young Catholics were trained as priests, and then secretly returned to England to spread the word from this very town. Perhaps the atmosphere had seeped into Kit's soul and changed him – her? Was it the woman now in Kit who had changed character, he wondered, but dared not say. Kit had made him promise not to bring up the subject of his 'womanhood'.

Or was Kit up to his old tricks? After all, he had insisted they find somewhere that overlooked the cathedral with its brooding, finely sculptured frontage.

Kit, smoothing the long hair that was now coiffured in tight curls and braided, approached Tom. 'Nay, Tom, do not stare at me so. It's not to gain absolution – it's to gain revenge. You remember what I said when we left Antwerp. Why else do you think I insisted on travelling to this den of devilry, a hotbed of Catholicism, with its college of fanatics, when all I dream of is the beauty of southern states, of Venice, Padua, Verona and Rome?'

'Oh, no Kit, not again? I know you said...but I thought you had finished with revenge in Flushing.'

'Indeed. In the Low Countries, I had, but there is one more score I must settle. Trust me, this will be fun. I have been watching and waiting. Now is the time.'

Fun! And what did Kit mean by it being time? Tom did not know what to do. He was beginning to believe that nothing would surprise him. When they had left Antwerp and taken the south-western road into France he had not questioned Kit. They had, after all, been warned not to travel in the German States, or use the normal Spanish road, being owned by Philip of Spain. The only other route to Italy was through France.

Tom questioned, 'Revenge? Fun?'

'You know little of my time when I was absent from Cambridge and some of it you will never know. You were good enough to trust me when I told you my life was in danger, and we set up that little escapade at Deptford. But this I tell you. Whatever I did, whatever danger I encountered, it was for my Queen and my Country.'

He paused.

'I can't tell you all, it's too complicated. But one of the places I visited was the seminary here. I found it hard to carry out my duty and I was nearly betrayed, by one man. Now I have seen him in his priest's robes and I will get my revenge.'

So, Tom realised, this was why Kit had been so careful about their choice of lodgings, so patient, so abstracted. He had been waiting for someone.

'No, Kit, what can you do, a mere woman as you are? And why should I help you this time? Not unless you tell me more.'

Kit ignored him, moving to the mirror, where he checked his woman's locks. Tom watched in fascination, noting the gently feminine movements of hairdressing. Truly Marlowe, or his aunt Bridget, had effected a wondrous transformation. He waited, expecting more. He was not disappointed.

Kit spoke quietly. 'When I left Cambridge in that first year it was because I was given an assignment by Walsingham; to find out who was being trained here and being sent back to England to incite rebellion among the Catholics, against the Queen's command. But I found something else: a plot against the Protestants in the Netherlands, a plot to discredit them with false coin. Well, you know about that.' He paused and laughed. 'It seems my life is surrounded by money from peculiar sources.'

As he spoke, he gathered his outdoor cloak and swung it round his shoulders, pulling the hood close around the face. Tom realised he was serious about going out and quickly tied the ribbons of his own jerkin which had been loosened in the comfort of their lodgings, pulling parts of his sleeve through the slits and smoothing his hose. He could not let *Christabel* go out alone, it would not be seemly, and he could see by Kit's determined air that he would go, even if Tom refused. As they left he reminded *Christabel*, 'You were telling me why you needed revenge.'

'Hush, dear brother and I will tell.' Tom grinned at the naming. They had agreed on the road from Antwerp that they would now be brother and sister, to hide any suggestion of untoward behaviour.

Kit raised his voice to a feminine high pitch, and explained as they hurried across the narrow street to the towering frontage of the cathedral.

'False coin was to be my undoing. You already know what happened there. I have had my revenge on the traitors.' He spoke quickly, staccato, as he measured his pace to that of a dainty female. 'Now I hunt a priest, Father Lawrence. I had known him here in Reims where he bethought me a good pupil. I saw him in Flushing, by a strange coincidence, when I too was there to work on the Catholics; he spotted me from my time in Reims. He wondered aloud why I was always where there seemed to be trouble. I tried to counter this with accusations against him. He denounced me to the Catholics there and claimed I had betrayed his protégées who had been sent to England. Even though I denied it, his accusations meant that I had to leave and not complete my work. The accusation against me for falsifying coin came from him. It was true, of course, it was our English plot to discredit the

Catholics in that country. I was perforce arrested, my cover blown, and the good Queen sent me to the Tower to try and save me. Any spy of Elizabeth's is no good if they are discovered by the enemy, you understand that?'

Reaching the entrance to the cathedral, Tom shivered, as they stepped out of the sun into the dark shadow of the great building. Kit lowered his voice. 'I was lucky to escape without being hung, drawn and quartered.'

He paused as they entered the dark interior. Inside, there were gloomy corners where the sun did not penetrate, but the main aisle was bespattered with red, purple, gold and blue spots, light deflected through the multi-hued windows.

'Time in the Tower is not pleasant, dear Tom – and now I will get my revenge.' He spoke quietly for the high interior and cold stone made voices echo. Tom shivered again, for, despite the sun rays, all was cold in the great space with towering trunks of columns reaching to the high roof. They made their way down the southern nave towards the altar and found the confessional. There were only a few people kneeling in prayer in the nave, as if frozen in that position. A few couples hid behind the giant columns, their whispering voices carrying like the twitterings of starlings. A votary busied himself at the altar, cleaning the chalice with a linen cloth and replacing a wine container. A young woman held a baby before the Virgin Mary asking the statue to intercede for her. A crone lifted her face to the same statue, hands in prayer, her face skeletal and still.

As they walked Kit whispered, still using the woman's voice, 'Leave me, but wait inside the porch.'

Tom nodded and watched as the man who was Christabel ducked under the dark cloth that hid the confessor's seat. Tom sniffed as he retraced his steps. Brought up a Protestant, the dull stale smell of incense made his nose twitch and he felt alien in this exotic place. He would wait as instructed. He was tense and the stillness of the place disturbed him even more. But he would be ready to help his friend, and he put his hand on his sword hilt, hoping he would not have to use it. What was Kit planning?

*　　*　　*　　*　　*

'Forgive me Father for I have sinned…'

'All will be forgiven child, if true forgiveness is sought, tell me…'

'I have lain with a man, Father. A man not my husband, for I am not yet betrothed. I have committed carnal sin.'

'Tell me about it, child.' The priest hesitated before he answered; then he spoke as if breathing was hard for him.

Kit smiled as he recognised the excitement in the priest's voice. He had not expected the old rogue to bite so easily.

'I…I, nay I cannot say…'

'Dear child, you know the rules of confessional. You must confess all.'

'It started with us praying together, Father, for he said that friends must plight their loyalty before God.'

'But that is not sinful, child, unless your loyalty to each other is greater than your love of God.'

'As we prayed…' Kit took a deep breath, and continued, hesitantly.

'As we prayed, he turned to me and placed his hands upon my breasts, finding the gap in my robes. I, I did not know what to do, but felt so yielding towards his friendship, I lay back…'

The priest interrupted him.

'Yes, yes, and then?'

'All the time, he spoke about a close friendship and I wanted it so…he, he told me that in the eyes of God such close amity was not sinful and I believed him. Oh, Father, I allowed him inside my clothes. He reached for my depths and I felt so soft, so yielding…'

Once again the priest interrupted. 'Tell me more, child, tell me more.'

Kit hesitated.

'Go on child, go on.' It was said quickly, breathlessly. Kit hid his smile by looking down at his folded hands.

'My lover, convincing me that his actions were holy, released

69

his holy organ – that was what he called it - from its constricting clothes and placed it gently between my legs, Father. It was warm, and, as it moved closer and closer, his whispered endearments and licked light kisses on my ears, made me feel faint. And Father, he moved it so slowly, like a gentle snake's head, caressing my inner secrets.'

Kit, with all his drama-producing skills, suddenly speeded up in his description. 'Father, suddenly, he found an eager opening. I was beguiled. I would do whatever he would ask. Then, like a cold shock to me, he thrust eagerly against me.'

'It hurt Father, for this was the first time, and he approached as if this was his holy grail, for that was what he called it, Father. He feared that he was too big for me. At first he was gentle and hardly moved at all, resting there inside me. I was surprised at how large it was. He left it at the entrance, and but gently stroked it into what he called his holy nave of friendship. Oh, and, Father, I never knew such a magic feeling deep inside me which seemed to make me all soft and giving. As I felt such pleasure, he moved deeper up my soft nave and it seemed to be easier, and again he kissed me, gently but with an insistence which meant that his tongue mirrored what was happening below. He moved further inside as if to worship at the altar, and the pleasure I felt became more intense.'

Kit paused again. He knew all the tricks of how to arouse his audience. Indeed, the description was making him feel hot. If he were not careful he might well reveal his hidden manhood and would have a need to massage it into dullness again.

The priest gasped and said, 'Go on, oh go on.'

His breathing was becoming staccato, and through the grill Kit could see that the hands, which were originally held together in prayer, had slipped down and one had disappeared beneath the priest's habit. The head was thrown back and the eyes gleamed through the grill. A dull thudding regular noise could be heard.

Kit smiled. 'Then he pushed deep inside me and oh, the pleasure, Father, the pleasure. I could feel such a weight of tingling inside me, on my lips, on my breasts, I did not know what to do but suddenly a spasm passed through me and I raised my hips to welcome him into the deepest, secretest part of me and he thrust again, and we moved sinuously together. He was becoming larger and the tingling was becoming unbearable, I felt as if I was losing myself in a multitude of senses all over my body. I did not know what to do except to take into myself his deep friendship.'

Kit sighed; the priest was moving.

'Child, I must come to you, to give you absolution…' With surprising agility the priest slipped out of his area of the confessional in a side-stepping movement, one foot already into Kit's section. He pulled his cassock up and his erect penis was clearly visible, a hand clutched around it as if he would thrust it into any available cavity he could find.

Kit did not hesitate. He stood and called as loudly as he could, in the high-pitched woman's voice, 'Rape, help, rape! Help me someone, the priest has gone mad!'

The young mother looked up, the crone turned, the young couples ran from their hiding places and made for the confessional. The priest, as he tried to stand, whispered desperately, 'Hush, child, hush, it is not for others to know what shall happen. I will give you absolution.' As he spoke he still made useless thrusting movements.

Kit lurched forward suddenly and pushed past him, knocking him down so that his cassock rose above his head for all to see him in his shame, even though it was now rapidly shrinking. Tom came running and grabbed Kit, 'What in hell's name are you doing?' Then he realised others were gathering. 'Dear sis, what has happened?' he said loudly and with concern in his voice.

Kit leaned on his shoulder to hide his face, as if in shame and whispered quietly, 'Oh Revenge is sweet!' Then he gave a great sob and said in a stage voice, echoing Tom, 'Oh, brother, dear brother, take me away from this place, for it is a very hell! I was making my confession and this devil tried to ravage me; he claimed it would give me absolution.'

The crowd gathered around the priest muttering, 'Disgraceful.

Fiend.'

Father Lawrence tried to protest but Kit did not give him a chance to speak. 'He came at me, and I have never seen such a thing before, me, an innocent, a stranger in the town.'

Kit glared down at the priest and for a moment their eyes met. A dawn of recognition broke.

'You...' but the rest of what he was about to say was lost in the first kick he received from the crone who had been praying not far away.

'Wicked, wicked...' she screamed.

The priest gasped and tried to say something but one of the young men, holding the hand of his girl, also kicked the priest as he lay before him.

'You old lecher! How dare you!'

The old crone muttered, 'That's right, kick him where it will hurt most; such a man should not have such weaponry to attack a young maid!'

Another beau, to show he was brave to his belle, jumped on the priest's parts, and the priest yelled in agony. Then they all joined in like wild beasts, tearing at the dishevelled cassock so that pieces of cloth were thrown into the air.

Tom watched for a moment, but realised the danger; if the churchwardens came they would insist on an investigation, even a medical inspection of the so-called ravaged girl.

'Come, come away; leave it to the locals.' He said it loudly and one of the young men nodded, 'Aye take her away, she must be deeply distressed. We will deal with this wickedness.'

As they crept away they could hear the agonised cries of the priest lessen as his parishioners laid into him. There were screams of, 'Defiler! Devil! An insult to God! And you a consecrated priest. Burn, burn in hell!'

Tom said, 'I do verily believe you may not be the first he has so-called ravaged, dear Christabel. Their anger far exceeds what I would have expected.'

Kit chuckled then. 'Truly what a revenge – but now we must

needs depart, what say you?'

As they reached their lodgings, Kit added, ''Tis not safe to stay; they may well, as you say, want to ask questions. He recognised me for an instant, which was wonderful. He had such a stare of surprise before the first kick turned his thoughts from me.'

'And what gave you such an idea? What did you say to him? '

As they hurriedly packed, Kit spoke in short bursts. 'Never you mind, Tom, for I swear you will think I am but a crude and wicked woman if you heard the detail. It was just such a scene as a play could be made of...'

Tom left coins on the table for their landlady as Kit laughed again. 'Oh, what sweet revenge. For the last of my enemies.'

Tom, whose heart was racing and who wanted to depart as soon as possible, stopped his packing and stared at his friend. 'I hope you speak truly. I don't want you to do anything like that again. We could both have been arrested if they found out about us – what would they think? Promise me, never again.'

Kit sobered. 'I promise, Tom, but it could not be resisted. Now, to the south, to Rome, and then onwards to visit the seats of great learning; the universities of Padua and Milan, and to see the sights of that watery town of Venice.'

Tom laughed knowing that Kit was being ironic about the dream city of licence and republicanism, which they believed was floating on water. But it was a nervous laugh. Could he really trust Kit to keep his promise?

Chapter Seven

'Tom, I feel so fresh and excited. Imagine, neither of us have been so far south before. I tell you, if my parents thought I was alive, they would never dream of all that we have done – and will do.'

Tom nodded, looking with wonder on the strange terrain of high, snow-capped mountains that surrounded their path through a valley of terraces, with grassy knolls in the near distance.

'Indeed, and it is all so strange. Look at those goats grazing. Hardly enough for them to eat with that sparse grass, and yet they scramble on the slopes with such energy. In England...' He trailed off. He would not think about England, which was so far away. They had left the French and Hapsburg lands far behind too, like excess baggage. They were now looking down on the flat plains of Piedmont from a high vantage point. If they carried on eastwards they would reach the city states, Milan, Turin, and onwards to Padua and Venice. They had been travelling with a caravan of merchants for safety, Kit well hidden in a sedan, and the group turned south towards the Eternal City.

'We'll have to stay with them, Tom, a sojourn in Rome won't be so bad, although I long for the excitement of learning in a university town.'

Tom leaned forward to hear what Kit was saying. 'I agree, it's not safe for us to travel alone.'

Each city had its own ruling class, its own despots, and any one time one city state could be at war with another. Tom had heard Kit talk about these cities so many times in their Cambridge days as if they were but dreams.

Elizabeth and Ralegh and the England of their student life were a dim memory fading over the year and half they had been away. Being in a country where neither of them was known felt liberating. It was safer that way. They could be whomever they wanted. Certainly, Kit was now accepted as a woman wherever they went.

They now followed their travelling companions down the slopes. Soon they would reach their destination: Rome.

It was nearly winter. They would reach the Holy City after a long and arduous journey through deep valleys of sharp contrast where the sun tinged the tips of mountains but never penetrated the deep ravines where the roads ran. On sunny days the high snow had glittered as if clustered with diamonds but had been brownish slush along the passes where they made their slow way. Kit insisted on moving with donkeys carrying great panniers of luggage; his great trunk of clothes - *it is essential for a woman, Tom*, he'd explained. Tom thought it best not to argue; Kit had the money to pay for such luxuries. So they moved slowly, Kit leaning over Alpine balconies, enthusing at the views of high peaks and passes, not moving on until, he claimed, he was rested.

Few travelled at this time of year, and it had become increasingly difficult to find companions. They had joined small groups of desperate merchantmen and their wares; dried raisins from Spain, Valencia oranges and preserved lavender to sweeten the air of Rome.

Tom, shivering despite a thick fur cloak wrapped around him, stared at the wide plain before them, and was surprised at how cold it was this far south. Then he remembered the Alps behind them, which they had crossed, slowly, with trains of packhorses and donkeys. He realised that the high altitudes froze the winds that swept down from the mountains they constantly saw to their left as they travelled ever south into the Italian lands.

Then they saw her: the great Holy City lay like a great jewel in the valley below. Rome! They saw her pinnacles and domes some distance away before they came to it, like a mirage to a thirsty desert traveller. From afar, with the wintry long-horizoned sun glinting on the edifices and roofs, it seemed a golden enchanted place. As they approached, the buildings became great clusters of orange-tinged roofs, interspersed with campaniles and domes, all sloping on the seven fabled hills. They were surprised to see large cypresses stretching above the low roofs, and a lot more greenery than was usually seen in such walled places.

They entered the great north gate, expecting to see fine houses bedecked with pilasters and decorations exhibiting great wealth, only to find the place dilapidated with ancient columns standing alone in detritus, their capitals lying drunkenly at their sides. Cheap shacks huddled against broken down walls, skinny dogs scavenged in nooks and crannies. The great avenue they travelled along edged against the river Tiber then suddenly lost the river among ruins. They reached a deserted square and bid farewell to their travelling companions who were heading for the Vatican City. Tom looked around, not sure which way to go. Few people were about but columns of smoke rose from distant buildings. Thin scrawny cats slunk away among the fallen columns. A beggar, cloudy eyes blind, approached them unerringly as if he could smell them, holding a cage with two pigeons in it.

'Buy my pigeons – wonderful for carrying tales back home. Buy, so I can feed my wife and children.'

Kit shivered at the words 'carrying tales back home'; it was as if this stranger knew his innermost secrets.

'We have no need for such carriers, sir.' Priedeux was polite but spurred his horse and led *Christabel*'s sedan onwards, as a man protective of his woman.

'But they will always fly home – try them.'

Christabel couldn't resist bantering with the man, 'Aye, always home – to you! Come, sir we are not innocents you know.'

'Nay, but you have need of a guide in this place, yes? Do you want to know where to stay?'

The two friends exchanged glances. It was true they had no idea where they should go but could they trust this tramp? Was he truly blind or was it some trick? He spoke Latin they could understand which belied the image. He seemed to know exactly where they were but the clop of hooves on the rough paving

76

would tell him that. Anyway how would he know where to take them?

As if to read their thoughts he explained, 'A person who is a stranger in this city is as blind as me.' He laughed, a deep sound as if his throat was as cloudy as his eyes. Suddenly he turned somersault in front of them, holding the cage miraculously upright. The birds trapped inside didn't move except for a quick blink of the eye.

Kit also laughed, a tinkling sound which he had been cultivating. 'Come, dear bro, the man is right.' She turned to the beggar, if that was what he was and explained, 'My brother and I are indeed strangers here. We are at a loss in these ancient places; if you don't lead us astray another will, so let us throw our fates in with you.' She reached into the pockets of the voluminous skirts which billowed over the horse's flanks and threw the man a silver groat.

'Come man, lead us to a good place where we can take lodgings; where there are stables for our horses and the donkeys, and none too cheap; we are the Medicis of England.'

Priedeux shushed. 'Now we can guarantee to be jumped upon and all our baggage taken.' But the clown was jumping around them now, in exaggerated somersaults and high kicks.

'Come, the lady needs a discreet and honest place. She is wise, and her brother should listen to her.'

Kit laughed at the odd juggler's display of insight, and raised his eyebrows at Tom, but before he could say anything, the blind man was leading them down a narrow alley. 'I'll take you to Pensione Inglese; they will be able to accommodate you. There you will meet with compatriots. We will leave this square. 'Tis a bleak place; it will soon be a new piazza facing the Vatican. The Pope for his greater glory has razed all the old Roman pomp. The Pope's glory, I mean, not God's.'

He pointed to a grand sweep of steps which seemed to finish in rubble after the first few as if he could see them and explained, 'The Spanish Steps - designed by the great Michelangelo; started but not finished. Just like many things in this great City of the world. It is said that God does not like perfection; but that is a saying of the East. Even so, the Popes can never finish what they start because they have such grand schemes that they die before it is ended and the next Pope has other ideas. Much better to stick to simple things. Like training pigeons to fly home.'

The travellers listened politely as they followed. The area he led them through was more respectable than other parts of the city, and the buildings well-kept.

'But I rattle on. Here we are; a respectable place for respectable travellers.'

Before them stood a solid building stuccoed in bright yellow and white. The windows of the property were elegantly curved with heavy white plaster patterning.

'I will introduce you and then you will soon be assured that you will be cared for.'

The man was as true as his word. At the ring of a distant bell, the heavy door opened and there stood a woman, taller than any woman that they had seen before. A black lace veil was pinned over her hair which was swept up and topped by an elaborate headdress. The veil did not hide her penetrating eyes which were so dark they seemed black. She inspected them, her face remaining still. After what seemed an age, she grunted, and said, 'What do you bring here, Gabriello? More pilgrims or itinerant wanderers?' She did not wait for an answer but gestured to show they should follow her. Gabriello pushed past Tom and Kit, before they could move, and spoke to her in a patois much too fast and strange for them to understand. The proprietress, her heavy rusty black dress rustling and keys clanking from her waist, shuffled behind her counter, squeezing past a cabinet with many small drawers, nodding as he spoke. Tom and Kit waited. She answered in the same patois, but with short bursts, looking from the tramp to them and back again. Eventually with a larger nod, she called behind her and a young lad appeared.

Gabriello turned to them and explained. 'Giordano will take the horses to stables; if you, Sir, go with him you can negotiate stabling and fodder for them and Madame Gisella here will take your sister to the rooms.' He tapped Tom on the arm as if to push him the way the boy was moving.

Priedeux followed the lad with the horses, while Kit was led through the entrance hall and up an elegant staircase, pausing at a first landing to look down over an exotically carved balustrade, but the woman continued upward to reach a smaller landing. As they climbed, the stairs became narrower but were still made of elegant marble, so that Kit's outside shoes made a slapping sound. The banister which he clung to, because the stairs became increasingly steep, was cold beneath his hand, and he realised it was made of exotically wrought iron. The woman turned and spoke direct to him for the first time, as she reached for her keys. 'Do you speak Latin?'

Kit nodded.

'Good; we will be able to get by. These are my best rooms. The bed is furnished with the best mattress I have. You have a view of the new Vatican buildings, St Peter's and the River Tiber. There are two bedrooms, that is right, yes? The young man is your brother.' She spoke as if each point was a statement not a question, but Kit realised she was also checking. He knew he would have to give explanations.

'Yes, our parents died leaving us alone so my brother wished me to accompany him on his travels. He is very good to me.' He minced slightly, lowering his eyes and smiling, all the time playing with the belt at his waist, as if shy.

The woman nodded, not returning the smile. She lumbered to the window and opened the shutters. It was only then that Kit realised the room was stuffy with disuse. As the sun was let in through the windows he saw, through dancing dust motes, heavy furniture swathed in greying sheets. The chill from outside freshened the room immediately. He watched as the proprietress moved slowly, removing the sheets in a theatrical way as if she were performing a conjuring trick. A heavy carved table was revealed, covered with a brilliant Persian rug; four high-backed chairs carved in the same pattern were ranged against the walls; there were side cabinets and a large mirror on the wall, spotted with brown tarnish, which reflected the wintry light from the window.

'Come, I'll show you the room which I think you should have; your brother can have the smaller one over there; men don't have so many accoutrements.'

She opened a side door with a flourish; on the opposite wall in the middle room where they now stood, was another door which, Kit assumed, led into Priedeux's room. He followed his hostess.

This chamber was the same size as the sitting room but dominated by a large carved canopied bed with a carved trunk at the foot. The shutters were closed in here, too, but once again the woman strode straight to them and opened them with a flourish, obviously proud of this elegant chamber. She stood to one side, expecting her houseguest to say something. Kit could now see the room in all its sumptuousness. There were heavy velvet drapes either side of the windows, pulled back with elegant ribbons that looked as if they had never been undone. They had layers of dust on the upper folds. The walls were decorated with tapestries, the like of which Kit had only seen in the country house of Francis Walsingham. He exclaimed, 'What richness.' But the woman, seemingly satisfied that he was so impressed, stopped him by walking past him into the main room. It was a gesture of dismissal. He dare not ask how this richly furnished mansion had become a place to be let out to strangers. The woman said over her shoulder, 'When your brother returns I will send up refreshments. I will discuss price with him?'

Kit nodded; he had learnt that ladies were not supposed to deal with money although he had also noticed during their travels that it was usually the woman of the household who was the most businesslike and open about such discussions. The men seemed to sidle off into the back room or be full of bonhomie, offering wine whilst their womenfolk glared at them for being so generous.

'Good, I'll send Maria to clean a little when you are both out. As you can see the rooms haven't been used for a while. Is that all right?'

Again Kit agreed, although he could not see that the place was especially dirty, except for the dust that accumulated with lack of use, and a little musty perhaps but the opened windows would see to that.

*　　*　　*　　*　　*

After a few days Priedeux and Kit settled into a routine; in the mornings Marlowe would write and in the afternoon Gabriello would show them the places of Rome; the basilica, the great ruined coliseum and the outside of the Vatican, where Swiss soldiers barred their way.

'You cannot get in unless you have a pass from one of the Cardinals. You can only visit on official business. Or if you have letters of introduction.'

Tom wondered why they were here. Had it really been just to keep safe with the caravan of merchants? In every other town they had stayed, Kit had been up to something, so he waited, sure that something would happen, but their lives seemed to have become calm. Too calm perhaps, and when they first met some of their fellow guests, he was pleased. On the ground floor, behind the counter, were some miserable back rooms occupied by a Gilbert Ardingley and his tutor. Kit and Tom soon learnt all about the boy from the tutor, who had introduced himself, one day as Kit and Priedeux passed by to go out, waylaying them with a loud 'Yoo-hoo, you have just arrived, yes? My name is Simon Pyper.' Priedeux hesitated. The man was pale, with lank blond locks and, as he gestured to shake hands, Priedeux imagined them to be coolly damp and somehow oily. Before Priedeux could stop him, Pyper had taken his two hands in his and shook hands with him enthusiastically. Priedeux's guess was right; the hands felt damp, as if the tutor was nervous of meeting new people. Now he was bowing low to Kit, talking all the time.

'My charge's father is a retired sea captain, rich from piracy, I understand. He lives in the valleys of Devon near the famous Drake, you have heard of him? Yes, of course, everyone has! But my master knows that the way to get on is to emulate other landed gentry, so has sent his son abroad to be educated.'

Kit and Tom moved away, but Tutor Pyper scuttled by their side, rubbing his hands as if they were cold. He lowered his voice confidentially. 'Waste of time, of course. The boy is a dullard who by lunchtime has dulled himself even more with this cheap wine of Rome – which I must warn you against. It is most strong.'

They were out in the street now, but Master Pyper continued to scurry along beside them. 'I spend my time reading, especially in the afternoons when the boy sleeps.'

His voice was loud and echoed in the road, against the stuccoed buildings. 'It is a thankless task I have taken on but at least I have time to myself.'

Kit, in an effort to change the subject asked, 'And who has the other floors? Have you met them?'

'Indeed I have, young lady. Below you is Marshall, he is waiting for a commission from some Italian Count.' Pyper lowered his voice, which made him seem even more oily. 'He is a mercenary you understand, who can raise a small army somehow. It is beyond me, his work. Then on the same floor is a Hungarian who keeps himself to himself; his Latin is heavily accented and I cannot understand him.'

He walked by Kit's side and lowered his voice even more.

'And you would be well advised to stay away from him; Professor Erhard, that is his name. He is peculiar. You will not see him much but often we can hear him chanting and talking to himself. His room is just below yours. Sometimes there are strange smells emanating from his room. When he has been out, and I have had occasion to see him, he scuttles past us with strange bundles. He told me once that he had met and worked with Dr Dee in Prague.'

'Prague? But that's in Bohemia. I never knew...' Kit stopped as Tom elbowed him but Pyper waited.

'So sorry, I am dreaming. It is so far away is it not?'

Pyper nodded and continued scurrying by their side, taking a deep breath. Kit breathed a sigh of relief that he had not given himself away. One of his jobs in his previous life, as Marlowe, had been to maintain connection between Dr Dee and Ralegh without anyone knowing.

'Well you might be shocked young lady. Dr Dee's reputation is known even to you then?' Kit nodded and felt Priedeux pulling his arm.

'Come dear sis, it is not done to gossip and we must not keep Master Pyper any longer.'

They swept down the street, the tutor standing watching them. When they reached the corner Priedeux turned; the man was still standing, nodding and smiling at them, even giving them a little wave.

'We will have trouble with that one, you mark my words,' said Tom. 'He has not asked us about ourselves but is sure to do so, and then he will want to know whether we are connected to families all over the country; he will try to place us, Kit, I am sure.'

Kit, holding his arm gently on the sleeve, laughed. 'We'll have to be mysterious then.'

*   *   *   *   *

Shortly after, they were introduced by Mr Pyper to Marshall. He gripped Priedeux's hand as if he would break it and bowed slowly to 'the lady'. His eyes were hooded, his face lined and hard.

'Good to meet you – enjoy your stay.' He stared slowly at Kit as if he had not seen a female for many a long year. Kit kept his face lowered, for the man's eyes were piercing and judgemental; such a man might see through his female garb. But then the military man, as if he had reconnoitred his battle and decided on strategy, bowed and walked rapidly away.

Pyper said loudly, as if he wanted Marshall to hear, 'A man of few words, you understand.'

*   *   *   *   *

It was February and Gabriello, their blind pigeon conjurer,

explained about Carnevale. 'There is to be a great festival in the ruins; you must all come, including you, dear lady,' his head turned towards Kit where he sat at the desk in the window as if he could see. 'All wear masks and some men dress as women.' He paused, turned to Tom, 'Women dress as men...some dress as weird animals. It is all to do with losing your identity.'

They were in their sitting-room. It was suddenly quiet, as if the noise from outside had been muffled, and the English occupants did not know what to say. Surely this blind beggar, friendly and accommodating as he was, hadn't guessed *Christabel*'s secret? He couldn't *see* so how could he guess? The exiles exchanged glances but the tension was broken when Gabriello turned away from them suddenly and did a somersault so that he faced them again, without knocking against anything in the room.

'But of course you do not do such things in your country? You are shocked? I hear about your habits. You do not celebrate Mass? You do not believe in Purgatory, is that not so? And you believe heaven is here on earth? So if you do not have good things to do you cannot do the wicked. Is it not so?'

Tom laughed, 'Indeed, it is so. But I'm not sure we should go.'

'Oh, but dear brother, please, I beg of you, we must.'

The Italian nodded, his head moving from one side to the other, as if he would take in both of them, even though Kit said no more.

'Good. Tomorrow then, as dusk falls.'

* * * * *

'Come, Tom, let me dress as a man for this. It can be tiresome, especially when walking, to have skirts flowing around you. And how can I dance with all these petticoats? Dear Bridget taught me the hard work of women, but none of the fripperous ways. I can dance but need my legs free. If we are to wear masks, if others are dressed strangely, no-one will mind about me, surely?'

'No, it cannot be; if you wear such apparel I am sure others will spot that you are really a man. Supposing a story gets back to England of a woman who looks too much like a man; and your enemies in England find out? We already have nosey house companions and it is getting dangerous. We are in the very city of a thousand cardinals or so it seems. You know we stand out; it is rare for a brother to take his sister on tour with him. 'Tis not safe.'

They argued for some time until Priedeux said, 'I cannot guarantee your safety and if you persist and you put me in danger, I'll return to England without you.'

Kit answered ironically, 'Tom, you always were able to see my point. Very well. I promise not to put you in danger.' He turned away and said as if the conversation was closed, 'Thank you. We'll have great fun, you'll see.'

Tom tried to protest, but was interrupted. Kit had the last word. 'I must be allowed a free hand when I am there; promise?'

Tom was speechless. Kit was the very devil to argue with.

Again Kit smiled and quickly raised his hand to his mouth, in a very feminine gesture, to hide his smile. Tom knew that he had sounded so like Pyper that Kit had the upper hand. He realised Kit had achieved what he wanted; he would go to the festivities.

* * * * *

'I want to go, why can't I go?' The question was followed by the sound of smashed glass. The just-broken voice of Gilbert Ardingley, but now, in his petulance, with the high-pitched whine of a child, drifted up from the open windows below, echoing from the high walls of the building opposite. The lower voice of Pyper was steady and clear as he tried to explain logically why his charge could not attend the Carnevale. Kit looked over his shoulder at Tom, arching pencilled eyebrows at the unwanted interruption to their working morning.

'That old goat Marshall is going, why can't I?'

'Silence. How can you be so rude as to imply Marshall is the devil, it is unconscionable.'

Kit put down his quill and sighed.

'Sounds as if young Gilbert is giving that tutor of his a hard time'.

Tom nearly didn't answer. The arguments that drifted up to them seemed a mirror image of what he had gone through a few hours earlier. Kit waited, leaning on the back of his chair, sucking his quill.

'Indeed, Kit, he wants to make up another of our little party and Mr Pyper is much against it. It's one thing for the boy to drink himself silly indoors where he can keep an eye on him but he is terrified of losing his charge. He told me as much on the stairs; he is frightened that cut-purses will mingle with the crowd and slit young Ardingley's throat for his meagre funds.'

'Ah, Mr Pyper is not aware of the real danger then.'

Tom looked at him quizzically and Kit sighed. 'You might as well know, Tom, that Ardingley has been giving me the spaniel's eyes of love, and I wager he can't bear to think that the strong manly Marshall will be escorting me.'

'Oh, Kit, what have you been up to? Don't lead them on.'

'The young puppy doesn't need leading on, he's so straining at the leash that it could well break. He is such an eager young dog – and he has a pretty face and a pretty rump.'

'Kit.' This time it was a deep rumbling sound of warning. Tom had stood up and approached his companion who sat still, with a look of satisfied anticipation.

'Kit,' he repeated. 'No. You cannot seduce the young man. Just remember your cover. Where we are. How many times must I warn you?'

'All right, but see if you can persuade that churlish tutor to let his charge run a little; explain he'll be quite safe with us because you have to guard the party while I am in it. Something like that should suffice, but it *would* be great sport to show the lad how to really enjoy himself instead of swotting his wine all day.'

Tom laughed; Marlowe's phrase was so apt.

'Indeed the boy does study the wine too much. I wonder how it will be when they return to England? What will his father think of his son having developed into a full-scale drunkard instead of a studious gentleman? And aren't they supposed to meet with gentlemen, and advance themselves while on these tours?'

Kit was not taking any notice but was tapping with the quill now, eager to return to his writing. When Tom had finished, he looked up at him with such an air of persuasion that Priedeux could hardly resist his request to persuade Pyper that his charge should accompany them. Once again he was struck at how Kit had taken on the ways of womankind; teasing, fluttering eyelashes, looking down modestly and then looking up, wide-eyed as if totally innocent. He tried to read the writing before Kit; the paper was covered by a scrawl that was crossed out, over-written and hardly legible. Kit seemed to have many different personae; when writing, all was calm, except for the noisy scratching of the quill, but he would suddenly turn into this wheedling feminine creature.

Tom thought. They had not been to a great masque or play or such entertainment since they had left England and it might be a welcome diversion. He also was becoming a little bored with their purposeless existence and still didn't know why they were in Rome. Other than the trips with Gabriello, all Kit seemed to do was write quietly while Tom walked the streets on his own, or with Pyper and the boy.

If they were to go, it would be better if there were more in their group; there would be safety in numbers.

Kit was still holding his gaze, his dark round eyes seeming to become larger, as if he were bewitching Tom. Eventually Tom turned away.

He poured himself a glass of wine but then thought better of it and offered it to Kit, who shook his head. Tom sipped at it and nodded, 'Very well, I'll have a word with Pyper, but Kit...'

'I *know* – no seductions. I promise.'

* * * * *

Nightfall came early in February. It was certainly less cold than it would have been in England but still chilly. Tom was relieved that long cloaks, hats and gloves were part of their costume, as well as the masks and fantastic disguises; such fancy clothing could hide a wealth of problems. The party was gathering in the street before their lodgings; Marshall rode a large white horse and seemed remote, looking up and down the road, as if preparing for battle.

Ardingley was smoothing his costume, and trying his mask, holding it against his face and then whipping it away in what he evidently considered to be a sophisticated gesture. His mask had no sophistication about it, being merely a plain face, in gold, on a stick. A sedan had been found for Kit and he was now being helped into it by Tom. Pyper stood in the doorway, watching anxiously whilst the lady of the house, Signora Gisella, leaned out of the downstairs window, a small smile playing on her face.

'Oh, you look just like a shepherdess with your hair all loose and those country flowers in your hair,' minced Ardingley when he saw Kit emerge.

'Yes we picked the daisies and dandelions this morning. Just look at my brother,' she patted his arm with her mask, a plain black affair, 'dressed in an old sheep's skin. It might be all flea-bitten and moth-holed, but he looks the very picture of an old shepherd, does he not?'

Tom turned round to comment but stopped and stared at the lad.

'What have you got on, Ardingley?'

Ardingley answered, as if he were excusing himself, 'Well, I decided to decorate this awful plain student's black. Aren't the ribbons wonderful? So many, and I decided to tie one on every part of my doublet and hose, I think it makes a great show don't you?' He'd ribboned his shoulders, elbows, chest-piece and codpiece, his knees and even his boots. The total effect was clown like.

Ah well, thought Tom, he certainly didn't measure up to the usual standard of Kit's friends when he'd been at Cambridge; such a boy would have been treated with disdain and teasings. Tom hoped this would be the case tonight although the conversation they had had that morning still echoed in his head. He vowed to be extra vigilant.

Suddenly Marshall was cantering back up the narrow road.

'He's coming – and just wait till you see; the man's gone mad.'

They all craned forward, Kit leaning from between the drapes of the sedan. Before they saw Gabriello they heard music and from round the corner a troupe appeared, with the blind man in their midst, waving a large shepherd's crook to the time of the music. The stick was twice the size of the beggar and striped red and white, with silk banners hanging from the curved handle, the banners billowing as he waved it to the sound of the music. Behind him were a troupe of players, with pipes, string instruments and a drummer who was almost hidden behind his instrument, which hung from his neck. A tiny monkey sat on the drummer's shoulder and played a miniature drum in tune with his master. They were lit by two identically dressed men who held aloft great sconces, which glimmered and reflected on the bright ornamentation of the musical instruments. As they reached the waiting party Gabriello abruptly halted and hit the ground with his crook. The music stopped. Gabriello stepped forward and chanted,

> *'We come to wend you on your way*
> *To spend an evening at such play*
> *As heaven above can only offer*
> *All we ask is that you fill our coffer.'*

He then produced a wooden begging bowl such as was usually proffered by hospitallers and grinned, his blank eyes shining.

Marshall rode between him and their party.

'We did not order such entertainment, Gabriello; all we ask is that you lead us to the masque.'

'Ah, but this will set you in the right humour for such as you shall see tonight. Come, it is all part of it.'

Kit jumped out of the sedan and looked up at the horseman, his eyes wide in an appealing gesture. 'Oh, dear Marshall, don't spoil our night before we start. 'Tis meant well I am sure, and I for one think the little monkey must come with me wherever I go tonight.'

Marshall slapped the side of his horse with his gauntlet, and looked embarrassed.

'Dear lady, you must understand.' He trailed off, for Kit had his hand on his knee and was smiling up at him. He looked down at the pretty feminine creature but 'Christabel' suddenly wheeled away and turned to Tom and Gilbert who stood together. Still smiling, the gesture took them both in and they responded to the appeal. Tom agreed. He had already reached for his money bag, well hidden within his cloak.

'Yes, Marshall, my sister is right. We should enter into the spirit of the game, and I for one hope that our musicians will accompany us. The more the merrier.'

Marshall looked from one to the other, his last gaze resting longer on Kit and then he nodded slowly. 'So be it, let us leave now. I'll follow behind where I can keep watch on our party.'

With this, they set off slowly, the sedan bearers bending gracefully and walking steadily forward as Kit climbed back in and closed the drapes but only after he had smiled again at the escorts. The music started again and Tom noticed neighbours looking from balconies grinning and calling down in the local vernacular. Gabriello's face was beaming and eyes-blank-upwards at the voices, swinging his crook to the sound of the music. Tom caught up with him and asked, 'Where are we going?'

Gabriello, still conducting his musicians answered, 'We head to an arena on one of the hills; set up in a pastoral setting for the shepherds' masque. You will see one of the wonders of Rome, I assure you where all the great people of this city gather.'

Oh, no, thought Tom, were they showing themselves too much? He hoped Kit would behave. They moved through the busy urban streets towards a hill which could be glimpsed tantalisingly through the narrow streets until they reached an ancient Roman arena, now in decay, with trees sprouting from damaged arches. Inside was a wide expanse of roadway, winding up in a great curve around ornate statues and fountains that gushed out red wine, and the party made their way through the throngs, upwards to rows of galleries arched by columns. Inside each gallery was a party, each lit up with their own great flares. Some had ornate chairs and benches and tables while others spread themselves on couches or on the ground. Still other groups were making their way along the roadway, trying to find space amongst the ruins where they could seat themselves.

The whole place glowed with what seemed a million different lights. The air was smoky with the scent of perfumed tallow and a richer smell from cooking meat. Most people held masks to their faces; some of the women held plain fans to hide their features.

Kit jumped out of his sedan, and grasped the hands of Tom and Ardingley and exclaimed, 'Now this is something. I've never seen anything like it before.' His high-pitched voice was raised against the general rumbling and the music of Gabriello's troupe.

Marshall rode up and addressed Gabriello. 'Where to now?'

The beggar responded, 'Follow me. Fear not, for I have reserved you a place; I have organised men to be there, with lights and soft cushions. When all are settled the masque will begin. The players will wait for all to come, as you will see.'

They made their way along the circular path as it wound round the hillock. Tom whispered to Kit as he walked beside him, 'You should be in the sedan, sis, it is not seemly for a woman to walk…'

'If you think I'm going to be hidden away from this…never. Please, Tom, don't always try to spoil my pleasure.'

Tom looked round; Marshall was watching them closely and whatever he said to Kit he was sure would be overheard. He took Kit's arm and held him close, as if to protect an innocent girl from the attentions of strangers.

Gabriello guided them between two columns where there was a natural platform of ruined stones from some fallen monument, and they fanned out. Marshall dismounted and one of the musicians took his horse and led it away. Where they sat, were thick cushions and rugs, a small side table and a brazier beside which was a mound of roasted capons, pigeon and other small birds piled high. On the low table were bowls of sweetmeats, fruits and bread. Behind the brazier a burly cook stood, with irons and a large skillet.

Gabriello nodded to him. 'Now that we are all here Francisco can start to cook the feast; it is always good to eat at these events.'

They spread out but the men jostled to help *Christabel* and sit near, as 'the young lady' spread out petticoats in a dainty movement. Again Tom marvelled at the maidenly modesty of his friend, but was perturbed by the obvious admiration of Ardingley and the old soldier. In the end Tom shrugged and sat opposite the group and watched as Ardingley glared past Kit at Marshall who stretched out, dignified and slow, on the other side. Tom tried to hide his worry, suspecting that Kit would lead both men on. How would this evening end? He could not let his friend out of his sight, afraid of what he might do.

One of the musicians produced a flagon and moved to the nearest fountain, where he filled it. Goblets were produced, and the group of Englishmen watched as these were filled and each of them handed an overflowing cup. Another musician handed out a plate of sweetmeats, little pasta parcels of vegetables and meats.

When they were settled Gabriello pounded his crook again and the musicians re-formed and started to play again. A low clapping of appreciation came from other galleries.

'Surely we're not providing the music for all of the gathering?'

It was Marshall again, but Tom shushed him. 'Nay, I've been assured there is public entertainment – it starts late though; these Romans like to play into the night.'

Kit was careful to sip the wine in a manner expected of a lady and toyed with the food that was handed to him. The massive curve of the coliseum-like area meant that the buzzing conversations of the other groups echoed around them, the music of their troupe making only a small impression on the general hubbub.

Suddenly there was a flickering flare in the sky, and then another, followed by a brilliant shower of colour and explosion of noise.

'Fireworks.' Ardingley screamed. 'Oh, I love them; I saw them at Kenilworth when I was a child.' He dropped his mask and his eager face was illuminated in one sharp instant and then there was darkness again before another flare lit the whole assembly.

As the fireworks shot into the air, there was a great trumpeting from the walls around them and all the party looked up. From every crevasse in the ruins there was a trumpeter, with huge headgear, standing aloft. The crowd fell silent, awe-stricken.

Then a voice, eerily resounding, proclaimed, 'Hark, all ye shepherds and shepherdesses, welcome to my pasture. Tonight we will seek out the animals of prey that ravage our flock and put them into sheep's clothing themselves and truly we will teach them how they shall nibble at grass and be content and never eat us again. What say you?'

There was a great roar from the crowd, 'Yee-es, let us to it.'

'But wait! There must be rules to our masques and no man must act outside those rules.'

There was a derisive roar from the crowd.

Marshall muttered, 'This sounds ominous. I do hope you will be careful, Christabel; we will all protect you but you must stay by our side.' He glared across at the young lad who moved closer to 'Christabel'.

Gabriello assured them, 'Nay 'tis innocent merriment, I assure you; watch.'

The magnified voice came again. 'Rule one: no trampling underfoot.'

The crowd rumbled.

'Rule two: no kicking, biting, stabbing or such mayhem!

Rule three: No carrying off the ladies of your party!'

The crowd were in uproar now, laughing, gesturing, a hundred voices all calling at once so even the great voice was lost amongst the hubbub.

'Now let us begin.'

There was a great whoosh of sound and a hundred rockets exploded in the air above them. Tom was stunned and stared into the sky, forgetting about his need to watch Kit.

When he looked down again the arena was crowded with bizarre shapes of giant wolves, lions and foxes. Their misshapen

93

bodies indicated that they were men dressed in great costumes, with giant heads. Some of them spat fire from their great mouths; others glowed from the eyes. They jumped around and travelled through the horde of guests, snarling at the picnic groups that they passed. Only when they were roaring near him did Tom notice that Kit was not with them. He jumped up and looked around.

'Kit, where's Kit?' He shouted above the hubbub. Marshall heard him and with a quick look round answered, 'and that young whippersnapper, Ardingley?'

They both jumped up and pushed past the parade and as they looked around, a great whooping sound followed by the roar of clattering wheels made them start. Approaching the main arena was a great horde of men led by a golden horse-drawn chariot and the crowd was parting to allow them to reach centre stage.

'Come on, Priedeux, we must find them, even if we have to force our way down there.' He ran, agile for a man of his height and Tom followed, ignoring the driver who was now proclaiming himself a god, ready to rescue the sheep from the wild animals. 'Behold the rescuer of all sheep. I come to drive away the dragons of the old age.'

'Now he is mixing up his terrible creatures,' Tom grimaced. He felt himself nearing hysteria. Marshall stopped as they reached the writhing throng in the centre of the arena.

'Keep calm, young man, and keep your wits about you. We must find them.'

Tom nodded, immediately sober. Marshall was his usual solid self and Tom saw how good he would be in a battle.

'And we must go among them if we're to find the young lady.'

They ran towards the chariot with its supporting brigade of men, and as a mock battle took place Tom and Marshall ran between them, always keeping close. The throng were laughing and jeering and pressing forward. When Tom tried to push through the crowd, he was repelled; everyone wanted to do the same. He and Marshall worked together; Marshall was head and shoulders above all others and pushed his way through, always looking from left to right for the errant pair.

'I can't see them at all,' he shouted.

Tom only just heard him and yelled back, 'Keep looking. We must find them.'

Chapter Eight

Priedeux yelled, as he elbowed his way through the exultant crowds, 'Keep looking; I *knew* my sister would try a jape such as this.'

His voice could barely be heard among the screeches and laughter of the masqued company, but he felt he had to justify himself to Marshall who glared at him. 'She promised she would behave. Women can be very foolish at times.'

Marshall's face was impassive as they continued to shove their way through the writhing throng. The 'battle' was now becoming a free-for-all with the whole crowd joining in, aping the entertainers, some dancing with them and others taking the hand of someone from the crowd and leading them into the melee. Both Tom and Marshall had to pull themselves away as they too were grabbed, so they could continue their frantic searching. Eventually they reached the end of the arena where they climbed onto a high wall with trees growing from it creating a natural boundary. They stopped. They both looked down on the crowd below.

'What to do now?' Marshall asked.

Priedeux watched the crowd.

'The only person who can help us is Gabriello I think – let's return to him. I assume he would not desert his post.'

They pushed their way back up the causeway, a painfully slow process, to where they had left the musicians. They were still there; in some disarray and resting, picking at the remains of the food. When Priedeux explained what had happened Gabriello grinned. 'Have no fear. In such a crowd as this she will be safe. But I will send my boys out to find her; it would be no use me searching for the myriad noises here would confuse me like a dark woodland of many trees would confuse you.' He turned to his troupe and explained with many gestures what he wanted them to do; they nodded and moved away in different directions, one of them patting Priedeux's arm to comfort him.

Gabriello stood, his head cocked on one side until he was satisfied that all his men had gone and then gestured for them to relax.

'Sit, eat and don't worry,' he repeated. 'She will return safe, I assure you.'

It was growing late into the night and there was now a chill as dawn approached. Priedeux and Marshall discussed what to do. They considered leaving and returning to their lodgings in case the errant pair had returned there, but the whole party were still dancing, music still wafted on the air, and fireworks sparked the whole into a glittering array from time to time.

Gabriello interrupted, 'Nobody leaves until the fountains run dry of wine and I cannot imagine that the young lady and young man would be able to find their way through the crowds.' He went on, 'Some even stay to sleep off their overindulgence, despite the early morning mists, which could well endanger their health, even though sometimes it is tinged with frost at dawn'.

As he spoke they saw some of the musicians returning and with them a dishevelled Kit and Ardingley, laughing and looking into each other's faces, seemingly oblivious to the two angry men, Marshall and Priedeux, who now stood up, in unison, hands on hips, ready to give them a great dressing down.

Tom started, '*Christabel!* How dare you...'

But he was interrupted by Gabriello, who whispered, 'Nay not here. It would make a spectacle that all would turn to watch. Wait until you get home.'

Priedeux and Marshall looked at each other in despair, but agreed. Still Priedeux grabbed *Christabel's* wrist as soon as they left the light of the now fading flares, and when he was sure he would not be overhead, hissed, 'We go home now dear sis, for you must be very tired.'

'Indeed, bro, I have had such wonderful dancing and cavorting

97

I believe I will sleep for a week.'

He winked, but Tom did not respond, turning away to Gabriello. 'Fetch the sedan and horses. We leave this instant.'

* * * * *

'How dare you, Kit, how dare you? You promised.'

They were in their apartment, the door slammed on a laughing Ardingley who cried outside, 'Ooh, don't be cruel dear Priedeux, I want to stay with my dear 'Christy'...*please,* let me in.'

Tom shouted through the closed door, 'Clear off, young sir, for I would have my sister to myself.' He turned to Kit, but still spoke loudly for the sake of the idiot suitor. 'I need to speak with *her*. She has mightily displeased me.'

Kit sank into a chair.

Tom still spoke. 'And you need to go home to sleep off the wine and your foolishness in placing my sister in such jeopardy. Tomorrow I will have talk with your tutor.'

Tom banged on the door to quieten the still protesting young lad. Suddenly all was quiet. Tom turned to Kit, who was now grinning, totally unabashed and wide awake. Before Tom could remonstrate he excused himself. 'All I promised was no seductions, Tom, and there were none. A little innocent teasing, lovemaking with words and dancing. Mind you, it is mighty hard to pretend to be maidish when dancing. And not to quaff at one's wine, I must admit. But look you...'

Tom tried to interrupt. The man who was a woman approached him coquettishly, laying a delicate hand on his clothes, dishevelled and smelly now after the night's events, and went on, 'He is but a boy. I promise not to go further. But sometimes,' he turned away and again Priedeux was struck by the seeming feminine modesty. 'Sometimes 'tis devilish hard to keep up this pose and it was good to escape and be carefree with that drunken sot – indeed I hardly think Ardingley will remember all that took place - the free wine will ensure that.'

'Kit, you didn't?'

'What?'

Tom was exasperated.

'Come, come, you know…'

'I repeat. No seductions you said. I promised. So none. Just some kissing.'

At this Kit approached Tom and gave him a great dramatic kiss just short of Tom's cheek. Tom backed away; they had been friends at Cambridge but never lovers; maybe that was why their friendship endured. Tom found his pleasures with women only but knew of Kit's preferences.

Kit continued, 'Nay, I say, just kissing and I felt his manhood rising when he caught me as I accidentally fell into his arms in the high dance. I brushed him slightly with my buttocks, and felt him sigh but as he pushed against me with such hard desire of which he should be proud, I coquettishly danced away. The chase was the great thing. After that, we fully joined in the whole of the masque. I have learnt my womanly wiles well, have I not Tom?'

Tom couldn't argue. He was tired and beginning to feel hungover. All he wanted to do was to go to bed, and sleep. With Kit so excited he wondered if he could; would Kit go out again? Would he *ever* be able to relax, travelling with this strange companion? And what had tonight been all about except for Kit to display himself when Tom truly believed they should travel quietly and not draw attention to themselves.

* * * * *

There were repercussions. The first came with a determined rap on their door just before lunchtime; they were both still dozy from the night before. Kit had not even dressed and was still in a loose gown. He scuttled into his room to tidy himself. Tom, in hose and shirt, waited until Kit was behind his shut door and then answered the knocking, which was now becoming insistent.

'Coming, who is it?'

'It is I, Marshall, I would have words with you.'

Tom hastened to the door and opened it. Marshall marched in, his usual large strides taking him to the middle of the room before Tom had time to shut the door. He glanced from right to left as if he would ferret out the enemy before making a fatal blow. It was impossible to mistake him; so obviously a military man he looked now as if about to enter battle. His eyes gleamed, his shoulders back, his arms held at his side, with his fists clenched. Ignoring Tom's discomfiture, he spoke briskly.

'I'll not beat about the bush, young man. Something has to be done. You cannot carry on like this.'

Tom raised his eyebrows but before he could say anything the man continued, 'Your sister will be shamed and not able to make a good marriage. As for returning to England to take her rightful place...well if the tales being told in the taverns of this place reach our home country, she will never be able to show her face again. You are young and seem sensible, but do not know in what danger you are letting your dear little sister become embroiled.'

Tom tried to interrupt but the soldier carried on, his campaign well on its way now; nothing Tom said or did, even offering him wine, could stop his advance.

'I can save her from moral degradation and I will take this first opportunity of approaching you. As I understand it, you are her guardian as your parents are dead, so I will ask you'. He paused, as if he would review his troops before charging in. He looked embarrassed, but, like the last charge of a desperate man, almost gasped, 'for permission to marry her. I have a manor in Rutland, a house in London. I can easily support her with my success in my military expeditions.' He was in full battle now, marching up and down, totally ignoring Tom who was trying to answer.

'I organise things you understand; rarely do I find myself in the front of a charge so I expect to live for some time. I can leave her well provided for if I should die. If she bears me a son I will ensure he is well catered for. What say you?'

Tom reached for wine himself, not only as 'hair of the dog' but also as a delaying tactic. If Marshall did not want any, he certainly did. If he hadn't been suffering from a pulsating headache he might find himself laughing outright. He just hoped *Christabel* could not hear, although it was highly likely that she could. The man's voice was as loud as a cannon. He just prayed that the feminine toilette that was required, and usually took some hours, would keep *Christabel* discreetly hidden in 'her' chamber for a while. Tom was thinking rapidly, but his stomach churned and his head thumped. What could he say? In the end he prevaricated.

'Marshall, you hardly know my sister. You do not know her character at all. Last night she was swept away with the excitement of it all; I rather suspect…' and here Tom raised his voice. 'She is so shamed that she will not show her face this morning.'

'Indeed, I am glad to hear it. It shows that my esteem for her character is correct. I believe her to be young and innocent, but impressionable. With me by her side she could become a good woman, a wonderful housekeeper with servants at her bidding, and mother to strapping children. I accept that the strange ways of these Romans can turn a young girl's head, especially if she has no parents to guide her. I realise that I am a little older than her but…'

He stopped as if embarrassed by the unusual length of his speech.

Tom sipped his wine to stop himself chortling. Marshall must be forty-five if not fifty; his beard was grizzled and the sun had hardened his cheeks into great deep wrinkles. He was also surprised that Marshall thought his 'sister' so young. *How old did he think 'Christabel' was?*

He continued. 'But her youth is no bad thing. I can guide her and protect her and train her in the ways of the world.'

Tom proffered the wine again, but Marshall was not to be deterred. 'No, today I wish for a clear head. I have spoken: what say you?'

'I cannot speak for my sister. I have never been privy to the secrets of her heart. But although she is a little older than when most girls marry, the loss of our parents means, I believe, that she is not mature enough for such a serious matter as marriage.'

Marshall, taken aback by the common-sense answer, said nothing for a while. He was obviously reflecting. The battle had not turned out the way he had expected and it seemed as if he were reviewing his options. After a while he nodded. 'Perhaps you are right. But a betrothal? I would wait…'

Tom was tempted to agree, and make sure his friend heard. Of course they would have to move on but perhaps it was no bad thing. The attentions of two such very different men as Marshall and Gilbert were dangerous in themselves; *Christabel* being what *she* was made of, it would be even more catastrophic. Perhaps if he agreed to a betrothal it would put paid to any other man paying such attentions and curb his friend's flirting ways. But how long could he keep the man dangling?

'I cannot make up my mind – your suggestion is too sudden. You are quite right that I am my sister's guardian and I must be allowed to think about these things. Can I have some time to consider it?'

'A day? May I return this time tomorrow?'

Tom was shocked; he had been hoping to suggest three months, time enough for him and Kit to enjoy Roman life before they moved on.

'Nay, a day is too short. Give me a month to think about it; I would write to England for counsel with advisers there. Do you mind waiting that long?'

'I will wait as long as you say if I hope to be successful in my suit. I am leaving soon for the south, and I will return in three months' time.' He took Tom's hand and started to shake it. 'Thank you, dear boy.'

Marshall rhythmically pumped Tom's hand, squeezing it so that the fingers went white, grinning like a silly schoolboy. Abruptly he turned and was gone, like a siege that disappeared in the night as winter came. Tom ran out of their apartment and called down the stairs after him, 'That is only for me to think on things; it does not mean that Christabel will say yes.' But the man had disappeared and all that greeted Tom was the greenish face of Ardingley looking out from his door on the landing below. Tom ran back quickly; he couldn't cope with a visit from him as well.

When he returned he found his friend slumped in his

customary chair near the window, still in dishevelment, sipping the wine poured for Marshall and grinning.

'Another conquest. Well, Tom what say you? Shall I marry the burly man who will protect me?'

'Idiot. Dunderhead.' Tom nearly threw his glass at Kit's head. 'Don't you realise what you've unleashed? He'll not leave you alone. Those sort, once they set their sights on a *woman* they take it seriously. He will treat it like a military siege. You mark my words, I swear he has never made such a proposal before and it cost him dear to do so today; he will not give up.'

'But I did nothing; he was not the one I dallied with last night, as you well know. And he will protect me from myself.' His obvious enjoyment of the situation infuriated Tom, who did not know what to say. Tom glared at his companion, taking in the untidy dressing-gown, the unkempt hair, and despaired. How could he get it through to Kit? He knew Kit was enjoying the whole mix-up. Eventually he came up with the only solution as far as he was concerned, 'We'll have to leave, move on. If you refuse him, I'm sure he will spread stories of you and if gossip reaches England of a coquettish girl called Christabel travelling with Priedeux, how long before your enemies are on to you? All that dashing from Deptford - our decoyed plan - will come to nought.'

'Oh, Tom, you worry too much. It is public knowledge that I am dead – Christopher Marlowe is dead, long live Christabel, maybe soon to become Christabel Marshall, what say you?'

It was impossible. Kit was prancing around like a silly girl, proud of her conquests. Tom turned and stalked out; he couldn't bear to stay with his friend for the moment and had to clear his muddled head.

As he stalked down the stairs Ardingley emerged from his lodgings. Priedeux grabbed the lad and pinned him against the wall. 'Leave my sister alone. If I return and find you anywhere near our apartments, you will meet me at dawn, daggers drawn.'

The fact that he whispered the threat made it doubly intimidating for Ardingley, who nodded, his face white and frightened-rabbit like, eyes popping. As Priedeux stomped out, he scurried back into his lodgings.

*　*　*　*　*

Tom returned calmed, after a great ramble through the City, which had led him to the site of last night's revels. It was as if he would go back and try to stop Kit from running away and causing the mess they were now in. He stalked around the ruins where the artificial settings were being dismantled. Tom thought it looked a sorry sight now all the revellers had gone. He made his way back to the pension, considerably freshened.

His head no longer thumped and his stomach had settled. The cool fresh air of mid morning had made him realise that the matter was not so serious; all they had to do was persuade Marshall that his suit was unsuccessful and all would be well. After all, he must realise that a young person might not want an old man as a spouse.

He took the stairs two at a time, ignoring the half-open door of Ardingley's rooms. As he reached the landing of the apartment, the door opened and a man sidled out. He wore the dark clothes of a clerk, the long beard of the Jew and nodded to Priedeux as he slipped past him, saying nothing. He carried a parcel under one arm.

Tom's good humour disappeared. *Now* what was up? He had almost grabbed the man but, slippery as an eel, he had gone before Tom recovered his composure. Tom stormed into the apartment.

Kit was sitting at the desk, scribbling and blotting as if finishing letters. Beside him was a half-opened parcel, as if he had checked the contents and then put it to one side. He looked up, his face all innocent greeting.

'Oh, welcome back, I was just becoming bored with my own company. Better now?'

'Who was that?'

'Who…oh, no, you saw him. Tom, sit down, have a drink. Now don't get upset.'

'Stop humouring me.' Tom shut the door behind him and said quietly but firmly, 'I'm not one of your spy companions to be

104

pandied to, remember. What are you up to? '

'Tis harmless, I assure you. There are enough intervening for it not to be known…'

'*Kit.*' It was a sharp warning.

Kit stood up and started pacing, swishing the long skirts as he turned. He was dressed now, his hair in an elaborate coiffure, the white powder plastered on, and acted the part of a woman in deep thought. It was some time before he said anything.

'Do you think all we do is travel? That last night's entertainment was merely entertainment? Do you not trust me to know what we do, where we go? And for a reason?'

'That's the trouble. You never tell me the reason, Kit. All you do is ask me to help you and then throw it in my face.'

'To protect *you,* Tom, please believe me.'

'Then why write? Why try to communicate with the world?'

Kit said slowly, 'What you cannot understand, Tom, is this burning inside me for finding new places, new experiences, to help me write plays. All around us are scenes, characters, actions that I would put into other people's mouths to see how it all develops. A tramp with some doves….asking for help from a great tyrant…I will call it Titus Andronicus.'

'What are you on about? Please, please explain.'

'You know I write in the mornings. What do you think happens to my writings?' He waved a sheet before him as he spoke.

'I assumed you were collecting them. You and I are travelling with them; that big trunk…'

'Indeed, it is true I keep copies by me. But it is no good if a play is just words on parchment, is it Tom? It needs to be born, to be brought to life by those who speak the words, who walk the stage…'

'All right, shall I see if we can find a way here?'

Kit slumped back in despair.

'Tom I know you to be intelligent but sometimes you are as dense as that new-famed Sargasso Sea.'

'You're not being fair. All I do is done to protect you. You know how much I...'

Kit interrupted. 'Tom what did you see last night? A great play or a silly dalliance?' He didn't wait for a reply but hurried on, 'Yes, it was but a pale shadow of what I have already had performed in England. There is no real drama here; and I must write in English, not this Romish language. Even if I used Latin, the words could not be twisted to my meanings.'

'Yes, you always magicked your words.' Tom was now becoming interested, as he would have done at their college, by Kit's explanations. Suddenly though, he shook his head. 'No Kit, don't do this. You think you can change the subject. The man I saw – I still want to know what he was doing.'

There was a pause. It was obvious Kit was weighing up his answer. Eventually, he shrugged and explained, in a slow measured way as if speaking to a child. 'He is a carrier. He takes my plays and other works and they travel via various circuitous trade routes. They go with other papers, such as bills of exchange, letters of credit. I discovered that about the Jews; they travel with all the papers of commerce in their packs. And now my manuscripts.' He paused, and then as a whisper, he said, 'Back to England.'

'What? This is mighty dangerous, and anyhow, they cannot be performed under your name. The players will know you are alive; some of your enemies will find out.'

'Nay, I have found a way; I write sonnets in code to a friend of mine and he helps. That is all I will say now and you must trust me.' He turned away and started to write as if the subject was closed but Tom was fuming. This time Kit had gone too far. Tom had risked his life and future to help Kit but always dreaded being stalked by the vengeful enemies Kit mentioned. He knew he did not know all that had gone on in Kit's life. All those times he had disappeared from college, for months at a time, and each time returning with money to purchase good wine and fine lace for his collars. And when he did return, he had been generous, inviting his friend Tom out for drinking binges but never explaining where he'd been. Tom had been too young and inexperienced to ask, just enjoying the times they had together.

Then there'd been the times that Kit had been angry. He'd been known to draw his dagger at the least provocation, and fight, being goaded by irrational, drunken arguments, until blood was drawn. Marlowe had made enemies in his secret life; Kit had told him *that* much to inveigle him into their adventures in the first place, warning that at any time an assassin's knife might be the end of him, unless he could escape somehow. With Tom's help that had been achieved and he would not want it all to collapse now. He strode over to the desk and grabbed the hand that had taken up the quill again.

'*No*, Kit, I need to have all the information. You cannot expect me to support you if I do not know all the truth.'

'The truth? What is the truth? If you really want to know...'

But they were interrupted by a hesitant tapping on the door to their apartment.

'The bells of hell. Who comes now?' Tom was exasperated.

''Tis me, Ardingley, can I come in?'

Kit stopped Tom as he tried to speak, laughing. Whispering, 'Oh, let him in, let us have some sport to lighten the air.' Aloud, before Tom could respond he called, 'Come, come in.'

He glided to the door before Tom could stop him, smoothing his already immaculate hair and his skirts, and opened it in a sweeping movement that showed Gilbert he was welcome. Tom was tempted to walk out but knew such impropriety, to leave his 'sister' alone with a young man would be totally foolhardy.

Instead he decided to ply the young man with drink, and perhaps that way he would deflect any romantic notions.

'Come in Ardingley, would you like some wine?'

The young man shook his head; he still looked grey even in the mid afternoon.

'Nay, I would try to stay sober.'

There was an unladylike snort from *Christabel* who turned to the desk and put down the paper he had been holding, making a pretence of tidying the desk. Tom coughed and said, 'Forgive me, but what can we do for you?'

Ardingley hesitated. Eventually he stammered lamely, 'I wanted to see if Christabel was all right?'

'Yes she is fine but needs her rest today, do you not, dear sister?'

'Oh but I am always pleased to see friends, dear Gilbert.'

Tom sidled towards the young man and intervened before he could edge further into the room. 'I thought I told you...' he whispered.

Gilbert seemed to gain confidence from Kit's reaction. He said in a loud voice, 'Your brother is displeased with me for leading you astray last night, dear Christabel, but I have come to apologise – to both of you. I realise it was wrong to be alone with you in such a way, and that I may have damaged your reputation by allowing you to be taken from your chaperon. My tutor has warned me that I may have put you in grave danger of losing your reputation and if the offer I would now make can recompense for that then...'

Tom interrupted, 'What offer, young man, what are you attempting to say?'

'I am a poor gentleman and it may not seem a good offer at present but my father has many lands, and a house in London. We are friends with Sir Walter Ralegh and other great men; Frobisher is related to us...'

'Yes, yes, but?'

'I would ask for your sister's hand in marriage, and that we return to England and marry in my parish, for I know you are parentless.'

Christabel who had been holding a delicate lace handkerchief to his face suddenly wheeled and ran into the inner chamber a snorting noise erupting again.

Priedeux realised his friend could no longer stifle his laughter, and he himself found it difficult to keep a straight face. It was obvious Pyper had given in to the young puppy and tutored him on what he would be expected to say if he was so lovelorn.

Perhaps Pyper had been advised by the father to get the young whippersnapper married to a girl of good family before he returned. Priedeux knew little of the West Country but imagined it to be sparsely populated and that this was how farmers and yeomen in that distant place found their wives.

He thought carefully before replying, 'You can see my sister is overcome by your offer. She is but young, as you are, and such thoughts could not yet be considered by her or by me. We are travelling. May I suggest that when we return to England, whenever that will be, we make the acquaintance of your family and proceed from there? I am sure my sister would agree with my proposal.'

Ardingley grinned as if he had been handed all he could desire. He had no idea that the reply was so nebulous that it meant nothing. He stepped hurriedly towards Priedeux, and for the second time that day Priedeux found himself being grabbed in two hands and a similar pumping motion being used as before. This time however his fingers did not turn white for the handshake was but a pale imitation of Marshall's. The boy was grinning so much that Priedeux could see the bad molars at the back of his mouth.

'Thank you, oh thank you, you have made me a truly happy man. And I promise I won't drink again.'

With that he turned abruptly and left, as if he would flee to his tutor and tell him the news.

As the door banged behind him there was a small click of the latch of Kit's room and with a swish of skirts Kit returned.

'Tell me off, Tom, but that was not of my making. You've encouraged both of them now. What are we to do?'

'We leave as soon as possible and continue our travels.'

*   *   *   *   *

Tom's nightmare had not finished yet, however. As they spoke they heard a shuffling noise which made them stop and turn once again to the door. This time there was no rapping or knocking or attempt to open it.

They both watched as a thick parchment was slipped beneath.

It was pushed through slowly, deliberately and the movement hypnotised them both. Neither moved to do the obvious which was to open the door and find out who was delivering the missive.

Chapter Nine

'Go on Tom, as my protector *you* ought to vet such papers. You will need to censor any letters to me, surely, as my chaperon?'

Tom glared at his friend, who was obviously enjoying the intrigues and events of the day. This was yet another diversion giving Kit the chance to avoid telling him the truth.

As they stared at the package, it seemed to grow before them. Neither of them moved towards it. It was thick and had been squashed to get it under the door with a slow and deliberate movement. It couldn't have been easy to get it through the gap. 'If we hadn't been arguing, we would have opened the door, and discover who had delivered it' whined Tom.

Kit shrugged, still not moving but staring at the letter. 'It would have been an anonymous boy, and he would have run.'

Tom nodded, now making a move, but as he did so, Kit pushed past him. He watched in slow motion, afraid that Kit would get the upper hand again by hiding the missive, and he would never know who it was from. He watched fascinated as his friend bent down elegantly and swept up the thick bundle, like a woman picking up a playful kitten. He stood turning it over and over. Eventually he stopped with the seal uppermost. Instead of breaking it open, Kit studied it, passing the tips of his fingers over the raised seal, as if to feel the quality of the ring which had impressed it on the parchment.

'It is expensive paper. The seal is a good one, large, almost big enough for a bishop's. It contains quite a large bundle.'

'*Kit*! Stop teasing.' Tom couldn't help laughing, the tension eased between them now that the letter had been collected. His friend was so mercurial; one moment a vivacious feminine temptress, now a scholarly type studying a manuscript in detail.

'Let me look at it before you break it open.'

Kit passed it to him, grinning. Tom peered at the seal; it was indeed a large one; the signet ring would cover a knuckle at least. The imprint was quite clear and depicted a long-tailed two-legged creature grinning maniacally, showing fierce ragged teeth, holding what looked like a fork. Around his feet, flames.

'The very devil himself' exclaimed Tom, quickly handing it back.

Kit nodded. 'Now shall we open it? But before we do, I'll wager you a night out on the town – dressed as a man – that I know who pushed that under the door.'

Tom stared at his friend. Kit was still holding the packet, and could easily break open the seal. It was foolish to take Kit's wagers; he always weighted the dice in his own favour, he probably had good reason to know. Either it was another message from England or…? He put his head on one side, considering. He was interested in whether Kit really could guess, but his suspicion that his friend had been plotting quietly behind his back anyway decided him.

'Nay, you'll not get round me like that. This may not be the first packet you have received.'

'But indeed it is dear friend, at least like this. I swear by all that is holy.'

'Your oath is not worth much, Kit, when you profess not to believe in anything. Come, stop teasing and open it.'

Kit did not answer but proffered the packet, tapping it. Tom shook his head and looked away.

'No, you open it, it is addressed to you, I can see that.'

Kit took the knife he used to sharpen his quills, and said, 'Very well, I'll stop playing tricks. I say it comes from the good Professor who keeps himself to himself.'

'How say you? What do you know now?'

'I only guess from the seal, it is one that a necromancer might use. And remember what Pyper said: strange smells and mutterings.'

Tom couldn't help laughing at the memory.

As Kit spoke he broke the seal and flattened the folded sheets inside, and started to read silently. Tom waited but still Kit read, not saying anything, his face emotionless. Tom swore to himself; the man was impossible.

'*Kit*. Read aloud.'

'My dear young people…'

'Oh, who is it from first – are you right?'

'My dear young people…I deem it incumbent on me…to warn you…'

Tom grabbed the papers from Kit. 'If you won't tell me…' He scanned the paper, until he found the scrawl at the end which was completed with many flourishes and tiny drawings in the loops of the letters.

'You were right: Professor Erhard.'

Tom handed back the paper. Kit took it, placed it on the table as if it were of no consequence and reached for the wine and poured two glasses. 'Come Tom, let's relax and I'll read it aloud. With suitable inflexions as well.'

Kit grinned and slouched in his chair. Tom gave in and watched as Kit positioned himself, no longer a woman; now a student, ready to show off. He held up the paper and read, in a deep sonorous voice.

'*I deem it incumbent upon me to write to you. As a man who knows what has happened, what may happen and what will happen in the future – and you must not wonder how – and I have seen dark things in your past and I can tell that you are not named correctly in this world now and your true name will cause you great troubles because it is the name of the very devil's familiar. The four-legged wicked ones that walk in the dark and screech into the moon when the devil walks. I know them too well! You are like them – tempting all men as I have heard for I hear all things.*'

Kit broke off and said in his practised feminine voice, 'But *Christabel* – how could he interpret that to be the devil's name? Kit, maybe – if the meaning he has is that of a cat - but he should not know me as that.'

He read on before Tom could comment.

'And your so-called brother who would leave you alone to your machinations; he will be accursed and blame you and he will need to gird his loins against your machinations. Go, young lady, leave this place before I predict terrible shakings of the earth, which shall lay all prostrate before you when the devil takes your heart.'

Kit stopped and shook the paper as if to shake off the curse. The two friends stared at each other and said nothing. Tom could not make out from Kit's demeanour what he thought. Was he scared? Amused? Interested? Kit looked down at the parchment. 'There is more, shall I go on?'

Priedeux sat forward in his chair. He nodded, saying nothing.

'The devil incarnate that is neither male nor female – that can take on the guise of an animal; that can be ruthless, heartless and greedy of souls – has gripped your essence. That I can truly see. If you do not leave this place I foretell great disaster for all around you.'

Kit stared at Tom, dropping the parchment. 'We'll have to go and see this person. Find out what he knows and kill him if he knows our secret. Then we can leave, Tom.'

'Kill him, Kit? We'll be discovered.'

'He lives on his own and doesn't seem to go out or have visitors. He may not be found for some time. We must find out about him. These walls are thick and sound does not travel, surely he could not have heard us in our private talk?'

It was as if he was thinking aloud. Tom grabbed the pages and read the missive again. 'Are you sure you've had nothing to do with him, Kit?'

'Nay, I swear it – this time on my pipe of tobacco.'

Tom grinned; that was probably a more reliable confirmation than Kit swearing on anything holy, but Tom turned serious again. 'It is important that we find out what he knows. And how far his influence stretches. Remember you must remain dead if we are to be safe. No hint must get back to England and your enemies. But I cannot agree to murder.'

Kit said nothing for a while. 'Very well, but a visit is imperative.'

'We can't just walk down and confront him. Someone is sure to see us.'

'I agree. Let us consider. Young Ardingley is usually sleeping in the early evening if he is not out carousing; Pyper is a bit more difficult and we do not know the habits of the mistress of the house.'

'We could perhaps climb down from the balcony and surprise him.'

As Tom spoke he moved to the window and leaned out.

'We can't use the window, not at the front. We'll be seen by all those nosey neighbours.'

He turned to see Kit walking up and down, this time the skirts moving awkwardly as he fell into a masculine stride.

'If I dressed as a man...'

Tom shook his head, still thinking. Kit sidled up to him. 'Why don't we just visit him and be done with it? Wait, of course until a quiet time, perhaps when the young pup sleeps and Pyper is well into his books; I warrant you he dozes over his reading as well as the youngster sleeps.'

Tom thought a while. Why not? It was only Pyper who had warned them against their neighbour. It may just have been fear and prejudice on his part. They had both seen foreign scholars lecturing at Cambridge and knew that, with their long locks and sombre robes, their dark skin and preoccupied manner, their clipped broken English or mutterings in Latin, they were objects of derision with the locals who thought them necromancers. Such men would scuttle in the corridors of the colleges, afeared to go into the commercial part of the town, having heard stories of their fellows being pelted with rotten turnips and greens, or worse, beaten up. Pyper, despite being a tutor, might well have such prejudices or at least view such a man with suspicion.

'And if I am dressed as a man anyone who sees us might just think we are strangers.' It was said so quietly, while Tom was thinking, he nodded without really taking in what Kit had said.

'Good, we'll go tonight. We *must* find out what he is about.'

*　　*　　*　　*　　*

Tom couldn't say anything when he saw Kit in doublet and hose, a great cape wrapped over his shoulders, his hair pulled back in a knot. He was girded with dagger and sword, the dagger tucked into the top of his soft leather boots. It was the first time he had dressed in such a manner since the escapade at Bridget's house, and Tom was taken aback at the transformation. Truly not only did Kit transform action on stage, he transformed himself.

'Wait, I'll see what's afoot. I know it's only one landing but that boy is always skulking in the hope of catching you – or rather our lady friend.'

Kit pulled him back. 'I've an idea. If anyone should ask who I am, why don't you say that Christabel has had so much excitement in the last few days – not only with the carnevale masque but our dear brother from England has turned up for a visit?'

'And you're the brother?'

Kit nodded. Tom shrugged and strode to the door. The sooner this escapade was over the better. He lent over the banisters and into the depth of the gloomy stairwell. He listened. All was quiet; the lulling quiet he had come to expect of a late Italian afternoon, even early in the year as it was, before the hot summers forced people inside. It would be an hour before people started stirring to find supper or night-time entertainment. No sun penetrated the stairwell. He gestured for his friend to come out and they skulked down the stairs, keeping to the wall side until they reached the landing beneath theirs. What if Marshall should come out now? He was more of a danger than Pyper and his charge, and they both knew it.

Tom whispered, 'Do we knock? It might echo – in this quiet it might sound like hell has been raised.'

Kit considered. He pushed past his friend and shook his head. 'Let's see if the door opens first.' As he spoke he lifted the latch and then hesitated as the panelled door slowly swung open.

It was the smell that hit them first. It was sulphurous, as if they had indeed entered a hell on earth. A dank fog wafted around the

116

room in thick swathes. Kit led the way and they both moved inside quickly and shut the door behind them. Behind a large bench, cluttered with glass phials and bulbous glasses sat the shadow of an old man, who continued in the act of pouring a steaming liquid from a phial into a bowl. He seemed oblivious of their entry and muttered to himself as he read from a large leather-bound tome to one side of him. All they could see of his features in the grey gloom was that he had a flowing beard which fell over the bench before him. With one hand he held it aside as he read. His experiment was obviously at a critical point and both visitors stood quietly, fascinated. Through the thick haze, they saw the man continue to pour, very carefully, and they had a chance to look around the room. It was the same size as their sitting room but seemed much smaller, cluttered as it was with piles of books and astronomical instruments. Tom recognised an astrolabe. A large globe took up one corner. There were scrolls, all lain higgledy-piggledy on shelves, and an easel which held a map of the skies. The shelves held skulls, both human and animal.

As they waited, the bowl with which the man was working, started to fizz as more liquid was added, and the air cleared, as the old man placed the phial onto a tray and, quite calmly, as if he had invited them to tea said, 'Welcome, I knew that awful letter would excite your curiosity.'

Kit gasped, for now he recognised the man. His hair might be whiter, and longer, the eyes more ingrained in their sockets but it was so obviously the man he had seen at Ralegh's School of Night, albeit only once.

' Dr John Dee, I believe?'

Chapter Ten

Dr Dee; one of the most fascinating and perceptive members of Ralegh's circle. Marlowe was too young to have known him well, but he had been much talked about after he had left the country. Tom grabbed Kit's arm, still staring at the old man.

'What say you? How can it be?'

Tom was astonished. Everyone who had been at Cambridge or, indeed, in the intellectual circles pandering to the Court had heard of Dr John Dee. Favoured by the Queen at one moment, banished the next, his ideas were too individual for most tastes.

'Yes, I only met this good doctor once, at a meeting of the School of Night, before he fled to the Continent. Others plotted against him and the Queen soon turned her wrath on his memory, is that not right sir?'

'Indeed, Master Marlowe, you know as much about me as I know about you.'

'It was said you travelled as far as Bohemia and charmed kings and princes in that far, almost magical land.'

'Yes, and I sent letters back with my ideas. Were they not discussed at your meetings?'

Kit strode towards the old man, and shook his hand. 'Indeed, the ideas you set out in those letters generated great discussions. You were called a conjurer by some. '

'And you, what did you think?'

'As you know, I keep an open mind, like you, and am always interested in new ideas.'

Tom listened to them talking, and remembered the old rumour that the character of Dr Faustus, Marlowe's most famous play, was based on this man, so he watched him now with interest and not a little fear.

After that first 'welcome' Dr Dee returned to his experiment and even Kit, usually so discourteous, said nothing as he continued to mix potions. The man did not acknowledge their presence at all and neither of them felt confident enough in his imposing presence to interrupt what he was doing. Eventually, the experiment complete, the old man put down his instruments and slowly surveyed them again.

'You may wonder why I induced you to come down, because I do wish to remain incognito. But I have a special message for you. You're playing a dangerous game, *young lady*,' he exaggerated the last words and Tom and Kit looked at each other and then back at the alchemist. He gazed quizzically at Kit, who could not hold the piercing gaze. Dr Dee's voice was cracked. It made Tom think he spoke little.

'I hadn't thought to have to protect you on your travels; your job was to write and produce those plays of yours, of which I have heard so much, not to dally with nonentities. We all had and still have great faith in you, but to get muddled up like this! It is too dangerous. Rome is a dangerous place even though you are outside the Vatican.'

'But how did you know I would come to Rome? You were here before us.'

'There is a saying, *all roads lead to Rome*. In any case the couriers you use, I use. It takes but a few days for news to travel on our line for it is efficient, but, I assure you, discreet. I would not have introduced myself, if all was going well. As it was, you need a warning.'

Tom coughed, feeling left out of the conversation but also wondering if Dr Dee included him in his warnings. The doctor had not even looked at him and Tom wondered if he would stop his revelations if he realised that Tom was also present. Dr Dee turned to him and continued in the same rebuking manner. 'And you, young man, should be ashamed of yourself. I'd say you need tuition in how to care for a young lady.' As he said it the good doctor had a twinkle in his eye. 'Already there is gossip and

Gabriello brings me stories.'

Tom interrupted: '*Gabriello*?'

'Yes, he is in my employ. A good man, who perceives more than any of us who can see with our eyes. I told him to bring any English travellers to good Signora Balzatti's place. Unfortunately, he brought the nincompoop Ardingley and the gossip Pyper whom I frightened away with my mumblings. Then he brings Marshall – a much more dangerous man. Silent but with eyes that not only see but understand, with ears that not only hear but listen. Luckily I find he has his own preoccupations further down, in the boot of this peninsula, and will soon be sailing away.'

All the time he spoke he moved phials, measured strange mixtures, and ambled to and fro between his instruments.

'But enough of these.'

He moved round the long table and came towards them, and suddenly spoke quietly and insistently, 'Kit you know I have read your stars and you know what I saw there. You know I have heard angels and what they say of you; don't lose your destiny like this. Remember who you are.'

He turned back to his work, taking a fizzing glass from a flame and holding it to the light, continuing to speak in an ordinary voice. 'You must both leave soon, for the great beauty who is living in this house is being talked about and I have it on reliable authority that the English Catholic ambassador in Rome – albeit unofficial – has been asked by other ambassadors to seek out the *lovely lady* and present her.'

Kit twirled, using his cape to drape elegantly around him, obviously pleased that his female persona had set the City a-gossiping, but Dr Dee frowned. 'No, Marlowe, it will not do. You must realise there may be some who would recognise you. I can see you revel in your role, and, whilst it is an excellent disguise, you are now known as a beauty; there will be serious suitors soon.' He smiled, a twisted awkward smile, and continued before Kit could say anything. 'But it would be dangerous and foolhardy. Now, I need to know from you if the system we have set up is working.'

Suddenly Kit was serious and stared at Dr Dee; Tom felt uncomfortable, knowing that Kit was trying to warn the doctor; who obviously had no idea that Tom was not privy to all Kit's secrets. He was becoming increasingly annoyed with his friend. All he was, he felt, was a servant. Never told what was going on, only getting the undercurrents and having to deal with the repercussions. But this was not the place to air his views. Instead he would act on what the necromancer said, and, ignoring the fact that Kit had not answered, changed the subject. 'I think the good doctor is right, Kit, it is time for us to move on. I, too, am worried about the proposals you have received and feel they will warrant unnecessary attention.' He paused. The doctor looked surprised. 'Yes, he has received two marriage proposals, which I hope I have effectively delayed for some years.' He turned back to Kit. 'If what the good doctor is saying is true, we must disappear.'

'Kind Tom, would you give me a few minutes with Dr Dee on our own? We have matters to discuss.'

Furious, Tom looked from one to the other of them. At first he was rebuked for not looking after Kit, then he was used by Dr Dee to persuade Kit to move on and, just as the conversation was turning to matters of which he needed to know more, he was being dismissed again like a servant. He did not know whether to storm out and pack or refuse to leave. He hovered but Dr Dee rose and approached him stiffly, gathering a stick to aid his walking as he moved round the table. Tom realised he was even older than he had first believed.

'Kit, I would have words with Tom first, you must wait.'

Kit nodded and walked out. Tom was surprised but then realised that for once, Kit truly respected this old man. Dr Dee watched him as he minced away and then turned to Tom. He rested his hand on Tom's sleeve and Tom could see that twinkle again.

'I have had good reports of you, lad, that you are a good friend to our genius here, Marlowe. I wager he has tried your patience from time to time? Yes, I see he has. I cannot tell you all, but your friend was born in a magic year, 1564, and forms a triumvirate of valuable men who, between them, will change the world, one by revealing the stars, another by spreading the word about those stars to the whole world in a way that the world can understand, and a third is the mercantile man who trades those words, for the good of mankind. Your ultimate job is to put these three men in contact; already two of them have those lines of communication but your job, from now on, is to make sure our Kit there meets the third. You will know who he is, when the time comes.' Dr Dee stopped speaking, breathless and licked his lips. Tom suspected that he rarely spoke so long now, living on his own as he did. 'I would say to you that it is the lesser men in life, forgive me for saying this, like yourself, who are instrumental in making large events happen.

'So, you must be a little more patient, and use your intelligence and good grace as you have been doing up to now, and do not get too angry with our genius, here, whom we both love and want to protect. I will always know what is happening and will guide you.'

Tom asked, 'How? How can that be?'

'As you have been guided so far. But you must accept that messengers come and go, and say nothing of it, agreed?'

Tom was calmed by the old man's words, which made him feel truly involved in Kit's adventures even though he did not understand of what the man spoke.

'Very well, I agree.'

Dr Dee patted him on the arm and nodded. 'Now send that *young woman* to me. Let me have quiet words with Kit and I will warn him that if he is to use you as he is doing, then he must be kinder towards you.'

He smiled as he spoke and Tom accepted what he said. He turned and left without looking back. When he reached the apartment, he simply said, 'Your turn now, he will speak with you.'

*   *   *   *   *

When Kit finally sidled into their rooms it was late into the night. Tom was dozing in the chair, one side of his face reddened with the shape of his hand, where he had slept awkwardly. The candle was spluttering, the wax hardening on the table, his clothes dishevelled. He awoke slowly, his face setting into a resentful line, as he noticed Kit.

'So, you return. What further devilish tricks have you been cooking with that old man?'

Kit ignored his friend. Dr Dee's words hung with him now, haunting, warning, '*Most people only have one life. Marlowe; you have been granted a second and there was a reason for it. Do not waste it. Do not take advantage of those around you who have made it possible; least of all that young man Priedeux who has thrown in his lot with you. My charts tell me what his life would have been; your charts tell what it is. You must cherish him.*'

Kit felt a corresponding sense of resentment towards this friend of his, upon whom he had to rely upon. Sometimes the burden of being a dependent woman was too much. When he had first come into the room, with Tom still half asleep he might have been able to charm him, but now Tom was wide awake and waiting for a satisfactory answer. And Kit did not want to tell him all.

He stood at the side of the door, arms crossed, one leg pressed against the wall, his cloak nonchalantly slung over one shoulder. A small smile on his face, he waited for the onslaught of abuse and anger that would surely come.

Tom said nothing. Even from a distance of yards between them Kit's magnetism reached him. This was the magic of Christopher Marlowe, even though he was silent. Also Dr Dee's words still hung around him. Tom remembered the great plays he had seen in London, sometimes from the wings or the music gallery, the magical poetry wafting up to him and floating away into the sky, leaving the colours, emotions and effects behind them. They had evoked the magic of other worlds, of history in Dr Faustus; a magic Malta in the Jew of Malta, the splendours and strangeness of the east in Tamburlaine. The man who had created these worlds stood before him. Tom had faith in him. Dr Dee had faith in Kit. He rose slowly and approached him. Without speaking the two friends clasped each other, a hug of forgiveness, friendship, of promise for the future.

Eventually Tom pulled away and faced his friend. 'You are the very devil himself, I vow, but I accept it. Whatever you want to tell me you can, whatever you want to keep secret, you can. But,' and his voice was raised, 'We leave tonight, no ceremony.' He moved to the table, and emptied his pouch. 'There; we'll leave that for the good Signora and we go now. When we settle we'll send for the trunks. You are too important to be embroiled with scheming ambassadors.'

*   *   *   *   *

It was easy to leave the house for all the other residents were sleeping after the events of the night before. Even so, the city did not sleep. They made their way through streets which still clattered with the sound of carriages and crude laughter, as revellers made their way home. Tom and Kit walked boldly, carrying their clothes in great bundles over their shoulders, Kit still dressed as a man. Leering whores stepped out of dark doorways to offer them service; curs ran alongside them before diverting off to kitchens where cooking smells attracted them. They hoped to find a berth on a ship at the mouth of the river Tiber. They didn't care where it would take them. They had no plans, except to leave. They would take the next ship out regardless of its destination.

Chapter Eleven

They headed for Florence. 'Come, I *will* see that great fabled Michelango David,' insisted Kit. 'I'm sure we can get there by boat.'

But in the end they had to go by both sea and land, finding that the River Arno was dried and silted in the late spring.

The captain of their vessel laughed at Tom as he asked to be taken to Florence. 'I'll not get my ship up the Arno now. After the mountain snows melt a great torrent of water rushes through, bringing with it debris. Didn't you know that Florence is landlocked now?'

Tom shrugged and accepted what the man said, explaining that he and his *sister,* because he had insisted that, before they boarded the ship, Kit should become female again, were strangers to the area.

To reach Florence from the port of Pisa they had had to hire a carriage for *Christabel* to ride in, with Tom sporting a great charger by the side of the rude four-wheeled conveyance that pretended to be a carriage. Kit smarted inside, not able to express his disgust at being hidden 'like a woman' once again.

Tom laughed, a cruel sound to Kit's ears. 'But dear Kit, you are a woman, even the good doctor said so. And if a woman wishes to visit Florence she must go accompanied and in the right manner, in these dangerous times.'

They travelled along the banks of the river, the countryside largely flat with a few hills highlighted with the campaniles of churches and friaries, like exclamation marks against the sky. It was a long journey, taking a full day as the cart lumbered along. Then they reached a bend, a slight incline in the road and Kit, peeping through the carriage's grubby curtains, gasped at his first sight of the City he had so longed to see.

Boccaccio, Plutarch, Machiavelli; the great painters, da Vinci and Michelangelo; he had heard of them all but most of all he wanted to see the famed statue that stood many men's heights in the main square. *David,* made of one great slab of marble; a creation in stone, as famed as his own creations of Dr Faustus and Tamburlaine, Tamburlaine the shepherd boy who had conquered the world; David the shepherd boy who had conquered a giant and become king. The sky before them was gloomy with the impending close of day but the roofs glittered from the low sun behind them, Boccaccio's dome reaching up higher than all the other roofs and campaniles.

'It is dangerous in Florence; the Medicis are losing their power, there are whisperings and rebellions in every street, it is not safe. There is no-one like the old masters now.' So said the Pisan who had taken them to the city gates.

'Trade is now done by river when it is not silted up, we do not go into the City,' he explained. The carter stopped; he refused to go further; Tom, after haggling, gave up and paid him off and they continued on foot. It was not far and they reached the gates as bells tolled for the evening's closure. They found a wayfarers' inn immediately within the gates, facing San Lorenzo church. They would find more permanent lodgings the next day and send for their baggage when settled.

*　*　*　*　*

Next morning, Kit chafed and argued but eventually stayed at the inn while Tom left to find lodgings. Kit watched his friend pass by the side of the church and turn into the street at the east end. He waited to see if Tom thought to return but he didn't.

Quickly he stripped off his woman's dress. He was used to the bows and ties by now and although there were many underskirts and lace, he was soon free of them. Beneath he wore doublet and hose, easily disguised as undergarments. The only item of menswear he lacked was sword and dagger but he thought that, in a strange town, it might be better to go unarmed in any case. He rubbed at his face to remove the traces of rouge and mercury which hid his man's stubble, and then swept up his long hair beneath a large cap. After checking himself in the mirror, he shook his head. He was not quite right; his face looked riven of all character now. Looking around the room, he strode over to the fireplace and reached up into the chimney. He found what he wanted; soot. He covered the lower part of his face with it, rubbing it in, again checking the mirror. This time he was satisfied; he had achieved a stubbled chin with makeshift makeup.

He listened at the door of their rooms. It was mid morning and most wayfarers had moved on. There was no bustle of horses jingling outside, harnessed and ready to ride on. There was no odour of old ale or baking bread. Hesitantly he moved out into the galleried hall, but saw no-one. All was quiet below. He could see the front door, wide open. He moved rapidly down the stairs and out, into the warmth of the honey coloured streets.

There was a market in the piazza at the west end of the church.

'Which way to the Palazzo Vecchio?' he asked a leather vendor who seemed half asleep.

He was directed towards the river. It was but a short walk past the Baptistry and the imposing Duomo, through another square and a long street before he reached the great palazzo in front of the Medici Palace.

And there it was, his dream, his David.

At first, from where he stood at the edge of the plaza, it was not that large being in proportion to the square which was magnificent enough to hold a thousand. As he walked slowly towards it, he gasped. The marble glinted in the late spring, slanting sunlight. The figure stretched its shadow across the square. The magnificent body, in all its muscled nakedness, aroused feelings of envy in Kit. How he wished he could create a great hero like this, but he only had skill with words; this statue represented a man's vision made tangent, hewn out of nature itself by hard physical labour.

Groups of merchantmen stood around chatting amongst themselves. How could they be so oblivious to the magnificence dwarfing them, Kit wondered. Women with baskets scurried to their markets for their daily bread. Schoolboys loafed by, loath to get to their studies. None of them seemed to notice the huge wonder before them. Kit wanted to sit before it, but there was nowhere to do so in the main body of the square. To one side was a long galleried shadowed walkway with a stone bench that ran all along it. Here, old women sat staring; pot-bellied grey-haired men puffed at pipes. Kit joined them and they shuffled along, sighing to give him room. He sat in the shade for most of the morning, watching the sun play on the marble, changing the facets of the statue's muscles as it moved round, so that the arm holding the club seemed to shimmer and move; the leg, loosely held, might step forward at any moment. The face took on different features, sometimes it seemed as if David had a small smile playing around the full lips, at other times there was a cold stare; the stare of determination to kill.

Kit dreamed on. He was already behind with a mission that the dark ones brought him and he did not know how to start, but he let that worry drift away before the overwhelming beauty and grandeur of this great marble. Truly this was a thing made in heaven, a statue that could come to life if given words. He would be a great hero who would inspire nations…a great king who would lead his people…*Once more unto the breach, dear friends.* It came into Kit's mind from nowhere and he knew he had to get back to his rooms, and start the political play he had been asked for. To flatter the Queen and her forebears, that was what he had been told. He hoped that Tom did not return before he got back. He had to start writing something immediately.

As he strode away he found his way barred by a robed man with a turban, the face dusky, the lower half hidden by a curly, oiled beard. Kit thought he was not a serious threat for he did not reach Kit's shoulder, being more round than tall.

'I saw you staring at the great statue; it interests, yes?' The man held a great ledger under one arm, and a heavy purse hung from his thick leather belt that gathered his robes around his waist. A merchantman, Kit guessed. The man continued. 'You were staring so hard, it was obvious that you….' He stopped.

'Indeed, it is a great marble…'

'And you like the shape of the man, yes?'

He was attempting to take Kit's arm now, trying to lead him away.

'Perhaps you would come for a sherbet with me.'

Kit laughed. 'Indeed, I like the shape of man,' he answered the first question, ignoring the invitation, gently extricating himself from the man's hand. With a glare at the man he added, 'Indeed, I like *young flesh, strong muscle.'*

The merchant's eyes narrowed, he recognised the put-down, for his belly hung over his belt, the face was sweaty with a middle-aged man's efforts to move in the heat, his eyes hidden in a welter of furrows even before reacting to Kit's words. He looked round to see if anyone else was watching their encounter, and then shrugged and let go of Kit's arm. 'I was only seeing if I could help a stranger; never having seen you in the Square before.'

Kit relented, the man might be useful. 'Indeed, I apologise. But I was on my way home. I have been out long and have work to do myself, as I am sure you do, too?'

The man lowered his head in assent, and said nothing more as he glided away on soft shoes.

Kit hurried out of the square, now preoccupied with the words that sang in his head, not bothering to see if he was being followed, and, as he made his way back to the inn, looked for a stationers. There were many and soon he had purchased quills and paper and ink and blotters and could hardly wait to return to start writing about the great monarch, Henry V.

He was unlucky though. Tom was waiting as he slunk in and immediately complained. 'No, Kit, not again. You go off on your own, I know not where. We cannot be doing this. We will be discovered; how could you, after what Dr Dee said?'

Kit ignored him and swept off his hat, shaking out his hair and unwrapping his parcel as he loosened the buttons of his hose. As he placed his writing materials on the table he enthused, 'Tom, I have seen the wonder of the world today. You must go and see it while I write. Go, go to the Palazzo Vecchio, past the Cathedral – the Duomo – and then on; you cannot miss it, and I will write.'

He sat down and primed his quill, opened the ink and poured a dab of water into it. Tom pulled him upright by the collar of his undershirt. '*Kit*. Listen to me. I have found lodgings, we are not staying here. We cannot now, I don't know who saw you come in like that – and how am I to explain that there is no-one else in the room when we leave, if someone saw you, as a man?'

Kit sat back and shrugged. 'Tom, you worry overly. I am careful. Nobody saw me I assure you. This is a drab of a place, empty all day, as you can well note if you listen and could suit our purposes. There's no-one else here, I suspect, not even the landlord. And a city of nincompoops who can ignore a ten league size statue as they go about their business are not going to notice the actions of two strangers such as us.'

He was fired up now, and went on, while Tom stood there, arms folded, frustrated. 'I assure you, I sat in the square and watched as well as admired. There are many different nations here; many Afriques, dark of hue, and strangers from the Arab lands with flowing robes. French and some Germans too; truly this is a cosmopolitan city, with its great Bibliotecca which I must needs visit soon, either as a man or a woman, I care not, so worry not. A young man coming and going would not be noticed, neither a young woman – well perhaps a pretty woman...might be noticed.' He grinned as he turned back to his papers and started writing rapidly.

'All right, Kit, I give up. But do not turn away. At least you'll hear what I have found and what we must do.'

Kit, a bored look dulling his face, stopped writing and leant against the back of his chair as Tom moved around the room, stuffing belongings into bags, and explained about their domestic arrangements.

Eventually Tom stopped what he was doing, dropping a

stuffed bag on the floor. 'Oh, come on, just collect your scribbles, get changed into your woman's guise and let's go.'

As they had no heavy luggage with them, it was a matter of paying the bill, and leaving. It was but a short walk through the City and across the river to their new rooms near Santo Spirito. Tom avoided the great squares and led Kit round narrow alleys but they could not avoid crossing the river on the Ponte Vecchio. As soon as they reached their lodgings, in a back street behind the Carmine convent, Kit left Tom to supervise the arrival of their trunks. Without even looking around, he unpacked the small parcel he had brought with him, made himself comfortable at the wide table, spread out his writing materials and started scribbling.

* * * * *

A few days later Kit persuaded Tom to take him for a walk; he had written for long into the nights, and Tom had left to wander the streets alone. One day, as he returned with food, Kit was pacing up and down. 'I need to walk, would you take me? I know, I must be a young lady. So be it.'

Tom did not notice Kit place a large package in the middle of his writing table before they left.

As they emerged into the sunlight, Kit took his protector's arm and tripped daintily beside him. For a short moment, Tom felt the pride of a man who had captured a beautiful woman and they strode along the narrow street, peering into shop fronts selling silks, leather goods and furs. Tom was conscious that men turned to stare at *Christabel*. He conceded once again that Kit made a pretty woman. They were peering into a fur emporium, at the pelts that hung from long racks, at the made up robes with furs at the collars and cuffs. There were other robes made completely of furs.

'It cannot be cold enough here for such clothes, surely,' said Tom.

As Kit was about to remind him of the winter in Rome, further south than Florence, when they had first arrived in that city, there was a murmuring roar.

'What's that?'

Before Tom's query could be answered, passers-by started running past them, away from the noise: one woman, obviously a servant, with a large basket full of greens and new fashionable tomatoes, huffed and puffed, 'Not again,' she complained to them, 'Apprentices. Why can't they be content with their lot? I swear it is the heat of the sun turns their heads to rioting. I would run home, young man and take your belle with you.'

As Tom and Kit stood undecided a crowd rounded the bend, all gaily dressed in bright doublet and hose, carrying banners of yellow red and blue; the frontrunners had small drums and whistles and a discordant rhythm led the crowd into a determined march down the narrow street, where Tom and Kit were now the sole strollers. As they approached they banged on shutters lately pulled tight.

'Justice! Fairness for all. Give us our holy days!' The words of their chants could just be determined. As they approached, Kit turned up his nose in disgust; there was a strong smell of stale wine and sweat coming from the rioters. Some of them were jumping up and down, at the end of the crowd, using wooden staves to bang on shutters and doors to add to the cacophony. They were but a few yards from Tom who faced them, trying to hide Kit.

'What shall we do, Tom? I shouldn't really run.' Kit moved into the shelter of a shop porch. Suddenly a liveried man emerged from the doorway where he had been hiding.

He gestured to them to follow him and ran past them as if to confront the crowd, and then disappeared down a small side alley. The two friends shrugged, what else could they do? They ran to catch up and looked down the alley; sure enough he was waiting. The students were almost touching them and some of those in front had started to point. Tom heard one mutter, 'A goodly figure, what say you?' before he saw their guide gesturing for them to follow. Tom nodded and pushed Kit in front of him. Kit lifted her skirts and half ran, Tom following. He did not turn round to see if any of the rioters broke away to follow them. The man was standing outside what was obviously a shop with a canopy still open. As they reached him, he pushed against double doors and disappeared inside. A hand pulled Kit into the darkness beyond. Tom, surprised, followed. The shutters were quickly shoved to, and bolted.

Chapter Twelve

'Fools. Why did you not scamper like everyone else did? You must be strangers here, not to know how rough the apprentices can become when they are on the march.' He turned to Kit. 'They could have ravished you.' Someone was speaking in the gloom and, as their eyes adjusted to it, they could see a finger pointing at Tom. 'And stabbed you, young man, for knowing about it. Crowds are dangerous animals.'

Tom spoke first. 'We owe you thanks for our rescue. Indeed we are strangers.'

As he spoke, a taper was lit and a hand placed on Kit's arm to draw them into another room. As they followed, Tom noted that they had entered a cavernous place, with strange piled up shadows and he could only guess that it was a great emporium of a shop. They were led into a courtyard. Initially they were dazzled by the bright sunlight after the gloom of the shop, but as their eyes adjusted to the bright sunlight, they saw that the courtyard was kept cool by a fountain gushing in the middle and an arched covered walkway around the side. They had emerged from the side where the sun shone, otherwise the area was shaded so that it was cool and the fountain sent sprays of water across to them, cooling them more. Tom realised how hot he had become with the sudden fear of the rioters.

'Come, sit and share some sherbet with me until it is safe to go, I welcome strangers to my home.'

It was the word *sherbet* that made Kit gasp; he had been so taken by the suddenness of what had happened he had not really noted the man's voice in the gloom. Now he hastily glanced at their host and quickly looked down. It was the merchantman who had importuned him in the Palazzo Vecchio. Had they been followed? Was this a trap? Or just a ghastly coincidence? Had their rescuer been given instructions to bring them to this house in whatever way he could devise? Kit suddenly bent his head, as if shy, and would not meet the man's eyes. Their host was gesturing for them to sit down, still standing himself, hovering close as if, with a little encouragement, he would take Christabel's arm and lead her to the seats.

'Come, please, enjoy my hospitality, and perhaps you can introduce me to your dear lady, your wife.'

Tom interrupted. 'Not my wife, my sister. Christabel, say hello.'

Tom had seen Kit's sudden movement and wondered at his friend, but thought it was Kit being careful; even so, he was surprised when Kit curtseyed and kept his face averted.

'Indeed my sister is shy, and wondrous of the world we move in. Our parents have left us orphans and I am her only protector.' He thought it wise to explain.

'And I am Omar, silk and carpet merchant, and when I catch my apprentice, he will be on rations for a week for joining those rebels, for he is nowhere to be found. He will be whipped, too, for frightening strangers. I would apologise to you, dear lady, for the inconvenience caused.'

Now the man was skirting them, ushering them to an opulently covered sofa and chairs, placed in the covered walkway, clapping his hands to summon servants, all the time moving round them and coming back, his head moving from side to side in an effort to catch a sight of Kit's face as Kit sat down. Tom followed and sat beside Kit.

There was a silence as dark-skinned servants arrived with trays and extra cushions and all was made ready. The heat of the day made the scene shimmer in front of the two Englishmen's eyes.

Omar waved dismissively to the servants, who bowed to him, backing away and melting into the darkness of the house. When they were alone, their host positioned a chair opposite them and gestured with open palms, offering them the drink. He took a deep breath, his heavy beard quivering.

'I feel I know your sister, has she been here long? Does she talk?'

'Indeed she is shy, but yes, she talks.'

Tom looked at his companion and nudged him. Kit had never been so silent in the presence of others before.

'I feel that perhaps I have seen such as she, walking in the great square…'

Still Kit said nothing. Neither did he stretch out to take the fizzing drink that Omar placed before him. The Arab continued to stare at Kit's averted face.

'Perhaps the *young lady* admires strong men?'

This time there was no doubt. Kit jumped, he could not help it.

'At last, a reaction, so I was right.' He spoke, calmly, leaning back in his chair, satisfied. Then he continued, as if philosophizing. 'A man or a woman? What is it to be?'

Tom gasped. The man seemed to know all about Kit. How could he possibly have seen through *Christabel's* disguise when it had fooled so many others? Had Kit been up to something, again? He watched, mesmerised, as their host raised his glass, a delicate-stemmed work of art, an embossed glazed pattern of flowers on the bowl, and sipped slowly, like a lizard who anticipates his prey before whipping out the long, tendril-tongue.

He continued, in the same vein. 'I admire both; I come from the east but live in the west; it is all the same to me, so long as the face has character and charm and, indeed, young man', here he turned to Tom, 'your friend, sister, lover, whatever you will, has such a face; a face that could charm me for many years. How much would you take for such a creature?'

'Take? What do you mean? You mean you would pay me for my sister?'

'Indeed, if she is your sister. But you should take more care of *her* for she can seem well as a young man, and should not be allowed out to visit the great David statue, alone, and charm hearts as well. I was not the only one who saw his gaze and concentration, not the only one who admired his shapely leg, I assure you. You should be careful if you are to stay in Florence for a man who dresses as a woman, or a woman as a man, whichever it may be, is guilty of a great sin according to your Christian rites.' He paused, then continued, his voice now almost whispering, 'The penalty is death.'

All the time he spoke, it was measured, with no hint of threat.

He placed his glass down on the table in a decisive manner. The suddenness of it made both Tom and Kit sit back, startled.

'But no matter, you need a protector, a guardian, and I can be that one; for a fee. The fee can be easy and of joy to us all, if you would permit me to so hint, for I could spend many an afternoon's dalliance with our hermaphrodite here. If that is not to be, if you guard its chastity well, then it must be in gold. Or I regret the authorities must hear of this carnality.'

Tom jumped up, about to protest, but Kit pulled him down and stood himself. He towered over the rotund merchant, who seemed to shrink into his chair.

'And you too are a stranger in this town, and tales such as you carry might be held against you.' He spoke in a quiet deep voice, certain that Omar would only make such threats if no-one else could hear.

'We have little money, we are strangers, and if I choose to dress differently then it is none of your concern. Neither will I give in to your desires nor will we pay money. We will leave now, or I will scream and cry rape; whether as man or woman matters not, I would be bound.'

Omar tried to sit upright and answered, but his voice was strangled. 'You would not dare. It could work both ways, both of us would be convicted.'

Kit laughed. Tom was horrified and tried to restrain him but Kit brushed him aside. '*You* have more to lose than I and my friend. You know nothing of us. Perhaps we have allies here who could speak for us. Perhaps we are not what we seem, even if you think we are but strange lovers. Perhaps the Medici know about us….'

Tom was impressed now. Kit spoke with authority. He only

hoped that Omar was not in the pay of the Medici.

But Omar, so confidently sly moments ago, now cowered, all the calm cunning gone from him. He stood and edged round Kit. He glared at him as if in defiance but Kit knew well how to act not only a woman but a kingly man. He lived his plays as he wrote them and it was unfortunate for Omar that he was writing Henry V – a forceful king and strong leader. Tom was mightily impressed.

Omar backed away, holding his hands in front of him as if he would push the power of Kit away.

'I will call my slaves: you can go.'

He clapped his hands and one of the dark-skinned servants arrived. Omar whispered something to him and he nodded, gesturing to the guests. He led them back through the emporium but suddenly took a left turning and opened a door onto a side alley. All was silent as they left the house. There were no chants from the rebels, and all they heard was the clanging of the door behind them.

'I can't believe he would let us go just like that. We'll leave before he can get up to any more tricks.' Tom said as they hurried down the alley. He added, 'I don't believe we've heard the last of him.'

When they reached the corner Tom looked back but nobody seemed to be following.

*   *   *   *   *

It was the dead cat on the doorstep that finished them. There had been the arrival of a funeral arranger who at first refused to believe there was no body to be interred; there had been parcels of dung and dead beetles, a delivery of sour wine which had given them stomach ache; all of these might have been mistakes or coincidences, but the dead cat was serious. It was black and had been strangled, the rope still around its neck. Both Tom and Kit were aware of the superstitions that surrounded such a delivery, and if not truly superstitious themselves, knew enough to take it seriously.

'We have to leave, Tom, it is a warning. I am sorry, but you were right. I leave Florence with sadness, on to another life.'

The atmosphere was too sombre for Tom. He turned to their trunks and started packing.

Chapter Thirteen

They found themselves on a fast sailing coastal vessel going southwards, heading for the Bay of Naples. It was the first boat due to leave.

'We'll get on it and take our chances, what say you Tom?'

Tom had boarded before Kit stopped talking. It was not just the fear of Omar's stalking of them. They had both heard tales of the fabulous wealth of the King of that city. They would see for themselves, although they had agreed that they would not visit the court. They would lie low, pretend to be poor. No longer would *Christabel* wear exotic clothes to public masques; or parade the squares inviting admiring glances from passers-by. Instead, Kit had reluctantly agreed to wear weeds, dark robes where he could hide behind a pretended widowhood.

'It's the least you can do, Kit. We are going into territory where we might meet Marshall again. Remember he said he was going south? I don't want him hearing about us being here. We must make sure we are not noticed; you can always write, wherever we are, surely?'

Tom now accepted that Kit was writing plays but still wanted to know how they were performed and where. He waited for an opportune moment to confront Kit again, when he hoped he would not be able to wriggle out of telling him.

The vessel hugged a rocky coastline for a few days. It was now early summer and very hot. On board they kept to their berth. Kit was stretching into wakefulness after a long sleep, dimly aware of singing and a lute accompaniment. It came from the public rooms. The way the music drifted to them without definition irritated him.

'Let's go on deck and listen outside, Tom. It might inspire me. But I don't want to go in and join the other passengers'

Tom yawned, for he too had just woken. Kit, without waiting for an answer, covered his dull widow's weeds in a large man's cloak and they were soon out on deck. Tom followed Kit as he strode towards the sound of the music, realising he understood now what was happening; not only were they travelling and losing themselves on the Continent, Kit was constantly watching and absorbing, learning and noting all things new. He would transcribe these experiences into those new plays that Kit had mentioned. He could tell by the way Kit sometimes stopped and stared and then muttered to himself. Sometimes he would stand and gesture, then step to one side, as if he were answering himself, then return to his paper and scribble. He never showed his work to Tom and Tom never asked, awed by his friend's absorption. He wondered, though. Would they ever be performed? Or were they just being sent back to gather dust in some patron's grand library?

Tom joined Kit as he paused, leaning against the timbers, feeling the warmth of the day. It was early evening and the sun was setting in a sky of multi-coloured clouds which bubbled on the horizon as if the earth was a very cauldron. The sky was a varied easel of tints, the clouds glowing orange, magenta, crimson and apricot. The colours were even more vivid compared to the blue black of clouds untouched by the slanting rays of the evening sun, clouds that seemed to rise from the sea. Some were of royal purple, the colour mirrored in wavering lines on the sea. Kit moved away, and rested against the guard rail and stared, enchanted by the myriad shapes and colours. He was sure he could see them dividing and expanding and growing towards them. Tom joined him. Suddenly Kit seemed to tense, and put his hand to his mouth as if he would stop himself from speaking.

'What is it, Kit?'

Kit hesitated before he spoke. 'Look, just look at the sky. It is as if hell is attempting to swallow our earth.'

'So, it is beautiful.'

But Kit shook his head, and started pacing, looking at the sky and then behind them at the coastline which, suddenly, looked far

141

distant.

'It looks to me as if we are in for a storm. What say you?'

Tom was unconcerned.

'Even if we are, we cling to the coast. The Captain will find safe harbour surely?'

'I'm not so sure'. Kit spoke over his shoulder as he hurried to the captain's cabin.

As Tom followed he heard a cry. It came from above. The lookout in the crow's nest was gesturing to the crew on deck. At last he had also seen the warning sky and was now taking action. The captain emerged from the wheelhouse as if to greet Kit.

They turned now to look at the shoreline but it was all rocks and high hills, tinged with the last rays of the sun, and tiny bays with high seas smashing against great jagged promontories that were sometimes hidden by the waters and sometimes stood out like gigantic monoliths.

'All hands on deck,' he called in a voice that carried against the gathering wind. Tom and Kit stood frozen as the crew rushed to rope down sails, and follow the captain's barked orders as if they had become fast moving automata. As he swept past them he ordered, 'Down below, sir and your sister, if you please. No arguments. We are in for a storm and we will do what we have to do, don't you worry now.'

Kit shook his head, 'Nay if I cannot help I will pray. But on deck if you please, Captain. Otherwise I shall be sick.'

'Better to be sick downstairs Madam, for you'll be in our way up here and I cannot have my men put in danger by watching a weak woman and risking their lives to save you if you go overboard. Below, NOW.'

He had not shouted, but it was a command Tom knew they could not ignore and he pulled Kit away. 'We can watch from the porthole, Kit, come, we must obey the Captain, you know that.'

Even before they reached their cabin, the vessel lurched as if it had hit rocks. Kit realised what it meant now when sailors described 'hitting a storm'. The sun had been swallowed by the clouds which had gobbled up its rays as well so that it was almost dark. All that was left of day was a glimmer of light on the high seas which seemed to rush towards them and clash against the rough glass of the tiny window. The sea was lashing against the porthole as if it wanted to get at them, the waves breaking into a million foamy strands like grasping fingers. The noise of the crashing waves against the ship was horrendous. The whole edifice groaned and shivered as if it lived. Both Tom and Kit were thrown against their bunks and, trying to stand upright, grabbed each other. Before they could steady themselves, another great wave rolled the ship almost on its side. Water trickled through gaps in the ceiling of their cabin. A smell of salt pervaded the cabin.

'I can't believe such a storm would brew so quickly,' gasped Tom before he was thrown on the floor again. 'What do we do? Should we lash ourselves to our bunks?'

Kit was trying to stand and reach his tack. He held on as the boat heaved. Tom fell back again but watched as Kit pulled down the belt of gold that he had taken off and hidden while they were on board.

Tom could see it was double-layered and heavy. Kit yelled against the noise, 'Come Tom, you must have a layer of this as well. If we drown we drown, but if only one of us is saved at least he will have something to live on.'

''Tis foolhardy, Kit, it may take our lives.'

'So be it, but I'll not live a pauper's existence. If I die, oblivion will be my comfort.'

Kit was unbuckling the belt and, as if mesmerised, Tom helped. It seemed an age for them to clothe themselves over the belts, as they tried to steady themselves from the constant lurching. Eventually it was done; Kit's fitted neatly under his widow's weeds but Tom's thickened his waist under his doublet.

They turned to the porthole but outside all was a seething mass of darkness and hellish noises. Screams came from other passengers. Tom and Kit braced themselves against the side of the cabin, gripping each other's forearms.

Then it came; the end. A great cracking and rendering from beneath; they both knew instinctively what it was. The boat had hit rocks. They could feel the heart being torn from its undersides; they could hear the roar of the water as it torrented into the bilge; they could smell the saltiness and sourness of seaweed; they could sense the fear of their fellows, their screams and shouts.

Then silence. The silence that Kit imagined would greet him in his grave. He held on to his friend and felt, for the first time in his life, an eternal gratitude for the loyalty of this man who had followed him into exile and now, possibly, death. With the gratitude came a profound disappointment; they had not only travelled through danger and strange worlds together but Kit had experienced what it was like to be both man and woman, a privilege he felt so profoundly that he gave up a silent prayer, *if I live, I will put all of my experiences into my plays. My women as well as men will be as living creatures on the stage.*

As he breathed the strange incantation, he suddenly took in a new odour. He released Tom and said, so calmly it took his companion's breath away, 'Tom, that smell. It's seaweed. We are near land, I swear it. Let's try to make a light. Where is the taper?'

Tom laughed hysterically. The violent movements had stopped but the noises had increased. It was as if, after the strange silence and shock of being shattered, the ship was now collapsing into a thousand pieces of shard. He could hardly hear Kit for the roaring around them. To think of making a light in this hellish waterhole was absolute nonsense. He couldn't answer because of hysteria. Kit moved away. Tom stood still, afraid that the smallest movement would affect their haven. He could see nothing in the profound darkness. He could hear Kit moving back and forth, could feel water engulfing his feet, and moving rapidly towards the top of his boots. Should he take them off? Surely they would both drown and if the water swept them out to sea, the weight of their gold would pull them into the depths. Despite this previous hysterical laughter, Tom now felt strangely calm. He did not want to move.

Then there was a flicker from the tinder. It died. Another flicker and a candle flame fluttered as if new life had been given not only to Kit but to Tom as well. The two men stared at each other in the dim light. Kit grinned.

'We're not moving. We have light. We are alive! Let's go outside and see what's afoot. I'd rather be out in the open than drown in this place.'

They had to force the door. It was difficult for there was hardly room to stand side by side and the swirling water hampered their balance. It took them some time, but the water rising around them added determination. The door broke off its hinges and they almost fell out into the corridor. Here, water was swirling and great slivers of wood moved rapidly past; swirling garments caught between their legs as they waded through the sludge. Kit pulled his skirts around his waist and tucked them into the belt that held the gold, to stop the extra material pulling him down. Although the vessel still creaked and groaned it was strangely quiet of human sound. Where was everyone? Then their way was blocked by a great wet stone; not only had the boat caught on rocks, it had been seared almost in half by the great pinnacle which now reared through its timbers. It was jagged with scarred edges.

'Come, Tom, we will climb this rock and get out of this watery hell hole and wait until dawn to see what has happened.'

Kit had already found a foothold and climbed upwards. There were jagged ends of wooden deck-floor when he reached the top. He called down, 'There's a large ledge up here, we can rest here and wait until daylight.'

Tom followed and Kit hauled his friend through the jagged edges of what remained of the deck. The candle spluttered out in the wind of the night. Tom could just make out that the sky was still angry with clouds. They scudded now, with scars of lighter blue between them, and he could see a dark mass landward where the storm swept away. The sea was still roaring but the waves could not reach them; they were well above them on this promontory. Their ledge was slimy with damp and a sticky substance. In the sky great white birds, their wings catching the last of the fading light, swirled around them. They gripped each other.

'You sleep first, Tom, and I'll hold you; then I'll rest.'

That night Tom dreamt the great white birds were angels come to take him. In his dreams he was glad they were angels and not watery she-devils from below come to pull him down again into the hell from which he had escaped. He felt the angels grip him as he was being dragged down but he woke with a start to find that Kit still held him tight.

Then it was his turn to hold Kit. He was terrified. He could see nothing but dark terrifying shapes. As Kit relaxed, his head lolling, Tom felt a great sense of responsibility. Supposing he should fall asleep and lose his grip on Kit? Kit had not done so, and that gave him strength.

Slowly dawn came, Kit stirred, and they surveyed the devastation around them. Their rock was one of several, and it looked as if the boat had been tossed in the air and then thrown straight down onto it. The water was whitely fizzing around the rocks, and with horror they could see bodies floating, as if they were sleeping in the water and being gently lulled by the waves. One pinnacle had shot through the main room where most of their fellow sea-travellers had been revelling. Debris from the ship was all around. The only part that was recognisable was their cabin and both Tom and Kit laughed to see their trunks, all jumbled together against one wall which protected them from the sea.

'My papers. They are safe. Tom, truly the spirits protect me; Dr Dee was right, my works will go on after me.'

Tom took no notice, he was just relieved to be alive. Cold, wet, sticky, stiff, and surely smelling of seaweed, sweat and what else he could not imagine, but alive.

The rock they sat on lent at an angle. What they had not seen at night was that on the other side it sloped gently down to a sandy plain which then changed to a grassy slope; dry land. With a bit of effort, thought Tom, they could escape, simply by climbing over the ledge they sat on and walking away. To what, he did not care.

The sunrise was benign in contrast to the sunset of the night before. The sky became softly grey before turning to a clear blue as the sun came up, a bright yellow orb, silhouetting distant hills on the land.

Where they sat was covered with white bird ordure; it was obviously the nesting grounds of the great gulls that cried in the morning light, wheeling around them as if in anger at the invasion of their home.

In front of them was a sandy bay, with little runnels of water creating channels in the sand. It was semi-circular with softly rising hills around it. There were trees leaning from the top of the hills, as if trying to reach the sea. All this they took in. It was Tom who called out first, 'Look, coming down to us galloping: a party of horsemen. Friend or foe, what say you, Kit?'

Chapter Fourteen

It was strangely eerie to watch the cavalcade approach. The horses' hooves on the sand made little noise and the cries of the birds blotted out any other sound. They could not even hear the jingle of harness or clanging swords. They were like dream-men, ghosts. Could they see Tom and Kit on their rocky haven? The two sat, saying nothing, awaiting their fate. Tom whispered, 'We do not know where we are. Friend or foe I care not, for we cannot stay up here forever and must needs get some food. Shall we call them?'

Kit nodded. He was stiff with cold, despite the thick skirts and cloak he still wore and they were both still wet through with the spray from the sea.

The men were nearly below them now and wheeled their horses about, kicking up flumes of sand not a few yards from them. There were five, and they looked merely curious, pointing at the flotsam and jetsam that was being washed up on the beach. One of them dismounted and pulled a stout box from the foam onto drier land.

'I'll be a helpless woman – will that be safe, do you think?'

Tom watched the men; they did not look rough, and the way in which they rode about indicated idle interest rather than a desire to find survivors and kill or take them captive. If they had weapons, they were well hidden. Tom quickly made the decision. 'Yes, call out now. I'll edge further along the ledge and hide. If they attack you I'll come but I think it sensible for only one of us to be captured if that is what they do.'

Kit was aghast. He stared at Tom. 'You can't just abandon me like that.'

Tom moved away but as he did so he deliberately pushed Kit, so that he slipped. Involuntarily Kit cried out and grasped at nothing as he fell on to the shattered deck below. Tom fell back, shocked. He hadn't catered for the slippery slime of the birds' droppings. He hadn't expected Kit to fall, just to cry out in surprise. That would have made the men look up and see a lone woman. Tom was confident that he would be hidden by the craggy rock. Now he watched with mounting fear for his friend. Was he dead? He lay so still that Tom was almost convinced of it.

All of the horsemen wheeled round and looked up. Orders were given and two of them dismounted and climbed the hull of the stricken ship. Tom watched horrified as they touched Kit's face. It had paled and looked void of all character, with eyes closed fast. Was he faking unconsciousness or really dead? Tom could not tell. He could not understand what the men said but watched as one of them, obviously the leader, pointed to some jagged planks and ropes and his orders were carried out; a rough bed was quickly constructed and the still pliant and insensate Kit carried off, the makeshift bed strung between two of the horses. The group moved slowly away, never thinking to look back. Tom was relieved; Kit must be alive; he was sure that no-one would bother to carry a dead body away from this wreckage, especially as they left everything else.

When they had gone, he climbed down slowly, keeping to the lee of the rock so that, if any of the horsemen turned round, he could not be seen. The men were moving so slowly, and the horses' prints so clear in the sand, that, so long as he moved before the tide came to wash them away, he would easily be able to follow. All he knew was that, if Kit was alive, he had to be near him.

Soon the men were dots as they left the beach for harder ground, and he ran to the dunes peppered with rough grass, and started to climb, keeping to the shadows, meaning to follow the horsemen from on high. As he climbed upwards he found verdant woods with undergrowth which would hide him. Now he could hear the steady crackling as the group made its way through low undergrowth which snapped and cracked beneath the weight of the horses. They could not move fast with the makeshift hammock held between them. Every now and then he caught a glimpse of the group through the trees. As he came to an opening, he looked back at the view. The land proved heavily wooded on the cliff top but between the trees, he could see a myriad of bays stretching along the coast. He could not tell whether he was on an island or had landed on the Italian mainland.

His quarry was heading for a large wall of rock that stood out from the woodland scarring the sky like the end of the world. The horsemen had slowed even more and were going at a walking pace, with Tom following stealthily. Surely they knew a way through the cliff, perhaps a narrow chasm, even though it stretched as far as Tom could see through the large trees. Or would they skirt it? It seemed to stretch to both horizons and Tom was not sure how he would be able to follow. As the party approached the forbidding cliff, Tom lost sight of them for a moment as they disappeared into the dark shadow that the rock created. He noticed that it wasn't a sheer, blank cliff-face; it was covered with hanging creepers, which slowly moved in the breeze. When he looked for the party again they were gone and one particular stretch of the creepers was swaying more intensely than those around it. He rushed down the slope to where they had been, oblivious of his safety. Where had they gone? Where had they taken Kit?

He brushed past the creepers at the place he thought they had gone through, convinced he would find an entrance but there was none. The rock face, although jagged, had no scar in it to indicate a door. All he found was the scarred granite which was cold to his touch.

What was he to do now? He looked around for hoof prints but there were none; the ground was bedded with chips of the grey rock, as if the wall moulted. He looked up the sheer face. It was as tall as the castle walls he had played beneath as a child, if not taller. He guessed the promontory faced north, and this place never felt the sun. He became aware that he was cold and damp, the sea-spray not yet dried from his salt encrusted clothes. He was hungry, too, but he could do nothing about that. He walked up and down, touching the rock, pressing it, convinced there must be a hidden entrance but none would reveal itself to him. He looked up again. All his instinct told him to climb, even if it was to reach the warmth of the rays of the sun at the top. He pulled on one of the creepers. It was as thick as a man's wrist, the leaves a waxy emerald. It seemed strong. He gripped it with both hands and started climbing, pulling himself up, levering himself away from the face of the rock as he swung around. Then he gripped the rope-like creeper between his thighs and clambered up the steep cliff.

It seemed to take hours to reach the top, and there were moments when he thought he would just let go and fall to the ground beneath. As he climbed higher, the wind increased and swung him back and forth so that every now and then he had to loosen his thighs' grip and kick himself away from the granite face. Then the pain in his arms became unbearable, as they took the full weight of his body. He had to rest, grip the creeper with his thighs to rest his arms. He started to mutter prayers from his childhood, in a desperate plea to the God he questioned rationally, to aid him. As he reached the summit, the rock was so sharp that he had to swing away and then, with an extra effort, yank himself over the promontory. He had wanted to peer over carefully to find out what was at the top. Supposing there were people, farming perhaps? He lay there awhile, panting and semi-conscious with the effort, on soft grass, his legs still swinging until he scrabbled, kneeling first and then half-crawling he was clear of the cliff top. He collapsed, exhausted, eyes closed, waiting until his heart stopped the frantic beating, his body thrumming with the effort.

His nose was being tickled by some wild flowers and he opened his eyes. To view flowers which he had never seen before. They speckled the grass yellow; the smell was of infinite sweetness and warmth. He lay there for some time, his breath coming in deep gasps which hurt his chest, before he looked further. The heat of the sun beating down on him as he rested, and the effort of the climb made him sweat so that although his clothes had dried out, he was damp again.

If there was anyone about they would see him and come for him, he thought, and for a time he did not care. His eyes drooped, his whole body ached. The exhaustion of the night and his climb overcame him and he slept, without even looking to see where he was. It was a comfortable, deep sleep as if the strange flowers were narcotic.

He woke with a start. He was being prodded by something blunt. He opened his eyes and saw thick hairy feet, the toenails black and talon-like, either side of him. He jumped to his knees and looked up to see the ugliest *thing* he had ever seen. For a moment he forgot where he was and thought that Kit had donned different pieces of fancy dress costume to scare him; he had been dreaming of losing Kit in the fated celebrations in Rome, where masked creatures in assorted costumes leered up before him and blocked his way. All thoughts of where Kit could be were dissipated by the realisation that this monster was not a dream, but real. It was horrific; scaley, like a fish but with huge shoulders, a head sunk into his neck, bulbous eyes and a glowering forehead. Tom shrank away, still staring. Yes, it must be human but what sort of horrors had his mother encountered as she carried him to make him born so ugly? The creature spoke first. The voice was thick, as if it was unused to speech. He spoke in thick Latin dialect.

'What are you? What you doing here?' As Tom tried to get up he was pinned down again with a large thick club held firmly against his shoulder.

'Where am I? What are you?'

'No, you first; you in my land. A stranger. Speak.'

Tom found himself stuttering, not able to answer easily, being winded by the club pressing into him, 'My name is …is Tom…I was shipwrecked. I have lost my friend. Kill me if you will but if not, remove your club and let me breathe.'

There was a moment when Tom's chest was crushed even more, but then the pressure was eased and his captor jumped away quickly. 'Stand. You come with me. You be of use to me.'

Tom pulled himself to a standing position, edging away from the drop over the cliff, even though this meant moving closer to his captor. The creature ignored him and lumbered away gesturing for Tom to follow.

'Wait, please. What is your name? Where am I? What is this place?'

The creature turned and, pointing at his chest said, 'Nabilac my name. My mother and I banished here because of my looks. Mother died. Alone, I reigned supreme until the Duke came. Calls himself King now, but I know better. He is like you. He rules now. He made me show my island, all the watering places, the secret caves, where to find food.' He stopped and beat his breast in an agony and his face creased in pain. 'Then he chained me to him with oaths of loyalty. I fetch his water and fuel. A slave, me, Nabilac. One day I will avenge the wrong.'

Tom picked up on the first words. 'An island? I'm on an island?'

The man-monster nodded and turned, talking over his shoulder as if he would not brook any defiance. 'If you want to live you follow me.' The creature lumbered away. Tom followed, realising there was little else he could do.

*　　*　　*　　*　　*

Soft voices seemed to caress Kit as he drifted in and out of consciousness. All he knew was that he ached all over and didn't want to wake up. Every now and then soft hands held his head and forced a sticky liquid between his lips and he would dream again. He dreamt of a rich table of food, of fruits and sea-creatures, rose-pink and ochre; black and orange; crimson and purple. A dreamy emanation of the sky before the storm that had swept him away from his friend. His friend, Tom. In his dreams, Tom approached, but Kit could not hang on to the image; Tom drifted away. All Kit was left with was a feeling of violence that had knocked him about so much that he was a blackened and bruised, bloodied, inanimate unable to hold onto anything.

All he could think of now was the feast before him. The food cascaded over the table and great vines hung, opulently, over the side like the fringes of a tablecloth. There were people urging him to eat but every time he approached, the feast misted over and disappeared and his hands would be left hanging helplessly in the air. Sweet music enraptured him but he couldn't identify the source of the sound; not even whether the instrument was being plucked or blown. Sometimes, in his dreams, he thought he could smell the saltiness of sea-food, the sun-ripened savour of rich citruses; the cloyingness of over-ripe mango.

He tried to open his eyes but could not; as if his eyelids had been stopped by the same sticky substance that he was being fed. He thought hard; violence, that was where it had all begun. But then there had been a still time, a cold, stiff, time. Birds wheeling around. A fall, a fall that had led him here. Had he broken his back? Was he dead? Was the feast, so tantalisingly drifting towards him again now, part of his punishment in purgatory? Grimly he smiled to himself; nay, he didn't believe in such things. He was in pain; he was lying on a soft mattress, people were being kind to him. He was alive.

He was alive and slowly it came to him, how he had been carried away. Where was Tom? Had they caught him? Was he dead? Kit lay a-while trying to absorb the atmosphere. He was sure he could smell food, even if it was dream food. With a great effort, he tried to open his eyes. He blinked. Everything was misty at first and he blinked again, several times, to clear the dreams.

He thought the insubstantial creature before him was part of his dreams but then it smiled. A sharp little face with pointy ears, the earlobes transparent, curly light hair, the light shining through it so as to make a halo which circled the head. The eyes, as Kit became more conscious, were clearly-blue and large. The creature was so slim it might disappear. It wore a shimmering light gown, with no visible clasp. It was holding a gilt goblet and trying to pour liquid down Kit's throat. He gagged and coughed.

The creature laughed, a silvery musical sound.

'Good, you have come to. Come, try to sit.' With surprising strength for such a tiny creature, it put its arms around Kit's shoulders and levered him up into a sitting position and proffered the goblet to his lips again. Kit drank; a sweet strange-tasting liquid that had a tang of citrus in it. It revived him immediately.

After Kit had drunk all that was in it, the creature set the goblet down on a table at the side of the pallet and quickly jumped onto the end of the bed, crossing its legs underneath and crossing its arms likewise. It surveyed Kit from this stance, its head moving slowly from side to side as if assessing what Kit could be. Kit was bemused and lay back, waiting. He realised he still had his woman's clothes on, and he rubbed his chin thoughtfully; no stubble roughed his face. He could not have been long asleep. But what would the creature think if he started a beard?

As if to answer his thoughts, the creature explained, 'I am to care for you, whatever you are, wherever you come from. You have been down in the depths and I must raise you up again; my master will see you when you are fully recovered.' The voice was musical, like the laugh, gentle and soothing. Kit felt tired again. Only one thing bothered him.

'Thank you – but I had a friend, where is he?'

'I am sorry, I know nothing of your friend. If my master knows nothing about him, then I know nothing.'

'Your master? Who is he?'

'No questions, you must get better, that is my job.'

Kit nodded; he was helpless, although he wanted to know the name of this creature's master. He would wait until he was stronger before he questioned further. But he could find out more about this creature. 'What is your name, who are you?'

'My name is Leira, and I serve my master until this day is done; he has promised me. I am but a spirit of his will for the moment. But soon, soon I will be a free spirit.''

It didn't make sense to Kit but he was so tired, he could feel his eyelids drooping again and the figure seemed to fade before him. He let it happen; for once in his life he would not try to rage against the world or work towards his destiny, or try to determine his position in society. Wherever he was; whatever was happening to him; he would let it drift around him, as if this was another life.

*   *   *   *   *

For all his cumbersome bulk, Nabilac moved fast and it was as much as Tom could do to keep up with him. He led Tom inland, away from the precipitous cliff he had climbed and the growth became thicker, with trees stretching upwards through dense undergrowth of rich lush creepers with heavy scentful flowers.

'Here, we stop and eat. Eat. Quick.' The creature pointed to a slab of rock which formed a natural table. On the slab were fruits and crustaceans, some so large that Tom thought they had come from some giant ocean he knew nothing about. The very sight of the food made him remember that he was famished; he hadn't eaten since early yesterday. Nabilac was tearing a claw from the lobster and with the other hand pulling at a bunch of large grapes. Tom followed his example, but ate one item at a time. When he tore off a claw and extracted the flesh, it tasted like no lobster that Tom had ever eaten before. The food was fresh and delicious but before he had had his fill Nabilac had lumbered off.

'Come, follow. We not reach place yet.'

Again he set a fast pace but Tom, now fully recovered and his hunger assuaged, managed to keep up with him. They reached a clearing where the rich growth lessened and more rocks were exposed. Nabilac headed towards a large outcrop of grey stone straight into a large cavern through a slit which couldn't be seen until they reached it. As they left the sunshine Nabilac grabbed from a sconce in the wall a large branch which was glowing crimson. He waved it vigorously and it suddenly blazed into light, to reveal a green-covered corridor which led downwards into an interior so dark Tom could see nothing; just a black void. As they walked, Tom saw stalactites glistening from the high roof like frozen fingers and could hear the steady drip drip of water. He followed warily, realising the ground was wet with runnels of damp. He was losing his foothold, and the ground sloped steeply downwards. He could easily slip and roll, where to he knew not.

Nabilac was mumbling to himself and the noise echoed against the walls like the distant murmuring of invisible crowds. Should Tom turn and run towards the light or should he continue with his strange companion? Gingerly he slowed and turned round to see from whence he had come. They hadn't gone far into the cave but it was as if the entrance was a pin prick and he wondered if the creepers outside had rapidly grown, so as to cover the entrance. That was impossible. He shook himself, wondering why he was becoming fanciful. He turned back and followed the ungainly figure, the light he held being the only hope for Tom.

They moved onwards, ever down and soon the noise became greater as if Nabilac was singing to himself, or hidden hordes were gathering around them. The echo of dripping water became constant and rushingly loud. Then the air changed and Tom realised the way had opened up into a great cavern. The light from the flare could not penetrate to glitter against the walls now. It was but a sputtering tiny candle and Tom could discern nothing in the great void around them. Nabilac turned and muttered, 'Keep close to the wall. A huge drop if not.'

Tom nodded, but his agreement was not seen by the monster who blundered onward, sure-footed. Tom felt his way forward gingerly. There seemed to be a black chasm to one side, he could feel the chill of nothingness, and dark damp wall on the other, which he fingered as he went along. It was quite smooth. Suddenly he felt his foot slip and he yelled as he nearly fell, his leg slipping down. He grabbed wildly but there was nothing to grasp. He fell with one leg dangling, his body desperately balancing on the side of the narrow path.

Nabilac edged back to him and yanked him to a standing position. Tom could smell the monster now, a rich stench of fish as if he had spent his life netting sea creatures, gutting them and living with their rotting bodies. He wanted to pull away. The creature seemed to sense this, 'No, I hold you. Very dangerous. Not long now.'

He half dragged Tom along the narrow ledge and Tom could

see by the light of the flare that their path was only the width of a wide man's shoulders; to his right all was the blackness of a deep hole like hell. But the terror did not last long and the way opened up into a small cave or large passageway. The echoes lessened, the dripping of water was not so cacophonous and Nabilac released his hold and led the way forward.

'Safe now, nowhere to fall.'

Tom thought he could detect a different brightness in front of Nabilac which accentuated his lumbrous frame, and deadened the flare he held. Tom was not mistaken; the bright light became larger and soon they stood in a giant open area with high cliffs at a distance. Above them was open azure sky, and brilliant sunshine. The air was sweet. Tom stood on soft grass, blinking in the strong daylight which at first dazzled him. As his eyes accustomed to the glare, he saw there was a limpid turquoise pool fed from a misty waterfall, circled by rainbows along its length. Lush trees stretched up towards the light and there were brilliant emerald bays surrounding the pool. Then he saw that the place was populated with groups of people who were dressed in such vivid colours they looked like exotic flowers or magical birds such as Tom had only heard of. They were lying about, some with great baskets of food by their side. There was one woman being fed grapes by a smiling attendant, who, leaning over her and staring into her eyes, dropped them one by one into her mouth. It reminded Tom of a great picture he had seen somewhere. It was all too bright, too unearthly, to paradisal, to be real. Once again he wondered if he had died and was being led to his eternal fate, but could only follow the creature, who led him towards the throng. He stepped after him as Nabilac skirted round these people as if they embarrassed him. They, likewise, ignored him and Tom as if they were invisible. Nabilac guided him to the waterfall and led the way along a rock ledge behind the great flow of water. He paused and gestured, to make sure Tom followed. Tom turned and surveyed the bacchanalian scene with regret. He would like to have joined these beautiful people, but dared not ignore his guide.

As a stranger in this land he had no other option.

He was surprised to find that the path did not lead back into darkness. Behind the waterfall was a private glade, where the sun shone in a concentrated manner filtered through the water. This gave it a multi-hued aspect like a many-sphered rainbow. Inside were tiny hillocks and glades of strange tinted shades, as if the rainbow colours had imbued the very earth with violets, azures, emeralds, yellows, oranges and reds. People stood about, dressed in robes that matched the rainbow colours and fanned around them in exotic drapes. They huddled in small groups talking quietly, but with a half-turn away from their companions so that they could be alert when whoever they waited for arrived. It reminded Tom of the beginning of a university ceremony, where all the students waited for the dignitaries to arrive. It was certainly not Nabilac and Tom, who they all pointedly ignored. Tom had seen the crowds in London wait in such a manner before the Virgin Queen arrived in procession. Nabilac stopped just outside the gathering, a little to one side and crouched down, a look of fear on his ugly features. Tom stood beside him and opened his mouth to speak, but Nabilac shook his head violently. Tom shrugged and waited.

He did not have long to wait before there was a flash as of lightning and before the crowd stood an imposing figure, hands aloft, holding a great wand. He seemed to appear from nowhere. Nabilac whispered, 'My master, the King.'

The figure wore a great billowing robe and his long flowing beard and hair gave him an air of grave power.

'Bring the stranger forth, Nabilac. Welcome, to my land. Do not hide from me, for I know all.'

Nabilac pushed Tom forward. He realised all the assembly were bowing. Tom bowed and waited.

'You are welcome stranger, and your friend who is ill. We have watched you and you are safe here; you do not threaten me. Some have come who are dangerous and we will deal with them.' There was a general murmur from the assembly, in agreement with their

159

leader. 'We deal with them, but for those who are good, we have great feasts and laughter. Come, come and see your friend.'

He gestured, the great cloak billowing around him, for Tom to follow him, away from the crowd and into a chamber behind him, set into the rock. Tom turned to question Nabilac, but he had disappeared. He followed the king.

Inside the new cavern was a wide gallery lit by a million sconces so that the walls glowed. Around the edge were doors set into the walls and outside some stood soldiers such as Tom had seen carry Kit away.

'My friend, where is…?' Tom didn't know whether to say 'he' or 'she'. What had these people found out about Kit? Supposing they had stripped him. What would they have thought? 'Is ill? You say ill?' His voice sounded harsh in the chamber, echoing off the walls.

'Come, I am taking you to your friend, worry not, we have not touched her. She is recovering. I say she is your friend, for we have been listening to her ramblings and often she calls for you.'

Tom forebore to ask how they knew that Kit called for him, how did they know *his* name? He began to accept that whatever happened on this island was natural.

He was led between two guards who hurried forward to open one of the doors as they approached, both of them bowing deeply to him. Tom followed him into a chamber bathed with light, and there was Kit, leaning against a balustrade of thick pillows, a young nymph-like creature sitting on the bed beside him feeding him some brightly coloured fruits.

'Kit! How are you?'

'In pain but comfortable.'

The king interrupted, turning to the servant, 'We will leave you two to talk. Come, Leira, leave them be.'

Leira smiled at Kit, patted the bed, shuffled the pillows and glided out. As they departed the door was pulled silently shut behind them.

'Well, are we prisoners in some Arcadia, Kit, or will they let us

160

go on our way when you are well?'

'I know not, but my main problem is to maintain my womanly disguise; I thank God they did not see fit to strip and wash me. I feel as if I should be thrown into a hot bath but have resisted asking so far. But it is the face, Tom, the face, how do I stop my beard from growing?'

Tom laughed 'Perhaps you can wax it with candles? Or scrape it with one of these delicate fruit knives?'

'Tom, stop being cruel, what are we to do?'

'I'll find a way of nursing you and shaving at the same time, what say you?'

Kit lent back on the pillows, nodding.

'These people might not mind if I show my true colours, let me be a man for a while?'

Tom shook his head. 'Remember what Dr Dee said; you never know who is watching us, these people could always tell someone else and such a story as that would spread to your enemies; nay, if they believe you are woman, then let it be so, and I'll ensure you don't give yourself away with facial embarrassments. I admit it will be difficult if we stay a while so we will have to think of escape – when you are better.'

Kit moved uncomfortably. 'My back hurts badly Tom, I must have fallen some way. I can't remember it all although every now and then I have flashes. I think it was the jolting of the journey here that hurt more than the falling. I know I have been unconscious – I feel as if I have a new life, as if I have passed through a deep passage or river to another land. '

Tom said nothing to enlighten his friend, relieved that Kit couldn't recall everything, especially the fact that he didn't remember being deliberately pushed. He felt somewhat ashamed of this even though he had done it with the best of motives. So far, he hadn't been wrong. They seemed to have landed amongst friends.

'But how did you get here? Tell me.'

Tom filled him in with his adventures, telling him of the

strange creature Nabilac. As he was finishing his tale the door opened. The King appeared as if he knew that his guests had completed their stories. He smiled at them. Somehow he was less imposing than when they had first seen him.

'So how are you both? You are my guests until this young lady is well, and then we will see what you wish to do. Leira here will attend to all your needs and I have suggested a bed be made up in the alcove here for you Tom, if you would like that, or if you want privacy, or the young lady would prefer it, you can have the room next door. We are at your disposal.'

Tom nodded and agreed. Kit, with seeming womanly modesty said nothing.

For the next few days they were feasted and entertained by Leira and others who sang and played music. A strange lethargy overcame Tom and he was content to watch Kit recover. Kit grew progressively stronger and started to walk, striding back and forth in the room that was rapidly becoming too small for them. At one point he opened the door to leave but banged it shut.

Tom looked up exasperated. 'Kit can't you sit still? What happened to the writing? I'm sure if you ask they will give you ink and quill. What say you?'

'Write. Write? I cannot. Has it not occurred to you Tom? We are prisoners here, albeit treated like honoured guests. I suggest you try to go for a walk and see what happens. There are two guards outside and if you try to leave they smile and close ranks, barring the door with their swords.'

'But the King assured us he would see what he could do for us; he will find a ship surely?'

Kit strode to the door, all strength now restored, and opened it, standing back so Tom could see. The guards jumped to attention and, as he had said, crossed spears with smiles on their faces that belied their imprisoning gestures.

'I wish to see your King. We wish to ask him something.'

One of the guards nodded, and pulled the door shut.

Soon after, there was a fanfare and the door swung open. The

King entered slowly, a changed man, looking as if he had aged overnight.

'You called for me? What can I do for you?'

Tom spoke, before Kit could. 'My sister is much stronger now, and we would be on our way. If you could oblige us by hailing a passing ship, we would board and be no more trouble to you.'

The King sat down heavily on a chair, resting his elbow on the arm.

He said nothing for a while but then answered, slowly, 'It was no accident that brought you here. I would have something of you. You remember when you first came, Tom, when I said I know all.'

Tom nodded, waiting. Kit had returned to the bed and was lounging on it, as a compliant woman would, who waited to hear her fate.

The king continued, 'I am old, I have had my day, and my power wanes. Others will take up the work I and others do. But I would not be forgotten in the world. I want men to know of me, my magic; the way I can call up spirits, old mythic creatures like Ceres and cause storms to throw men in my way. I know that you, young *lady,* are not what you seem, that you have other lives to lead and I would give you your freedom, grant you your next life, but I would ask one boon of you.'

Kit had jumped off the bed as the King spoke and stood before him, his head on one side. 'What do you want of me?'

'I know you write magical scenes, and in a way you are like me; you weave dreams for people. I want you to weave a dream of me that people will watch and know the magic that I wove, for the good of all; to show both good and evil and that good will triumph. If you promise to do that for me, I will let you go. Not only will I let you go, I will find you a ship, with my last waning strength, and blow you with good winds back on your course. What say you?'

Tom laughed; nothing could be easier, surely, but for Kit to agree. They would soon be on their way. He started to gather their few possessions. But Kit surprised him. He burst out, 'I cannot do it. I write what I know about, what interests me, but also what I know people will want. I do not write of such things as magic and strange creatures.'

'You lie. I know you have a sacred aim, that you write what you need to write, what is needful for the cause. But think of your Faust, of your Helen of Troy, of your mocking of the pope. Was that all for your cause?'

Tom saw Kit look surprised. 'How can you know of those matters?'

'If I tell you I know that you were born in 1564, and that there are two others with the same birth year. That all three of you were put on earth to change the world?'

Tom burst out, 'That is what Dr Dee told me, Kit, but I've not said anything on this island about it.'

'Yes, Dr Dee, another one like me, but his powers are not so concentrated as mine were. He will live to make sure you succeed.'

Kit became very quiet, thinking.

'I am not sure I can write you, as I write other characters. I have to think very carefully.'

'You conjured up the devil in Faust; good angels and bad angels. Why can you not do this of me?'

'It would not be honest. I am not ready to write of such things.'

Tom turned and faced his friend, with his back to the King. 'Kit,' he whispered, 'Surely you can do this? Just promise and let us go, now. You, more than I, want to be gone.'

Kit strode backwards and forwards, thinking. Tom waited. The King watched his prey, eagle eyes boring into him as if, even now as he rapidly aged, he would still force his will on the young man.

Then Kit stopped and stood before the King, his shoulders slumped and his hands outstretched. 'I will do it. But you must trust me. It will not be soon. You are an old man; I need to understand that. You must wait until I am ready to write such a play.'

The old man stared at him, once again boring into him with deep eyes that sunk into aging flesh as they played the scene. Tom watched fascinated. The King and Kit were locked into a private battle of wills which made the air buzz. Time passed. Tom, standing, became stiff and wanted to move but was afraid to break the deadlock between the two; his young friend Kit who looked younger than his years with a beardless chin, and the old man who seemed to wither before him, the battle weakening him.

After what seemed an age, the King stood up in a rapid movement which made Tom jump. He knew that Kit had won. The King nodded. 'So be it, but my spirit will punish you if you die without doing what you have promised. Now we will find a ship for you to board. But before that you will leave this island as a man – yes, you. You will grow your beard and be my emissary for a while, for I would learn more of the world, before I die. Also I have orders to direct you.'

'Direct us? We go where we will,' Kit proclaimed as if it was a mantra.

The King leant back as if to avoid the words. He said slowly, 'You have a mission to complete and you have played long enough, toying with others in Rome, delaying for your own savouring in Florence. Now you must meet your apex, if I can call him that. You must head for Padua, and soon.

But you must avoid Naples, for there is a military man there, Marshall, who may well cause you trouble.' His voice was becoming fainter, and Tom realised it was with a great effort he added, 'It may be better to go by ship to Venice and travel to Padua that way.'

Tom listened and became increasingly agitated by what he heard. He was sure it meant danger and he was becoming tired of all the travelling. Kit, on the other hand, nodded enthusiastically. 'Something after my own heart, we will go where you direct, your highness, not just for you but for me. I too need such stimulus.'

'Very well.'

Kit then surprised Tom, 'But before we leave, I must know your name, for the play you understand.'

The King smiled. 'It is Orepsorp. Use it wisely.'

All seemed a-bustle after that and soon, they were escorted through the caves. As they reached the exit to the outside world, Orepsorp said to them, 'Try to keep me informed of what you do, who you meet.' He looked directly at Kit, 'Use the normal channels.'

Kit nodded as they moved out into bright sunlight, and the door closed behind them. They were at the bottom of the cliff that Tom had climbed, near the shore line. Tom turned to where they had come but the door was so closely fitted in the cliff he could not see it.

He turned back to Kit who was striding down to the sea, and thought that he looked quite different now. He realised that he too was different. Both of them were richly adorned with new clothes of velvet and fustian, great coloured feathers in their caps, gold-trimmed cloaks draped around their shoulders. Tom thought they looked exotic enough to be Slavic princes and he strode confidently after his friend. He laughed as he came alongside Kit, who was clearly revelling in his new image, stroking the soft beard that was framing his face. By the time they would reach the mainland, Tom realised, Kit would once again be a fully-grown man. More so than when they had left England so many moons ago. Did he need Tom now, he wondered?

They strode along the coast, to where the wreck still swayed in the tides of the sea. Just out of the bay was another ship and, as if by magic, a small boat was being rowed towards them. They waved. Soon they were on a strong barque moving south.

Chapter Fifteen

'Dottore, Dottore, now give him the olive crown;
Dottore, Dottore, not for him the life of a clown.'

The singing of the students rang out over the main square in
Padua, as they emerged from the bar, arms around each other, a
sheepish stooge in the middle with a great olive wreath wrapped
around his neck. Kit and Tom watched them from a corner,
strangers still shy of making themselves visible.

'So obviously a university town,' whispered Kit ironically as
they watched the group stagger between the stalls of the fruit
market, ignoring the protests of the stall-holders as they rocked
their wares, making oranges and apples roll.

'Different from Rome or even Florence,' commented Tom,
jumping back to avoid the students as they tried to grab him and
make him join their rollicking way down a side road.

He remembered Rome and Florence with a shudder. The
experiences had faded in journey around the foot of Italy and
along the eastern coast to Padua, after their sojourn on the island.
To Tom the island seemed a dream now but one that had refreshed
him and changed him in ways he was not sure of at the moment.
Now Tom recalled those other places and contrasted them with
this new town. Rome had been lively, with many religious
ceremonies. Every day there was some procession clogging the
streets, the cloying perfume of incense always floating on the
wind, the chant of priests rising above it. He had hated the
constant sombre religious festivals and the gaiety and masques
that followed, as if the hell of one encouraged the heaven of the
other. He remembered *that* masque in particular where Kit had
been so brazen.

By contrast, he thought, Florence had been secretive, political, dangerous, with Kit nearly being exposed.

Despite the rowdy students, Tom was glad to be here in Padua which reminded him of Cambridge with its colleges and students, some raucous like the group who had just passed them; others bent in thought and study. This, his first full day, seemed to bode well, despite the drunkenness of the students celebrating their graduation from the great university, which dominated the town. Tom felt relaxed for the first time in many moons.

As they made their way out of the square to find lodgings, Tom's first impression was of many open spaces where intense, staring-eyed men, dressed soberly, and sometimes thread-patched, hurried past. Scholars such as these ignored the markets, as if they did not exist, parchments and books tucked under their arms, as they rushed to their lecture or tutorial.

* * * * *

After a few weeks, they settled into a routine, with both of them attending lectures and Kit writing constantly.

'I tell you, Tom, I am so grateful I am not truly a woman. Not only could I not study at the university but I would be scrubbing my clothes now like those women down there. Look, Tom, how their backs are bent and the sweat pours off them.'

Tom came to the window, drawn by the sympathy in Kit's voice and looked down at the group of washerwomen, but turned away, not seeing anything special.

Kit continued, 'As we men scuttle about our learned business, carrying no more than a few books and hiding away in cool corridors, they carry those great bundles on their heads. But with such grace, Tom, they move like dancers.'

'But you don't see any ladies of the town,' countered Tom, 'They are kept hidden behind cool shutters.'

'Aha, so you notice that, do you Tom?' Kit turned from the window and eyed his friend. 'Are you looking for that sort of woman?'

Tom laughed, and picked up a quill pen from the desk where

168

Kit had been working. He started to pick at the thin remaining feather at the end of the quill and did not answer. How could Kit read his mind so easily?

Kit did not push it but turned back to the view from the window. Across the River Brenta could be seen the bare sandstone buildings where in the heat of the day the shutters remained firmly closed. The skyline was broken by turreted façades, and in the distance stood the viewing tower of the Collegio like an exclamation mark to the world.

Tom and Kit attended the lectures of the professor, Galileo. A man who already had a following.

Kit had enthused as they travelled to the city. 'He is the new man – Ralegh spoke of him and we must hear him. It is said he will find new worlds, or at least introduce his students to new worlds.'

Tom willingly agreed – he was becoming bored with their travelling life. Their escapades had left him jaded and tired. He wanted to stay in one place, not to have to worry about the exploits of his so-called sister. Or brother, now that his beard was full-grown. Even so he warned, 'We must be careful, Kit, I know we've not been in England for some seasons now. Your beard hides your features well, but we never know. You must promise to be a discreet student.'

Kit laughed. 'In this place, with students from as far as the steppes of Russia, Mongolia, the Arab countries and France, we won't be noticed; we'll just be seen as more foreign students. And anyway, we will call ourselves something different. I know. We can say we come from Ireland, that wild country to the far west where no-one from this land travels. My name will be Fitz and you will be my cousin, Rovea, what say you?'

Tom laughed at Kit's inventions. Kit added, 'No-one will take notice of us, just another two poor strangers eager to learn the new sciences and follow Galileo's methods of experimentation.'

But he was wrong. Even at their first tutorial, Kit could not resist asking pointed questions and after a few sessions, it was obvious that their fellow students were talking about them. Tom soon realised that with Kit's thirst for knowledge, his lack of any sensitivity to social mores, and his questioning nature, they were sure to stand out. Now that he had stripped himself of his women's guise, he had become an over-confident, loud man who ignored all others' feelings. All he seemed to do was to concentrate on the learning he could acquire from the great men of Padua and constantly strained the lecturers with more and more questions.

Tom was being waylaid by other students and asked, 'Who is he, your friend? He knows so much. When he questions the master it seems as if he has secret knowledge.'

Tom shrugged them off. 'He always shows off, take no notice. I know him not at all well; he is but a travelling companion.'

After one such interrogation, when he had been pinned up against the wall by three burly Germans and prodded and questioned, he became so disturbed he hurried home. He had to warn Kit that he should either keep quiet or word would surely reach England of two bright English speaking students and English spies might be sent to find out who they were. Tom dreaded that they would have to move on. When he reached their lodgings, he remonstrated with his friend, 'You should not keep interrupting the lecturers, it is not done.'

Kit just laughed in his dismissive way which so infuriated Tom. 'I don't do it deliberately, dear friend, you must know that. It's just that what they are telling us raises so many other questions in my mind, that I must know more. Especially Galileo; he knows so much.' He put his arm around Tom's shoulders and placated him. 'I will try but it's very hard.'

But the next day it was as if Tom had said nothing. At the very next lecture, as if to spite him, he saw Kit lean forward and knew what was coming. He watched in despair as Galileo looked up quizzically from his demonstrations, to answer the latest question that Kit threw at him. Galileo was not a good lecturer; he buried his head in his instruments, spoke hesitantly as if he wished he were not there, and, when he had finished, he gathered his books and ran for the door before any student could waylay him. When

Marlowe coughed and attracted his attention, Galileo looked up as if he had been rescued, even though it was not the custom for a student to interrupt the master. There was a smile on his face which all could see and know what he was thinking. *At last, an intelligent student, one that understands, who has an enquiring mind, one who wants to know more.* The other students turned in their seats and stared.

'And how can we see the stars with glass tubes?' he asked, as Galileo explained his ideas about star-gazing. He'd been experimenting with grinding glass and making it into convex and concave shapes and was explaining how such altered glass, if looked through, either accentuated an image or made things smaller.

'Unfortunately, the glass grinders, who, as you know, mainly come from the Netherlands, have not yet perfected the art. Glass-grinding is not precise and I experiment myself with trying to get a clearer lens to see the skies. It is said they know how to measure such magic in the east but they keep their secrets and we have to re-invent what is already known. '

The doctor explained calmly, now looking squarely at the enquirer. Tom squirmed but Kit was smiling and nodding.

Galileo continued, 'There are glasses that magnify, which, if ground correctly, so I am told, will see to the end of the earth and into the depths of the skies to the very end of the spheres.'

'And where can we find these wonderful magnifying glasses?'

Galileo sighed, 'There is a lot more work to be done, sir, as I say, otherwise I would be taking the whole class out in the night and showing them the wonders of such a thing.'

The class laughed at the mischievousness of their tutor and some of the Italian locals turned triumphantly and shrugged at Kit, as if to say, there, that puts you in your place.

It was high summer and classes were winding down. There were no lectures in the afternoons because of the heat. Tom and Kit had acquired the local habit of sleeping in the afternoon when the heat was most intense, and all was quiet in their lodgings. They

171

had not yet spoken of their plans once the university closed for the long summer break. But for the time being they slept the afternoons away.

Tom woke suddenly. A noise had disturbed his sweating slumber. Kit was not on his pallet. Tom sighed. Not again. His friend was always missing and refused to tell Tom where he went. 'I just wander. You have no need to worry, I'll not get into trouble. And if I do, you'll not be there to get involved.' Kit always tinged such words with an ironic toss of his head, which did not placate Tom at all. They had rented a small apartment, not far from the college, where there was only one room for them to sleep and a study room next to it; lodgings fit for poor students. They were careful not to let others know that they had money a-plenty although Tom realised the purse he kept was becoming lighter. He waited awhile but Kit did not come back into their sleeping quarters, so he rose and approached the door to their other room, and listened. He could hear low tones; Kit obviously had company but whoever it was spoke so quietly that Tom could not make out what they were saying. Another stranger, whom Kit would keep to himself. Tom had hoped that, while Kit was occupied with the new learning, he would not become involved in any more intrigues.

Even though he listened hard, all he could hear was the odd word. 'Packet.' 'Travel...take some weeks...avoid the low countries...'

He remembered the secret man in Rome. Kit had very cleverly deflected him and never referred to it again. Dr Dee had hinted at something and he remembered the advice given, to find a man who had been born in the same year as Kit, but how could he find that out? And Orepsorp had advised Padua. It was high time Tom realised that he should be taking the old men's advice.

He yanked at the door. He had to know what was going on. The conversation halted abruptly and both Kit and his visitor looked at him, an identical expression of surprise on their faces. Kit's companion was a dark bearded man, similar to the person whom Tom had passed on the stairs when he'd returned to their apartment in Rome, but he was certain it was not the same man. The stranger turned from the intruder and looked at Kit and then back to Tom, as if scared. Kit placed a hand on the arm of his dark robes by way of reassurance.

'Fear not, he is my friend. This is Simon, a merchant. He helps me here.'

'In what way?' Tom spoke English; Kit had used Italian. Kit stood and faced Tom, standing in front of Simon. 'I'll explain later, as I know Simon has to go soon. He travels far, he helps carry messages for me. After all, we promised Orepsorp we would keep him informed of our studies, you remember?'

Tom nodded. Simon too had stood and was folding something away into his robes. 'I will leave now, I will carry out your wishes.' He said no more but drifted towards the door and edged out with a sideways look at Tom. Kit tidied the papers on the table. Tom waited. Eventually Kit faced his friend.

'Tom, don't be angry with me. I have to use this method. My messengers are Jewish as I told you before; they know how to move across the continent silently and almost invisibly. So far none of my packages have been intercepted.'

'What packages, Kit? I seem to recall we had this talk some time ago and you very cleverly deflected it then. If you are sending messages to your family in England, that would be very foolish. And if you're writing to your old colleagues...'

'I promise you it is not to my family. I have no truck with them. If they could see me now they would have no idea how to deal with me. I was always trouble for my father; remember how angry he was when I was involved in that brawl the last time I was in Canterbury? He was none too pleased that I showed him up in front of his guild friends. I think he would have been glad to see the back of me; relieved at my death.'

Tom nodded but was impatient. Once again Kit was not giving him the answers he wanted.

'Kit don't take me for a fool.' Even though Tom guessed what was being carried, he needed to know where they were being sent.

'What is in the parcels? Where are your parcels heading for?'

Kit moved about the room, pacing up and down in the same manner as he had done in Orepsorp's magical prison. Tom knew he felt trapped but he would not relent. They might be friends, but he had risked much, and given up a pleasant life in England, to help Kit, and he knew he could not now return without a great deal of explanation. Kit owed him loyalty and gratitude. He would not let him bluff an answer this time. He crossed his arms and stood still. Kit sauntered to the exit of their chamber but Tom moved quickly and barred his way, shaking his head. Eventually Kit stopped and placed his elbow in one hand and his chin rested on the raised hand.

'Very well, friend, you will know. But not yet.' He paused and smiled. 'For your own safety, I promise you. I have heard that the Queen ails; if she dies, I know we will be safe.'

Tom looked sceptical. 'How so?'

'With the Queen dead, intrigue dies; that's all I am prepared to say.'

'Oh come on Kit, don't deflect me once more with side speculation. Tell me what the packages are and where they are bound.'

Kit answered. 'I know you have risked much for me, Tom, but if you knew all.' He took a deep breath. 'I was involved in some scheme – you recall I travelled to Scotland once? And if the Queen dies, I will tell you about it. It is connected with what I do now. But it is dangerous. No, I cannot tell you.'

'But you must. I'm to be trusted, you know that by now, surely?' Tom urged but Kit ignored him and gathered a short cloak around him.

'Of course I trust you, but the less you know, the safer you will be.' As he spoke he headed for the door. 'I must go out, the evening cool sets in. Soon it will be dark. I want to try an instrument that Dr Dee has sent me; it has just arrived and it excites me.' As he spoke he picked up a tube-like packet from the desk which Tom had not noticed before, and he assumed it had been delivered by the stranger, Simon. Kit was almost at the door when he paused and, as Tom made to follow, held up his hand, 'No, let me go on my own. I need to think. If it works, you will know soon enough. Anyway, if I am alone, I am not so noticeable; the two of us are well known.'

Tom gave up and allowed him to leave. He slumped in a chair, despairing. How could his friend run rings around him like this? He could never get Kit to be straightforward, always finding a way to change the subject. Even though his friend's mercurial nature was one of the reasons why he had agreed to join Kit's adventures in the first place. Always there was that magical novelty about him.

So far they had never been found out, except for the mysterious Orepsorp, who had known who Marlowe truly was. Tom was beginning to think that he and Kit had imagined the whole play on the island, a form of dream brought on by the hunger and thirst of the shipwreck, all to fade into thin air once they had been rescued. No-one in Rome, Florence or now Padua had suspected that Kit was the 'dead' Marlowe, even though his plays were known in Italy. They had even become involved in a bizarre student discussion when they had first arrived in Padua, when someone had loudly boasted, 'That Englishman Marlowe was the greatest playwright ever - how terrible that he had died so young. Just think what great plays he would have written.' Tom had watched Kit with bated breath but Kit had answered, almost angrily, 'Nay, that wicked man died deservedly. It is well known that he had cursed the true God, and called up Devils.'

So Tom was assured that their scheme had succeeded but only while they travelled on the Continent, where few knew what Marlowe looked like.

But if Kit was writing to who knows who in England then some people there knew he was alive. Such knowledge could flow through to his enemies and Priedeux was aware of the spy network that could find a priest hiding in an obscure university somewhere or a fanatical Catholic forging coin in the backstreets of a Netherlandish town.

And it was not only the spy network that concerned him; he was worried that Marlowe's continued contact with his old life would place them in danger and, Tom suspected, he would want to return to England one day to take up those friendships and acquaintances to whom he was writing. He had hinted at such in what he had just said. If they returned to England surely *someone* would recognise them?

There was something else that played on Tom's mind. He had been watching and absorbing the life in Padua, and had begun to realise he did not want to return to England. He basked in the Italian heat, which was at its height now. He liked the food and, if he was truthful, he also liked the women. Suddenly he jumped up; he too would go out, why should he not have his own life? Since leaving England he'd gone where Marlowe had led, had shared his adventures, accepted all. While Kit had gone out on his own, Tom also had found new interests. Now he would take his own path, and not bother how Marlowe fared. He'd been given an invitation to an informal debate by some of the other students.

He strode down the narrow streets until he reached the hall where the debate was to be conducted. It was an open meeting, and the public could attend; even women if they were chaperoned. He'd discovered that these Italians loved to meet and parade in the streets, especially at dusk, when the heat of the day lingered but did not stultify; when the body had rested and there was an air of excitement which was accentuated with the odours of bay, basil and other aromatics, scents released by the dewy air of evening.

The hall was heavy too with the sweet scents the women wore. Even though the young ones were accompanied by dour old maids who were supposed to look after them, the place was redolent with whispers and secrets. The women found ways of communicating and, as he sat at the back of the hall, he watched as notes changed hands discreetly while the elderly companions gossiped and laughed. Suddenly he felt a pressure against him and looked sideways. The meeting hadn't started yet; he found the Italian students' concept of time peculiar. No public meeting or lecture began when it was supposed to. The pressure was from the heavily robed body of a young woman who had sat down beside him. She smiled as she shuffled into the space pulling an elderly woman with her to sit down.

'Allora, Aunt Maria, we will sit here; yes this kind student makes the space for us, gracie, Signor.' Her smile was enticing and teasing and her eyes were dark like those of most Italian women. Her high headdress made her seem tall but the slender form, underneath the heavy robes, fitted beside him neatly in the small space, and told otherwise. He smiled back, suddenly totally content with all thoughts of Kit and his wiles gone from his mind. The warmth of the evening seemed to increase.

The debate began but most of the audience continued to gossip with their neighbours and even Aunt Maria saw an acquaintance in the row before her and, tapping the woman with her fan, was soon in agitated conversation, leaning forward and resting her elbows on the bench back before her. Tom found it difficult to concentrate and wanted to glance at his neighbour. Eventually he risked it and took a surreptitious side-glance, only to find her watching him, a small smile playing on her lips. She smiled at Tom and whispered, 'Truly, my Aunt Maria is a kind soul, but not a good protector. You are a foreigner?' She breathed the word, as if it should not be spoken. Tom inclined his head, with an answering smile, 'Not so much a foreigner that I cannot speak sweet words with you, young lady. For sometimes I am most lonely.'

The girl smiled and nodded. Encouraged, Tom continued,

'I walk alone, and have travelled far to study at your great college here at Padua; these debates are indeed inspiring and interesting.'

For a moment she looked up at the two serious students, dressed in the habitual dark gowns of scholars, flat hats on their pates, standing opposite each other; one talking while the other looked down at his notes. It was only a moment before she turned back to Tom.

'Indeed I am sure they are very learned, but I must confess that when I have listened to one lot of argument and then the other and then again their counter arguments, my head spins and I can never decide who was right and who was wrong.'

'So, why are you here, pretty one?'

'How else can we stretch our minds?' As she spoke, her slender form moved and pressed against him. Kit put his hand on his thigh near her skirts, moving his finger so the taffeta of her gown rustled, and she did not move away.

'You could read in the privacy of your own gardens, away from the hurly burly of a crowd like this.'

'Ah, but my dear Aunt would not then have a chance to meet her friends – and I to be seen and also to see. And you are very forward; how do you know I have gardens in which to read?'

As Tom was about to answer the girl's aunt leant back and whispered to her, 'Indeed I swear they make these seats uncomfortable to make us sit up straight and listen.'

Tom looked straight ahead and said nothing, until the aunt turned back to her companion. Then he answered as if there had been no interruption, 'A maid as pretty as you must be surrounded by such beautiful things as a good garden, with sun-kissed roses to compete with your cheeks for the light of the sun.'

The girl breathed heavily, 'Indeed you speak prettily for one from a foreign land. And where do you come from? What is your name?'

'Nay sweet maid, you have an advantage over me for I know you are of the warm south, and I will guess you come from Padua, born and bred. So I will trade names with you. But you first. That is fair, is it not?'

'My name is Gabriella di Capelli, my father teaches at the university. And your name?'

Tom held out his hand to shake hers, and told her.

'My name is Tom – perhaps you could call me Tobias – that is how you say it in your language?'

The girl smiled and nodded. 'Tobias, always walking with

angels, yes?'

Tom felt like laughing – he thought of Kit as his 'angel' for certainly he had walked far with him; if this young girl knew what sort of angel his companion was perhaps she would run from him.

By the end of the evening he had discovered the whereabouts of her sweet garden. England seemed very far away, cold and drear. If Kit insisted on going back, Tom would not go with him.

* * * * *

Marlowe soon reached the gardens where, at this time of day, couples strolled in the dusky coolness, chaperones following like shadows of death. The trees and shrubs kept the air cooler than the rest of the city. He was heading for a raised open space on a terrace reached by marble stairs on either side. The river flowed through the gardens below, and the sky overhead could be clearly seen. It was well away from the public walks where vendors sold bags of nuts, sweetmeats and oranges. He looked around and, when he saw he was alone, extracted the long parcel which had arrived from Dr Dee. With it was a letter, which he read again.

You need to hold this against one eye, closing the other. Stare carefully at the skies, and the stars should become clearer. I have been in communication with your Galileo and he knows of this; if you are satisfied, you can show him but do so privately. I would not have the whole world mock me again for an idea as they have in the past. I sent it to Robert Cecil telling him it would help him to see more but he has not answered. I fear I am out of favour with the Queen and her officers. She grows old and uninterested in new matters. Let Galileo test it thoroughly before we announce to the world what I have made by grinding my glass into these spherical shapes. If Galileo is impressed, I will send him my formulae for shaping the glass correctly. The tube concentrates the vision. I will call it a tele-scope for now.'

Kit experimented with the glass as instructed. At first it was too light for the stars to shine but, as he waited Venus became clearly visible in the south and he aimed the tube towards it. As he did so, the stars seemed to jump towards him and he moved his head and the tube to follow the constellations. It was amazing. Suddenly he could see the stars that formed the plough were not the only ones; there were a million more. So many more, at depths he could not comprehend. Surely, he thought, the stars are fixed in the firmament in their own sphere. He had been taught that at school and, although at college there had been hot debates – outside the hearing of the authorities – regarding the way the universe worked, even Kit, with his great leaps of faith, could not imagine such as he could see now. But with this tube – the *tele-scope* - he could see that there *were* depths to the sky and the stars stretched outwards away into a place he could not imagine. He was so intrigued and excited he almost jumped when he felt someone tugging at his sleeve.

'My student, Fitz, what are you so excited about? And what is that you are holding?' It was Galileo himself , a large cloak wrapped around him to keep out the chill which was noticeable now that night was almost upon them. Kit smiled to himself, these Latins felt the cold very quickly. He thought it was pleasantly cool after the humidity of the day. He did not answer but handed the instrument to his tutor. The man smiled and held it up to his eye as Marlowe had done. Galileo had been experimenting with something similar, as he had explained in the lecture. He aimed it at Venus, in the same manner as Marlowe had done, and gasped in the same way as Marlowe had done when he had first seen through it. After some time searching the heavens, he slowly lowered the telescope and inspected it. He shook it, peered up the other end and aimed it at Kit. He took it from his eye and Kit watched his face break out into a rare grin.

'Truly this is a miracle. I have been experimenting with glass and mirrors but have not been able to get such a good image. I could not perfect mine but this truly works; where did you acquire it, young man?'

'Firstly, I need you to confirm something for me. I believe we were born in the same year, but tell me, what year was your birth?'

'I was born in 1564.'

'Same as me and my...well, let us call him my alter ego. I have been sent to meet with you. This will explain.'

Kit pulled out the letter from Dr Dee and showed it to Galileo who read it slowly. Dr Dee had not addressed him directly by name in the body of the letter, and it was written in Latin, the language of scholars, so Galileo could easily understand it; Kit realised he was absorbing the information. Eventually he nodded and returned the missive. 'I have heard of this Dr Dee. You have studied under him?'

Kit shrugged. 'Not exactly, but he has been a kind of mentor. He guided me to you.'

'I would like to meet him but I understand he is an old man. Is that not true?'

Kit told him of the English conjurer, his hard life trying to find validity amongst his peers but finding only ridicule; his journey through Europe to find sponsors, his return to England only to find his home ruined, his life's work scattered.

'I think he despairs, but wants someone who understands to benefit from his invention.'

Galileo nodded. 'Come back to my home and we will talk further of this and I will show you what I have attempted. I have noticed your questions in class, young man, and know you as one with the same enquiring mind as my own. But it is dangerous. What I am working on could well rock the whole Church.'

Danger? Rocking the Church? Kit was delighted. He always liked to be involved in the machinations of those with 'enquiring minds' as Galileo put it. In England, he had courted the confidence of Raleigh, of the Cecils, and of numerous playwrights and poets, not only to practise his spying but because he found such men fascinating. To be a confidant of Galileo would stretch him he was sure.

When they reached Galileo's apartments, in the Borgo dei Vignali, Galileo ushered him into his downstairs chambers. The rooms reminded Kit of Dr Dee's chamber; the clutter of experiments, of books half-open, of piles of papers seemingly higgledy-piggledy, the paraphernalia of someone who had so many ideas he did not know which way to turn, but certainly not to cleaning and tidying.

'You live on your own, Sir?'

Galileo nodded as he roamed the room, picking up parchments and dropping them, as he searched for something. He did not look up as he answered, 'Except for the students who rent rooms from me and pay to have the privilege of private tutorials; it helps to support my family.' As he explained, he pushed papers aside so they could sit on two hard chairs.

Kit had heard rumours about Galileo's family; how a brother-in-law had proved profligate, and Galileo had had to support his sister, and how he tried to ensure his younger brothers had an education. Rumour was that Galileo needed far more money than a humble scholar would obtain from just teaching.

Galileo, after a pause, continued, 'Indeed I really live alone, but I would have it that way. I would not have a woman bustling and tidying my papers, as they would do.' He stopped then and seemed to sink into a reverie. He looked keenly at Kit and then confessed, 'Even so, the wish for heirs and the comfort of the female body does sometimes irk me. Do you have such longings? Do you have a lady you dream of in Ireland?'

Kit studied his companion more closely, he was so surprised at the softness in his voice. He was not a handsome man. Indeed, Kit would say that Galileo was positively ugly, except for his eyes which were bright and intelligent. He had a bulbous nose, a long chin and his eyes were heavily-bagged with long study late into the night, no doubt reading by cheap tallow candles. Not the sort of man, Kit imagined, that womankind would take to.

'Nay, I satisfy any lusts I have with the passion of studying. I would be celibate in that way.' Kit knew he had to be careful. Tom's fears were well founded. Kit wandered the streets at night seeking those men who practised as he did but he knew that sodomy in most states, and Padua could not be any different, was punishable by death. He liked the company of men, found them sexually exciting. Even so, he was careful and satiated any lusts with nameless ones who slunk away. But it would be too dangerous to admit to this, even to one such as Galileo, who Kit suspected was of such an independent turn of mind that he would not condemn him. Galileo's face did not change, and Kit realised that he was too much immersed in thoughts of the one he yearned for. Kit thought to bring him back to their conversation.

'Tell me Sir, it would be a great honour, who is she of whom you dream?'

'Ah, you come from a far-off country and perhaps do not know of our ways here. Where my true friend lives, women have to marry well; they have to help form alliances, they cannot marry poor lecturers who have a whole brood of brothers and sisters to care for. But Marina is like me and I lust for her because she has a good brain – for a woman – and I can talk to her about all things and she accepts me and looks serious but sensual at the same time.'

'Marina, Sir?'

'Indeed, that is her name. Marina Gamba, of Venice. That richest of cities, but also the most corrupt of cities. A place that floats on water, that is so safe and yet so unstable. Did you know they allow their citizens to make anonymous suggestions by placing papers in a hole in the wall at the side of the Doge's palace? Many an innocenti has been condemned in such a way.'

'But Marina Sir, why don't you just seduce her? If you think she looks at you sensually?'

'Seduce her, Kit, what do you mean? She would scream the house down and her brothers would rush in and slice me into a hundred pieces with their swords. You have no idea how jealously such beauties are guarded. No, I snatch but a few moments with her when she visits her aunt in Padua and they wander in the very gardens in which I met with you this evening.'

'Why don't you approach her father and ask him?'

'Ah, that is the problem, Kit. I do not have the status, the wealth. But stop. It is not just that. Although she has looked on me kindly, indeed, I interpret her looks to be sensual, I cannot be sure. I am known as an inventor, and I know some women are foolish to think that such men must be revered. Supposing she looks up to me just for that, but not as a man? You say I should seduce her – I confess, it is not just the sharpness of her relatives' swords that frightens me; it is the rejection. It is the look of horror that would appear on her face if I should stroke her long neck, as I long to do, it is the scream of fear as I touch her soft milky breast that keeps me cold when I am with her; it is the shame of being exposed as being a forceful unwanted suitor that makes me lily-livered.'

Kit had been selfish all his life, satisfying his wants and needs as he would, using his imagination and skill to be discreet. The reason he and Tom had never been lovers was because Kit was fully aware that, if they had been, some trust would have gone out of their friendship. Kit had sought his needs elsewhere with ostlers, messengers and playwrights on the London scene. The players were a wandering, independent band, outside normal society and that was why he loved their world so much; they had the attitude that lust should be satisfied and then forgotten. It would be too hard to maintain a sensual relationship with someone he knew and liked, such as Tom. Something in what Galileo now said struck a chord with him. He felt saddened that this great man, whom he recognised as a great enquirer, like Dr Dee, could not attain personal satisfaction. He knew it was no good saying to Galileo that there were many other females in the world and he could visit a lady who leant on the corner of a house, and beguiled men passing by to satisfy their lust for gold. Whores would not satisfy the dream of men like Galileo. Marlowe, despite his cynicism, recognised this.

He was also curious to see the woman who aroused such longings in a man as revered as Galileo.

'Have you ever thought of sending an emissary to this lady to enquire of her thoughts?'

For the first time since they had played with the telescope, Galileo became alert, enquiring, and Kit recognised the man he saw lecturing, a man always seeking the truth.

'What do you mean?' It was said with true humility; of true

enquiry.

'If you send someone to this lady who could ask her real feelings, she could tell *that* person what she thought of you. If it was done with tact, she might not even realise that such enquiries were being made on your behalf, and your emissary could return to you with good – or, I admit, bad – news and you would at least know what to do next.'

Galileo was nodding slowly and raised his hand in a gesture to indicate Kit should continue. 'If she gives every encouragement, you know you can proceed to - well, seduce her if you do not think it right to marry her – or you can resign yourself to the fact that she likes you not in that way and at least you can stop, well, brooding?'

Galileo smiled then. 'Indeed you are a wise man, as I know from my lectures. I respect you and know you would be excellent at such a task.'

Kit nearly fell off his chair. 'No, Sir, not me, I do not mean me. Come, I have only been here a term or two. You do not know me, how can you think I would be up to such a task?'

'Because you have just described it. You have thought of it, so you would have the words, the ways of explaining to my dear Marina, without her suspecting what is going on – please, dear Fitz.'

'I cannot, it would not seem fitting.'

Galileo stared at him now, the same quizzical stare he gave in lectures, which everyone noticed. He began to speak in a lower voice, as if he was confiding even more secrets. 'You know, Fitz, you fascinate me. You come out of the wilds of Ireland, so you say, with your friend, your *mentor* Tom, to study. Tom watches you and is always afraid. I ask myself why? It is as if he is afraid you will give yourself away. But he cares for you, he likes you. I like you. You are special, Tom and I both know you are special. You know Dr Dee, a dangerous man, a necromancer.

'*Who are you really?* I cannot begin to guess, but I could write many letters and describe you – do you think I would get an answer? I have an Englishman in my classes, a William Harvey. Perhaps he will know of you?'

Galileo paused. Kit could not but help admire him; his logic was unimpeachable. Kit had not heard of Harvey, but knew that letters back home might reveal his secret. He said nothing. Galileo continued, 'So, I would ask this of you, you have suggested it, and I can see it would be such a good idea. So, you travel to Venice, there is a canal, an easy boat ride there, and speak with Marina. Come back and report to me.'

Kit wondered what Tom would say. He didn't care. It would be interesting to woo for someone else. He would not tell Tom but just leave. It was easy enough, Tom was out a lot and he could just collect some spare clothes and go. What else could he do?

Chapter Sixteen

'You're what? Going to Venice? Why?'

Tom burst in just as Kit was leaving. The large bag had made him suspicious, so Kit thought it best to tell him where he was going. Kit for once decided to tell the truth. His explanation sounded lame and improbable. 'I'm going to woo a lady for Galileo.'

'*Oh, come on,* Kit, this is ridiculous.' Tom was unbuckling his belt, and threw the short sword that he had taken to wearing in the Latin manner, onto the table, not looking at Kit. He had found the Italian students more than willing to indulge in sword-play when they were carousing, even more so than in England.

'I know you like to make up stories and I am your most enthusiastic follower, but this cannot be. After all, you don't know the great master, except by sitting in his lectures.'

Tom said the last triumphantly but, before he could crow even more, there was a knock on the door. He swung round in anger at the interruption. Almost immediately, the door swung open, for they rarely locked it. There stood Galileo. Kit grinned. It was as if he had written the cue himself, Tom angry, he needing a diversion and there it was.

Tom shrugged in his usual way of resignation. He watched as the great man entered, as if he was expected. Since his island experience, Tom had learnt to suspend belief. It was as if he was a character in a book or someone Kit had made up, he sometimes felt, who had to carry out the author's wishes. So, he thought, I deny such a thing can be true and here is the man himself to vindicate Kit's story. Tom didn't even bother to turn to see Kit's smile of triumph. As Galileo sidled in, however, he was surprised to see the man looking sheepish. He nodded at Tom, as he would at an acquaintance, but looked warily around until he lit upon Kit.

'Good, you have not left yet. I thought afterwards that it would be fitting for you to take a small gift with you. I know women think highly of such things.' He rushed it out, as if he were afraid that, if he waited, he wouldn't say anything. 'It is but a trinket, but it may please her.' He handed over a small box, with a tiny catch, elaborately carved, on its side.

'You may open it if you like – perhaps you will be more eloquent with the lady if you know what it is.'

Kit took the gift and carefully slipped the catch to reveal a tiny ring lying inside on a bed of velvet. It would only fit the smallest finger of the most delicate hand. It had an insignificant dark garnet of oval shape, clasped in tiny hands, the fingers of which elongated into a thin circle of gold that held the stone in place. As he looked, Galileo took it back again, as if it was too precious to let go.

'It was my sister's but she died as a child. It is all I have to give my lady. Tell her that; it may melt her heart towards me.'

His voice broke as he spoke and Tom was surprised, although he said nothing. He had always respected his tutors at Cambridge, in the way they always seemed to be preoccupied with books, scurrying through the streets, disregarding family and such like comforts. He had never considered that they had sisters, brothers, a family. Because they were usually unmarried, Tom had thought of them as people apart. Holy Orders in the Catholic world still meant celibacy, even if it was lip service, with many cardinals and popes producing 'nieces' and 'nephews'. What also surprised him now was not the way Galileo spoke of love, and the seriousness of this great intellectual who so obviously wanted the woman, whoever she might be, but was too shy to ask for her hand himself. But Kit was saying nothing and Galileo was obviously discomforted by his own actions.

'What makes you think that...' Tom paused. He was just about to say 'Kit' when he remembered how careful they had to be. '...my friend will succeed? He will speak with an accent tinged with our home, and he knows not the habits of Venetian women.' Tom perhaps thought it best not to mention that Kit would prefer not to woo women, of whatever country.

Galileo turned the tiny casket over and over in the palm of his hand, thinking deeply. Eventually he replied, '*Your friend* is handsome and he seems to understand women. I saw him laughing and talking with the washerwomen in the square and it was as if he were one of them; they accepted him immediately. If any man can persuade a woman he can.'

'But how have you seen him with the washerwomen?'

'They come to the river below my window too, and sometimes their banter carries up to me and disturbs me. I usually yell down to them to be quiet but one day I saw your friend there, sitting on the bank, one hand on his knee in such a relaxed attitude. There he was, laughing and joking with them, asking about their work as if he would set up his own laundry.'

Kit was grinning as he turned away and collected the large bag he had been stuffing with spare clothes when Tom had returned early. He was embarrassed about Galileo's revelation. It was true, he often spoke to women around the town, asking about their lives, listening to their speech and watching their mannerisms, but only to turn the experiences to his own uses. It was lucky Galileo had not seen him scribbling in the side alleys as he made his way home. He also wanted to be going before Tom started his normal interrogations.

'And your friend is the same age as me, born in 1564, so my angel might be more inclined to...'

But Tom interrupted him.

'You are the same age?'

Galileo nodded. Kit was now very busy with filling his bag, but Galileo tapped him on the shoulder, and, as Kit turned round, he handed back the ring.

'Take it and stow it away safely. Remember it is of great sentiment to me.'

Kit nodded, and put the ring away in his breast pocket.

Tom said, 'Wait, be practical. How are you going to get to

Venice? I believe it is a hard day's ride through marshy country. Were you going to steal a horse?'

Galileo interrupted, anxious to please both men. 'Oh but there is a canal, it is fairly new but it is an excellent way for us Paduans to reach Venice, and it only takes a few hours by the barges. They are always willing to take passengers for a few coins. I have already spoken with my usual bargeman, Lorenzo, and he awaits your friend even now. That was why I was so worried about missing him.'

Kit smiled at his friend and headed towards the door.

Galileo called, 'I pray to God you will come back with good news.' Kit shook the man's hand and rushed out of the room, not even glancing at Tom who turned away, exasperated, ignoring Galileo who remained. A silence fell on them. Neither knew what to say. Now Galileo was embarrassed, it was obvious, and Tom was containing his anger. He wanted the scholar to leave, but he didn't seem inclined to go. Eventually Galileo spoke, using the hesitant tones he used sometimes in his lectures when he put forward a new theory, 'I am sorry if I have caused dissension. It is a terrible thing, this longing, have you never felt it?' Without waiting for a reply he continued, 'I have great problems with my family. My brother is a ne'er do well and we owe his wife's family for the good luck of marrying into them. I have younger brothers who must be educated. It is my responsibility as the eldest, to support them; and my aged parents. Marrying is not for the likes of me, I know that, but I cannot concentrate on my work until this matter is resolved.' He was stepping from side to side now, as if, by speaking of it, he had to demonstrate by physically moving about. It seemed he could never settle or be at peace again, his hands flapping.

'If you could but see her. When we speak it is comfortable; she is intelligent, she understands my work and listens to what I have to say and makes sensible suggestions. But I cannot - *I just cannot* – ask her if she will come to me. I do not believe I can support her in the way she is accustomed. I could not give her the sort of life she should have, from her station, I am being so unfair even expecting it. Yet my whole being trembles and wishes for her. I cannot sleep.' He stopped his jigging from side to side, despair freezing him. Then he looked straight at Tom, who said nothing. 'D'you know, in one way I hope that your friend, if he woos her aright, will turn her mind to him and then, as a lover spurned, I can mourn and continue with my researches. Is that not stupid? If only I could research the heart, rather than the stars.'

Tom saw a man tormented but one who had a sense of his own idiocy, a good man, a man with integrity. Tom remembered Gabriella, her warmth, his longing as he walked home in a daze. Yes, he could understand. He felt a sympathy with Galileo and forgot for a moment Kit's duplicity.

'Indeed, my friend will succeed for you. I know it, he can be very persuasive. He will not make a case for himself, that I can guarantee.'

'How do you know? I'm so unsure, so worried, my Marina....'

Tom stepped towards the man whom he had seen lecturing, and placed both hands on each of his shoulders, as if to still him, and kissed both cheeks. 'Because my friend Fitz is honourable, that is why.'

He turned away before Galileo might see something else in his eyes. Tom knew that Kit was not so much honourable as not given to such a task as wooing women for his own needs; Galileo need not know how safe his lady would be with Kit. It might be that, just because he was lacking in interest, but with his colossal arrogance, he might even succeed in his task.

'Shall we wait and see? When he returns I will send him to your lodging even before he eats; if he does not go to you directly. There, what else can I say?' As he spoke he ushered the man out of the door and slammed it firmly behind him. Tom leant against the closed door and sighed. What had his friend got into now? He was determined to find out the truth about what Kit had been up to and, now that he knew Kit was not going to return for some time, decided to investigate. In addition, he was elated at the fact that they had found the third person that Dr Dee had said they must find. Why hadn't Kit said anything? Tom became suspicious again and this made him even more determined, to find out what was behind all their travels.

A good start was to read through all the papers Kit kept hidden. He strode over to the large desk near the window and started to rifle through the cubbyholes, dislodging folded notes and other papers, and threw them on the table higgledy piggledy. It had always been unspoken between them that they never touched each other's papers, but Tom had had enough. He had to find some clue as to what his friend had been doing with all his writings. If he could find something concrete, he could challenge him with it, and maybe Kit would come to confess. Tom had to find out. He didn't believe for a minute that the trip to Venice was just to woo a lady for another man; he knew by now that Kit always had an ulterior motive.

Then their sojourn in Reims where Kit had waited, until that day he had decided to go to confession. Going to confession? No, it was to get his own back on a duplicitous priest. Rome? What had Rome been about? Travelling to Padua to learn more from Galileo? Tom remembered their mysterious meeting with Dr Dee and now recalled that Galileo had mentioned Dr Dee. *Had they come to Padua for Kit to make further contacts, to get involved in another plot?* To involve himself in Galileo's love life? That seemed highly unlikely. And what was the significance of these three men now joined, all born in the same year?

Now that they had been joined, Tom thought, he could find out what it was all about and leave, to be with his new found love, to give up the constant travelling and deceit. He threw papers on the floor, great parchments crackling as he rifled. He picked up some of the dropped manuscripts and held them under the sputtering light of a candle. All they seemed to be were scraps of poetic ramblings, some of which Tom had heard Kit read aloud, in an ecstasy of excitement at his own genius. Others he remembered from performances in England before they left. Some he admitted were new but they were mere scraps, just fragments of speeches, speeches of a Miranda, a Silvia, a Rosalind – the words demonstrating that they could be evocative women, so very different from anything that Kit had produced before.

Kit had explained it to him in one drunken evening. 'Once I was but a man who understood manly things, tobacco and Homeric discussion and the smell of men; but now I have lived as a woman I understand the clever undercurrents, the instincts, the strengths of women's hearts. Tom, they are a breed apart, who stand not on pedestals, but on heavenly heights that we men cannot hope to reach. They are full of contradictions but of great constancy, of honesty and guile, of emotions so strong that they might kill a man, like Judith murdered Holofernes, but with the heart to control those emotions for the good of those around them.'

Tom had laughed at him. 'You are but befuddled with this Italian wine, Kit.'

Kit shook his head. 'Nay, I will show you; watch that wench, the barmaid. She laughs and jokes with the men, but, yes, Tom, watch her, she never allows any man to touch her as she weaves her way through the crowd even though she carries that great tray of tankards.'

Tom followed Kit's gaze and watched the girl. She looked so young, her form so slight and men seemed drawn to reaching out to her as she passed, to catch her attention. But Tom could now see how she moved, cleverly ducking and diving, and laughing good-naturedly at the customers, acknowledging their attentions with a raised eyebrow, while her body sinuously moved so that the grab at her crotch missed, the clawed hand that meant to squeeze her tender breasts fell wide and brushed her shoulder. He nodded slowly; he could dimly comprehend, albeit through a haze of alcohol, what Kit meant.

Now he read the description of Silvia, a great beauty indeed, from the words before him. He could recognise how authentic it sounded. He thought back on the terrible plays that Kit had written while in Cambridge and London that had made his name as Christopher Marlowe, playwright. How dark they were, how sadistic. Even when he wrote about Jews or Protestants in France there had been a level of nastiness, Tom believed, about his writing that Tom could not see in this more recent work. Instead of using dark images of war these images were of flowers of the field, of tender countryside. Tom thought back; he was sure that the old Marlowe had never even referred to greenery or foliage in any play or poem. Now here he was referring to the lady being like a lily of the fields.

As he read the fragments he forgot his original quest and leant back in the deep chair. Kit would succeed in his mission, he was sure. Tom was suddenly envious. He grabbed his robe and dashed out the door, would he be too late to join Kit?

* * * * *

The barge was moving off slowly but Kit managed to board. If he had had time to think about it he would probably have jumped off and made his way to the City of Dreams – as he had heard Venice called – by any other means than this. The barge was full of rotting manure, and he was overwhelmed by the humming smell that rose from its flat bilge. It stunk so much that, he believed, his very core would absorb the odour and he would smell of it too, not a good idea when wooing a gentlewoman. If not that, he could catch some awful disease from the odour that wrapped around him like an evil spirit. Why had he agreed to go?

Apart from the veiled threat from Galileo, when he had insinuated that he had suspicions about Kit, he'd agreed to the task because he'd been intrigued. And he realised from what Galileo said that it might be difficult for him and Tom to disappear again. He was always aware of the protection he had gained from his secret network of friends and wanted to count Galileo amongst them. If he succeeded in this task, he was sure he would be able to add the man to his loyal network. And it was his curiosity that spurred him on. In these nation states, he'd discovered, very few couples wooed between themselves; there were always parents who organised a betrothal, or an older brother or an uncle, especially amongst the wealthy classes. He knew such dynastic alliances were made by the nobility in England but for most of his contemporaries, such as his sisters, they were free to love where they pleased; with some disastrous results, Kit was sure. In Italy there was another element though; secret letters passed between the lovers; intermediaries were used, and disguises and even young boys were encouraged to recite exotic poems. Minstrels were hired to sing under the windows of lovers, with specially written ditties. Kit had heard all this; now he would be involved in such a wooing himself.

He dropped his baggage and leant against the wall of the cabin on the barge. It was a flat narrow boat and a large horse was dragging it along the Brenta canal. Galileo had said the journey only took a few hours but at this speed Kit thought he might be able to walk to Venice faster. He stared over the marshy lands beyond and tried to dream himself away from where he was. In some ways the land was not unlike England, every now and then there were small coppices of willows, poplars, common alders and water elms; not unlike the banks of the Cam. But the smell, accentuated by the heat of this southern country, brought him back and it was difficult to forget where he was with the stench from the load rising like steam around him. There was no escape, the smell wafted around the barge like circling seagulls. Men worked stoically at their tasks, loosening ropes or calling to the horsemen in a rough dialect that Kit could barely understand.

He tried to address the task he had been assigned. How would he entertain the lady? Should he hire minstrels or would a direct approach, a visit, be more sensible? Galileo had given him a letter of introduction but warned that this might only result in a meeting with her parents, her father of the merchant class. He grinned; he knew his natural ingenuity would see him by and decided not to think of his future task; he had some time before they reached the lagoon and Venice.

He extracted a small book of poems, by Sir Philip Sidney, and lent on the gunwale of the barge as he immersed himself in the magic of the poesys, his head drooping slowly down in the heat. He was not aware of being stared at by a stranger.

Chapter Seventeen

"Leave me, O love, which reachest but to dust,
And thou, my mind, aspire to higher things."

They were the last words that Kit read of Sidney as the book nearly fell from his grasp. A sudden swell of the barge made him start and catch the volume before it fell into the foam. He looked around him, surprised to find that they had reached the lagoon and the barge horse had been released. He caught the eye of a fellow traveller and felt embarrassed; the man was staring at him, quite brazenly. Kit looked away and watched the oarsmen who were now rowing across a wide expanse of water. No longer was there a languid, tired feel about the vessel. Now there was a rolling and swashing, a pale reminder of his other times at sea, crossing from England and, more dangerously, the horrific storm-tossed interlude after they had left Florence.

No longer did Sidney's poems sing in his head, for all around him were new sights, new sounds. The banks had withdrawn; there were no shady places where willows lent into the water. The forests of rushes that nestled in the marshes either side of the canal had disappeared. There was a wide horizon of deep azure, punctuated with low islets. Kit's attention was caught by the view immediately before him; the place where the barge was heading. As the boat made fast headway, towards the large island, and in the haze of summer, the skyline was shot through with vertical campaniles, church towers, domes, and squat buildings. At this distance the shapes were dark purple against the yellow glow of late afternoon and he could make out no definition at all, except for the irregular squares and oblongs and ovals of the silhouettes against the glowing sky.

197

He looked down; the water lapping at the boat was a deep turquoise. Then it changed. They moved slowly through some small lumps of low land, almost mud-flats, where the water was still and murky, as if the barge stirred up the land. After this they were in open waters again and the water transformed back into the turquoise hue. Kit thought, like my life, murky and dark in narrow waters and then opening out into some great limpid open experience. He was still aware of the attention of the stranger, a young well-dressed person, which he was doing his utmost to ignore.

He tucked his book into his jerkin. Everything around him was much too exciting. His nose was accustomed to the smell from the barge's cargo, but some other odour now tickled his nostrils. A tang of salt. He realised that they must have reached open sea waters. Was he now in the Adriatic? He was excited at the thought that, at the other side of this sea lay the Orient; the great magical unknown of his Tamburlaine. He would soon be in Venice, the first foot in Europe from the east. After Venice came Constantinople; the gateway between east and west.

With the salt odour came other smells; the tinge of sewage, of many bodies, spiced with garlic, cardamom and cayenne. As they moved closer to the city, he realised they were approaching it from the west and he could now make out large sheds with workmen, dressed in heavy aprons and hats, shovelling at piles of rocks, or others working in detail on stone or wood or other materials. Stonemasons or carpenters, at least labourers of some sort, he thought.

There were barges delivering great bundles of fruits, some spilling from their sacks and falling into the waters; men ran up gangplanks half hidden by the loads they carried. One shed, open to the air, was a heaving mass of animal flesh, calves mewling for their mothers. Kit remembered; the Italians loved veal, the baby milk flesh. There was a-banging and a-shouting at these dockyards; it was obvious this was the working part of the city.

The stranger was standing before him. He could no longer

ignore him. Kit's hand felt for the daggers he had hidden about him.

'Aye, 'tis indeed a mess of noise and filth, is it not? The unacceptable face of a beautiful and rich city.' Kit now matched the man's gaze, but recoiled from the proximity of the man, who was nearly touching him. He was dressed in dark velvet in the Italian manner, an exotic velvet hat with a long matching scarf wrapped loosely around his head and neck, a protection from the hot sun, and he held out his hand for Kit to shake. Kit looked down at the hand. It was smooth, the nails clipped neatly. The man had the air of a confident gentleman. Kit noted the smooth but shadowed chin, the dark eyes and heavy brows; obviously Italian, of good family. His Latin was faultless. A cultured man. He relaxed.

He continued, 'I was with the Captain, when you first came on board. I cannot stand the heat of the day, but now there are some sea breezes I came up, and noticed you studying deeply.' He smiled. 'What were you reading?'

Kit showed him the book of poems. He did so with some reluctance. The young man's face creased as he tried to read the English. He shook his head and handed it back.

'Nay that is all foreign to me and looks ugly on the page; there is no rhyming. I can tell that the way the lines end.'

Kit shrugged. He knew what the man meant; the Italian poetry he had read not only rhymed because most words ended in 'i' or 'o' but also had a regular metre, something that Kit was now working away from in his own poetry. He said nothing though and waited. The stranger continued, 'My name is Val and I am on a trip for my father-in-law. You have never been here before, I can tell by the look of horrific wonder on your face.'

Despite his youth, Val exuded confidence, the confidence of an aristocrat. Kit wondered why he was travelling in such a strange way; the way only poor students or workers would travel, and why had he not introduced himself more fully? Kit was now used to Italians, especially the richer ones, giving their full titles, whether they were the younger sons of counts or archdukes or minor aristocracies from the East. He dismissed the thought of questioning him for now, thinking that it would be rude and might antagonise him. He would grab the opportunity of the proffered friendship, and hope that this man would prove a guide in the strange city before him.

'Indeed you are correct. I too am on an errand but would not know where to start.'

'Ah, you start by first going to St Mark's Square and having a drink with me. Once you have your bearings in the greatest place on earth – I swear it – yes, greater than Rome, although that may be heresy – then you can find lodgings, you can get to know the city.'

Kit could only agree. For once he felt inferior. With Tom he knew that, even dressed as a woman, he was the one in charge; now, in a city, strange in more ways than one, he would have to rely on the superior knowledge of this new acquaintance.

They disembarked and Val took him by the arm and led him away from the noise and filth of the landing stages. Soon they were side by side, too close for Kit's comfort, in narrow alleys, the sun blocked out by the tall buildings rising on either side. There was a foreign feeling in the air and at first Kit could not identify it; it was not just the tall buildings. Then as Val said, his voice resonating, 'This way, we turn left here,' Kit realised what it was. There was a silence in this place; there was no clopping of horses and yelling of men trying to clear their way through the throng of a normal city with heavily laden carts. No cries from hawkers or vendors; there were none in these narrow streets. The houses were heavily shuttered. No children played in the narrow alleys.

Every now and then they made their way across a small bridge over a canal, the water sluggish, no longer turquoise but a muddy brown, with debris floating on top.

'I know this place well, but it is easy to get lost in these streets; best to keep to travelling on the canal if you can,' explained Val. Kit nodded, wondering why they were not doing so now. He already had enough clues to realise that Val's trip was of a sensitive nature and decided to find out when the time was right. He recognised the signs from his old life, when he worked for Walsingham; avoid obvious entry into a new town, act as natural as possible. They were walking through a wider street, with a few houses, but still the sun did not reach them. Turning a corner Kit saw a bright stripe of shadowed sunlight.

As they approached this, the way in front opened out. As they emerged from the narrow alley Kit gasped. A greater contrast could never be found. In the alley the air had been chill, for the sun never touched the earth or the lower bricks of the buildings to warm them. Now they were in the bright sunlight of an open space, not a square as such but a piazza with balconied buildings on three sides. In front of them was a bridge which rose and fell in a beautiful arc over a wide expanse of water. Here people flocked; here were the vendors, dressed in vivid hues, with large panniers in front of them. Here children played, running between the stalls. Laughter and chatter, the high screech of excited youngsters, echoed. On the bridge were kiosks where well-dressed ladies peered into the tiny glazed windows and then wandered on. Now there was the slapping of water against the banks, gondoliers calling their fares, women laughing and men talking seriously, bags of money clinking as they changed hands.

Val laughed at the way Kit had stopped, almost open-mouthed.

'Yes, the Ponte di Rialto is a great sight is it not? But we have not yet reached the jewel of the Doge's domain – come, we cross over here and you can gawp if you like.'

As they reached the bridge and pushed their way through the crowds, bells started tolling; first a few and then many. Kit stopped on the brow of the bridge and listened, looking over the great canal which snaked around the buildings. The bells had a quality to them, a resonance and depth that he'd never heard before. He realised that not only was the sound echoing against the buildings but there was something about it wafting across the water to him, as if it bounced and resonated on the turquoise waves. It created a different multi-hollowed sound that seemed to penetrate his very innards. If he had believed in God he would say that he was being called. He stood entranced, until Val touched him gently on the sleeve. Kit followed as he walked away; he realised Val was obviously unhappy about being too conspicuous.

'Come, it will be dusk soon and we must find lodgings.'

Val led him criss-cross through more narrow walkways, across more canals, some putrid with wafting sewage. Then, with a quick dogleg and a right hand bend they came to the huge open space that was the Piazza San Marco. As Kit gazed; he was aware that Val watched him as if he owned the place and was waiting for comment. Kit's eye followed the black and white stone of the paviers, set in an exotic courtyard pattern, until he gazed at the eastern end where the great St Mark's shone. It was impossible to take in the full glory of the great square in one. Kit tried to hide his wonder at the sight, but knew Val could see his astonishment. Kit approached St Mark's, walking fast, as if he did not appreciate the evening light glinting on the five irregularly sized gold-encrusted domes of the great duomo; the slanting light accentuating the regularity of the arches of the surrounding buildings, which led the eye away to the campanile standing proud on one side, most of its golden-peach coloured brick shining in the sun. On the other side stood the clock tower. As they reached the entrance, the mosaics on the inside of arches of the duomo attracted Kit.

He stood for a long time, literally open-mouthed. Never in all his travels had he seen such sumptuous glory. He knew Val stood by him, waiting, but Kit could not move.

Eventually Val pulled him away, towards one of the arched walkways down the side and ushered him into a bar, where he sat down in a dark corner. He ordered a skin of wine then he smiled at Kit, 'I come from Verona myself which also has its splendours, but seeing you today reminded me of my first sight of the Piazza. I was only a lad – I have been here many times since – but it still entrances. Your face was indeed a very picture. You confirmed by your reaction that it is not just wonderful for me – it catches all men.'

For once Kit was embarrassed. He raised his glass and said, 'Salute!' They were both silent as they drank their first glass quickly. Val poured some more and asked, 'So, what is your reason for coming?'

Kit grinned. 'You will not believe me. But I will tell you anyway. I need help in this town, I can see that, and as you are the only one I know I must throw myself on your mercy.'

He paused and eyed his companion. He hoped that, by explaining his mission to this stranger not only would he get the help he needed, but he would also gain Val's trust. He wanted to find out about Val. He was also of the mind that any meeting with a stranger might not be coincidence. Kit reminded himself again that, despite Val being well dressed and looking prosperous, he had travelled by lowly barge and then had kept to the back ways. It would be interesting to discover his companion's reason for visiting Venice.

'Let me introduce myself; my name is Fitz and I am a student at Padua from where I travelled as you no doubt realise. I have been asked to meet with a lady and ask her…well, ask her intentions, I suppose, for a mutual acquaintance. He is shy and although he believes they get on well,' Kit smirked and Val smiled back, nodding, understanding, 'he does not know whether further advances would be repelled. I suppose that is it in a nutshell. A very unusual task and one I know not how to carry out. '

Val leant back against the wall behind him and laughed aloud. 'An unusual task. In other states the men are not shy, but very proud of their dignity; they would woo a lady gently and the family watch and smile, whereas here in Venice, you could be assassinated as you walked home for 'insulting' the lady of a house, where a girl's virginity is their most treasured prize. It is so dangerous to approach such a one direct. It is customary to send a messenger.' Val paused and took a sip of his second drink, then, placing the tumbler carefully before him, took a deep breath, and Kit realised he was in for a long explanation.

'Let me tell you a story, of how I won my wife. It is one of two friends, two gentlemen of Verona, let us call them, although one of them may not seem such.

'I was sent to Milan, which as you know is a great military state, by my father to advance myself. My best friend, let us call him Proteus, did not want to go because he professed great love for a lady of our home town of Verona. No, I was not involved in that courtship. Eventually though, his father insisted he join me – but only after I had had enough time to fall in love, and my love was returned, by the Duke of Milan's daughter. However, as soon as Proteus saw her, unbeknown to me, he too fell in love with her. And you know what this gentleman did then?'

Kit shook his head.

'He told the Duke of my plans to run away with his daughter, after promising to help me. I was banished and he was left free to woo the girl. Then he persuaded the Duke and the Duke's preferred suitor, an idiot called Thurio, to let him woo the girl on Thurio's behalf. Luckily my love was a sensible and wonderful girl and she saw through his wiles, and would have none of him, despite sweet words, music and poetry.

'In the meantime, Proteus' love back in Verona had followed him and she, the sweet thing, revealed the plot to the Duke and there was a denouement. So, I can reveal, because I believe you are truly a stranger to the politics of our city-states, I am now the son-in-law of the Duke and my dear friend Proteus lives in Verona with his love. We made it up you understand, once we both had what we really wanted; good sensible wives. So you can see what wiles we get up to all for the sake of love.'

Kit listened enraptured. He could envisage the repartee, the scenes between the various parties. Oh, what a play such a story would make. But he was curious too as to why Val was in Venice. And travelling incognito.

'A goodly story and a good outcome. But why are you in Venice now? And your way of travelling is certainly not that of a nobleman.'

'Shush, not so loud.' He looked around the room but the other occupants were all deep in their own conversations. There was a mixture of young bloods that looked like students and soberly dressed men, whose serious conversation showed them to be businessmen, transacting the last of the day's business in a convivial manner.

'I will tell you. Perhaps we can help each other? I need to go to parts of the town where there may be danger, and you can accompany me – for I see you wear a goodly dagger. In exchange I will help you find this lady, and perhaps, assist in the wooing of her. What say you?'

Kit nodded and Val, after another sip of wine, explained, his voice lowered. 'Milan fights the French this time. Always there is some border dispute, if not with Florence or the Pope, it is the French who invade from the West. We need to employ mercenaries.' He spoke even more quietly. 'In order to do that we need gold. Rumours fly if we are seen to visit the money-brokers in Milan or even in the nearby Cities. I am known in Verona of course, and in Rome and in Mantegna. Venice is a place where a stranger can get lost but can also be lost to those who know him. So, I am here to raise funds. I will find the Jewish Quarter, where the money is available and make terms.'

It all made sense now. He suspected that Val had questioned the bargeman about him and had approached him with the very intention of making him an unofficial bodyguard. Kit did not mind if it meant his task would be easier. Val would know how to woo an Italian lady. He felt as if he would reap the better side of the bargain.

They quaffed the rest of the wine before Kit raised another point.

'What do we do first? Your business or mine?'

Val, whose head was drooping, shook his head. 'Let us toss for it, and let fate decide, although no doubt I will be rebuked for delay.'

Kit tossed. Val called out, 'heads,' and when Kit revealed the other side, he shrugged.

'Come, I am too tired for this, tomorrow we will start with your a-wooding. Now, to find us lodgings.' Val stood, steadying himself on the table.

'I suggest we try the scuola; it is like a guild and they sometimes accommodate strangers if they believe you are one of them. I have a cousin who is in the Scuola Grande di Santo Rocco; they will put us both up, I am sure and I can say I am visiting him on family business.'

Kit could only follow as Val set a pace through the narrow alleys once again. When they reached the water he called for a gondola and they stood as the man rowed them across. Not long afterwards they were billeted in a sparsely furnished cell, a pitcher of water between them and a tiny oil lamp which gave them enough light to bed down before it spluttered out.

Val whispered in the darkness, 'Fear not for going to bed earlier than you would wish; there is early morning mass before breakfast and you will be expected to attend; it is a small price to pay for such clean and cheap lodgings.'

Kit groaned. He had attended masses before, in the name of his queen and country; he would do so now.

* * * * *

'This must be her house, the pink one facing the new church of St Georgio di Maggiore; look there are the triple balconies the herbalist described. I told you it was easy to find people in Venice, well, at least those who live here.'

Val was triumphant; he had shown Kit around the city with a proprietary air which irritated Kit, who liked to be in charge. In the end they had decided to find Galileo's sweetheart first, and then carry out Val's assignment. It had taken some days to find the place. Kit knew now that this maze was not one where he could have found his way easily without a guide. Val had used a mixture of questions and guesswork to find the house of the Gambi and they now stood on the wide pavement, edged by the lapping lagoon on one side and by tall, elegant houses on the other.

'Now all you have to do is knock and ask.'

206

Kit grimaced.

'I have letters of introduction, but what excuse do I use to be alone with the lady?'

'That is your problem; look, I'll wait over there at that kiosk.' He made to move off to a small wagon, whose side was open to the elements, except for a canopy which sheltered those standing at its counter from the strong sun. Kit had noticed many such small drinks-vendors, with their names or some description painted on their wagons, around the city. Before he reached the stall, Val sauntered back. He had seen something. He whispered, 'Wait, there's a courtyard garden round the corner.' He pulled Kit to the side of the building. 'Look, you can see it through this grille. Why don't you keep an eye out and if the lady appears, you can speak with her without the household knowing.'

Kit looked where Val was pointing and saw a luscious garden, filled with palms set out amongst walkways and sweet smelling jasmine and roses climbing over elegant arches, the gravel paths edged with brightly painted tiles. An arbour at one corner had an elegant wrought iron bench in it, covered with an arch of bright red roses.

Suddenly Kit jumped back, almost knocking Val to the ground. Val grunted but Kit put his finger to his mouth in a warning. A woman walked in the garden, and was approaching the path nearest the gate. Had she seen them? He was not sure, for she seemed immersed in a small book she was reading, her lips moving as if she spoke the words. She was tall, with dark hair caught in a simple lace head covering which fell about her shoulders.

'I'm going – see you over there.' Val grinned as he hurried away.

The woman looked up at the sound of the footsteps. Kit had no time to jump away to hide. She looked straight at him, all clear-eyed and innocent enquiry. Kit rattled the gate which, he was surprised to find, opened and he walked in, smiling. This was going to be far too easy, but he took the bull by the horns and asked, 'I believe you must be Marina? I come from a friend – here, I have letters of introduction.'

She lowered her book but still held it in both hands. 'It is normal for a stranger to enter by the front of a house.'

She made it as a statement, not a rebuke. She did not step away from him however and calmly took his note. She read it slowly and smiled.

'Ah, you are from Padua, come and sit down. Fitz is your name; a stranger from Ireland,' she read aloud. 'Welcome. Would you like some lemon drink? It is a hot day, and you look quite dusty.'

Kit was impressed; a sensible woman, not one to be hysterical or fazed by strangers. Instead her manner showed she was curious, interested to find out about him.

He nodded and thanked her. She walked to the end of the path to the door of the house and called within, then turned back to him.

'Come, we will sit in the shade and you can tell me all the news. How is my dear friend, Galileo?'

Kit walked beside her; she moved slowly, stowing the book away beside her.

'He is well and sends greetings from his home.'

He would have continued but she flushed and hurried on. 'And what brings you to Venice?'

'I have a duty to perform for a friend of mine. He waits impatiently for me to perform it.' He assumed she would know he meant Galileo but she merely nodded and waited for him to continue. She turned away at the sound of footsteps.

A maid approached with a tray holding a jug and two long stemmed glasses. She placed it before her mistress without comment, not looking at the stranger. Kit watched as Marina carefully poured a cloudy looking drink into each glass and offered him one. He took it tentatively and held it to his mouth, trying to smell it before he tasted it.

She smiled. 'It is a refreshing drink; made of lemons from my father's estates and sherbet from the east.'

Kit tasted the drink gingerly, remembering the last time, in Florence, when he'd been offered such a drink. Marina was watching him, so he took a sip. She nodded as he swallowed and then lick his lips, foaming with sherbet residue, in appreciation. Then she continued. 'You were saying; about a task for a friend?'

'Yes, he waits for me back in Padua. He…he wishes to know a lady's feelings towards him.'

'What lady is that? She lives in Venice? You wish for my help?'

'Indeed she lives in Venice and, yes, you may be able to help. She is as beautiful as he told me she was. And as charming.'

'Ah, so you have met the lady?'

'Only but a moment ago, and she is so charming as to accept me, a stranger, who imposes himself on her, and refreshes me with a wonderful lemon sherbet drink.'

Marina blushed. 'You mean, I am the object of your duty? And why will the man not come to me himself?'

'He believes he knows you not well enough to force his attentions on you, dear lady.'

'And I know him not, if he will not reveal himself.' She stood, in a movement so rapid, the glasses trembled and almost fell. She steadied them with both hands but looked at Kit, a clear honest glance. Her face had lost its genial, calm appearance. 'I will not countenance such second-hand courting. It may be good enough for others, but not for me. If your friend wishes to be my suitor he should come from out of his house and declare himself. You must go now; my father and brothers will be back soon.'

Kit did not move for a moment, so surprised was he by her change of mood. But she continued to stare at him, her dark eyes becoming stonier by the moment. He stood up; backed away from her and, when he believed he had reached a turn in the path, fled.

He almost ran to the kiosk to find Val. He found him laughing and joking with some of the locals, and took him by the arm to lead him away. Val was still laughing. 'Well, how did you get on? I hear from the neighbours that she is a cold lady, much immersed in books and has few suitors. She is considered too remote to make a good wife and mother.'

'I think I have failed miserably. She has sent me away with a flea in my ear, and I know not what to say to my tutor.'

'Oh, and I thought you would be good at wooing a lady. Did you not recite sweet poetry to her? Did you not try to sing to her? No, maybe not. Well, tell me all and we will see what we can rescue.'

Kit explained that Marina had been all courtesy itself but had suddenly become annoyed when he had said he was speaking for someone else. Val laughed, 'I think she is playing with you, pretending not to know who has sent you on your errand. Or she genuinely was puzzled by your approach. Tomorrow, we will think further on this.'

'She asked after Galileo, the friend I spoke of, so surely she knew I referred to him.'

'Perhaps she did not connect him with what you were saying. You must put this right, dear friend.'

Kit suddenly said, 'You don't think she saw you waiting, and walking away? You don't think she thought I was referring to you?'

Val looked serious. 'You must correct that, if it is the case, for I am a married man – happily at that, as you well know.'

'What am I to do?'

'Perhaps speak with her father, her brothers?'

Kit considered. 'No, Galileo made it plain that they would never accept him as a suitor. I must think of something else.'

'Look here she comes; heavily veiled and with a shopping basket. I would bet with you she is still curious and has come to find out more. And be careful, she has a chaperone with her. Approach her, but be careful.'

Kit saw that the chaperone was the servant who had served the sherbet, and he was certain that she was loyal to her mistress. He would have to take that chance.

As Kit looked doubtful, Val pushed him forwards. 'And I am going, no longer will I tarry here – I will meet you back at our lodgings.'

Kit followed the lady who had passed them without acknowledging their presence, and was heading down a dark alley. He knew he could not approach her in such a place. For a start, it was too narrow for him to come abreast of her and he would feel ridiculous trying to talk to her from behind. He followed, as stealthily as he could, until she reached a large square filled with stalls. It was market day and the vendors cried their wares, the sing-songs vibrating on the tall buildings surrounding the large area. This was not just a normal weekly food market, for apart from the usual trussed up chickens and baskets of eggs, tethered sheep and ducks, there were stalls draped with rich silks and ribbons; oriental rugs and metal belt clasps, pretty silken shoes and sensible pattens; stalls with rows of paper and pens; second hand bookstalls and weary looking men with old farm tools arranged on the pavement. A large stall on the church steps was manned by several monks who cried, 'Indulgences for sale, chips from the leg of St Sebastian; A cutting from Mary's veil.' Kit listened in distaste but hurried on as people clustered and moved and he nearly lost sight of his prey. Crowds pushed between the tightly packed rows but he could see that Marina moved sedately, greeting acquaintances with a nod or a smile. Kit was hard put to keep up, there was such a great milling and pushing. Then she came to the centre of the square, an open space, surrounding a water pump. She paused and fanned herself with her hand, dropped it discreetly in the water and bathed her forehead. Indeed it was hot and there was a rancid smell from rotting vegetables nearby.

Kit approached her. 'Signorina, a word, please.'

She looked surprised, and pulled her shawl around her head so that her face was hidden. She said calmly, 'I thought I had made it quite plain. I would not be trifled with. You could be arrested for following a lady, you know.'

Kit grinned; he knew it was true but also knew that it seldom happened, the Venetians being tolerant of such behaviour unless it was their own kin. Many a female visitor had been surprised by the sudden hand on her backside, a brushing that she could not believe had happened, but few made hue and cry. Even if they did, most of the assailants would suggest it was but an accident and the lady would be severely embarrassed.

'I fear I owe you an apology. I believe there has been a misunderstanding.'

'How so?'

She stood calmly, her empty basket slung over her arm. She seemed to have grown in stature since their garden meeting. She was nearly as tall as Kit; although he realised she now wore high-heeled shoes which would make her taller she seemed to have an air of gravity that made her seem statuesque.

'Firstly I must apologise because my Italian is not so good, no?'

She laughed, as he intended her to do; he had deliberately spoken in her language but broken and heavily accented.

'So, you see, you will understand. I referred to my benefactor, your suitor, as waiting at home and indeed he is; in Padua, up there in his tower in the skies. He stares at many stars, all more brilliant than the rest, even during the day he dreams of these stars, but there is only one here on earth that really attracts him and she is so much more brilliant.'

The lady turned away as if not interested. Kit thought to grab her arm but stopped, it would not be right. He moved round the fountain and faced her, staring intently at her face beneath the shawl. Then he realised.

'You're blushing. You know who I mean, and you know he will follow you all the way to the stars if need be; except that he is very proud, and shy – perhaps like you lady, for most women, as I have found, can give their men hope, can show them they would accept an offer – why has not my great tutor had such a sign?'

'Because he is so great?'

'So, it is you too – you are worried that you would be rejected?'

She leant against the side of the stone fountain then and looked straight at him.

'I am fully aware of his responsibilities; he would not want to take on another.'

'Supposing he sees you not as a responsibility but a helpmeet, a companion, someone he can rest with at the end of the day?'

She did not move. The crowds surged around them but for Kit and her, it seemed as if they were in a private chamber.

Eventually she said, 'Is that how he sees me?'

'Indeed, lady, I am sure. He says you can converse with him, you understand how he works, you are sympathetic.'

She laughed. 'Sympathetic. I need more than that.'

Kit paused. 'Oh, lady he craves for you; it is a surprise in one so great, I admit, but all he wishes for is one word and he would make the world change for you.'

Her face glowed and Kit waited.

Then he remembered the ring. It was so tiny, he had forgotten. He fished in his doublet and brought it out, holding it delicately between his forefinger and thumb.

'Look, this is his token. He gave it up willingly but then snatched it back; it was a young sister's ring, who had died. It is very precious to him but he would give up his greatest jewel as a talisman of his love for you.'

He proffered it and it was only then that she pushed back the shawl as she hesitantly stretched out to take the ring. But as quickly, she too, in a mirror image of Galileo, pulled back and hid her hand.

'Nay, I could not. I know how he thought of his sister, for he has confided in me.' She paused, not wanting to tell this persistent stranger more.

Kit continued to hold it out. 'Please, dear lady, here is something precious between you two; you cannot refuse it.'

She looked at him. Then that wonderful smile suffused her face. Slowly she took the ring and held it in her palm.

He was sure he could carry good news back to his friend although Marina was a sensible woman. Would she really give up her life of ease for one of struggle and shame with a poor academic

213

with great family responsibilities? He waited. Her face had set again, showing no emotion, though her cheeks were flushed rose. Time passed, but still Kit waited. The air around them stilled. Then she spoke. 'Tell him to come to me; tell him I would discuss how we would make a life together. Tell him I will keep this ring but will not wear it until he puts it on my finger.'

His task had been too easy. Or so it seemed.

He said no more but bowed and backed away, leaving Marina standing alone in the piazza.

Chapter Eighteen

He had succeeded. All he could think about as he sought out Val, was that he was free of that obligation. He found his friend at the Scuola, and, as they sought out food he crowed of his success.

'I must make haste and leave Venice. I promised Galileo I would bring back the good news as soon as possible. I also have to make up with my friend with whom I travel. I have treated him badly.'

But it was not to be that easy. Val caught him by the arm, his face changed from one of affability to scorn. 'Oh, no, dear friend, you cannot run away yet. There is an obligation to me, who helped you in your quest. You must now help me in mine.'

Kit protested but Val was loath to let him go.

'You are a good companion, and, I repeat, I need you. I have helped you and you should now honour the arrangement by helping me. Why else did I befriend you? It was not that Spenser you were reading; it was the way you held yourself, the way you hid your sword and those daggers in your boots. You would be a good fighter in case of need.'

Kit sighed. Once again he was under an obligation to someone. Val had been his unerring guide since he landed in this strange place. Simple courtesy meant he had to give something back. And then there was the veiled threat in Val's speech.

'Very well, I agree to stay with you for a few days. Will it be enough if I leave early Monday? I would catch my mentor Galileo before he becomes immersed again in his lectures. He must be told the good news.'

Val nodded, 'Indeed, I visit the ghetto on Sunday; all the good Catholics will be at mass and it should be easy to slip across the bridge when all is quiet. The Jews work while we pray. I too will leave on Monday, with good news or bad, with heavy purses of gold or disappointment for my duke.'

They shook hands on the arrangement, and, as they wove through tortuous alleys and streets, Kit regaled his friend with the detail of his conversation with Marina.

*   *   *   *   *

Sunday arrived, a grey day where the waters of the lagoon seemed to penetrate the air and all was quietly misty. The bells rang out solemnly in a two tone call to the faithful. Val and Kit left the Scuola after mass, Kit sneezing with the smell of the incense, Val patting him on the back in sympathy.

'We head northwards towards the working quarters; the Jews have their own island surrounded by canals, I am told, and we will know it by the small windows and tall buildings.'

It was easy to find; the rest of the populace seemed to be walking the other way and the two men had to duck and dive to work their way through the crowds. Perhaps that was why, Kit thought later, they had not realised they were being followed.

'Look; Hebrew writing, we cross this bridge and we should be there.'

Val led the way across another of the interminable arched bridges and they both had to bend down to enter a dark alley, the buildings overshadowing it completely. At the end of the alley they came out onto a square and once again Kit was surprised. It was as if they had entered another place with a different atmosphere to the rest of Venice. It still had the quiet air of the backwaters of Venice, it still had the central well head, but there were trees, and children playing, quietly. They did not screech or punch like Venetian children. The boys had dark clothes and kicked a ball to each other, in a manner that involved real skill. The girls leant against the walls of the houses, holding small dolls and whispering. Val paused to get his bearings. Above each house was a Hebrew sign. He studied each carefully. He had extracted a piece of parchment from a pocket and compared this with the signs.

'Ah, here it is, the sign of Benjamin Rothko – the banker. I want

216

you to wait outside and look inconspicuous; let no-one enter while I conduct my business.'

Kit laughed: 'Look inconspicuous. How can I do that, dear Val? Unless I pretend to be a large child and play with my dolls. There are no others with whom I can mingle.'

Val looked around. He had obviously been so preoccupied in finding the place that he had not seen what Kit had noticed. Now he shrugged. 'All right, wait for me outside. I expect no-one to come but if they do they will be Christians like us and you will have to waylay them and tell them to go on their way until I have finished. I suggest that, you whistle a tune to warn me and I will think of something. The main thing is that I must not be seen at this place.'

Kit nodded. It seemed an easy task – what could he fear from a few children in this large square? He had stowed his Sidney poems in his doublet and, as Val disappeared into the bowels of Benjamin's house, he took the book out, crouched down and started to read.

The sun had circled so it was at its mid-day height and Kit had moved to the shade of the trees. The children had been called in by mothers who appeared at doors and disappeared into the cool interiors, not waiting for the children to follow. A silence had descended on the square. Kit's stomach rumbled. He began to wonder if perhaps Val had left by a secret, waterside exit and abandoned him.

Then he was startled by the noise of a door opening, which echoed in the eerie mid-day silence, and Val emerged. He did not look for Kit, but moved off in the direction of the bridge, gesturing to him to follow. Kit could not tell from Val's countenance whether he had been successful. As he reached the end of the alley out of the square, he gestured again for Kit to follow as he walked quickly into the darkness. Kit sprinted the short distance and joined his friend in the gloom, but, picking up on Val's mood, said nothing as they made their way through the ghostly half-light of the narrow way out.

As they emerged into sunlight their way was barred by the slim rapiers of gentlemen's swords, suddenly crossed in front of them. Both Kit and Val were dazzled by the sudden glare after the dark of the alley and at first did not realise what was happening.

'Bon giorno, stranieri.' A man jumped out from where he had been hiding against the wall and stood before them. Two others stood either side holding their swords at arm's length creating the bar.

'What the?' It was Val who spoke. Kit felt the tip of the sword move rapidly to his throat and said nothing.

'We do not like our ladies being accosted in the street. We will punish such insolence.' The man who stood before them held his sword vertically before his face, as if he would jump back and then thrust forward to deal a deathly blow.

Val protested, 'I know not what you mean. I have done nothing, I am here on business.'

'Aye, indeed, business of a courting nature. We see everything and know everything.'

The two men who had hidden either side of the alley now moved round and joined their companion. All three faced Kit and Val making a human barrier. There was no way they could continue. One sword was still held against Kit's throat, the other prodded Val's chest, making an indentation in his velvet doublet. Kit assessed them, still saying nothing. All three were swarthy, obviously related with the same dark square chins and wide noses which, in a woman, might be interpreted as generous. Dark eyes which in a woman might be calm but in these three were revengeful. Kit sighed, remembering Marina's words; *'My father and brothers may be home soon...'* He had developed enough feminine instinct in his previous guises to guess who these three were. Avenging relatives of Marina. Surely she would not have sent them? And how were they to escape?

He left the talking to Val, fearful that speech might cause his assailant to lose his nerve and thrust the point into his voice-box. Val protested, 'I assure you we come on business, not to dally with ladies. I have no idea…please tell us…'

It was a delaying tactic. As he spoke, he moved quickly sideways and with his rapier suddenly out of its scabbard, he forced aside the blade against his chest. Both swords hung in the air, quivering against each other.

Kit's opponent, startled by the sudden movement, looked at Val. It was only a second but the point of his blade loosened from Kit's throat. He ducked, his antagonist's sword barely scratching his face as he moved. His guard tried to lunge at him but missed as Kit danced sideways, twisting and turning. When he came to a standing position, arms extended, he had a short dagger in one hand and a sword in the other. His foe's backed off, cursing.

Kit danced from side to side, and whispered to Val, 'A dagger in the boot is always useful. Back to back and have you a dagger too?'

Val laughed in his familiar joking fashion, 'Like all Verona's gentlemen, I carry many daggers. Follow my lead. A figure of eight with my sword to the count of three and take out the centre foe: what say you?'

Their opponents were looking from one to the other, puzzled by the verbal repartee, trying to listen. They seemed stunned and unable to work out what was happening, hypnotised by the swooshing sounds caused by the weaving weapons of Kit and Val.

Kit, swinging his sword and dagger before him, answered, 'I fear the count of three might be too much but I concur.'

Their assailants glanced from one to the other and then they crouched, ready to strike but still not sure how to break through the weaving weapons.

Val and Kit moved closer together, becoming a four-handed monster. They weaved their swords in the air so that the sound became a whistling. Val called, 'One, two, three.'

They lunged forward as if one, Kit weaving his weapons sideways while Val thrust towards the centre foe. Kit didn't see Val's lunge but a great scream, like a wild animal, from their main opponent was enough to tell he had dealt a fatal blow. The man leapt backwards into the water of the canal, blood gushing from his neck. The other two looked horrified, momentarily stopped in their tracks. Kit and Val, in harmony, grabbed the opportunity and pushed forward. Their foes tried to regain their advantage. Kit and Val remained together, easily sidestepping them. Kit jumped forward and then back, allowing his foe to lunge towards him and as he did, thrust at the man's body so that his blade hit on bone. He stumbled, holding the rib that had cracked.

'Well hit, for a foreigner.' yelled Val, who passed him to chase his foe along the causeway, and Kit saw that he, too, now held a dagger in his left hand and was double-parrying and lunging. The dagger flashed in the sunlight with rich jewels, further glints coming from the water; the multi-hued reflections dancing in the eyes of Val's enemy.

Kit and Val, fighting for their lives, dashed at the two men until they retreated. They only had swords; both Kit and Val had swords and daggers. It was easy to keep advancing on them. Kit admired his friend's skill and followed his lead. They forced the Venetians back along the canal, away from their floating friend. It was not long before one of them tripped on a jutting paving slab as they edged backwards. The other grabbed his arm and, stumbling in a dance-like movement, comical in any other situation, he gained his balance and both men ran, Kit thrusting forward in a last desperate attempt to finish the fray. All he achieved was a dark slash of the thick padded satin of sleeve without touching flesh. Then their enemies were retreating along the canal, heading for one of the many bridges that crossed it.

Kit and Val watched them go, breathing heavily, leaning on each other. Then they too ran, the opposite way to one of the other bridges near where they had been waylaid. As they reached the bridge they saw the body of the first man, caught in the debris that was caught beneath the bridge, floating, his face distorted by the blood that swilled around his neck and mixed slowly with the dull waters.

'I rather fear we are in deep trouble; the leader is well and truly dead.' As Val spoke, he brought out a rough cloth and wiped the blades of his weapons and gave the cloth to Kit. 'It has an oil on it that will clean the metal,' he explained.

Kit made to bend down to try and retrieve the floating corpse, but Val pulled him back. 'Come, there is nothing we can do for a dead man and we must make ourselves scarce. Remember we are strangers. It would be dangerous even to return to the Scuola for our things. Make your way back to Padua as best you can; I return to Verona, my job done.'

As he spoke he dragged Kit away across the bridge, and down an alley, half running, half-walking. When they came to the end they reached a small piazza. 'You go that way. When you reach the end of the alley, turn right, walk slowly, put your sword away now, and, dear fighting friend, if I never see you again, good luck.'

Kit, who was still breathing heavily from the fight, patted Val on the shoulder. Suddenly they were in an embrace and Kit whispered, 'Good luck to you too dear Val, I'll not forget you, and somehow I'll make sure you will know it.'

As he parted from his companion he muttered, 'And make sure your story is made immortal.' He was already forming the start of another play.

Chapter Nineteen

'I spoke with your lady, Sir, and I am sure she will welcome whatever proposal you wish to make.'

He was standing in Galileo's lodgings, and had spoken immediately, dropping his bag as he entered, seeing by Galileo's expression that he was apprehensive. Then he stood, like a sentinel, waiting. Galileo only stared at him but did not move. Slowly, he closed his book, slid away from the desk and approached Kit. He embraced him in a great bear hug and then stood back. Kit was so taken aback by this he said nothing more, afraid to give Galileo the full story.

'You made it quite clear?'

'Indeed; and she was quite annoyed that you used an emissary – she would have you woo her yourself.'

Galileo nodded. 'Yes, she can be quite stern. She is not a weak character, would you agree?'

Kit smiled, 'Indeed no, she is as upright as a man.' But Galileo was not listening. He started pacing up and down, and Kit could see he was planning how to approach her, now he was sure of her affection. How could he break the bad news? He was sure that he and Val had murdered some of her relatives; brothers, cousins or even her father. Would this change Marina's feelings? Surely she would not want to associate with the man she would hold responsible. Kit hesitated. As he'd travelled back, he had thought that perhaps Marina would never find out how her relative had died. And if she did find out that he had died in a sword fight, would she connect this with him? How could she? Perhaps he should say nothing. But he was sure that those who had escaped would have told her what had happened, how they had tried to avenge the insult to her by the stranger who had approached her.

Even if they did not, he remembered what he had been told of those secret messages, slid into stone mouths; the populace of Venice were secretive, sly and might tell. If it was public knowledge she would find out soon enough. She would know that her family were plotting, were revengeful. Perhaps, if she had protested, they had even locked her away?

Val's fatal strike might prejudice Galileo's lady against him, Kit had concluded.

'How seemed my lady? Did you like her? Yes, she is stern, but true, true as a well turned sword.' Kit winced at the analogy. Should he tell him? At the very least, the lady might be grieving and not want to think of love at this time.

Galileo stood before him again. 'You mean, she really would come to me? Me? With little money and a whole tribe to support?'

Kit nodded; he could find no other words to assure him and could not bring himself to disappoint the man. After all, his fears might be groundless.

'Then I must go to her.'

Kit shuddered; in his imagination, Marina was locked up, inaccessible now, and her avenging relatives watched over her, waiting for another approach. Kit could not let his tutor, whom he now considered a friend, be put in danger.

'There is something else I must tell you.'

But Galileo had grabbed a scrap of rough paper and a quill and was leaning over it, scribbling frantically. Kit could see figures being listed down the page. Galileo muttered as he moved his quill rapidly up and down, adding up the expenses of a journey, Kit guessed.

'Sir, I must tell you something else.'

He almost shouted it. Galileo looked up then, and came towards him with a concerned look on his face; he could see that Kit was really worried.

'I...we...I was attacked. I fought back for my life. But I killed one of my assailants. It was me or him.'

'So? What has that to do with my love?'

223

Kit continued, 'They accused us – me – of dallying with ladies. I – I denied it of course, but they were hell-bent on getting revenge for an imagined slight to their family. I can only assume that they were Marina's kin; for I did not dally with any other lady of Venice. Also, they bore a passing resemblance to her…I rather fear.'

'Oh, my God. Not her father, please don't make it her father. She would be honour bound never to come to me then.'

'No, not my father.'

The two men had been so involved in their conversation that they had not noticed the door open quietly. Galileo was the first to see her and his face lit up.

'Marina! Marina my love…'

'Wait; stay there and listen.'

Galileo stopped in his tracks, arms raised to wrap her in an embrace. Kit stood to one side, hoping to hide in the shadows, but Marina pointed at him and continued, 'you send this worm of a man to woo me and he does it so badly that I almost send him away – Galileo, why cannot you trust yourself to know the truth? A great scientist like you, who has already been reckless in his researches, so that the Inquisition and the Pope are asking questions about your investigations into the sun and the stars, and you cannot even ask a simple lady a simple question. Instead you send this *stranger*'. She said it as if it was the deepest insult an Italian could make to a person. 'This *stranger* to woo me and he makes a fine mess of it and breaks up my family, a kinsman dead, my mother in hysterics, my father so angry he threatens me with a nunnery. I am questioned until I am so tired I would collapse and then I am locked in my chamber and threatened with only food for peasants.'

'How have you managed to travel to me?'

Marina smiled grimly. 'I have very good and loyal maidservants, who would still help me, even though my uncle, a hard and jealous man whom I distrusted, was left lying in a murky canal.'

So, an uncle. And not one that the lady respected. Kit was relieved, but still worried. He watched as Galileo led her to a chair, pushing papers to the floor. He was smiling, and Kit realised he knew this woman well. Marina had escaped, made her way to him, to her new life. Galileo had his woman.

Kit stood helpless, watching. It was obvious that there was a deep understanding between them. He started to edge sideways. He should leave these two alone to resolve their own problems; he had his own. But Marina turned quickly as he nearly reached the door.

'Nay, do not leave, young foreigner. You owe me and I would have at least an apology.'

Kit bowed; every time he met her he was more impressed. Despite her obvious distress at the situation she found herself in, she addressed him with calm dignity, an assurance that normally came to women when they were older; he was reminded of Bridget, his tutor in womanhood. This young woman had poise and intelligence. He could see why the great academic was so enamoured of her. Galileo smiled, a secret proud smile, one hand on her arm. Galileo did nothing to stop Marina from talking and explaining what she wanted.

'An apology first – and an acknowledgement that you owe me a service.'

Kit inwardly seethed. Would he never be rid of other people's errands? He had so many schemes that he wanted to start, he had his own unfinished business with Tom, to see to and now this woman also wanted his time. He could not refuse her though. His ability to assess other's situations had stood him in good stead in other ways, and he knew she was right. He could always see two sides of an argument; that was why his plays were so good. He thought back on the arguments between the Good Angel and the Bad Angel in Faust. He bowed his head and humbly acknowledged her.

'Dear lady, I apologise most profusely for the loss of your uncle, which was not caused by malice but by self defence and utter shock at the sudden challenge by your relatives, if that be who I injured.' He would have stopped there but she had cocked her head to encourage him to continue; he knew what was expected of him, 'I am at your service, dear lady, whatever I can do to make amends.'

He trailed off.

She nodded and turned to Galileo. 'I am impressed by your emissary even though I do not approve of your method of sending him to me, dear Galileo. Do you think I can ask one *favour* of him before we release him?'

Galileo was puzzled but nodded.

'Thank you. I would have him return to Venice…'

'What? I cannot do that, it would be certain death if I were caught.'

'But you will not be caught. Return to Venice and collect some clothes from my servant. I told her to expect you. I will tell you the place. You will find her, sitting on the edge of the fountain in the main square on Murano, one of the islands of Venice, where she visits her family on Sunday. She will wait for the next four Sundays so you have plenty of time. She has agreed to wear a red scarf around her shoulders and carry my possessions in a large food basket. My jewels and best linen will be hidden in eggs, good pasta and a dried ham for her family. They are glass blowers and, like all their trade, have been banished to Murano because the furnaces are thought to be dangerous. It is one of the islands that many visitors go to on Sundays so you will not be noticed.'

Kit leant against the door, his escape if he would but take it, and thought. If he travelled with Tom, perhaps in disguise? Could he shave his head so that he had a monk's tonsure? Or metamorphose into a woman as he had been once? Or just walk out of this room and disappear again?

'If only it was February and I could disguise myself behind one of your exotic masks for Carnevale. I will go, madam.'

Marina was delighted. She looked up at Galileo and said, 'You see, your friend understands us Venetians. He will do it and then I will be worthy of you, dear Galileo, my star-gazer, and denounce my family for you and our future together.'

* * * * *

Kit was in a deep sleep when he was woken by the banging of the door. Kit, the recent sword fight still giving him nightmares, woke so suddenly at the noise that he was half-sitting, his hand reaching for his sword, before Tom entered the sleeping chamber. Tom was humming to himself, but stopped short when he saw Kit, dishevelled, so obviously disturbed. Then his face clouded over, he slung the packet he was holding into a corner and snarled, 'So, you've come back. Obviously exhausted. No doubt you've been drawing attention to yourself, wherever you've been, carousing and singing and shouting.'

He lurched to the window and pulled it shut; the outside shutters had been drawn against the heat of the afternoon by Kit but the sudden noise made Kit jump again and he sat up, wide awake, and smoothed his hair. After ensuring that he could not be heard Tom began his tirade again.

'Kit we cannot go on like this; you treat me with disdain, not telling me what you're up to. I know you're writing, you scribble away all the time, but what do you do with it all? Then you take off like that. I just cannot believe what you get up to anymore.'

Kit did not interrupt but slowly swung his legs to the floor. He stood and straightened his undershirt, reaching for his doublet and continued to dress as Tom vented his anger. Kit knew his friend well; he rarely lost his temper, indeed this was the first time he had really seen him seethingly angry. He might be peevish, complaining, but never white hot; that was Kit's way. Perhaps it was time he told him about his secret life, the life he had not revealed because he feared Tom would not understand. He would at the least think it highly dangerous.

'And you never have told me why you are visited by your dark friends, who come so mysteriously. Kit, I need to know what is happening.'

He slumped down onto the trunk where they kept their clothes,

227

his hands held out before him as if in supplication.

Kit approached and touched his shoulder. Tom shrugged him off. Kit dropped his hands at his sides. He wasn't quite sure where to begin. He knew he still had some work to do for Marina and Galileo. He'd thought of a way but it would involve Tom again, and with Tom in this mood, how would he ever persuade him? The only thought that came to him was to him the truth.

'If I tell you, I must ask one further boon of you.'

Tom walked towards the door. 'No, no more. I tell you I have had enough.'

Kit ran around him and stood between him and the door. 'The last task, Tom, I promise.'

Tom tried to push past but Kit held him. Tom tried to push him off but Kit was always the stronger.

'Very well. Tell me, first, and I will decide what I will do.'

There was a pause while Kit studied his friend. Tom looked different, but Kit could not quite say how, except that he seemed to be taller, more dignified. This rebellion was unusual for him. Yes, he could become tetchy and be exasperated with Kit's behaviour, but Kit always knew he could talk him round. This time he knew something was different. There was an added determination about him. Kit noticed that around his friend's eyes were wrinkles and there were a few grey hairs tinting his head.

'Nay, I'll have one more promise from you, Tom, and then I'll tell you all.'

Tom turned away in frustration and grabbed his cloak and attempted to leave again. Kit once more noted the determination and leant against the door to block him. He smiled at this friend with whom he had had so many adventures as if to say how ridiculous they looked, jumping around each other. Usually, such antics brought a smile to Tom's face but this time there was no reaction. Kit remembered what Bridget had said to him long ago, almost in another life. *Remember that men like to think we don't know about things; they must believe in our innocence.* It suddenly occurred to Kit that Tom was in love, but he knew that, if he accused his friend of a liaison, he would get no more out of him, at least not now. He would say nothing until they had resolved his present problem.

'*Please,* Tom, for the times we have had together. You have proved a good and loyal friend in the past, why stop now? Our lives are bound together and I wouldn't know what to do without you.'

But the cold air continued to surround Tom. Kit realised he had hurt him beyond endurance by being so cavalier, by disappearing and not involving him in his affairs, except when he needed to. Tom had always been there. Tom had rarely asked questions, and when he had, was soon satisfied with what little Kit told him. Kit knew he could be persuasive; after all, he spent most of his private life creating mythical creatures which some said were totally believable. Faust, the Devil; the Jew of Malta or Tamburlaine. And all the others, so many others, since their travels together.

He moved away from the door, as if to let Tom go. 'I'm sorry, dear friend, I have tested you beyond endurance, have I not?' He did not turn round to see if Tom departed or waited to hear what else he had to say. He knew by the silence that he was still there.

'I have, and I am sorry. Tom, are you in need of money if we part? What do you wish to do? Are you tired of our carousing? You say you are. Of our travelling? You already know that we must soon leave this place. Will you come with me?'

Tom, head down, was still facing the door as if at any moment he would go, but his cloak had fallen to his side. His whole demeanour indicated defeat, but there was still the stoniness about him. Slowly however, he turned to face Kit.

'Where do you wish to go? Do you want to return to Venice?'

'Just for a while, and I promise you that, once I have carried out my commission there, I will give you all the money I have left and you can do what you want to do.'

'And what will you do? How will you live?'

'Dear Tom, perhaps you would put your *sister* into a nunnery in Venice. I hear they are wonderfully social places with gossip and scandal surrounding them. Perhaps that is the place for me.'

'Are you serious? That would be a safe place for you to hide, if you would don women's garments again.' Tom brightened, he could see a way to escape from Kit's influence. He added, 'So, you will go to Venice as a woman?'

Kit grabbed the chance. 'Yes, I would, to carry out this last commission and then I promise we will settle this once and for all.'

* * * * *

'Dear Gabriella, forgive me for deserting you for a while, I have to travel with a friend but I swear I will return.'

She pouted, her lips pursed, and Tom loved her for it. He loved the way she didn't like him leaving her; every time he kissed her hands, her lips, her face in farewell she would sigh and her brows knitted in disappointment; all this he saw as he tried to leave, but she pulled him back to her.

'Tom I do not know what your countrymen are like; are they uncivilised, like we are told? Our priests tell us you do not celebrate mass and that you are all wild and crazy, not led by the rules of God. You have wormed your way into my heart and now you would go. How can I trust you to return?'

Tom removed the small talisman from around his neck, which he always wore; a family heirloom the meaning of which was lost in time. Slowly he hung it around her fine neck and gently stroked the curve below her ears as he gathered the chain together and fixed the clasp. She lent against him, but still kept her face tuned from him. He could see her bosom gently heaving and the stiffened lace collar of her silken gown around her neck became crumpled.

'I would not part with this ever; I give it to you as a token of my faithfulness, and confirmation of my return. I have travelled this far with my friend but I swear I'll go no further with him than Venice; and only for a few weeks.' He gently pushed some stray hairs away and kissed the down at the top of her spine, and whispered, 'I could not bear to be away from you longer. When I return I'll ask your father for your hand in marriage, what say you?'

She pulled away from him and faced him then, her sultry eyes all soft and they clung to one another; a long joining which was full of promises for their future.

Chapter Twenty

They travelled by exotic barge to Venice and this time docked before the Doge's palace. It was mid morning and all was a-bustle with merchantmen and officials scurrying from one office to another. Women paraded in their finery, men flirted with them and urchins skipped between the crowds, openly grabbing at loose silk handkerchiefs or discarded food before the dogs could steal it. As Kit's party stepped onto the quay, all heads turned to look.

Kit was dressed in full feminine regalia, with puffs and gewgaws enough to draw attention. Mid morning, for the Venetians, it would seem, was not a time for rich accoutrements; Kit, in rich attire, was a sight for everyone to stare at and admire. The dress was of cream shot silk embossed with thin gold chains; at the neck and wrists was the finest Brussels lace. He wore the most delicate slippers of cream satin, great pearled buckles on the front matching the pearls at his throat. *If there is a great outward display people won't notice the insides,* Kit had explained as he described how he wanted to arrive in Venice for the second time. He wanted to make sure that none of Marina's kin would ever know he was back in their city. His hair was elaborately coiffured and decked with tiny pins of butterflies and leaves. Indeed, Kit looked more like a flitting butterfly, catching the glint of the sun on the richness of the clothes.

Whilst he rested a delicate heavily be-ringed hand on the arm of Tom, not for support, but as an affectation, he glided along the quay. This was a creature so different from that of the much less sophisticated *woman* who had used Tom's arm to board a boat from England. This was a *lady,* who needed no man, except for adornment.

Behind them came two child-negroes, dressed in shiny silk

pantaloons and half-shirts, all in a blue-purple silk which shimmered and changed shades as the Venetian sun caught the sheen. They held great ostrich fans, which waved over the heads of Kit and Tom.

'Men are not observant, Tom, take my word for it; they will be so enamoured of the gilding they'll not see the man beneath. I'll use white powdered mercury to hide the blue shadow – we will travel in style this time.'

Tom had protested at the expense of it all; he hadn't liked buying the slaves either. Hiring servants was a matter of negotiation with the person who was going to work for you; he wasn't even sure whether the negro slaves knew Latin or any other language by which they could be ordered about. And he hated having to negotiate with a slave-dealer. He had been used to dealing with free men. The dealer had assured him that the negroes were conversant with foreign languages but had not allowed Tom to speak with them or do anything else but test their calves for strength. Tom did not know how to treat someone who was handed to you with chains locked around their ankles.

He had walked home in silence, the two young lads following him, the only noise being the clanking of their chains as they walked in unison.

When he arrived home with his purchases, Kit had been delighted and rubbed his hands through their tight curly hair and given them sweetmeats. They had both smiled back, showing pearly sets of teeth with numerous gaps in them.

'Break the chains off and let's go and dress them to fit that shiny ebony skin.' ordered Kit. Tom had protested; the children had cost him nearly all their savings but Kit insisted. They had found a local smith who had also protested, astonished that someone who had newly bought slaves would release them but Kit insisted.

'They'll not run away, they know who is good to them,' he said. The smith, shrugging, had swung his heavy hammer onto the middle of the chain which rested on his anvil, and it only took a few blows before the twins were separated. Kit was right. They did not run away. Instead, they smiled broadly and one took the hand of Kit and the other squeezed in between the two men and took each of their hands, and both were laughing, as they all walked back to the lodgings. When the door was shut, Kit swung them both in front of him and bent down so he was crouching, his face at their level.

'Now, young ones, can you speak? Do you understand me?'

They had bowed to Kit, and then to Tom. 'I am Dromio.'

'And I am Antipholus.'

They spoke together in clipped accents, as if they had been taught what to say. After their speech they bowed in unison, taking off their plumed hats and swinging them low. Then they had laughed together and bowed again.

'We are at your service because you give us our freedom.'

Both Tom and Kit had been delighted, perhaps Kit more so because he had proved to his friend that freedom meant loyalty.

The cortege glided past the Doge's Palace into the great piazza, Kit walking so much more gracefully in the high heels than he had done in the past. He haughtily ignored the great promenade of people, the cooing pigeons which strutted in multitude around him, and the gulls which glided low around his head, screeching in the breeze. The young blackaboys held his train high and played up to his strutting by copying his stance, their high-heeled shoes clacking.

'Where to, Tom? Where do we go? We must stay in the best places.' He spoke out of the side of his mouth, not daring to let the staring crowd think he knew not where he was headed.

And that was another of Kit's whims. Tom had been sent on to find sumptuous apartments, outlining exactly what he wanted. He had negotiated a small terraced palazzo, squeezed between two great mansions on the Grand Canal, in accordance with Kit's instructions. He was sure Kit would be pleased with it. He had found something that fitted the description; within full view of the nobility and the busy traffic on the Grand Canal, but with back stairs leading not only on to a small backwater at the rear of the house but also on to an alley, so there were three ways of exit and entry. He led Kit towards the Rialto Bridge and then, when they were past the main way, with its gaudy shops, took him down a side alley that led to the quiet, secret entrance to the palazzo. It was a dingy narrow place, with mould on the lower walls of the houses either side, where the sun never reached. The slaves stopped their excited chatter, awed into silence by the gloom.

They entered their lodgings by an unobtrusive wooden door, which slid shut behind them without creaking or banging. All four stood, close together, before Tom moved on, showing the way. They were in a dark large hall, and he crossed it to a wide stairway which circled away to rooms above. As he showed Kit around, Kit nodded in approval; when he opened the shuttered windows and stepped on to the tiny balcony, with its ornate metal balustrade, he smiled, and Tom knew he had chosen well. The view showed a curve in the Grand Canal, with the Rialto Bridge forming an arched boundary at one end. All the river traffic passed up and down at this point.

'Indeed, we will show these Venetians how to display themselves. And we must prepare for a little trip to the nearest of islands; on Sunday morning perhaps, what say you Tom? Our little lads here look too peaky.' He had swept one of the boys onto his lap as he sat at a chair placed strategically to one side of the great windows. He played with the other's curly head as he leant against Kit. Tom turned away in disgust and busied himself with taking in their luggage as the baggage men scurried up and down the stairs from the barge which had docked at the front of the house.

Sunday came and Kit had his way. Tom was sent off to hire a boat. 'Not one of those nodding gondolas, Tom, a proper boat with a boatman who can take us to the islands. The lagoon can be choppy. But make sure it is hired just for us, I'll not travel with lackeys and strangers on their day out.'

Their day started early for it would take several hours to reach the island of Murano in the rowing boat, even though there were two oarmen, and then they had to find the Byzantine church where Donatella, the servant would be waiting by the door. Kit vaguely remembered the servant who so silently served her mistress. Would she be shocked to see him in disguise? He would risk it, for here in Venice, for the first time in his life, he felt as if anything was acceptable.

Kit had not told Tom why he was going to the island and, when they landed, they wandered along the canals, the two boys running ahead and looking in the windows at the brightly coloured glass ornaments. The heavy smoke of ever-burning fires drifted across the canals from large-doored shops, where the furnaces glowed like so many hells.

'Surely they would not be working on a Sunday?' Tom queried.

An old workman, sitting on a barrel outside one of the furnaces answered, 'Nay, the glass-workers do not work on a Sunday, but we cannot let the furnaces go cold because it takes too long to fire them again. Would you like to see?'

Kit whispered to Tom, 'No, Tom, it is a ploy to get us into his workshop and then we'll find ourselves trapped, impossible to leave without buying some of his wares.'

Tom shook his head, smiling and followed as Kit moved away. The two of them ambled along, the young servants following, until they reached a large square which was obviously the meeting place for the locals, where there was a buzz of conversation, children running around and old dames resting on long benches. Kit saw the fountain that Marina had mentioned. As soon as they reached the west entrance of the church which dominated one side of the square, he immediately spied the woman waiting, the basket seemingly weighing her down, a dead chicken resting on top of brightly coloured vegetables. He gestured to the fountain in the centre of the square and suggested, 'Tom, take the boys and buy them a drink and come back to me. I'm going to wait for you at the fountain. I have business to conduct.' He walked away before Tom could say anything. As Kit approached the maidservant, he thought, she may remember me as a man; now I have to persuade her to trust me as a woman.

Tom and the boys hung back and watched as Kit walked confidently towards the entrance of the church. Suddenly Tom saw him halt, not far from a woman and speak to her. She looked startled, glanced from side to side at other passersby, and then lent forward as if she would study the person who addressed her. Then her hand went to her mouth, Tom guessed to hide either astonishment or laughter, he could not be sure. Kit's hand went out to her, and grabbed her arm in a gesture which could be both rebuke and warning or a hurried explanation. Then the two moved off together, ignoring the crowds of Sunday revellers who seemed to fall back to give the servant girl and the grand lady space. They looked as if they were laughing, heads together, all the world as if they were old friends, and would catch up with news from childhood.

Tom turned away, exasperated. What was Kit up to now? He entertained the two lads, buying them an iced sherbet each and, when they reached the fountain, splashing them with the water from it so they giggled in delight. Even so, he could not stop himself from time to time glancing over his shoulder, to keep Kit and the servant girl in sight. He saw the basket being handed over, and Kit pushing the chicken further down, so it would not fall out. The woman looked longingly at the basket and Tom watched as Kit removed a bunch of grapes and gave it to her. What was Kit doing buying a basket of food?

Then they kissed in the Italian fashion; a peck on each cheek and a moving away, hands leaving hands in a sliding away movement. Slowly Kit walked back towards him through the crowds, a lady not to be hurried. Tom viciously collected some water from the fountain and as he neared splashed it at him. Kit saw it coming and ducked, the basket leaning perilously. The water fell short and splattered spots of water onto Kit's skirts. He laughed in the high pitch of the woman he pretended to be and cooed, 'Oh, sweet gentleman, water me not, for you will ruin my silks. Come, it is getting hot, let us to lunch, and the youngsters can come too.'

He handed the basket to the slaves who took it willingly and held it between them, just keeping it from scraping the ground. Tom wondered what was in it, it seemed so heavy.

As they made to move away Kit stopped short, pulled down the veil around his headdress, and took Tom's arm; whispering, 'We must away, no lunch here, I fear, for I see a familiar face; much like my friend Galileo's lady.'

Tom looked round but could see no-one in the crowd who seemed suspicious or was following them but Kit pulled him forward and carried on whispering, 'The nonchalant one in green hose and blue doublet.' Tom tried to look from under lowered brows and soon spotted the man from Kit's description. 'I know, he is as bright as a peacock but look at the dark shadowed eyes and sharp chin – if you meet Galileo's lady you'll see the resemblance although the features in her present a much more pleasant visage. I told you how I was attacked in Venice; he was one of them.'

Tom looked horrified and started to hurry; the man had pulled himself from his leaning position and was making his way towards them. Kit slowed him. 'Tom, stop worrying. I am a woman, remember. He may ask us how we know the servant girl, but I can say I am a long lost cousin; or we can get one of the slaves to say so. It matters not, I am sure.'

Kit continued on his way in the same confident showy manner he had used since he had arrived in Venice. His foe was almost face to face with them now but Kit stared ahead. Tom turned to make sure the slaves were following and chivvied them for laughing together. Kit protested in his feminine pitch, 'Dear brother, leave the lads alone, they do their duty well enough. You are too strict.' With that, she smiled at the peacocked man who was just passing, as if she would ask for his sympathy and agreement to her thought. He answered with an embarrassed look and hurried on. Tom turned once more as if to attend to the slaves, and watched the man scurry into a tavern. He breathed a sigh of relief and turned back to Kit.

'I insist we leave this hellish island, for the sun's heat and the furnace's heat combine to make a reeking inferno. We'll return to Venice and as soon as we can we will return to Padua. I have had enough.'

Kit stared at Tom whose face was furrowed in an angry frown. Tom avoided his gaze and walked firmly ahead, and it was as much as Kit could do to keep up with him in the high-heeled ladies' shoes. The lads behind called out, the basket was heavy and they would drop it. Tom slowed but continued to walk to where they had left their boatmen. He was muttering, 'I'll not rest until I get away from these watery places. The damp atmosphere seems to addle my brains.'

This time, Kit realised the best way to deal with him was to remain silent and let him burn out his anger. They boarded the boat, the boys handing down the basket to Tom and then jumping down causing the boat to rock, and the boatman was soon away.

* * * * *

As they journeyed back no-one said anything. Even Dromio and Antipholus were silent, leaning against the basket. They did not even attempt to steal an orange or grape. Tom stared away to the horizon as if he would be there and be gone. Kit, sighing loudly, eventually took from a pocket of his skirts his Philip Sidney and started to read. Not even the boatmen spoke as they disembarked and proceeded to their palazzo, sensing that their passengers were at odds with one another.

When they were alone Kit said, 'Tom, we will have a serious talk tonight. I suggest we ask the boys to organise a dinner for us; good wine, good food – and then we will talk. I promise.'

Tom needed no further encouragement. He said nothing but called for the slaves and gave orders. Great preparations were made and eventually the table was heavily laden with candelabra, all sconces filled with expensive wax candles; the chicken had been cooked and stuffed with figs and grapes which gave it a rich sweet taste, there were salads and greens, a great bowl of fruit and fresh bread. A flagon of wine was on the table and had already been used to fill two elegant Murano glass tall-stemmed goblets.

Antipholus and Dromio were dressed in the best uniforms Kit had insisted upon and served them, bringing up more foods from the kitchens. They took their duties seriously but kept grinning at each other, obviously enjoying the job of running to the cookhouse and collecting hot meats, capon, chicken and light sausages. Then pouring wine or handing an extra sweetmeat to one or other of their strange owners.

'How like you Venice, Tom? Apart from the job I have had to do would you now like to stay for a while?' Kit was breaking bread and dipping it into the chicken sauce.

'I've told you, Kit, I wish to be back in Padua.'

'You love the studying? The heat and the sweat as we pour over those heavy old books?'

'Kit, I did; but you may as well know…'

But Kit wasn't listening, he was carrying on, 'Yes, I can understand but surely the same town, the same lecturers, apart from Galileo of course, they are all so mundane.'

'But it's not the studying.'

'Such new experiences…'

Tom threw his bread at Kit's face and yelled, 'You're not listening to me. It's not the town or the studying. I have met a woman. It is time and I would marry.'

'*Marry*!' Kit made it sound like he was swearing. First Galileo, now his old friend. What was happening to the world? He stared at Tom, long and hard. It was a long time since he had even noticed him, so familiar and easy was their relationship. He saw again the wrinkles around the eyes, the thickening of the skin and greying hair. Indeed, he felt as if he had never really looked at him. Tom did not flinch as he was studied.

Eventually Kit turned away, stood up and studied himself in the mottled mirror into which he would gaze as Dromio and Antipholus dressed him in all his finery; *his* face was slack beneath the thick make-up, but he did not have the dark beard line, nor the darkly ringed eyes of his friend. He looked like a dissolute lady of uncertain age. Tom joined him now, standing behind him, and Tom's reflection did not waver, he stood waiting, a determined, strong man. Kit thought on his night-time escapades, hidden entirely from Tom, with the ragamuffins of Venice, of Rome and the other big cities they had lived in. Kit would never marry; the thought of such a venture made him shudder.

He realised that time had taken its toll. How long had they been travelling? Two, three years? They had discovered that their sojourn on the island of Oresorp had distorted time and a year had passed although it had seemed but a few weeks. Certainly many seasons had passed. He saw himself as he was, a dissolute man of no morals who sought all the time for new ideas or situations to turn into words and the words themselves into plays; things of no consequence, which would be played out and disappear.

Behind him he saw the reflection of Tom, an honest, decent man who would be a faithful husband and good father, who had grown out of dreaming and wanting, who had found what he wanted and was firm in his resolve to obtain it and keep it. Kit recognised it was time they parted. He wanted no truck with the decent life of a married man, children, and work to maintain the family. He'd seen how Galileo was weighed down with the obligations of kith and kin. He shrugged and turned to face Tom.

'So be it my friend, you and I must go our own ways.' Then he coquetted, 'But what is a young maid to do without her protector? How can I live? What will become of me?'

Tom snorted, as he watched Kit slide back into his seat at the table. Despite his determination he could always be amused by the way Kit acted the woman. Before he had a chance to answer, however, there was a loud rap at the door and Dromio went running before Tom could stop him.

Dromio returned quickly and they could hear the heavy boots of the person who followed. 'Sirs, a Venetian visitor.'

The man followed him so quickly Dromio did not have time to introduce the guest in the way he had been taught. In strode a stranger, who quickly moved into the centre of the room, and spoke as he stood, one hand on the hilt of his sword. 'I come to seek a favour of you.'

Kit stared and suddenly raised his napkin to his face, in sudden mock humility. He recognised the intruder immediately. It was the man who had followed them in Murano. Marina's relative.

Chapter Twenty-one

Tom, still standing, stepped back involuntarily and nearly knocked his glass off the table. He steadied it and pulled himself upright, his hand also on his sword, matching the man's aggressive position.

'What can I do for you, interrupting a family at their supper? Who are you?'

The man circled around him and glanced at Kit before turning back to Tom. 'I would speak with you in private, for what I have to say should not be said before women.'

Kit, delighted, half rose to leave the room and then hesitated; playing the perfect subservient woman. Tom nodded and Kit slid off, banging the door so that the handle did not catch, leaving the door slightly ajar. The man strode around the room, as if he could not find words to start. Like a lion, thought Tom, ready to pounce if any weakness was exhibited. Tom said nothing but stood still, his hand resting on the hilt of his sword, watching as the visitor reconnoitred the room. Tom could see the man taking in the remains of the chicken, the salats, the wine goblets half full. Eventually he sat and helped himself to the remains of Kit's wine. Then he began, 'I admit I have been following you and your good lady...'

'My sister, yes...'

'Your sister. Ah, I understand.'

'No, you don't understand, she is my sister...'

The man smiled. 'No matter. I have been following you because I was present when your sister met with a servant from our family today. Can I ask how your sister knows the woman?'

'I think that is none of your business, sir. *If my sister met with someone.* As far as I know we visited Murano to refresh ourselves

243

from the foetid air of Venice...' Tom hesitated seeing the reactionary movement of the man, and corrected himself, 'I apologise, you are justifiably proud of your great City. Yes, then, it was to take a trip in the lagoon and, I admit, she purchased some fresh food from the island. We have been partaking of that food, as you can see.'

The stranger swept his explanation aside. 'It is important to me...it involves the death of one of my family and the honour of my family. I am looking for a man, a foreigner, a real devil. He killed one of my kin and stole one of our daughters. We know not where she has gone.'

He paused and said, in a dead pan manner. 'You too are a foreigner; you may know of this man.'

Tom wondered. Could he have seen through Kit's disguise? Surely not. Tom was almost sure that, if he had he would not be speaking like this; he would have drawn his sword and killed Kit immediately. Tom guessed that such a nobleman would deeply despise a man disguised as a woman and would not have hesitated. Tom came to the conclusion he was genuinely seeking information.

'Sir, I assure you I know nothing.' Tom stopped, and waited. The man looked at him enquiringly. Tom realised an explanation was required for his being in Venice but did not know what to say.

The man whispered, and the whisper was more threatening than any shouting or posturing with swords, 'So many men from the north cannot be a coincidence. So many strangers contacting members of my household cannot be coincidence. What is going on? You must know something.'

Tom thought quickly. He remembered Kit's words, *Put your sister in a convent.*

He sat down opposite the man, as if comfortable in his presence and gestured for him to sit too but the man brushed the invitation aside and remained standing.

'May I be frank with you sir? You are a Venetian so must be fully aware of the many convents here. Indeed, their reputation has spread across to our country, even though we are Protestant.' Tom lowered his voice, 'My sister has been very ill-used and is still pursued by someone with whom she will not consort. He is powerful, and has many spies everywhere. She feels she is not safe anywhere except in a convent many miles from her home. She is prepared to lock herself away, devoting herself to God; this was to be our last night together.'

He took a sip of his own wine, put his hand to his brow, as if upset, and continued, speaking slowly, 'In truth, I am very sad at her decision and was hoping that these last few hours, a journey out to your beautiful island of Murano, and a trip on the lagoon, followed by good food and fine wine might persuade her that the ways of the world are worth following.'

The Venetian listened, his eyes down, considering.

'Who was this man? Was he in Venice recently?'

Tom jumped up and almost shouted, 'Indeed I hope not, for all our plans could be jeopardised. I'd hoped he would not be able to find us so easily. Perhaps it is best that I prepare my sister for her last journey in this world tonight. Tomorrow I will take her to the convent of the Sisters of Mercy.'

'I have a cousin there, we have paid for her to be the next mother superior; would you like me to help you?'

'Nay, it is better that my sister and I face this alone.'

The man nodded and gathered himself up, shook Tom's hand, 'I am sorry not to know you better. You will lose a sister tomorrow; I have lost a cousin and a sister, I know not where. I will not trouble you with my name and I'll not ask yours. Farewell.'

He strode out. Dromio, who had stood immobile at the side of the door during the interview, followed. Tom listened until he had heard the main door bang and Dromio returned. 'He is gone?'

'Yes, he's gone.' It was Kit who spoke as he emerged from the bedchamber. The servant boy was dismissed with a wave of the hand. Kit continued, 'And you would cage your sister in a convent, say you?'

'I had to think of something, and you know what? I believe I must do it. For that man may be satisfied, or he may not. What do you think?'

All anger between them was dissipated in thoughts to save themselves. Kit nodded, impatiently moving the flowing skirts away from his legs so he could stride about.

'I believe he will continue to watch the house…'

He moved to the window and peered through the closed drapes.

'Indeed, he is watching now, poor man, in such a way as to call attention to himself. These Venetians! They have no idea how to spy do they?'

'They don't need to if what you have told me is correct; all they need to do is put a name on parchment and place it in the mouth of the Doge's letter boxes and anyone they suspect will be arrested. Kit I think we are in real danger here.'

Kit was still pacing as he put his hand to his chin and skipping a few steps as he tripped on his skirts in his excitement. He was smiling, his whole face lit up with anticipation. Tom despaired, thinking of his darling back in Padua.

'*You* are in real danger, not me. He thinks I am but a woman. I can see the danger for you. Tomorrow you will take me to the convent.'

'If I am in danger, Kit, it is your fault.'

'Exactly, as I know too well. That's why we must do it.'

'Very well. All I will do is take you there, as early as possible. The servants – slaves – whatever you will, can stay with you, for I'll have no use for them. I'll tell the Mother Superior you must keep them with you because you took them in as babes, orphans or whatever.' He turned and started to tidy the few items they had in the room, filling his bag.

Kit strode across and stopped him with a hand on his arm.

'There is one thing you must do when you return without me.'

'I'll not do anything, once we part.'

'Tom, you must. I promised Marina that I would return with her possessions.'

'What? Where are they?'

Kit gestured to the kitchen. 'In that basket. Why did you think it was so heavy? You must take it with you and give it to her, for me, please.'

Tom continued to pack and said over his shoulder, his voice muffled, 'I will take your basket back to Marina and then I am getting away. I have had enough – from tomorrow, once I have delivered you to your convent, I will take no more responsibility for you, Kit, whoever you might be, woman, man or beast.'

Chapter Twenty-two

'Goodbye *dear* sis, please God and your Mother Superior...'

Tom hugged his friend, and kissed him on the cheek. Kit could hear the irony in his friend's voice but it was to be expected. Would their ruse work? He responded in like manner, knowing they were being watched.

'You really are leaving me, Tom?' He leaned on his 'brother's' breast. 'I'll not believe it, you'll be back.' He whispered.

He did not wait for Tom to answer but stepped away to stare out of the barred window and continued in hushed tones, as if day-dreaming. 'Maybe in another guise, another time, but we've been through too much together, lived too many lives, for you to just walk away and never be involved in another escapade again. I'm sorry it has to end this way, but do not believe you will leave me here forever.' He returned and hugged Tom tightly.

It was Tom who pulled away this time and backed off to the door.

'Kit, I'll remind you once again what Dr Dee said; we had to find the third man, born in the same year as you. We have done that, and so far as I'm concerned I've done as much as any man can for a friend.' He tapped on the door to be let out, watching for the door to be opened, to make good his escape. Did Kit suspect his real intentions? He called to the nun who stood outside who had not responded to his gentle tapping. Kit and Tom, sister and brother, had been allowed this one last time alone but Tom could feel eyes on his back, even as they talked. He was sure they were being watched by inquisitive eyes, if not by the Mother Superior, then by her spies. After his call, the nun immediately unlocked the door. It was obvious she had been standing to one side, perhaps with an ear pressed against the wall. She opened the door and led him through the cloisters to the exit.

As he reached the multi-chained door, that he knew would be barred as he left, he turned to see Kit standing, clothed in the dark robes of a novice nun, all finery stripped away, the two black boys standing either side. *They* wept and waved at him. Kit stood stiff, hands held demurely together, not even a slight rise of the hand to acknowledge his departure.

Tom gripped the great ring of the door, swung it open before the nun could do it, and with one final look at his friend, closed the door behind him. It clanged with a finality that made Tom's heart sink. Could he really leave Kit to the sterile life of a convent? A place where another man, ironically, might be in his element but for Kit would be pure torture – a hell on earth.

Tom thought of Gabriella waiting for him and continued his determined walking. All the resentments against his friend, all the risks Kit had taken, welled up to give Tom the justification he needed. Now he wanted Gabriella, like a great ache in the pit of his stomach. All he could think about was his future with her; long languid siestas in her arms, the laughter of a happy family at festivals, and the gurglings of their children, when they arrived. A settled life where he could study and smoke a pipe with friends in the cool of the evening as Gabriella hovered around them, offering sweetmeats or wine. He wanted sons to teach and care for.

The agreement with Kit was that he would take him to the convent, leave him there, and, a while later – a month or even two, certainly before she was forced to take her final vows – he would return and claim his 'sister', explaining that a relative was seriously ill and she was needed as a nurse.

But Tom had no intention of returning. Kit could go hang, or languish if that was a better way for a 'woman'. He should have died at Deptford. Tom remembered all those times he had let Kit run rings round him; he might now guess where Kit's writings ended up, back in England, but still he did not know *why*.

Tom had read the sonnets, which passed back and forth, he knew Kit's writing of old. Even now as he composed his speech to

249

Gabriella, it would end with 'Oh, come, lie with me and be my love'. Such magical words could sway his lady, he was sure, if she needed any more persuasion.

News from London, had reached them, but never of plays by Marlowe being performed. The rising star had been Shakespeare; all the talk was of Shakespeare and Tom wondered if Kit ever felt jealous or angry at this, for Kit had never had much respect for the country lad who lived on the edge of the players' troupes, begging for minor parts. Tom grinned; he didn't care what happened in England any more, he would never go back, he was sure he could woo Gabriella and he would find a teaching position in Padua.

He would leave Kit to play a waiting game. He found he was walking with a bounce in his step as he felt a great weight falling off him. He grinned even more; Kit would be hard tested with just waiting. How long would it take him to realise that Tom was not coming back? That he must eventually give up waiting; then what would he do? Kit was resourceful, devious, adept at talking his way out of situations as Tom well knew; he would find a way of leaving the convent without his help.

Thus Tom assuaged the small twinge of guilt. Kit officially had one bag of silver, but that was the rules of the Order; the money should be paid to the convent and personal funds not allowed except for a little pocket money. Tom knew that Kit also had the jewellery and some small items that he might be able to sell; he would be able to find money. And anyway, Tom reasoned, it was Kit's fault that they did not have much more than that between them; it was he who had insisted on the grand house in Venice and the purchase of the two slaves.

Tom continued to argue with himself, he was sure that Kit had another source of funds delivered to him by the mysterious Jewish messengers; something to do with that original venture of delivering the pirated gold to Antwerp. Kit would find a way, even in the convent.

Tom did not question the incongruity of a novice being in contact with Jews. It never crossed his mind that it would be impossible, even with the slaves, who would be allowed some freedom. Dromio and Antipholus would be able to run errands but would be monitored by the Mother Superior. He would not be entirely isolated from the world. Tom wondered as he made his way back to their lodgings for the last time where the funds had come from. He knew they had spent most of the horde they had been given by the Antwerp money merchant. Surely Kit could not have made money from his scribblings? He had no patron, not whilst they had been in Italy, Tom was sure.

His musings were cut short by the realisation that he was being followed. Out of the corner of his eye he saw his late night visitor hovering in a corner. Tom knew then that he had been correct to deliver Kit to the convent; the man had not believed his story. He was so obviously following Tom that he agreed with Kit; the Venetians made hopeless spies. Would he leave Tom alone, now he had seen him deliver his 'sister' into the hands of the convent? Tom hurried to the lodgings; he would close them down, and leave, to return to Padua. He quietly thanked Kit for choosing lodgings with more than one entrance. Even if the man had accomplices and he was followed to Padua, then he would see Tom settle down to a life with a local woman, not one of Venice; surely that would stop the spying? He would conjecture that Tom was relieved to be free of his sister, with his new responsibilities of a bride.

*   *   *   *   *

It had been three months, he had celebrated the complicated Mass and St Stephen's day in the convent and the days were lengthening and still no word. Kit kept to his cell, ignoring the giggling overtures of the younger nuns and the stern warnings of the older ones. After a while they left him alone and he was known as truly devout; always writing. The two black boys ran errands for him and the Mother Superior overlooked their comings and goings, believing that the worst they were buying for their owner was pen and paper.

'Be careful, boys, don't bring any money back; tell the

messengers that I will collect when I leave the convent'.

Antipholus and Dromio nodded as they took Kit's parcel.

'And tell Sister Conventua that it is my dirty washing you are taking to the laundry. I'm sure she will not expect me to do my own washing. She will not want to inspect it further.' He instructed as he wrapped his precious manuscripts carefully within bales of linen.

The twins grinned, bowed and scampered off. By now, they were objects of great admiration and fussing. Lace collars were always being tried on them; little seed cakes presented to them 'to try' and the cook always gave them the choicest cuts of meat. The boys loved the attention but stayed loyal to Kit. It was as if by cutting their chains and releasing them, he had bound them to him even more. One day in the garden Kit overheard one of the sauciest novices quiz Dromio; what was his mistress like, from where did she come? But Dromio said nothing. Kit watched him; he stood, his ebony face quite still, his hands by his side, and just looked at the girl in a sad way. Eventually the novice gave up. 'We know you are not dumb so you needn't pretend, but if you won't say then you won't and there's enough of it.'

At first Kit was patient, sure that Tom would keep his promise and not abandon him despite what he'd said. They had been through so much together that Kit could not believe that Tom would just walk away.

In the meantime he occupied himself in the garden of the convent, avoiding the other nuns by making friends with the old gardener, Anatello the older of the outside gardeners who carried out the heavy work the nuns could not do. He moved great composts of earth to where they directed, carried out winter pruning of the vines that curled and climbed around the cloisters, and stoically used an old plough to churn the solid earth. Usually Anatello avoided the nuns who could be coquettish and silly. He was a man of middle years and middle build. He always worked in yellow buckskin clothes, a wide-brimmed hat to hide his weather-beaten face from even more punishment from the hot sun, and thick heavy clogs. Kit would work alongside him in the herb garden, quietly and efficiently. Anatello had said one day, 'You're almost like a man the way you say nothing and concentrate on your job. I can see why you don't mix with the others.'

Kit smiled and carried on working, his face hidden by a similar wide-brimmed hat to the one that Anatello wore, but held on by a long scarf tied beneath his chin.

As they worked the old gardener started telling Kit about his family, how his wife dropped babes like a clumsy conjurer, and how they died soon after. 'Only one has survived, my son Anatellilo and he is now growing quickly into manhood.'

But as the winter turned to spring and the hard work of planting out was imminent, Tom could wait no longer. He sent Antipholus to find Tom in their lodgings on the Grand Canal. Kit had ended a great creative urge when he had written several complex plays. He was beginning to feel stifled, the food was boring, the warmth of the spring was making his skin prickle in the rough habit he wore and he realised he was now middle aged. How long had he to live? And would he ever see his plays being performed? He began to think of England, of the easy life of theatrical London compared to the ascetic life he had lived, for a short while, in his college at Cambridge, which even then had been more exotic than the life he lived here. He had plenty of time to think now, between the services and he wanted to know what was going on in the world. He waited anxiously for the boy to report back.

There was another problem. Soon his novitiate would end and he would be expected to take full vows, where the other nuns would dress him in the customary white and he would attend the service where his hair would be cut off. Such ministrations by the nuns would prove embarrassing. He had to avoid it.

Anthipholus returned with a furrowed forehead, the whites of his eyes hidden by the frown.

'What is it, little one?' Kit asked.

Antipholus shook his head. After a while, he sat on Kit's lap as if he wanted comfort. Eventually, in a whisper, he explained, 'The house is shuttered and the cook from next door came out as I banged and banged. He recognised me. He called, "Well met, young fellow. I never thought to see you again. All was sold and your master shipped himself off some time ago. We were told he put his sister in a nunnery. She deserved it, the wench, she was always giving herself airs and graces. We heard the house is to be let soon to others for the summer. So we know the other Signor will not be coming back.

"We wondered why he was doing all the hard work, closing down the house, instead of you two." Then he was horrible and said he guessed that me and my twin had proved unsatisfactory and you had sold us on. Or we had run away. He said you were a foolish northerner to unchain the likes of us.' Antipholus was weeping.

Kit stroked the close curls on his dark head and neck to comfort him. Stroking the boy also comforted himself. So it was true, Tom *had* abandoned him. He said nothing, thinking frantically. Tom had always threatened to leave, he was always complaining about Kit's actions.

It was the woman, he thought. He had taken Tom for granted, but had not foreseen that a woman would give Tom the strength to leave. What sort of life would he carve out for himself?

Kit shook himself. Why should he worry about that? He turned towards thoughts of his own predicament. How could he get out of this place? Could he continue as a woman without a chaperone? Perhaps he could send out messages to find Marshall, that old soldier, and ask to be rescued? He considered this, while all the time stroking Antipholus' wiry curls. No, that would be no good, Marshall would expect marriage. He guessed that Pyper and his charge had returned to England long since and anyway, they would be equally problematical. No, he would have to deal with this on his own. First he would have to be sure he could collect the money that had been sent from England for the plays.

'Antipholus, you are to go to the man who holds my money

and ask him…' But he stopped. He knew he could not allow any of the money to come into the convent, it would be sure to be found. And how then would he be able to go? It was not possible for him to tell the Mother Superior he was leaving, it would not be allowed without a family member to collect him. He needed someone to send for him. How could that be achieved? He knew both Dromio and Antipholus were watched and suspected that his cell was searched when he left it for services and meals. No, he would have to use some other means and leave the two boys to be innocent bystanders.

Anatello, he was the one Kit would have to approach.

He explained that he needed money and had jewels to sell. He could not trust them to his young slaves; would Anatello help him to sell them? Would he deal for him?

Anatello refused. 'Nay. I won't get mixed up in such matters.'

Kit persisted and one day Anatello softened. 'On Friday, instead of attending the special saint's mass, slip away from the others and meet me in the little court on the north side of St Raphael's Square. I will escort you to someone who can help, but I'll not be seen by the others to be involved in this intrigue. Once there you'll have to find your own way back. Do you think you can do that?'

Kit nodded, excited. Going to church was a great occasion. He had learned quickly how to genuflect and bow and sing like a devout novice, although he sung silently. During the week, the priest would come to the convent to attend a meal and give blessings but all the nuns attended church outside the environs of the convent for feast days. The nuns filed quickly across the square, with its usual fountain in the middle, and down a side road to reach the local church. They scurried, heads down, some lingering and smiling quietly at youths who lounged and made lewd remarks. The older nuns would be on the outside of the group, chivvying the novices along.

It would be easy for Kit to slip away; he was usually one of the last to join the group and the others largely ignored him, even the supervisors, for he was not considered at risk, being too studious to take any notice of the banter.

Friday came. It was late spring now and the sun was still low so that long shadows made cool areas in the squares and alleys as the nuns filed out and headed for the church. Kit hovered at the back, as usual. No note was made of him, for his character, Sister Catherina, as she had been christened in her new life, was known as a dreamer. The others hurried onwards as he drifted off to one side and left the square through a narrow alley where he could see the mustard yellow of Anatello's customary clothes. The gardener said nothing, but gestured to him to follow and they moved silently through narrow alleys. Kit realised after a while they were heading north east; he guessed to a place he had been to before. He remembered Val's visit to the Jews to lend money and realised this was probably the only place where he could sell his jewels secretly.

Eventually Anatello stopped before a bridge that led over a canal. On the other side of the canal were gates, open at present. Kit had been right; the Jewish ghetto.

'Over there, through that narrow archway, turn left, and look for the sign of Shylock, but be quick - you only have an hour 'til dusk.' Anatello pointed as he spoke and then took his hand off Kit's shoulder where it had unconsciously rested, and turned away before Kit could ask him for any more help.

As he left Anatello turned and said by way of explanation, 'It's Friday you see,' Kit remembered from his dealings with the messengers he had used throughout his travels; the Sabbath started on Friday as the sun went down. He sensed the urgency in his friend's voice and hurried across the rough wooden bridge, so unlike the large stone bridges over the Grand Canal. Here there was a tiredness, a closed-in feeling, a secretiveness, accentuated by the afternoon sun. It seemed even more oppressive when he remembered his fateful visit with Val, and the sword fight. He thanked his Christian god, in a kind of blessing that he did not really believe in, that, dressed as a woman, and a veiled nun at that, he had not been followed.

When Tom had left he'd watched from the grills; it was Tom they followed, not bothering about the poor 'sister' now tied to God and hidden from Society. Never would it occur to the spy that the new nun would find a way out. Or was anything but a woman.

He passed the close-fitting gates and into the alley that was truly dark because of the height of the buildings either side. None of the buildings facing onto the canal had jetties or doors for the taking in of goods and he wondered how the occupants of this area had their daily needs delivered. But he was through the dark opening now and into a large paved square. It was not the one he had visited with Val; he had entered further along the canal, but it was similar, with the familiar fountain in the middle. This time it did not have exotic lions' heads gushing water; it was very plain and no movement was to be seen, although the basin was full. All was quiet - there were no flocks of ladies parading or shops exhibiting their wares and flowing over into the walkways. No birds sang. The buildings on all sides were tall as if the owners could only build up and up. In other parts of Venice it was possible to come across small gardens and elegant walkways but here all was high plastered walls with no break except for shuttered windows. He looked up, trying to find the warmth of the sun, and saw a collection of strange shaped windows all joined together at the top of a storey. Where did he need to go?

'Can I help?'

The words were said so quietly that it was not until Kit turned to find a black-robed creature, with long beard and locks flowing from beneath his tricorn hat, that he knew someone had spoken. He had the air of a teacher, from the pile of books under his arm. A fellow academic Kit was sure. Then Kit pulled himself up short for the man kept a distance between them, and Kit realised the man saw him as a woman and would not get too close to a female.

He responded gratefully, 'Yes, I am looking for Shylock. I was told he might help me.'

The man's eyes hooded over, as if a woman who sought such a man was not to be trusted. Marlowe had seen the look before, and recognised it. A woman doing something they would not normally be expected to be doing. He looked down, at the ground and explained, 'I am in deep trouble through no fault of my own. I do not like doing what I must do.'

He could see the man relent. In the same quiet voice, he pointed.

'Over there, in the corner. The shutters are painted a darker colour - because he can afford new paint.'

And others can't. That was the implication. But Kit nodded by way of thanks and glided away, to indicate the embarrassment he imagined a woman would feel in such a situation.

He reached the door and turned round but the man had vanished, his steps making no noise. Kit could see no-one in the square, although he had the feeling that he was being watched even though all the buildings were shuttered. He knocked at the closed door of the place and waited. It was a long time before anything happened.

Marlowe was about to knock again when there was a noise of heavy bolts being scraped back. A heavily wrinkled face appeared, dark-rimmed eyes, a full-lipped mouth surrounded by a scrappy grey beard. The nose seemed to stand out as if it would smell Kit and his reason for being there. The eyes were what struck him; suspicious. He almost walked away. He reminded Kit of the eastern merchant in Florence. He would find the money somehow; he did not want to deal with this person, even to raise the funds to allow him to escape from the convent and get back to England.

Get back to England? He was surprised at the thought for, up to now, he had no thoughts to travel north. He sometimes daydreamed about England and his old life there but he had not formed a definite plan to return. So long as he enjoyed his work while he travelled, he had no plans except to hone his craft. His immediate aim was to escape from the nunnery and continue his travels. He would reserve consideration of the idea of England until later. He stepped back but the man was speaking now.

'Have you come with news for Shylock?'

'News? What of? I know you not, but, if you are Shylock, I would ask a boon of you.'

The man still stood, holding on to the door as if he would shut it quickly if something Kit said decided him.

'You, a nun, what would you want of Shylock but to tell him.'

As he spoke, he looked over Kit's shoulder and, without warning, opened the door, shot out a heavily robed but skinny arm and grabbed Kit's hand. With a movement that seemed too strong for an old man he pulled Kit into the house and slammed the door behind him.

'I'll not stand on my front door discussing family business. Go in. In there, my parlour.'

Inside it was so dark that Kit could make out very little. He obeyed the man's instructions and glided into a side room. He found himself in a cluttered space, the shutters pulled tight and the only light coming from a tallow candle on a large table in the middle. The candle sputtered and sent out a dark feather of smoke as the air from the opened door caught the flame. The smell of tallow lingered like the thin wisps of smoke. Surrounding the candle were parchments and writing materials. Shylock slid behind the table and gestured him to sit opposite.

'So, you have news of my daughter? Please?'

Kit decided to find out more and asked obliquely, 'What was the last you heard of her?'

The old man put his head in his hands and sighed. 'Only that she has left me for a gentile and I am bereft. Woe is me, my only child. I loved her and she betrayed me.' He did not look up.

Kit could not help feeling sorry for him.

'And why should you think I have news?'

'The young man who took her, I would not trust him. I can only hope my child has been helped by your kind.'

'Sad to say, sir, I know nothing of this, but, I believe you help people – financially?'

'Help people?' He spoke softly, without interest. He continued, 'I did not think such as you want *help*…you are more likely to give help than take help. Like my child? Have you helped my Jessica.'

He paused, eyeing Kit with a dim look of hope. '

'I repeat, I know nothing of your daughter Jessica.'

Shylock stood up, leaning heavily on the table.

'Get out. Get out if you come here to mock me. None of your kind would even deign to look at my type in the street, but you and your kind seduce my daughter and carry her away and lock her up so she is dead to her father. And now you think I can help *you*. You mock me.'

He sat down and rocked, once again holding his head in his hands.

Kit thought rapidly. The man was obviously demented at the loss of a daughter; could Kit make use of this for his own ends?

He had worked with many Jewish messengers to keep in touch with his colleagues over the continent and had learned to respect their discretion, the way they lost themselves in the streets of great towns but could always be found if needed. He knew that they were forced into the trade of money lending, as he had used them himself in his early career. He also knew they were usually honourable in their dealings, so long as they were treated fairly. They dealt with kings and great dukes and had access to great secrets and because of this Kit felt a kinship with them, as they helped him in his work.

Very few of them would convert, even when threatened with death. He had respected that. He knew some of them gave lip service to the prevailing religion of the place they lived in; Protestant in the northern lands, Catholic in Italy, Spain, and Portugal, but Kit also knew they carried their prayer shawls hidden in their robes, their Talmud ready to be read in secret.

Now here was a man who was alone and had been treated badly if what he said was true.

'I will find your daughter if you help me. I am but a poor nun but we do hear of others in other convents from time to time.'

'How do you hear? Behind bars, locked away?'

'But it is not always like that. The other nuns have visitors, men who come to admire them; the men think it great sport to visit nunneries. I will ask…but you must help me in exchange.'

Shylock was silent for a while and Kit could see his face fall into repose, as he considered Kit, who tucked his hands into the sleeves of his habit and looked down, so that most of his face was hidden. He doubted that in the soft light of the single candle, even detailed study of him would reveal the real truth.

'Very well. I will expect you to find her or let me know of her…now what do you want?'

'I need to know where your messengers are in this town, I have use of them.'

'Messengers? I know nothing of messengers. I deal in loans. If you have security. Or exchange of information, information of my daughter. That is worth more than trinkets as security.'

'Look, I know there are messengers. If I give you the name of Robstein of Antwerp?'

Shylock lent back then, and eyed him, his head on one side.

'Robstein? You know Robstein?'

He stopped talking and played with the papers before him. Kit watched him but could make nothing of his face. It was a blank, all the look of loss gone as he reflected on what he had been told. There was a long silence. Kit waited, the candle burnt down a thumbnail's length and was flickering, as if there was silent argument going on between their two breaths.

Eventually the Jew sighed deeply and spoke as if he were a teacher.

'You know, there are many types of Jew. We were dispersed, some to the Far East; some travelled west, trying to keep ahead of the persecutions. I know some who have taken their wares to the new lands across the ocean, risking their lives with the Spanish or English in the new colonies. We are not all alike. My forebears came from the east, after Constantinople fell; they helped the Venetians with trading. That is why some of us are left in peace in this great city.

'We know of the other tribes but we do not mix and, indeed, I

261

would say that Robstein is not well liked here; his power spreads too far. Our trading in Venice is small. Even so, Robstein uses his great influence to stop us…so my young pleader, it means nothing to me, that you know such a one. I cannot help you.'

Kit was devastated. How was he to find the messengers? Dromio and Antipholus were always told to use different houses, or meet men in the streets, in taverns, now that he could not risk *them* visiting him. How was he to find them? And get his money? He tried another tack, 'I have jewellery to sell…I have to raise money for a sick relative…'

He pulled out the bundle he had hidden beneath his robes and opened the string, pouring out the pearls and the butterflies that had once adorned his coiffure.

Shylock lent forwardly eagerly. This was something that interested him. He studied them, rolling the pearls between fingers and biting them between crooked teeth. He shook his head, ´Nay, these are of no use to me, it is what they call paste. What else do you have?'

Kit thought of the jewelled missal, in Latin, a rare hand-painted book of hours that he had found on a stall, in a market in Padua. Now that most books were printed, even Bibles, many people considered old vellum books worthless. But Kit knew enough about Jews to know they valued books and learning above other worldly goods; would Shylock be the same?

He slowly produced the manuscript from his pocket in his habit, and laid it on top of the jewels.

'I will ask that you take this as a pledge. It is my most precious possession, and I would return to claim it if I can raise the money.'

Shylock's face lit up involuntarily before he quickly recovered. He stared at the book and then up at Kit. The greed in his eyes said all.

'Yes, I can see this is your most precious item, especially for a nun.'

He offered a price that was a quarter of what Kit had expected to receive. Kit refused and they bargained, a ducat at a time.

Eventually Kit exchanged the few jewels that Tom had bought for him to impress Venetian society, the missal and some lace for enough gold coin to get him back to England. Kit knew he was being given much less than the items were worth, even after the bartering, but had to take it, aware that he would not be able to deal anywhere else.

In addition to the low price, Shylock made him sign a pledge that he would also find Jessica, or at least news of her, and return for his goods within three months or forfeit the same. It was not until Kit had watched him write out the pledge and he had signed it that Shylock handed over the gold. Kit hurried away. As he left as fast as would be expected for a nun, ideas mingled and he knew he would write about the man.

He smiled to himself. Shylock would never find the nun he had bargained with. But Kit would fulfill his side of the bargain by making sure Jessica lived, even in a fictional sense.

* * * * *

'I have received this missive from my family and must away for a while. I would seek your permission to leave the Convent.'

Mother Superior took the note from the strange Sister Catherina, as if it was tainted. She was a small woman by any standards but Kit towered above her; another reason why he had been shunned by the other sisters. She held a delicate lace handkerchief to her nose as she read, and Kit noted that it matched the lace that peeped from the cuffs of her habit and at her neck. Her wimple was also edged with delicate lace. He watched her as she read, her lips moving slightly and a frown developing on her forehead as she wrestled with the handwriting. Kit held his breath, hoping she would not guess he had worked on the note the night before by the light of his candle as others slept. It informed him (as Novice sister Catherina) that his dear father was ailing and *she* was so desperately needed to nurse him and other members of the family who suffered. Plague was rife and she must come. Kit had worked on the letter as if it was a play to be sold; he could imagine the playgoers at the Rose weeping through sympathy with the poor nun who had to give up her vows, so unwillingly, to help her family.

Mother Superior looked serious and dropped the paper, as if it too, held the plague.

'It is not good that you should leave now you have nearly finished your novitiate. You must promise to obey your vows, even though you are still a novice.'

She was going to let him go. He knew why; she was scared, like most, of the plague and would want him, and his letter, which might be tainted, to leave, and quickly. Kit kept his head bowed, as she looked up at him. She seemed to soften then. 'Of course, you must go, dear girl. It will be a test for you. You must keep yourself pure, but you have been quiet and good here, unlike some of the other flighty girls. Will you be safe travelling with your two servant-boys?' She turned and threw the parchment onto the fire that blazed in her room, another luxury like the lace that belied her dedication to her vows of chastity. Kit thought for a moment that she would open her money box and offer him some gold to use for his journey, but she returned to him and patted him on the shoulder, an odd gesture for she almost had to tiptoe:

'It is a long journey, I understand, to the very ends of the earth. You will come back? I will keep the dowry that was left for you to ensure your good welcome on your return. I see that there is money in this letter, for your passage, but no luxuries.'

She handed over the meager coin that Kit had included in the packet.

Kit considered protesting, but he was so pleased that she had accepted his forgery of a letter he would put no barriers in the way. Indeed if he insisted on the money, not only would it be unfeminine but would certainly indicate that his intention was not to return. She could not know of the Jew's money hidden in his habit. He bent and kissed the large ring of office on her hand and scurried away in as dignified a manner as possible. He reached his cell to find Antipholus and Dromio packing. They said nothing; he nodded and they continued.

'I will say farewell to my dear friend Anatello…'

He found the gardener working, as usual, in the vegetable garden. The path was of gravel and the gardener heard him approaching and looked up. He stopped working, bent his back to ease it and leant on his spade

'I have to go, Anatello, to help my family…'

'And you will not return.'

It was a flat statement. Kit stared at the man, and realised that, although others might just see a gardener, behind the peasant garb, was a perceptive and intelligent person. Kit did not hesitate. He answered quietly.

'No, I'll not return. But, Anatello, I thank you from the bottom of my heart for your friendship; whatever happens, I will remember that.'

Anatello nodded and turned back to his digging. 'Sad, I had hoped you would be a good wife to my Anatellilo. You may be a little older than a maid, but you are sensible and strong. He needs someone like that and you are not made for a nun; you would make a good sensible wife.'

Kit turned away grinning. Even such as Anatello had not seen through his guise; again he relished the fact that he had succeeded in becoming a true woman.

But now he was curious about England. The thoughts he had had when he was with Shylock resurfaced. News had reached Italy that the old Queen was dead and the Scottish James was now on the throne. Kit felt satisfied and excited about that, remembering his secret trip to Scotland all those years ago. So Burleigh's plans had ripened, but not without help from a many others, as Kit knew.

It was time to claim his inheritance.

Chapter Twenty-three

'You what? You have abandoned Kit?'

'No, he is in a nunnery, quite safe.' Tom was squirming under Galileo's angry gaze which was so much of a surprise when all he'd expected was grateful thanks for Marina's jewels.

'Quite safe? Do you understand what you have done, young man? You have ruined the plans of many across Europe, so well laid for these long years.'

Tom sat down, and looked at the tutor as he paced up and down, ignoring the basket, which he skirted around as he walked. He answered the man quite calmly, confident in his future and freed of Kit's influence at last, 'I have travelled with Kit Marlowe for many years and he never told me what he planned, or why he did what he did. I need to know. Now you say I have ruined his plans. What are they? Will you tell me?'

Galileo stopped his pacing and came close, so close that Tom could see the individual grey hairs in his beard. They eyed each other and neither said anything. Then the professor stepped away.

'It is only fair that you know, now we are so close to achieving our aim. Have a glass of wine before I tell you all.'

He poured out the drink, and handed it to Tom. 'Perhaps you are right, perhaps Kit's usefulness is at an end. He was always a risk, but the benefits far outweighed that. Now I have another, William Harvey, who may be able to complete the task.'

Tom stood up, putting the beaker down heavily on the table.

'Now you speak in riddles. Just like Kit. I'm sorry, I'll have none of this, I must go if you won't tell me straight. I've done what I promised.'

'No, wait. You deserve to be told, after all your pains.'

'Well?'

Galileo stroked his beard and looked at Tom, appraising him, and Tom realised he was working out whether Tom could be discreet.

'Let me tell you, Galileo, I have met a woman, here in Padua, and would settle down. All I ask for is a post at the university and to live a quiet life surrounded by my family.'

Galileo nodded. 'Yes, I can see that, and of course I will try to help you in that. So, I will tell.'

He took a deep breath.

'You know that Kit travelled to Scotland?'

'I had a hint of it.'

'As early as that, Kit was working to continue the Protestant kingdom. Do you know that the Scottish king, who now sits on the English throne, has a daughter who is soon to become the Queen of Bohemia? All Protestants of course, these people.'

'Well, what of it?'

'Has it not occurred to you that a peaceful succession to the throne of England was surprising? Why did not the people rebel or question it?'

'I have no idea. I haven't been in the country these long years.'

Galileo leaned forward. He whispered, 'Because the people have been encouraged, through culture, *through plays* to be prepared for it. *That was Kit's job.* To write plays. If you see his plays now, you will interpret them differently, you will see the magic lines now I have told you. But he also influenced others across Europe, working his diplomacy amongst the Protestant elements, persuading certain royal families to join with others.'

'So why are you involved? It still doesn't make sense.'

'Ah, my job is to teach rationality, to show that we are on a circular world. Soon I will be challenged by the Catholic Church; I have planned it so. And my rational answers will echo around the world, and all the peoples will talk about what I have discovered and, once they are all talking, I will not mind what happens to me.'

'But why you three? And who is William Harvey?'

'You met Dr Dee?'

'You know I did, I am sure.'

'He saw all in the stars, a rapid changing in the world but the change needed like-minded men to get together – he saw the year when the important men would be born, 1564, but had to work to get us to meet. Kit brought the tele-scope so I could see more and thus develop my theories. Printing is now so easy so that our knowledge can be known to all men. As an astronomer I see progress in centuries, and my colleagues and I work towards a logical future. It will come to fruition and in the meantime our diplomats work on the kings and queens who all believe they are reigning supremely. Little do they know they are but pawns in our aim. Even those Spanish kings who intermarry, and breed idiots, and rule badly so that the Dutch rebel.'

'So what happens now?'

'I need someone to continue the work in England, to keep the pot boiling so to speak and I have one here that I can train, and am sure he will be willing.'

Tom remembered the name. 'William Harvey?'

'Indeed, yes, he is young but he reminds me of reports of Kit when he was young; an enquiring mind, willing to take risks. Even now he undertakes secret anatomy research, looking at how blood flows. If he were caught, he could be condemned but his enquiring mind puts such thoughts aside. Like me, *he has to know.* He is well connected and we will ensure he returns to England and finds a place in the King's Household.'

'We?'

'Indeed, there is a large organisation working towards our aim; to make men see clearly; a future age of enlightenment if you like. Some who help us know exactly what we aim for. Some, like you, are not aware of how you help, but I am telling you this, Tom, because of your loyalty and assistance to Kit these past years.'

'So, what about Kit?'

'If we need him we will go and get him. Finish your wine, and go to your lady, now you know all.' It was said kindly and Tom remembered that Galileo had his lady now, and would understand

Tom's need.

He stood up, feeling he was dismissed, but he shook hands with Galileo in a gesture of thanks for the explanation and left.

But as he walked down the stairs he paused, and retraced his steps and went back to Galileo who was picking over papers.

'Wait, there are other matters I would ask you.'

Galileo looked up slowly. 'Well?'

It was not said unkindly and Tom sat down again where he had sat before. He put his hands on his knees and asked, 'The priest, in Reims, do you know about that? What was that all about?'

Galileo smiled a rare smile. 'Ah, Yes, I heard.' He picked up a paper as if to read from it but looked at Tom, again assessing him.

'That priest knew too much, he was dangerous. He had got into the inner circle and knew exactly what Kit was involved in, so he had to be stopped. After that debacle in the church, he was defrocked and nobody in the Catholic Church would listen to him anymore. He died a broken man, in a hospital run by the Franciscans. Sad, but necessary.'

'And Rome?'

Galileo hesitated. 'Rome was one of Kit's diversions I'm sorry to say, and we really did have to get you both away. That's why Dr Dee made himself known.'

Tom nodded. It made sense. He said nothing for a while. He suddenly felt deflated, and knew that his job was done.

'Thank you for being so open with me. I hope to meet you, Galileo, as a fellow academic but I'll never refer to any of this again.' He looked at the great man. 'I'm tired of it all. I am, after all, just an ordinary man.'

Galileo came over to him then and took his arm, as if to help him up and Tom stood. They eyed each other and Galileo's look was kind.

'No, Tom, you are not *just* an ordinary man. For a start, no-one is just ordinary, all have their special place, even the lowliest servant. You have been patient and loyal and one day you might know how important such people as you are to the great movement of time and development of mankind.'

Those words buzzed in Tom's head as he walked away from the house. He strode through the narrow streets of Padua in a daze, trying to absorb what he had been told. Could there really be a worldwide conspiracy to make the world Protestant? No, that was not what Galileo had said; it was something about enlightenment, as if no worship would be of use. But would it ever come to pass? He could never know. He admitted he did not care. All he wanted was to live a life like others, to have children, to eat and drink with his wife and have a worthwhile career. As he reached his love's area, somehow he felt the past fading and anticipation of the future made him walk faster.

Chapter Twenty-four

England. 1609.

'Shakespeare, here, I need words with you.'

Shakespeare was striding through Southwark High Street, confident in his new clothes and with an authoritative staff in his hand, when he heard his name called.

The voice was croaked and hesitant, although the words were clear enough. Until he turned to see who had called him he could not tell whether he was being called by a man or a woman.

What he saw filled him with surprise. At first he was inclined to go on his way, supposing the woman to be a prostitute who had heard his name and thought to take advantage of the knowledge. A common enough ploy. He was not unknown in these parts.

But something about the creature made him look closer. The woman's appearance was not that of a street-woman. The clothes were exotically foreign, and the creature was unusually tall, and surely the lustrous hair must be a wig, of such crudeness it could only have come from a props cupboard, and the white powdered face was a parody of the old queen. Too richly dressed to be a beggar, the clothes were somehow too garish to be that of a lady.

He was inclined to stride on but something made him stop, and approach the apparition. He moved slowly, reluctantly. When he was closer, he saw that the rich clothes were grubby, torn at the hem; some of the lace at the cuffs was ragged. He shrugged, what was he doing? He turned and started to walk away but the crone followed. Shakespeare lengthened his pace. She too strode out and he could hear her breath coming heavily.

'Wait, I *must* speak with you.' The voice was now a croaked whisper but nonetheless it carried to him. *Like a good actor.* She was

271

trying to keep up with his strides but could not. Her skirts kept catching between her legs and she would stop and untangle them and scurry to catch him up. Shakespeare could see that the creature chasing him had caught the attention of passersby. Eventually he stopped and turned in exasperation.

'What do you want, hag?'

'I would have words with you, from a dark lady to a gentleman…'

That stopped Shakespeare in his tracks. He stared. The words resonated down the years; the sonnets, the plays, the magic words before him that he had turned to gold. All his London confidence disappeared; for the first time he remembered his origins. He remembered his first hesitant treading of the boards, his first excitement at reciting the words of the well-known playwright, his thrill at meeting the creator of those words, and then the tremors that had engulfed him when he had agreed to take part in a conspiracy.

All show now disappeared. He felt middle-aged, spent. The stranger watched the transformation with a malevolence. *He knew he had been found at last – found by the only person who could take away all that he had acquired.*

Christopher Marlowe, the writer of the plays William Shakespeare had claimed as his own.

'Ah – ha, so now you are going to listen to me. Where do we go?'

Shakespeare could see his ever-growing fame, wealth and status disappearing. His shoulders sagged. His first thought was to run away but he knew his challenger would find him. Shakespeare was well known in these fleshpot areas outside the city. Even in London town across the river, with its many crammed streets and multitudinous population, he could not escape.

He imagined those cumbersome skirts being lifted up, as his assailant tried to run after him; ugly, stocking-less, hairy legs being revealed perhaps; people wondering, pointing and laughing.

He nodded. 'Follow me, we cannot speak in the street.'

By this time a few boys had gathered and were staring at the well-known playwright and his peculiar companion. Workmen on their way to their mid-morning ale pushed by urgently; some women in groups, watching their lads squabbling became interested in the confrontation between the well-dressed jaunty gentleman and the scruffy old woman and started to wander towards them, curious.

Shakespeare strode off and did not wait to see if he was being followed. He led them through the market, dodging rotting cabbages which sent up a poisonous smell. Kit mimicked Will's skip and little run, keeping step with him. Will gathered pace, not caring now, fear giving him energy. He strode across the wooden bridge that had been erected across the Thames to give access to the new bear-baiting halls and theatres on the south side of the river for the City dwellers on the north side. Then they were in the City, passing some of its many churches, until they reached Cripplegate, where Shakespeare's house lay under the eaves of St Paul's.

So, thought Kit, he hasn't far to go to the publishers, to bicker and barter to see his words in print. Shakespeare slowed as he reached his lodgings. Kit saw him pause before a large terrace house in a newly built road, the white plaster between the timbers glistening in its newness. So he must be truly wealthy if he owned this. Kit remembered this place as spare burial ground around the great St Paul's. So the City's populace had swollen even more than when he had lived there.

Shakespeare said nothing as he ushered his guest into the house, looking around to make sure neighbours did not see. Inside, he led Kit into the front parlour, with its newly cut glass windows and panelling.

'Wait here, I'll get us some ale.'

He did not listen for an answer but shut the door behind him. He found Nell, his housekeeper and sometimes mistress, and asked for two tankards and a jug of her best.

'I have an important guest; don't disturb us, will you, dear

273

Nell?'

She tossed her heavy curls and moved away as he attempted to stroke her buttocks, her bulky frame not quite touching the kitchen table as she moved around the small scullery. She scooped the jug into the barrel and placed the brimming vessel on a tray without wiping it, leaving damp slops on the tray, collected two tankards off their hooks, her grubby finger and thumb gripping them inside as she swung them onto the tray. She handed this across the table to him and shrugged; she was used to his secret ways. A Londoner herself, she really despised this countryman who wheeled and dealt in words, but his obvious wealth made her stay, for the time being.

When he returned to the room his guest had made himself comfortable in the most luxurious chair, a heavy wooden upright with a red velvet seat. Dirty shoes rested on the opposite chair. Will could see now that the heels were worn down and there were small holes in each of the soles.

'Please, remove your shoes, you could have dog shit or spittle on them; they are expensive chairs.'

Shakespeare pushed the feet off the seat as he passed, and brushed the crushed-down velvet with his hand, as he placed the tray on the table, moving some papers as he did so. He did not pour at first but turned and leant against the table surveying the female form before him.

'Well, Kit, 'tis really you. I thought you had died of the plague these months back when no words came. I was about to close up shop and return to Stratford, for my ideas have dried up recently...'

Kit tensed but did not rise to the bait. Instead he baited back. 'Yes, you would make a good alderman, a big fish in a little pond, being spoon-fed from others. But now, now is my reckoning, not that stupid event at Mistress Bull's house all those years ago; it is time. I will have my dues. For many months now I have had no delivery of funds.'

'Because I did not know where to send them; as I said, I thought you dead these many moons.'

'So, I will have the money I am due. Now.'

'What do you mean? Just because you have helped me twist lines in a few scenes…'

This time Kit did rise, and thrust his painted face before Will's. He kept his voice menacingly low. 'twist lines in a few scenes? I have been to the playhouse, Will, I have been watching all those plays that have been performed. I have heard how you let them publish *your* plays; even using your friend Field from Stratford; I have watched these few months as you strut and preen yourself before the players and suck up to the King's Men and the others. It makes me sick.'

Kit reached for the jug and poured himself a healthy measure and slurped a mouthful.

'Twist lines in a few scenes? I *wrote every line,* and you know it!'

He waved his wine around, noting Will's worried face.

'And besides, you have not kept faith with what was planned. You have made yourself rich…All you are concerned about is whether I stain your precious carpet.'

'But I did make sure your plays were performed, sometimes at danger to myself. The queen did not like your Scottish play you know, that was a low point.'

'You are just a country bumpkin! I realise that now. But the time comes when our work will be done, and I will not need you.'

Will turned away, hiding the panic he felt, picking up a quill which was on the desk under the window and playing with it, as if he would start writing the plays that Kit was now referring to. Kit noticed that the quill was unused, no ink staining the sharp nib.

When he spoke, Will sounded sulky, 'It was Richard Field who suggested we publish the sonnets; to gain some recognition, otherwise the great ones would not have come to the plays.'

'Don't go off the point, Will; I want my just rewards for all the hard work.'

He held his tankard as if he would throw it over Will but stopped and took another draft of the ale and slammed the empty tankard onto the table so that the funnel of quills and piles of papers on the table shook. Then he continued bitterly, 'In every line, I see my work; in every line I remember how I stared out of strange windows and dreamt and then, when the muse came, how I scribbled. How I plotted and planned to send my plays to you. I never even let Priedeux, my dear friend, know what I was up to, for I feared it would give him sleepless nights. Every word of the plays was written by me – not one amendment by you.'

'But I sent money, Kit, you know that. I haven't deprived you.'

'Nay, but you have stolen my fame. The fame that should be mine.'

Will smiled then, relaxing. 'But it cannot be, can it? You are dead. If you tell men now that you are the great playwright Marlowe, what do you think they will say? You will be laughed out of town, or locked up as a mad woman.'

He was confident now. By the look of him, Kit was impoverished. Surely he had just returned to re-establish the links which had been broken somehow? Then he would be on his way, and the old relationship could continue. Will was being pushed for another play. It was high time that they established the old pattern.

He turned back to the tray, taking Kit's tankard from his hand without asking, and poured two more drafts of ale. 'Come, drink with me and we can talk, you are not going to get anywhere arguing.'

Kit took the frothing tankard, and fell back into his chair. They both took great drafts and eyed each other.

'And anyway Kit, I heard you upset too many people before you disappeared. Ralegh is still strong; he came looking, you know, did not really believe you were dead. He quizzed me once, said my plays were so much like yours. I was hard put to dissuade him.'

'Aye, he suspected me, I know that, but it wasn't him I was watching. I had a job to do, Will and I carried it out, but afterwards I believe Walsingham thought I was too dangerous. I know I spoke rashly but it was my cover. They told me to act the loudmouth and when I did they betrayed me.'

'They?'

'The Queen's secret men. They were working behind her back for years to make sure the succession was smooth. I travelled to Scotland, just the once, but it was enough. Perhaps I can claim my reward from the new King.'

They carried on drinking. Kit thought it best to leave Will in the dark of the far greater aim of his life. After all, he would be betraying many across the continent. Having met Will again he could see he was debased coin; the fame had gone to his belly and now he reminded Kit of Tom; a man with a family, who thought of worldly wealth and not of greater things.

It was Will who broke the silence:

'You make a good woman, Kit, I was hard put to it to see through…'

'I know, and I must remain so…but we must discuss how I live now, Will. I have no money left. Tom Priedeux abandoned me. I do not blame him. I am older and wiser now and know I treated him badly. I had to pawn the last few things I had to get here. And I won't tell you of the hardships of the journey which has taken many months. It is not easy travelling as an old woman alone, without a chaperone. I need lodgings, a good bed, and a place to write.'

Will stood and turned to the window to disguise the grin on his face. He realised from the way Kit had spoken that he would always need to write, he couldn't stop. Hel also realised that Kit could not live independently as a woman and would need help. He couldn't live as a man; there were many still alive who might recognise him.

'You can stay here. It is my house.' Will could not stop himself. He was prone to boast. When he had said he was about to go back to Stratford, it was not untrue. He knew from his wife Anne that his fame had spread to the small town, made rich by wool, where he had been born. His father had died a few years ago and all the estate was now settled; his eldest daughter had an admirer, so

Anne said; he should return. If he went back, she'd already assured him, he would be revered. There was a large house in the middle of the High Street that awaited him; he had purchased it some years ago and he could well afford to retire. He was tired of London and persuading others of how the plays worked. It had not been easy; when the producers had suggested a new scene, a funny interlude, he had had to procrastinate, disappear back to Warwickshire, until Kit's parcels had arrived. Kit had jumped up, though, at his words.

'Your house? Indeed you must be wealthy. I heard you had a share in the Globe as well, or was that just gossip? Sending me the odd bag of silver was like sending crumbs?'

Will squirmed and stroked the heavy brocade curtains that hung either side of the window. 'It wasn't like that, Kit. It was difficult to find messengers at first. Then to visit the Jews was quite difficult. They live secretly you know and there have been riots against immigrants; you know that…'

'Oh the Dutch in the City and that silly poem. Nothing to do with me Will.'

Kit stopped. He had almost forgotten about that; it had been the catalyst that had led to his initial arrest and interrogation. It all seemed so many years ago now. He'd managed to get away that time but knew his luck could not last. And now the years in between, and all the plays he had written. And all the plays he still had in him.

'I want to get back to work. I think I would like this house. I have two servants who can help me. Show me your quarters.'

'Kit, it would not be advisable…' he hesitated. 'I have domestic arrangements, you understand. I can let you have the back quarters.'

'Oh, no, Will I know too well what they are like. I insist on having the best, as you know.'

'I cannot agree to that. It is not just me…there are other considerations.'

Kit grinned. 'You also were a bit of a philanderer. Got yourself

278

a convenient housekeeper here, have you?'

Will squirmed at Kit's direct hit.

'Indeed, she is convenient. But a gossip and a shrew. I will need to dispense with her services; can you shift for yourself until then? Give me a day or two.'

'Indeed, but I insist you show me your quarters now, it would be most interesting.'

His host shook his head.

'It's not easy at present, I say, until I dispense with…'

Kit wheedled and cajoled and eventually Will gave in. He opened the door and looked out carefully. He could hear Nell bustling around in the kitchen and realised how much noise she made. She was a common enough wench, good in bed, but dispensable. He would rid himself of her, it was necessary in order to hide the secret of the connection between him and Marlowe. He moved to the bottom of the stairs and gestured to Kit who followed. The stairs did not creak as they climbed them; a woodworker would approve, noting they were well-made.

'This is Nell's room.' Shakespeare hoped to confound Kit with the insignificance of the rooms; perhaps he wouldn't notice the large door at the end of the corridor that led into the master bedroom, perhaps he could pass this off as a cupboard. He moved on. 'This is the second room where I sometimes sleep.' Even now he could not find himself to lie.

Kit grinned; he had spotted the layout of the house and realised there was a large room at the front, above the parlour where they had been drinking and he had also noted Will's discomfiture as they faced the last large door in this corridor, albeit in the gloom of an unwindowed passage. Shakespeare was always a second rate actor, he did not have Marlowe's penchant for dissembling.

'And that room there' he pointed. 'Is that where you *normally* sleep, with or without strumpet Nell?'

Will moved from foot to foot, not knowing how to react at being found out.

'Come, Will, be not embarrassed, show me your best room. I

have two boys, slaves who I freed and are now most loyal servants. They need beds and a good home. They are still with me. Indeed they refuse to leave me, no matter that I travel to ever colder climes than they are used to. They would welcome the two rooms you have so far shown me as theirs. I would need something much more sumptuous.'

'Kit, you always were the very Devil's man for comfort, always liking the best – that's what got you into trouble in the first place let me remind you. Very well, I'll reveal to you my pride and joy.'

He unlocked the door with a great key he pulled from a slit in his doublet. As the door opened with a slight creak, he stood back and allowed Kit to enter first, as if he acknowledged his prior right to the riches inside, or, more likely, in pride at the manifestation of his own wealth. Kit stepped through the carved doorway. He paused, looked around the room and for the first time was speechless at what he saw. The room was not overly large; he had seen more splendid sized rooms, but its rich hangings of Brussels tapestries hiding most of the oak panelling – which Kit could see was well polished and well carved - the sculptured plaster on the ceiling with its coat of arms interspersed in square patterns, its burnished wood furniture and the cast iron moulded fireplace – Kit recognised the scene, Diana the huntress shooting the moon – all highly polished, all this demonstrated such wealth as only a lord or duke would have. *How rich was William Shakespeare?* Good wax candles in their sconces, a heavy table beneath the leaded window, with its papers, almost a mirror image of what Kit had created in his many homes since he had left England. The bed itself was the great centrepiece; with its coverlets and posters and curtains and wonderful carved balusters.

Kit stared at it, and turned to Will. 'I would insist on what is evidently your best bed; I'll hazard it has fine covers and a good bolster.'

Will said nothing, he would think of something. 'Please, why don't you sleep here tonight? Stay awhile to savour what you claim is yours.'

Epilogue

So here I sit, having at last discarded my women's robes and hidden now beneath a great beard, snowed by the years of bitterness...I am writing although it is hard with my crabbed hands and bad sight. I am, at the last, fulfilling my promise to Oresorp, now I am old enough to understand his wisdom and frustration at losing his powers. I feel that I too will lose the power to write, with these stiff hands and dulling eyes. I have had the last laugh on those islanders of dreams however. For I have reversed all of them; he is named Prospero, Leira: Ariel and Nabilac, I will call Caliban.

I feel my powers waning....Now my charms are all o'erthrown and what strength I have's mine own, which is most faint......'

* * * * *

Shakespeare entered the room quietly and saw that Kit had fallen asleep over his quill which was all broken, the ink spattered on the words which trailed off. He approached him carefully even though he knew Kit would not wake up from the drug-induced sleep from the wine he had drunk. They had both grown old and intolerant of wine, even if it was not tainted with poison. Will read the pages scattered about. A new play, almost complete, *The Tempest*. He quickly gathered up the sheets and stuffed them into his pockets. He could sort them later. He had got rid of Nell some time ago and he and Kit shared the house. Tonight, apart from the sleeping Kit, Will had the house to himself, suggesting to Kit's two young servants that they have an evening to themselves and giving them money for the bear-baiting.

He'd spent some time working out what he would do and, one day at rehearsals, when there had been a dangerous blaze that had spread fast from a fire scene, it had come to him.

Now he held a flare in his hand. Still he hesitated. Could he really destroy this room that he loved? The best bed? But the danger from Kit being discovered, would mean he could lose all in any event. Yes, he loved it all, the adulation, the fame, what this room represented, with all its wealth, but it had to be sacrificed. He could not afford to have Kit so close to him for surely their secret would be discovered. He wanted his fame to last into eternity: William Shakespeare the great playwright.

He would not put it past Kit to effect some wondrous return and he would be shamed before the whole world. If he gave up now and returned to Stratford to live with Anne, he had enough money to retire and his fame would endure. She could look after the aches and pains that had been growing on him with age. He had respect, wealth and other properties and he would not have to worry about producing more plays. There would one more, *The Tempest*, and all would be ended.

Fires in these new wood timbered houses were frequent, another would not be remarked on and, if he were lucky, neighbours would help to put out the fire before the whole house was consumed. It was, he thought, a quiet damp night so the flames would not spread rapidly. Except that his guest would unfortunately die in the conflagration, his body so roasted no-one would recognise him.

As he torched the bed hangings, and Kit's clothes, one last thought came to him. It was a shame that he would only be able to leave his second best bed to his wife in his will.

Also available from Goldenford

Esmé Ashford - *On the Edge*

Tramps with bad feet, a sheep rustler, a busker invited to dinner; a weird monster who devours a nasty husband and a child who learns from a visit to the fun fair; limericks and blank verse; it is all here.

Irene Black – *The Moon's Complexion*

Bangalore, India 1991. Ashok Rao, a young Indian doctor, has returned home from England to choose a bride. But who is the intriguing Englishwoman who seeks him out? Why is she afraid and what is the secret that binds them together?

The lives of two strangers are turned upside down when they meet and the past comes to haunt them. *The Moon's Complexion* is a tale of love across cultural boundaries. It is also a breath-taking thriller played out in the mystical lands of Southern India and Sri Lanka and in the icy countryside of winter England.

Irene Black – *Darshan: a journey*

The year 1999 is drawing to a close and the advent of the new millennium harbours danger, even in Oxford, that most English of cities, where a naïve but spirited Indian student sets out on a physical and emotional quest to reassert her British identity. She is determined to find her estranged Welsh father and to escape the prospect of a safe but passionless arranged marriage in India.

Her turbulent journey takes her through three continents via a morass of perilous affiliations, betrayal and heartbreak before coming to a momentous conclusion.

Irene Black – *Sold ... to the Lady with the Lime-Green Laptop*

The author, based in the UK, has used the experience gained over five years of trading on eBay to describe one hundred of her most interesting, entertaining, sometimes lucrative and occasionally disastrous sales. Each page is devoted to one item and carries a photograph, a description, the purchase and sale price, and, as the author says in her foreword "some additional trivia". The "trivia" consists of hilarious, fascinating and sometimes useful observations.

Jacquelynn Luben – *Tainted Tree*

A surprise bequest from an unknown benefactor leads American adoptee, Addie Russell, to Surrey on a journey to discover more about her mysterious English family. She does not know that her search will uncover secrets that will both shock and thrill her. Nor can she imagine the emotions and events that await her.

Jacquelynn Luben - *A Bottle of Plonk*

It's 1989 – a time when Liebfraumilch, Black Forest gateau and avocado bathrooms are all the rage, and nobody uses mobile phones.

When Julie Stanton moves in with Richard Webb one Saturday night in May, everything is looking rosy. She certainly doesn't expect their romantic evening together to end with her walking out of the flat clutching the bottle of wine with which they were to toast their new relationship.

But then Julie and the wine part company, and the bottle takes the reader on a journey through a series of events revealing love, laughter and conflict.

Jay Margrave – *The Gawain Quest*

Priedeux – a character who changes the course of history …

In the first of a trilogy Priedeux sets out for the wilds of Wirral on a quest to discover the writer of *Gawain and the Green Knight*, a seditious poem with a hidden agenda - a call to rebellion against Richard II. Can Priedeux find the writer in time to stop the rebellion and save his own life?

Jay Margrave – *Luther's Ambassadors*

In the second of Jay Margrave's exciting trilogy of mystoricals, Priedeux becomes the companion and mentor of the scheming Anne Boleyn.

info@goldenford.co.uk
www.goldenford.co.uk